The Pleiadians
by William A. Guillory, Ph.D.

First Edition, 2012
ISBN 0-933241-26-7

Printed in the United States of America

Published by The Center for Creativity & Inquiry
5442 South 900 East, Suite 551
Salt Lake City, UT 84117

This is a work of fiction. Names, characters, places, and
incidents are the product of the author's imagination or are
fictitious, and any resemblance to actual persons, living
or dead, organizations, groups, events, or locales is purely
coincidental.

The Pleiades

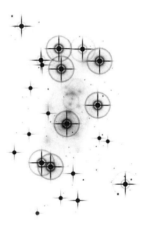

The Pleiades is a seven-star cluster called the Seven-Sisters. The stars are named after the seven sisters of Atlas and Pleione in Greek Mythology. The cluster is located in the Taurus constellation 440 light years away from Earth. The number seven associated with this star cluster conveys the energy of philosophy, wisdom, and spiritual enlightenment.

To Galina

Foreword

Bill Guillory has written a tale that is prophetic yet palatable. In a time where many of us prefer distraction over enlightenment, Bill expertly uses the medium of fiction to gently nudge the reader into an awakening. The great accomplishment of this book is that he achieves this without sacrificing any of the suspense one would expect from a fast-paced thriller. It is clear from the interaction of the characters that Dr. Guillory's intimate understanding of the dynamics of human relationships is well earned and his description of the conspiratory dimensions of the novel are well informed. This book beckons anyone with a pulse to open their eyes to what's facing all of humanity. It takes away our excuses.

—Pedro Silver,
Former Intelligence Analyst, Blogger, and Seminarian

Chapter**One**—The Arrival

"**W**ell I made it in record time, Bill!" he said, as he "appeared" next to me in the Casper, Wyoming airport waiting area.

"Where did you come from?" I asked, in a state of shock.

"Pleiades," he replied, calmly.

"Pleiades? Where's that?" I said, trying to hold down my voice. I could feel my heart beating at a significantly increased rate.

"Let me sit down and catch my breath." He plopped down in the seat next to me and let out a deep sigh. "It's in the Taurus Constellation. You can see it in the night sky with the naked eye."

"How did you get here?" I asked, looking around to see if anyone else might have seen his appearance. Fortunately, the airport was relatively empty at that time of day; except for an elderly lady who probably witnessed his arrival.

"I teleported through the space-time portal," he stated. "That was quite a ride!"

"You teleported? Through the space-time portal?" I repeated.

"That's what I just said. Teleporting is routine on Pleiades," he said. "But teleporting through the space-time portal, and in record time, now that is altogether different. I'm quite proud of myself."

"Are you looking for someone in particular?" I said, trying to establish the fact that we weren't traveling together. Just in case the elderly lady was monitoring our conversation.

"Actually, I'm looking for you," he said.

"Me? Why me?"

"I'm not exactly a stranger," he said, looking surprised at my reaction to him. "We've been in communication for more than 10 years. I thought I would 'drop in' and do some real-time coaching."

"You mean you're the one who's been sending me all those transmissions for the last 10 years?" I asked.

"Of course. Me and other members of the Pleiadian family. Not only transmissions, but most of *your* creative ideas," he said, with a conspiratorial wink, which seemed to imply, 'but that's our little secret.'

I chose to ignore his remark about *my* creative ideas. Particularly, since I would be considered a fraud for taking credit for someone else's insights.

✪ ✪ ✪

Just then an announcement was made over the public address system, "Flight 4915 to Salt Lake City will be leaving from Gate 3 at 2:06 p.m."

"Look," I said, "I'm sorry but I have to catch my flight to Salt Lake. Perhaps we can continue this conversation in a more private place." I'm sure he could sense my discomfort in giving the impression we were travelling companions.

"If you wish," he replied, becoming more formal. "I thought you would be delighted to see me. After all, you've been requesting a new mentor for some months now."

"I meant someone from this planet. At least, that's what I thought I meant," I replied feebly.

"Well if that's the reception I get after travelling all this distance, I'm not sure I want to stay. Let alone serve as your mentor!"

"I didn't mean it that way," I quickly interjected. "I really want you to stay. I just wasn't ready for you to show up so suddenly, and in a public place."

"I thought I'd surprise you, Bill. Hey! I bet you can't tell where I'm from. My country of origin, as you say here on Earth."

He was rather nondescript with blended features. Someone you saw, but forgot one minute later. He appeared to be the type of person who was simply born to populate the planet, but had no real purpose in being here. He was about five-feet-nine with surprisingly quick movements. He looked about 35 years old, although, his eyes were timeless with infinite depth. Something like a black hole. My impression was that if you engaged them, you would be lost in his world until he decided to release you.

He was right. I couldn't tell where he was from or his race for that matter. He looked more Western in terms of his facial features, but I could also detect some Asian influence. He spoke English perfectly and without an accent. He also had a continual smile on his face. The kind of smile a person has who simply appreciates being alive.

As I got up to go through security, I said, "Why don't we meet in Salt Lake at my home. I live alone, so no one will bother us." I realized this arrangement suited me best because of my discomfort with our public association. Like a long lost relative who shows up at your upscale office looking like he just got off the boat.

In any case, if he teleported all the way from Pleiades, he could certainly teleport from Casper, Wyoming to Salt Lake City! In addition, if he'd been telepathing with me for 10 years, he certainly knew how to find his way to my home in Salt Lake.

"I've never flown on an airplane before," he said excitedly. "I wouldn't miss it for the world. By the way, I'm sitting next to you. But don't worry, I promise not to make you feel uncomfortable."

How did he know I was feeling uncomfortable with him? Could he read my mind? If so, this was going to be a difficult relationship for me.

All I had left in terms of *true* privacy were my unspoken thoughts that I rarely revealed to anyone. I'd never had a relationship where I was "completely open." I think it's called transparency. I did wonder what such a relationship would be like and whether I had the courage to be in one. If he could read my thoughts, then courage was a moot point. I'd often thought, it would be a relief if the world knew everything about me; no skeletons in my closet.

I went through security without incident, although the elderly lady was eyeing me suspiciously. I had the feeling that anything I did out of the ordinary could be a disaster for me.

I continued to smile at her every chance I got, which I think made matters worse. I was trying to figure out what I'd say if the security people asked me where my friend was. Perhaps I'd reply, 'Oh he decided to teleport past security.' However, nothing interesting happened and I found a seat in the security area.

Just then, he reappeared next to me—from nowhere. "When do we leave?" he asked.

"When the flight attendant calls your row number," I replied.

"I think I'll board now. I get impatient waiting in line." And he was gone.

The elderly lady immediately got up and went to the head of the airport security detail. He was seated at an elevated desk carefully scrutinizing entering passengers. No wonder my *friend* decided to skip security.

After consulting with her for a few minutes, he approached me and asked politely, "Sir, can I have a few words with you over here?" He pointed to an empty area away from where other passengers were seated. He lowered his voice and asked, "Do you have a friend traveling with you?" He looked at me in a penetrating way to see if I would break eye-contact. I assumed he rarely had the opportunity to practice this look he probably learned from Homeland Security training.

"No. I'm traveling alone." We continued our "High Noon" eye-contact duel, until he finally broke off. I sensed I had won.

"What's your business here in Casper?" he asked, more politely.

"My name is Dr. Bill Bradley," I replied with equal politeness, flashing my million-dollar smile. I thought I'd pull out the big ammo right from the start and discredit the nosy old busy body. "I was here to deliver the keynote speech at the state SHRM luncheon—The Society for Human Resource Management. I'm returning to Salt Lake City where I reside," using my high-toned speaker's accent. "Is there a problem Officer Hendricks?" I noticed the name on his TSA badge. There's nothing like the personal touch once you've established high and low positioning.

"This lady says you have a friend who keeps appearing and disappearing," he said, obviously embarrassed.

"Excuse me? I have what?" I asked, looking astonished. "We can call the mayor to confirm that I am travelling alone if you like. He introduced me at the luncheon." I sensed he was in full retreat after my mention of the mayor. Frankly, I was surprised that name dropping worked with the TSA. I guess small towns still have respect for elected authority.

"No sir, that won't be necessary, I'm sorry to have asked you such a question. We have to follow up on every complaint we get, no matter how far out it may seem." He glanced at the elderly lady with a scowl. "Maybe there's been a misunderstanding here," he said apologetically.

"No problem, officer," I said. "These things do occur with age." I figured I'd discredit her once and for all. After all, TSA people have to take *everything* seriously these days.

The elderly lady looked at me like "You just wait." Then she said, "Are you telling me there was no one talking with you in the lobby area?"

"Of course there was," I smiled warmly and kicked it up to two million dollars. "He told me he was local. His job was to interview airport travelers about their experience of Casper." Fortunately, I'd seen two people in the lobby asking travellers, how they had enjoyed cowboy country?"

It was clearly time to end this *interrogation*. People were starting to notice our conversation, which was embarrassing. So I said, "If you don't have any other questions, I'll return to my seat Officer Hendricks."

"Okay," he said. "And again, I apologize if I've inconvenienced you."

"No problem." As I walked away from the two of them, I noticed the look on the elderly lady's face. This was one time I really appreciated rigorous security checks for firearms.

❁ ❁ ❁

When my row number was called, I boarded the plane. The plane was a four-seater across. As I approached my assigned seat, 5B, my friend was sitting in 5A. The elderly lady boarded after I was seated. My *friend* smiled at her as she approached us.

I looked at her as if I had no idea who he was or how he got there. My look didn't appear to make any difference. I got the impression she wanted to be as far away from us as possible. She probably thought he could disappear from the plane and who knows what might happen to us. Frankly, I had the same thought!

William A. Guillory

Chapter**Two**—The Identity

I have no idea how he bought a ticket and got a seat assignment next to me, if in fact, he did buy a ticket. He seemed to be delighted to be in flight and continued to smile throughout the short 45-minute trip.

Finally, I had to ask, "What do you think of flying on an airplane?"

"Slow," he said, "Very, very slow. It's great for me, though, because it helps to slow down my thoughts. If I don't slow down a bit, I think this body might self-destruct. I'm still adjusting to it."

"You mean this isn't your real body?" I asked.

"Of course not. On Pleiades, we have transparent energy bodies. I had to create a dense, semi-permeable body for my visit here. You know, to fit in. What do you think of it?" He asked, smiling proudly.

"I think it's fine. And you're right, I couldn't tell your country of origin."

He just smiled broadly, like a child presenting his first painting to a parent for refrigerator posting.

"By the way, what's your name?" I asked.

"I was hoping you could help me with a name. You know. Something nondescript. Like someone who is simply here to populate the planet, but has no real purpose in being here." He looked at me and smiled innocently.

I responded with an annoyed look. "I have no idea what your name should be. I have no idea who you are, except you seem to read my thoughts," I felt as though he had invaded my private space. I tend to be paranoiac about private information. Although I'm sure the CIA has been collecting information about me since my Berkeley college days.

"You don't seem to realize, Bill. You *project* your thoughts. Especially those with great emotion. Sometimes, they are so intense, I simply can't block them!

I just sat there trying to figure out how I might have non-emotional private thoughts that he couldn't detect. In a fit of frustration, I concluded I couldn't. When he smiled, I assumed he had *read* my conclusion.

✪ ✪ ✪

"Let's get back to my name," he suggested. "I would like something that might fit anywhere on this planet. We have so many places to visit while I am here."

I'm not sure he realized that I had a job, bills to pay, and a mortgage. I couldn't just visit many places although the thought sounded great.

"A name something like yours," he said. "William in English, Wilhelm in German, Guillaume in French, Liam in Irish, or Viliam in Slovak. And you are simply Bill everywhere. Do I look like a Bill?"

"Frankly, no you don't," I said. It felt good to say something that I thought would deflate his ego. But he seemed unmoved by my comment, as though he had no ego.

"What about Gregory?" he asked.

"No, that doesn't fit you. It sounds like a medieval pope."

"Chien?"

"No, that's 'dog' in French."

"Satorio?"

"Where did you get that from?"

"It's a Japanese Anime character. I'm thinking globally."

I just responded with a global facial expression that communicated my opinion. He understood perfectly.

"Well, what do you think fits me?" he asked. "Just say the first name that comes to mind."

"John!"

"John?" he asked. "Isn't that too biblical?"

"Not necessarily. In detective stories, John is used to describe unknown perpetrators," I said, with a smile.

"What?" he asked. "How does that fit me?"

"Well, nobody knows who you are. And I'm sure before you leave, you will break at least one law involving our legal system; starting with eavesdropping. Don't worry, John fits you perfectly. It's plain and, of course, nondescript. Nobody ever remembers a John. *And* it's universal."

"I kind of like John, even though it is biblical. Just plain John. John what?" he asked. "My last name?"

"Let's just stick with John for now. At least until we need a last name for legal purposes," I suggested, with a smile.

✪ ✪ ✪

When we deplaned, John felt like the trip had taken forever. He decided to meet me at my home rather than have me drive him; so he teleported.

When I arrived, he was watching television in my living room.

"I think this body is hungry," he said, quizzically. "It just doesn't respond as it did when I first appeared to you in Wyoming. What should I do to get it performing again?"

"John, your body needs nourishment, exercise, and constant care in order to function properly."

"Oh dear, this is more than I bargained for when I took on the assignment to mentor you," he stated.

"Well, that's what dense bodies require. By the way, as you take in nourishment, such as food and liquids, you also have to get rid of the residue that you don't use," I said, smiling.

"I seem to remember something of the process you are describing during my briefings. It seemed rather unpleasant."

"After you get accustomed to the process, you tend to ignore the unpleasant part. Let's put it this way, if you didn't have a way of getting rid of the excess residue, it would be much worse. By the way, we have an expression for that condition." I smiled.

"You do? Is the condition serious? He asked, with a look of concern.

"No, John, I was just kidding." It felt good confuse him a little with one of our colloquial expressions. But I was more interested in how they functioned on Pleiades. "Tell me how you nourish your transparent body?" I inquired.

"We have central energy sources fed directly from our major star; which you call the sun. This energy is distributed throughout our planetary communities where anyone can get as much energy as needed.

"How often do you need a new energy supply?"

"Once a week. Transparent bodies are extremely efficient. How often do I have to feed this human body?" he asked.

"That's your choice, John. I would suggest you feed it only when you're hungry. Just use your intuition to *feel* when it needs to be nourished rather than a mental signal that you need to eat something."

"This body is really complicated. I have to eat when it's

hungry. Yet, I have to know the difference between real hunger and eating as a diversion. Then I have to feed it two or three times a day. Preferably with nourishing food! How do you keep up with this complicated process for simply nourishing your body?"

"You'd be surprised how much money is spent on figuring out that question. We really have no clue! As humans, we also believe eating food goes beyond just nourishment. It's also a ritual of pleasure."

"Maybe I'll learn that ritual before I return to Pleiades." he said. "But it sounds very confusing."

William A. Guillory

Chapter**Three**—The Quest

"**B**ill, you remember when I appeared yesterday and I told you I was here to serve as your mentor?"

"Yes, I remember," I replied.

"There's more to my visit than simply serving as a teacher." John looked serious, like he had something important to tell me.

"You are fast approaching a point where You are seriously threatening your continued existence here on Earth," he said, engaging me with those timeless eyes of infinite depth.

"Are you serious, John? Nobody I know is worried about humans going out of existence," I replied in a humorous manner. I was wondering why John had become so dramatic. Up to this point, our relationship had been light-hearted and fun. I was actually beginning to enjoy having him around.

"Nothing lasts forever," he continued, ignoring my feeble attempt at humor. "All that exists is subject to a living and dying cycle: plants, animals, and You, as humans. The problem is that your dying stage is being accelerated *unnaturally* by your resistance to evolution as a species."

"What do you mean?" I asked.

"In simple terms, your development of technology is far greater than your ability to manage it. Much of your technology is designed for the destruction of people and property."

"John, that's because we live in a world where we all feel threatened by each other. The only way we can guarantee our survival is to build better weapons than those who threaten us." I could tell that this conversation was going to require patience on my part for John to understand the realities of our planet. He didn't appear to be "getting it" by the frown on his face.

"That sounds like a strategy with no resolution—just more technology and more weapons, endlessly."

"Of course, we also use diplomacy as a way of handling crises," I added, defensively. I was wondering how we got from mentoring to defending ourselves against the world.

"Will diplomacy avoid a global catastrophe?"

"Not really. But it is our best strategy for achieving global compatibility."

"I'm afraid global compatibility requires something more than your practice of diplomacy," he said, neutrally.

What I found most receptive about our conversations was how causal John was, as if he had no attachment to my responses. "Like what?" I asked.

"It requires transformation from a survival way of thinking to accepting the differences among you. This is what I referred to earlier as evolution."

"What does that mean, in practice?" I asked.

"It means to stop viewing your major differences in religion, politics, and values as threatening to each other. But most of all, it means to stop trying to force your way of thinking onto others. If you can do this, you can transform this planet."

"I'm afraid what you are asking of us is impossible. I can't imagine any group of people accepting the fact that their beliefs are not better than what others believe—especially about religion, politics, and values."

"Then your fate is sealed," John said. "It's just a matter of time."

"What do you mean? It's just a matter of time?" I asked. I was taken aback by how detached he seemed to be about our apparent self-destruction. Furthermore, I wasn't the one he should be having this conversation with.

"As more countries develop weapons that could annihilate all of you, along with increased tensions, your self-destruction is just a matter of time. That's what I mean," he ended. Again, no emotion. Just the facts. As an afterthought, he said, "Do you remember the book by Tom Clancy, *The Sum of All Fears*?"

"Yes. The one where there is almost worldwide nuclear destruction?"

"That's what I'm talking about."

John's simple statements made such sense that I was momentarily speechless. Then I asked, "So, what does this have to do with me?" The instant I asked that question, I knew I had made a mistake.

❁ ❁ ❁

"The reason I was sent is to prepare you to deliver this message to everyone who is willing to listen," he said like a coach preparing me to take over as quarterback.

"What? You must be kidding!" I almost shouted. "No one will listen to me. And there will certainly be no 'transformation to human compatibility' because of anything I have to say. Whatever that means."

John replied calmly, "Maybe, maybe not." He appeared to be unmoved by my protest.

"I admit I've had 'delusions of grandeur' of how important my writings were in the past. But more recently, I have come to my senses. Very few people are even remotely interested in the acceptance of evolution as you have described it. Certainly not those who have vested interests in keeping things exactly the way they are."

"Bill, so much depends on the *timing* of the message as well as the message itself in terms of acceptance. And communicating the message once or twice is not enough."

"In my opinion, most people don't want to read or hear anything that involves a change in what they already believe, let alone transformation. We only change when we have a crisis. Like hurricanes, earthquakes, or tsunamis; or even an economic depression. And I emphasize *change* not *transformation*."

"I am aware of that fact. That's what I meant when I described your unnatural resistance to evolution as a species. I am not asking you to discredit what most people believe. I am not even asking you to suggest *how* people should live their lives. I am simply asking you to share with others your planet's resistance to evolution, such that there is a clear understanding of the choice You are making; and the probable consequences of that choice. One final thought to remember is 'revolutions in consciousness' are never started by a majority."

"What do you mean?"

"Revolutions usually result from a *small spark*, something like the *Big Bang* from a very small singularity. Then an entire Universe emerges at blinding speed."

"And you think something like that is possible here on Earth?" I asked. I was beginning to have a sinking feeling that the more I engaged this conversation, the more I was getting sucked into a whirlpool.

"If a strong underlying feeling of dissatisfaction exist where people see no solution with the way things are, then evolution is possible. That's what we experienced on Pleiades."

"What happened on Pleiades, John?"

"We were headed to our own self-destruction because we

ignored regulations that restricted technology development that were threatening to the public health."

I looked at John without commenting, so he continued.

"Our economy is based on the element Tellurium, as yours is based on oil for most of your energy needs. Tellurium is a major source of our solar energy collection systems on Pleiades. It is also toxic when mining is conducted in an unregulated way."

"So, what happened?" I asked, partly guessing at his answer if it compared to our "exploration and mining" of oil.

"Eventually, the environment became hostile to our health. We still don't know the exact details of how it happened. But many Pleiadians contracted strange diseases that led to an epidemic."

"What was the public's reaction?"

"At first we looked to government and business to find a solution. But nothing substantive happened to stop the epidemic; except to call it a national emergency and establish treatment centers around the planet."

"Then what happened?" I asked.

"That's when the spark occurred. Someone simply pointed out that we were the cause of the problems *we* were having. That *we* were creating a more toxic planet because of our insatiable demand for more energy. And until *we* accepted responsibility for that demand, there would be no solution"

"So, what did you do?"

"We decided to return to a simpler way of living. A way of living that required less energy than we had become accustomed to using, all because of the spark."

"Didn't that feel like going backwards?" I asked, honestly.

"In truth, we had more energy than we needed. We simply didn't know how to manage it for everyone's benefit. Some regions of our planet used excessive amounts while others had practically none."

"And?" I asked, urging him to continue. "What happened

then?"

"Something very simple. We began to help each other. We found we required less energy when we worked together, rather than competing against each other. The idea caught on and took on a life of its own."

"That sounds like a rather simple idea for the complicated situation you were dealing with." I almost laughed at John's simple-minded idea. He simply ignored my response and continued.

"That spark eventually led to the evolution I was talking about. We began to stop thinking about getting ahead at the expense of others. We began to care for others as we did for our own families. It was a grassroots movement led by ordinary people. Government and business had no choice but to come along."

"Are you trying to tell me that something as simple as 'helping each other' led to a transformation in how you operated as a planet?" This idea was so simplistic that I almost started to laugh aloud, except John looked dead serious.

"That's exactly what I'm telling you." He appeared to be unmoved by my reaction to his solution. So he continued, "Have you ever noticed what happens when you help someone with no expectation in return?" he asked, with a look that demanded absolute honesty and deeper reflection than an off-handed, snotty reply.

"Yes, I know what it's like, mostly with people close to me." I reflected on how little I extended this way of living beyond my family or those closest to me.

"You change as a person without even being aware of it. But the change is permanent." He paused as if gathering his thoughts and then continued. "Usually, people have to see that nothing else works before considering the kind of change I'm talking about."

Even though I found our conversation interesting on an

intellectual level, I finally asked, "John, what does this have to do with the transformation that saved you?"

"It has everything to do with our transformation! With each small positive change, we became closer as a people. Not only among ourselves, but with people who were very different. We discovered our problem was not about energy conservation after all, but about establishing *trust* among ourselves; one *small* step at a time. Figuring out how to sensibly manage our insatiable need for more energy was the easy part."

My thinking was, as smart as John was, how could he possibly think such a simple idea could work with people here on Earth! So, I said, "John?"

"Yes, Bill."

"That's quite a story. Let me sleep on it and we can talk some more in the morning. It's been a long day."

"Okay."

✿ ✿ ✿

I didn't sleep very well. In fact, I didn't sleep at all! I shared this with John the next morning.

"I'd be surprised if you did," he replied. "After all, Bill, my arrival is not an everyday thing."

"You know, I was thinking about something we talked about last night."

"What's that, Bill?"

"I was thinking about how we live our lives here on Earth. Constantly wanting more of whatever it is we don't have. Always needing to be *doing* something. As though we are always searching for something *outside* of ourselves that will bring the satisfaction we want *inside*. But most of all, I was trying to understand why we resist change from within. What you call evolution."

"And, what conclusion did you come to?" he asked.

"Fear. We live in a constant state of fear. Driven, in part, by the uncertainty of what *might* happen next. 'I might lose my job,' 'I might discover I have cancer,' 'I might be rejected by the person I love,' 'I might lose everything I have by the risks I have taken,' 'I might discover my relationship no longer works,' 'I might fail at what I want most in my life.' And the list goes on endlessly. But most of all, I think we fear each other."

John looked at me with a deep sense of compassion and said, "That's because *survival* is the dominant consciousness of your planet. You also experience empathy, compassion, humility, and love for each other."

"That's true. I guess the question is, 'How much are they part of our everyday lives?'"

"For some of You, it is an everyday way of living."

John continued. "Some of You even experience a deep spiritual connection that naturally drives you to help others, with no expectation in return. I am speaking primarily of ordinary people, not necessarily those You put on pedestals or elect to public office."

"Why aren't we this way most of the time, John? Why can't we simply get along with each other?"

"Because the fear You experience is greater than the love you feel for each other. In all fairness, Bill, all intelligent species go through the survival stage—in their own unique way. Even our Pleiadian civilization went through this stage as I described to you last evening. Fortunately, we did so in a *natural* evolutionary period of time, when it was clear where we were headed."

"Are we so different? Why is a survival mentality such a dominant part of our way of thinking that we refuse to change?" I asked.

"Actually, it's part of your original genetic programming that was necessary for your survival as a species. When physical survival is no longer a reality, evolution to a higher state of consciousness is a natural transformation. Previous Earth civilizations like

Lemuria and *Atlantis* experienced the same challenge You are facing. They were both destroyed by their own resistance to evolution. You are presently headed in the same direction. That's why I am here," he replied calmly, "to help prepare you to assist in the evolution of this planet. Let's just call it the 'Quest' for the time being."

❂ ❂ ❂

"Wait just one minute, John. We never discussed anything about a quest. And if I understand your original motivation for coming here, it's to be my mentor and Guide for personal growth. Do you agree?" I asked.

"Yes, I agree, Bill. But somehow, I sense there is more you have designed for yourself in terms of how you would like to influence the direction of this planet."

"John, I'm only one person. I appreciate all you think I might be capable of. But I assure you, I don't do planetary transformation," I stated emphatically.

"That's perfect," John said. "Because all you need to be is the spark. The people of this planet will transform themselves if they decide to do so."

"So, what does being a spark mean?"

"It means giving a speech, facilitating a workshop, writing a book, and most of all blogging to the world community. These are just my ideas. I know you can be much more creative once you commit to the Quest."

John quickly continued. "Just for the record, you're not the only one involved in the Quest on this planet. We have a network of six other individuals being mentored for the same role you will be playing."

"Then why do you need me? I can do what I do naturally. I give speeches. I do workshops through our non-profit—*The Center for Creativity and Inquiry*. I write books. And my blogs on

The Voice are very popular. What more do I need to do?" I asked.

"You can move to the next level—beyond *The Voice*. You can say those things you *really* want to say about the human condition on this planet—that if You don't change in a dramatic way, there won't be any human condition."

"I can't say stuff like that. They'll think I'm crazy! Why don't you say it?" I asked.

"My role is not to *directly* interfere in your planet's chosen path. It is to *influence* certain individuals in promoting human compatibility. And support their sharing of this way of living with the rest of the planet for change."

"John, I understand your commitment to my personal development. But what you're asking of me is just too much."

"I understand and respect your reluctance. In part, that's why we chose you for the special role."

"Chose me for a special role? What special role?" I asked.

John laughed and said, "The special role here in North America."

Somehow, John was not a masterful liar. I assume lying was not part of social relationships on Pleiades. Every time I asked him about why he was here, he kept coming up with something different—and bigger. I sensed there was something way beyond what he was telling me!

I didn't realize then what started as an innocent, fantasy relationship would turn into a global adventure that would threaten my life as well as anyone who associated with me.

Chapter**Four**—The Opening

I'm a divorced father of two teenage daughters, 16 and 14 years old. I am the third of three siblings, an older brother and an older sister. I was raised in New Orleans, Louisiana. My parents instilled in us education as the key to success in life. As a result, the sequence of high school, college, and graduate school was like transferring from one bus to another— culminating with a Ph.D. from Stanford University.

I earned my Ph.D. in chemical physics in three years. After a two-year postdoctoral fellowship at the University of Frankfurt, I began a teaching career at one of the premier universities in the western U.S. My single-minded pursuit was the achievement of awards and recognition by my peers which often resulted in long hours of laboratory research, and time away from my family. (After all, I was doing for them!) This single-minded commitment to success inevitably led to a strained marital relationship.

My eventual divorce and separation from my children were more traumatic than I could ever have imagined. These events set into motion a reexamination of what my life was all about and what was truly important to me. Since I got on that first bus as a teenager, I'd never stopped to think about such questions. Fortunately, now, I had no choice.

I began to look inside myself to discover the direction my life would take. It was a period of emotional upheaval, confusion, and transformation. People and events that were previously important fell by the wayside as I began to experience a new reality.

In spite of the separation from my children, I devoted considerable attention to their upbringing. By the time they were adolescents, I had established a strong bond with each of them that serves as a lasting foundation for our relationship. A foundation based upon providing support and commitment to *their* happiness and success. I often wonder if I've become a better "divorced father" than a "live-in" one.

In retrospect, those events served as preparation for the journey that was about to take over my life. One night while experiencing a fretful sleep, I was abruptly awakened; by what or whom, I don't know. As if in a trance, I went to my home office and began writing as though my hand was guided by some mysterious force.

There was no mental thinking involved. Just "thought-forms" that appeared in my mind that I wrote down, as if taking dictation. When the download was complete, I went back to bed and a sound sleep.

The next morning, I was astounded by what I had written. The transmission implied that our descriptions of life were an illusion. That reality was something that could only be experienced, not described. Furthermore, our way of living would only lead to more conflict and destruction. We should look within ourselves, beyond what we have been taught to believe, for *a small still voice* that is common to us all. Therein, we would discover a way to live in harmony with each other.

I had no intention of showing *anyone* what I had written. "Did I write it?" I asked myself, or was it simply a dream. After all, dreams were not reality, I reasoned. So I decided to keep secret what had happened and assumed it would soon be forgotten.

Except the following morning at precisely 2:00 a.m., I was abruptly awakened again. I went to my office and began writing. This time the transmission described a whole new world of human existence where people were driven by giving instead of getting. Where there was abundance instead of scarcity. Where there was cooperation instead of competition. And ultimately, there was love instead of hate. This ideal world seemed so real, I imagined I could reach out and touch it. Afterwards, I went back to bed and to a sound sleep once again.

The following morning was as upsetting as the previous one. I couldn't deny that I had written these things. And amusingly, I had done so without the aid of any legal or illegal drugs. I was fairly certain that my sanity was intact, by the fact that everything was normal during the day. It was the sleep state I had to worry about. "Where was this stuff coming from?" I asked myself. I concluded it was my dreams that were probably the source. After all, dreams are fantasy. Aren't they?

After several weeks of these nightly liaisons, I had to make a decision. Either I was going to be receptive to these "perfectly sensible" transmissions or mentally shut them down. After all, there was no one else I knew experiencing stuff like this except for some homeless people I'd seen from time to time.

There was a secret part of myself that looked forward to these nightly messages. The more I wrote, the more this way of thinking began to make perfect sense. This acknowledgement led to my decision to "totally open" myself to these inner messages; and stop pretending to be a reluctant participant. After all, they were descriptions of how the world vowed it wanted to be, but didn't seem to know how.

While driving through my small university town following my latest nightly session, I stopped at a bookstore. It was as if someone else took control of my car and steered it to that location. I entered the bookstore and encountered a skinny, weird-looking guy with a broad smile. The experience was surreal because the guy welcomed me as though he had been waiting for my arrival.

"Hi, I'm Bill Bradley. I've been living here for more than ten years and I've never noticed this bookstore before."

"Yes, I know," he replied.

"How would you know?" I asked. I had a quick thought that I had entered the "Twilight Zone."

"I meant you looked like you wandered in here not knowing exactly what you were looking for."

"Or why," I added, with a nervous laugh.

"I'm Weldon Prescott and I own this bookstore. I've been here more than 20 years. What do you think you might be looking for?" Weldon asked. He continued to smile as though he knew my questions before I asked them.

Somehow, I felt I could confide in Weldon; particularly, since there was no personal connection. So I said, "I'm looking for something that explains how to interpret dreams."

"What kind of dreams?" Weldon asked.

"Dreams where it appears you're having conversations with someone, but you can't make them out. Unlike real people you normally dream about," I replied. I wanted to keep a few cards close to my chest. I didn't want to reveal everything in the first few minutes of our conversation. Apparently, he had other ideas, because he took over.

"Do you get unusual messages from this person you can't make out?"

"Yes, I do," I replied, reluctantly. "The messages are unusual for me. They are quite different from my normal dreams. In fact, the messages come so fast I have difficulty writing them."

Weldon's eyes lit up, and he said, "Oh, I get the idea."

"What idea?" I asked. I was thinking this whole conversation was moving far too fast for me.

"You've been channeling."

"Channeling? What's that?"

"It's when you get messages from your intuition. Except, you soon learn that the inspiration is from someone invisible."

"I'm not sure that's what is happening to me." I could feel myself retreat into a deeper state of denial. I don't like to be led about what I'm experiencing. Suggestions are fine. "I've simply been dreaming about stuff I don't know anything about or have any real interest in."

"Then why do you continue to write them if you have no interest in it?" he asked. Somewhere in this guy's history he must have been a lawyer. Because I felt confronted by almost every question he asked.

"Because it's like the pressure exerted against a dam, except the pressure is inside of me. There's no thinking on my part. My pen simply uses my hand."

"That's channeling!" Weldon said more emphatically. "Tell you what." He walked over to a bookshelf, selected a book, and gave it to me. "Read this book, and see if you 'connect' to it. If so, come back and we'll talk some more. If not, it was nice meeting you." He turned and walked away to help another customer.

❁ ❁ ❁

I drove home and immediately began reading the book Weldon had given me. It was a book of channeled writings by a woman who had lived in upstate New York. Her name was Jane Roberts. She claimed to have channeled an "entity" named *Seth* while in a trance state. The process was called *trance channeling*. The book was titled *Seth Speaks*.

As I read the book, it appeared everything was directed to me. It was like a recollection of events *I* had experienced. I could feel myself being drawn into a whole new world of discovery. It was like coming home.

The whole idea of channeling would have been absurd just a few months ago. Now I found myself drawn into this mysterious world that was not subject to scientific explanations. Statements about reality were literally taken out of the air from mystical sources. Statements not found in any traditional psychology book.

The problem was most, if not all, of stuff made perfect sense at an intuitive level. But science does not deal with intuition, except as a proposition you ultimately have to prove using scientific methods. The simple process of *engaging* the *Seth* transmissions, without immediate rejection, set my head spinning. Which I assumed was the point.

The transmissions explored human consciousness. Code for something bigger than your mind. The transmissions explained why we behave in irrational ways. The conversations engaged me as though I was taking a private workshop. I didn't feel threatened, put down, or preached to. Just someone explaining the "facts of life" and concluding with, "Now you decide what you really believe, not what you have been taught to believe; or even anything you've read in these conversations."

For example, the implication that there is no purpose or

meaning to life would be rejected by most people I know. We seem to have an overwhelming *need* to believe that our lives have meaning. Without it, we would probably conclude that we are, in fact, also meaningless. An unthinkable thought for most of us!

These are the kind of mazes that *Seth Speaks* led me to struggle with. Except that Seth's mazes have no exit. Only dead ends!

As I found myself drawn into this new reality, I was simultaneously leaving my old, familiar one, creating a temporary void in my life. The void was soon filled with people and events that reflected my new way of thinking. Weirdos! Or as the popular saying goes, "We attract those who are mirror-reflections of ourselves."

While strolling across campus a few days after the bookstore incident with Weldon, I ran into a good friend at the university who worked in administration. Her name was Sue Robbins. She noticed that I was carrying the Jane Roberts book. She asked, "Are you interested in books like *Seth Speaks?*"

Feeling an immediate sense of embarrassment, I replied, "I thought I would do some light, non-scientific reading." I had gotten accustomed to carrying the book around with me to read in case I was in a line or waiting for an appointment. No one else had ever paid attention to it.

"That book is hardly light reading," she replied, laughing.

"Yes. It has turned out to be more in-depth than I thought," attempting to maintain my professorial air. In fact, I was beginning to feel even more embarrassed, wondering how Sue knew so much about *Seth Speaks*. Maybe she was a weirdo too.

Sensing my discomfort, she said, "If you have an interest in similar reading, let me know. I'll suggest a few books I've read. Got to run, see you soon, Dr. Bradley." And she was gone.

After reading *Seth Speaks*, I followed up with Sue. She recommended a book titled *2150 AD* by Thea Alexander. The descriptions of the Earth in that book matched perfectly the recent dreams I had been having. The Earth's population had decreased to less than a billion people. The dominant activity was devoted to teaching and learning since everything humans wanted or needed was handled. Survival no longer existed as the dominant Earth consciousness. Ten percent of the people no longer felt compelled to "own" ninety percent of the planet's resources. I finished this book in a couple of days since it matched so closely what I had been "dreaming."

I returned to Weldon's bookstore. Again, it was like he was waiting for me. "Hi," he said. "How did you like Jane Roberts?"

"It was perfect," I replied. "It felt like coming home."

"I thought it might."

"I also read a book someone recommended to me, titled *2150 AD* by Thea Alexander."

"I guess I can put this one back on the shelf," Weldon said, smiling. It was a copy of *2150 AD*. So where do you want to go from here?" Weldon asked.

"I'd like to share some of the things I've written with you. I brought a few of them with me. Maybe you can give me some idea where to go next. I'm tired of doing this alone, and in secret."

❂ ❂ ❂

Weldon sat down and read some of the first transmissions I had written. He asked a few questions here and there, but absorbed their meaning fairly quickly. "This looks like introductory material to me. Probably in preparation for some more advanced channeling to come."

"I can't imagine writing more advanced stuff than what I've already written," I replied.

"Don't worry, *you're* not writing it anyway. You're just the channel. Remember?" He smiled. "I think your next step is the world outside of the reality you've lived in most of your life."

"What does that mean?"

"I think you need to discover the world outside of traditional Western thinking."

"Like where?" I asked.

"Not only where, but with whom," Weldon replied. "The Elders of China, the Zen Masters of Japan, and the Shaman of South and North America might be good places to start."

"How do I make a contact with them? Can you recommend anyone to me?"

I had never felt so lost and undirected in my life. There were always rules of how you progressed in my profession. Rules I had learned to use according to my objectives and goals. I had an instinctive feeling that this journey neither followed those rules nor yielded predictable outcomes that matched my objectives. I was definitely swimming in unchartered waters.

After a few weeks of confusion, frustration, and anger, the first step I took was to figure out what I wanted. If my journey required me to experience the total opposite of Western thinking, then my first thought was China or Japan. I had had a graduate student from mainland China who was now on the faculty at one of their prestigious technical universities in Nanjing. I contacted him and the result was an immersion experience on a commune in China in exchange for 50% of my time being devoted to teaching advanced courses in chemical physics.

I felt like I had stepped back in time to familiar surroundings. I had questions running in my head all the time. Something told me to keep my mouth shut and slow down my thinking. So slow, that on rare occasions there was nothing there! No thoughts! The commune experience taught me the value of *silence* and how to listen below verbal communication; bordering on telepathy.

I made a similar professional contact in Japan at the University of Tokyo. I had presented several seminars there in the Department of Molecular Physics over my scientific career. They were also eager to have me join as a visiting faculty member to collaborate with their scientists in the area of molecular beam energy transfer studies. This appointment provided me the opportunity to be taught by a Zen master. I learned *discipline* and how to use my *strengths to maximum advantage.*

Most of all, I learned to improve my weaknesses as a person. The most outstanding one is *patience*; learning how to let things come to me and then taking the appropriate action. During my Zen exercises, I had the extraordinary experience of "perceiving" without words through meditation with koans. Koans are paradoxical stories used to master intuitive thinking. One of the most famous is, *"What is the sound of one hand clapping?"* If you're thinking *silence*, that's the wrong answer.

Upon returning to the U.S., I spent several months with a Shaman in Southern Utah. These experiences involved both hallucinations and realizations that accompany *sweat-lodge* sessions. During one of my sessions, I experienced leaving my body and exploring the surroundings. I was unbounded in terms of freedom and exploration. I experienced that fine line where hallucination and reality become one. The hallucinations were similar to the archetypes described by Carl Jung, the Swiss psychoanalyst in early part of the 20th century. Jungian archetypes, which are innate personalities, help in defining one's role in life.

The most powerful realization I had was the result of a *vision quest*. This experience involved spending several days alone in the Southern Utah desert with very little food and water. It also led to the discovery of my totem animal being an eagle. In fact, it was an eagle that led me to water and edible plants in the desert. At the completion of my vision quest, I began to sense the direction my life would take; a direction which, at first, appeared to have little relationship to my vocation as a scientist.

I returned to the university after my year-long excursions into discovering this new way of thinking. I was sitting at my desk working on a research paper when a question popped into my mind: "What are you doing here?" It was one of those "aha" moments where life-changing shifts occur. Where making sense becomes irrelevant and answers appear to come from nowhere. In fact, I wasn't even sure *I* had asked the question in the first place.

"I don't know what I am doing here?" I mumbled to myself. Just for a moment, I thought I might be taking the first steps to joining those who live in alternate realities. Although I knew something significant had happened, I didn't know, at the time, what form my aha would take. That night, I experienced a restful sleep secure with the realization that my journey of exploration, triggered by my divorce and separation from my children, was finally coming to an end.

The next day I wrote my letter of resignation and submitted it to the president of the university. He asked me, "What do you plan to do, Bill?"

Before I could stop myself, I said, "I don't know?"

He looked at me like most people look at my homeless friends. Then I smiled and words came out of my mouth before I could stop them, "I think I want to take a sabbatical from life."

At which point the president stood to indicate our meeting was over. He simply said, "Good luck," and turned his attention to the papers on his desk.

I had a feeling I could no longer depend on him as a personal or professional reference in the future.

Shortly thereafter, I established a human resource

development firm based on personal and organizational transformation. I felt like singing, "I can see clearly now, the rain is gone...but there were still obstacles in my way."

$$\odot \; \odot \; \odot$$

During a span of five years, following my resignation, I continued to write channeled transmissions, at least two to three times a week. They involved a variety of Guides covering subjects from the nature of the universe, to spirituality, health and wellness, service, consciousness, past lifetimes, Love, and the future of humankind.

To celebrate my five-year anniversary as a consultant (which Steve Martin says in the movie, *Father of the Bride*, is code for unemployed), I had lunch with a friend I had recently met. Her name is Gala Korol, an immigrant from the Ukraine. Although we had known each other for a relatively short period of time, there was an instant emotional attraction. At first, it was like reconnecting with an old friend, like a sister. Then as I began to focus more on her shapes and curves, our friendship moved to the next level.

"What are your plans now that you've written all this material that you keep hidden from the world?" she asked.

"I'm not sure. I want to share it, but I'm concerned about how publishing it might affect our consulting business. Most of our customers are not only conservative, but they like the present business system exactly as it is."

"What do you mean? They have complete freedom to run their businesses as they choose," she said, puzzled by my response.

"The problem is that I've written stuff that questions some of our most cherished beliefs about business operation. Like greater cooperation instead of competition. Competition is the engine that drives capitalism. The transmissions suggest less emphasis on individualism and greater emphasis on the collective welfare of everyone. That sounds like socialism to some people. And most of all, they propose placing a limit on individual wealth, such that 10% of the people don't own 80% to 90% of the planet's resources. How do you think those ideas would be received?" I asked.

She looked at me with concern and said, "Just do what your heart tells you. Don't make it complicated."

Then a *Voice* whispered in my ear, "Hi, Bill."

"What did you say?" I asked Gala.

"I didn't say anything," she responded, looking at me with concern.

The *Voice* said again, "I'll come back when you're not so preoccupied with your dilemma."

"Are you okay?" Gala asked.

"Yes," I lied. "I'm fine."

Little did I realize, at the time, that my life had just taken another irreversible change in direction. The appearance of the Voice was the opening act of the adventure I referred to earlier. An adventure from which there would be no return to my previous life.

William A. Guillory

Chapter**Five**—The Journey

"**I** didn't mean to show up at such an awkward moment at your luncheon with Gala," the *Voice* said. "But I was testing our connection."

"So, I wasn't just hearing things? You are real?" I asked.

"Yes, you were hearing things. More like 'perceiving' things. But I'm not real. That is, I'm obviously not a real human being."

"Who are you then?"

This conversation began quite unexpectedly while I was on a flight to Rochester, New York to give a keynote speech. The guy next to me turned and asked, "Did you say something?"

"No," I replied. "I was just thinking out loud." I smiled as though the entire incident was amusing. I'm not sure he thought so. The truth is, these unexpected appearances in public were getting just a *bit* annoying.

"Look, Bill, I have thousands of other clients I'm overseeing besides you," the *Voice* said.

I turned to look at the passengers sitting behind me to make sure someone wasn't playing a trick on me by using "voice projection," like a ventriloquist. When I ruled out that possibility, I decided to pretend I was actually having a conversation with an invisible person.

I thought I would start in response to *Voice's* last statement. "Did I ask to become a client of yours?" I whispered softly so that the guy next to me couldn't hear what I was saying.

"You don't have to whisper," the *Voice* replied. "I understand your thoughts perfectly clear. In fact, if you could think a little faster, it would keep me on schedule."

"What exactly is the service you provide for me?" I thought quickly.

"That's much better. I was beginning to feel this assignment was going to be a long drawn out process of millisecond responses. Now, to your question, you have been asking for a new teacher for some time now. So, here I am."

"No. I was asking for a human teacher. Someone I can see, feel, and touch," I thought.

"Let me check, maybe I've made a rare mistake. Give me a moment to go back to Pleiades and review my listings. No, it's you," the *Voice* replied. I had the feeling there was disappointment in its reply.

"I thought you were going to check on me?"

"I did. I'm back already," the *Voice* said.

"Look, I've never had a conversation with an invisible person before. This is new to me," I thought.

"We'll discuss that later. For someone with the experiences you've had I assumed we would move a lot faster through our initial connection."

I immediately felt the *Voice* was expressing impatience or that I lacked quickness. "Just give me a few minutes to adjust to you. I'm not stupid," I thought, without thinking.

"Don't get me wrong, you do think a lot faster than most humans on this planet, but mostly about the same things, over and over again. What would *you* call that?" the *Voice* asked.

"I'll try to be more diverse in my thinking," I thought.

"Not only diverse, but out-of-the-box sometimes would also be interesting. Think how boring my job is to answer the same dumb questions I get asked."

"Like what?" I thought. I was also thinking that I had moved from just receiving intuitive messages to now holding conversations with an invisible person!

"On this planet, the most common question I get is, "Are we the only intelligent beings in the universe?" the *Voice* said. "How would you respond to that question, Bill?"

"I wouldn't know how to respond. But that's not a question I would ask in the first place," I thought. This conversation was unnerving since I had no idea what the consequences would be if I gave a wrong answer.

"I hope it's not about 'world hunger' or 'global warming'," the *Voice* responded. "I'm a little tired of those. Particularly, since it's so obvious what you need to do."

"No, none of those either," I thought.

"I think our time is up for this introductory session. Let me *tell* you how this mentor-protégé thing works. Your job is to have questions for me, preferably thought-provoking ones." When I didn't laugh, the *Voice* said, "That was a pun." When I didn't reply, it went on. "My job is to answer the questions you have and provoke you into asking more in-depth questions. On very rare occasions, I will communicate out-of-the-box ideas, if I think you're ready. That rarely happens on this planet. Got it so far?" the *Voice* asked.

"Yes, I think I got it," I responded.

"Good. Let's stop here for now. Like the old *Candid Camera* TV show, 'When you least expect it, I'll be there.' By the way, feel and touch mean the same thing."

In response, I wanted to tell the *Voice* that it was confusing the old TV show with a famous Michael Jackson song. But it was gone.

⊙ ⊙ ⊙

When I returned from my Rochester speech, I immediately called my friend, Gala, and asked her to meet me for dinner—a long dinner. She could tell by the desperation in my voice that something significant had happened. So, she rearranged her schedule to accommodate me. I was also hoping she could use her soothing touch for an after-dinner message. And the rest would be left to our imagination.

We met at the New Yorker restaurant in downtown Salt Lake City. The New Yorker is an upscale restaurant where table-talk conversations could involve anything from bribes for the Olympics to taking Federal money while simultaneously being against government spending. No conversations were off limits such that you get a dirty look for hearing "voices," more like curiosity.

I had made sure we got a private table, off the beaten path, which immediately made us suspicious. Gala arrived after I had been seated for five minutes or so. She looked at me with concern and gave me a tighter hug than usual. "How are you?" she asked, with her cute Ukrainian accent.

"I'm fine," I lied.

"What's going on? You sounded upset. I know these things you know?" she said. Gala has this way of looking at me that is far more than just looking at my exterior expression. She goes inside my head to my brain synapses and intercepts private messages being shared back and forth. I'm not sure whether this is a "female thing" or something that's indigenous to East European women. Her name, Gala, means *calm* in Russian. Her name and personality are a perfect fit unless she wants to know something that is being withheld.

"It's a long story," I replied.

"Can you make it short?" she asked impatiently, looking so deeply into my eyes that I thought she could see my soul. It was clear that subtle lying wasn't going to cut it.

So I said straight out, "I've been hearing a voice whispering in my ear." Depending on how she responded would determine if I would reveal more of what had happened to me.

"You mean the one that whispered to you last week when we were having lunch?" she asked.

"You picked that up last time?" I asked naïvely. Maybe there was more to her synapse interceptions than I had discovered, so far.

"Of course, what do you think, I'm stupid?"

One thing about speaking second languages where one is commonly limited by vocabulary is that you usually get the right word but with no subtlety. *Stupid* was the right word because it means unintelligent or lacking perception. But I would have softened my response by using the word *distracted*, which means preoccupied or a lack of concentration.

In any case, I ignored her "stupid question" and moved on to explain my dialogue with the *Voice*. "The *Voice* said it was my new teacher that I had been requesting for some time and I was its client."

"You mean a client like in a business sense?" she asked me with a confused look.

"I guess so, except it was dictating all the rules of our relationship. I don't think it knows or cares about customer satisfaction. It didn't mention any 360° surveys. In general, it didn't appear to care about my opinion." I was paying close attention to how far I should go in explaining my telepathic journey. I was ready to change the conversation the instant she began to frown as though I was a freak. But instead, she continued to pursue the conversation with heightened interest.

"Are you going to cut it off or continue your dialogue?" she asked.

"The truth is I got the impression that it felt like it was doing me a favor. So I guess I ought to be appreciative for the opportunity I'm getting. I don't have any other friends who are walking around hearing voices. At least, any who are not institutionalized."

Gala laughed and said, "I think Americans are too sensitive about how they're treated. Who cares if the *Voice* thinks you're an idiot. Maybe it's trying to test you to see how you respond to criticism. If it were me, I'd simply focus on what I could learn that would benefit my life. That's it," she ended.

I didn't care for her referring to me as an idiot, particularly since that's not exactly what the *Voice* said. But I assumed it was the language thing again.

That was when we had an uninvited visitor join our dinner conversation.

❂ ❂ ❂

"May I join you and Gala?" the *Voice* said.

"Do we have a choice?" I thought. I have a problem when uninvited guests just "show up" at private affairs. This was obviously not the time to discuss the next steps of our mentoring relationship.

"I can leave if you like and return in another ten years. My arrival at this time was because I wanted to meet Gala, since she will be crucial to our future activities," the *Voice* said.

"What activities?" I asked, confused. "And, I think it's my decision whether she is involved with our *arrangement* in any way," I thought. I was becoming a little perturbed by the *Voice* making all the rules like I was supposed to follow like some mindless idiot.

"What are you discussing?" Gala asked. It was obvious that I had ignored her for the last few minutes. It was equally obvious to her that I was also holding a conversation with someone and becoming progressively upset.

"Is it the *Voice*?" she asked.

"Yes, it is."

"What did it say?"

"It said it wanted to meet you." I left out the part about her being crucial to our future activities, which I was hearing about for the first time.

"What else did it say?" she asked, with that look.

I really didn't want to pursue this line of questioning until I completed my exchange with the *Voice*. But, I was dealing with Gala. "It said something about you being crucial to our future activities," I added.

"What activities?" she asked.

"That's what I asked when you asked me what was going on," I said. This whole thing was getting out of hand. Or more precisely, out of my control.

The *Voice* said, "You are both getting ahead of yourselves. Perhaps, I shouldn't have mentioned the future. It can wait."

"That's fine with me," I thought.

Feeling left out again, Gala said, "Why can't I talk directly with the *Voice*? Why do I need you to translate?"

I could see she didn't like "go-betweens," particularly when she felt perfectly capable of handling things herself. Her calmness was fast disappearing.

The *Voice* said, "Tell her she's not ready yet."

"What?" I thought. "I'm not telling her that."

"What did it say?" she asked becoming more upset at having me as a translator.

"It said you're not ready yet."

"What do you mean, I'm not ready?" she replied. Her eyes started flashing, her color visibly darkened, and the calmness associated with her name disappeared.

"I didn't say you weren't ready. The *Voice* told me to tell you, you weren't ready."

Apparently my communication didn't get through because *her* voice went up several decibels in reply, "Why are you ready and I am not? I've done as much spiritual work as you or more."

People were beginning to look at our off-the-beaten-path table with me holding two conversations; one with someone who wasn't there and another with someone becoming unhinged.

Finally, I said with equal decibels as her last comment, "Look, I'd gladly switch places with you. But I'm not running this thing, the *Voice* is."

Then the *Voice* said, "Just like the old days, nothing has changed, as yet."

"What did it say, now?" she demanded.

So I told her. "What does that mean?" she asked.

I could feel myself asking, "How did I get into this situation? I just wanted to have a nice calm dinner. And maybe a little sex afterwards if I got lucky. I concluded at this point that luck wasn't in my stars.

The *Voice* interceded without my translation to say. "Tell her the two of you have been involved in dramatic relationships for several hundred years. So this outburst isn't anything new. Tell her I've enjoyed meeting her and now I must leave to serve my other clients."

And with those last words, the *Voice* was gone.

✪ ✪ ✪

At 2:00 a.m. the following morning I was abruptly awakened from a sound sleep. "It's time to begin our first project," it said. It was the *Voice*, of course.

"What project?" I thought. "Not anything involving Gala I hope?"

"No, not Gala. That's for later."

"Then what project?" I thought.

"We have to write our first book of the channeled materials," was the reply.

"You mean all that stuff that I've written for the past five years?"

"Of course, and more that we'll write in the coming years."

My first thought was, "What is this 'we' stuff? Any published channeled writings will be in 'my' name regardless of the source." My fears of how my reputation would be affected began to arise again. Although, I attempted to imply that my concern was for how my consulting business would be affected.

The *Voice* said, "You may not know it, but this is your destiny. This is what you were born to do. This is what you have been preparing for. Why write these things for five years if not to share them with others?"

"Do you realize this material not only implies the way we live today is archaic but also that our fundamental beliefs do little to preserve the welfare of most human beings or the planetary ecosystem," I thought.

"That's exactly the reason we must begin to have humans look at themselves with new eyes. Soft subtle messages don't work. This is only the first step of a long journey," the *Voice* ended.

❁ ❁ ❁

The next five years were primarily devoted to writing new material, publishing, and continued learning until the appearance of John; who, not surprisingly, was the human form of the *Voice and* who was also my original source of the channeled messages. The Trinity! The Channeler, *The Voice*, and John; one and the same!

With John's arrival, I was at another transition point for the next challenge that he called the Quest. In spite of my dilemma, John seemed quite pleased with the human experience he was having. But he was also impatient and easily bored, given how fast he processed his experiences. So I wasn't surprised when he *unexpectedly* told me that he wanted to visit other cities that were important to our success.

Great! That would give us time apart. Time that I could use to process all that had happened to me since his arrival. What I didn't know was John's agenda about when and where he wanted to travel and how it involved me.

Surprise!

ChapterSix—The City of Light

"About a week after his arrival in Salt Lake City, John informed me that he had made first-class travel plans for our visit to Paris.

"Paris!" I exclaimed.

"Yes, Paris," he replied causally. "I told you there were other places I wanted to visit while I'm here."

"When?" I asked him.

"Tomorrow, of course," was his reply.

"John, I can't just take off without giving advance notice to my co-workers or making preparations for such a trip."

"I sent a memo to all of your co-workers a couple of days ago informing them that I was planning a surprise trip for you to Europe. I told them I was a childhood friend of yours."

"You told them what? You were a childhood friend? Where did you get that from?" I asked.

"I've known you since you were born. You were much more spontaneous then, by the way," John replied. "Now you have to think through everything."

"What are you talking about, John?"

"When you played as a toddler, I helped you build log cabins, put together puzzles, and choose crayons for the pictures in your coloring book. I even helped you learn to read."

"That's hard to believe."

"How could you possibly think you learned so much as a child with no one to help you? He replied. "Your mother and father were busy working."

"I never thought about it. I just assumed I learned most things on my own." As soon as the words were out of my mouth, I felt stupid about saying them. How could I possibly learn *everything* on my own?

In fact, my mother often told me about imaginary friends I played with as a child. But I didn't want to have that conversation now, so I replied, "Back to the memo you sent to my co-workers. What exactly did you say?"

"I asked them if it would be okay for us to be gone for about two weeks."

"And what did they say?"

"They all thought it was a wonderful idea for you to take a break. So giving advance notice is handled, as well as our preparations. I didn't tell them about our work together, of course."

"We are not working together!" I stated definitively. "Not until I am clear about what's involved in this Quest thing. Is that understood, John?"

"Sure, Bill," John replied with a look that implied, 'Whatever you say!'

That was two days ago. Now we were in Paris walking down the Champs-Élysées. So I decided to forget about how we got here or the circumstances involved. I decided to just *experience* the most exciting city in the world.

✿ ✿ ✿

As we continued toward our destination, The Arch de Triomphe, John said, "There's someone I'd like you to meet."

"I thought you told me this was your first time visiting this planet."

"It is," he replied.

Then how could you know someone here?"

"Because, he is not from here, originally," he smiled.

"Where is he from?" I asked, dumbfounded.

"Pleiades," John replied.

After pausing to let my reaction set in, John said, "Let's sit at this Bistro. It's the one nearest the Arch. Antonio will be here shortly. What would you like to drink?"

"I'd like something very French," I replied, "Grand Marnier, the elixir of the Gods."

Just then, from literally nowhere, this bald-headed guy "shows up" just like John did when he first appeared. I assumed he was Antonio. A gentleman from an adjacent table dropped his fork as well as the food in his mouth. Everyone else who witnessed Antonio's arrival pretended he was there all the time. After all, this was Paris.

John said, "Tony! I haven't seen you in years. You haven't changed at all."

John and Tony looked at each other in a funny kind of way as though some exchange of a greeting occurred that only they were privy to. I just watched. I was learning to not be surprised by anything that might happen. Except for John disappearing and leaving me to explain any "mess" he left behind.

The waiter showed up and asked what we would like to drink. Both John and Tony ordered white wine. John also ordered a Grand Mariner for me. The waiter took our order and walked away.

✪ ✪ ✪

"I am delighted to meet you, Bill," Tony said. He extended his hand with a firm shake.

"It's nice meeting you also, Tony," I replied hesitantly. "How long have you been here on Earth?" My last statement sounded like I was speaking to some "spiritual visitor," which maybe Tony was.

"My assignment started shortly after you successfully exploded the first atomic bomb. The Pleiades Council concluded that you had taken a serious step toward your own self-destruction as a civilization. Particularly, when you used it against others of your own kind."

"How did you come to that conclusion?" I asked, "The part about our own self-destruction." I thought I would I skip over his comment about using the bomb on our own kind, since history had shown why we *had* to use it. But the part about our own self-destruction concerned me more. That comment involved the present and the future.

"I think John began answering that question with you. Basically, this planet values knowledge more than wisdom— particularly scientific and technological knowledge. Your knowledge of destructive ways to use technology has far exceeded your wisdom to manage it."

"What, exactly, is your assignment?" I asked, becoming a little irritated that some extraterrestrial being, looking like the former Father Guido from *Saturday Night Live*, could judge our management of the planet.

"I don't presume to judge You. I'm simply expressing an observation. My assignment is the same as John's. That is to assist in having You realize that You are headed towards human extinction and what's necessary to have you avoid it. That's it. What You plan to do about this observation is entirely up to You.

It is not our role to directly intervene, in any way, into how you manage this planet."

I forgot that Tony could also pick up my thoughts as well as my verbal responses. "So, there are people that you have been working with the same as John has been working with me?" I asked. I remembered John saying there were others like me involved in the Quest.

"Yes, I have worked with many individuals during my time here on Earth, for more than sixty years. As you can tell, my efforts have not been successful in turning the tide. You continue to develop weapons for human destruction along with increasing planet-wide conflicts," Tony replied, dejectedly.

By this time, the waiter had returned with our drinks and left menus with us. With an unspoken signal, we each picked up a menu and began browsing for a choice.

My mind was processing Tony's statements in spite of my reaction to what he'd suggested. I realized that everything he said was probably true in spite of my inclination to deny his statements. For the most part, when we experience global disagreements, we assume we are right and those who disagree are wrong.

John said, "That's what we are talking about. Your systems of thinking are dominated by *polarized* points of view; all presuming to be right. And, You tend to resolve your differences by attempting to dominate each other through fear. When fear doesn't work, You resort to violence."

The waiter returned, right on cue, and we each ordered a meal.

Then Father Guido, aka Tony, took the microphone again, "Our assignment, which John and I volunteered for, is to form mentoring relationships with those of you who are receptive to transitioning from a survival mentality to human compatibility. Then we hope you will use your own creative ingenuity in communicating this message to others who are receptive."

"You expect us to start a grassroots movement in terms of human evolution? I asked.

Tony simply replied, "Yes." Then, after pausing, he stated, "You see the real question is whether the *people* of this planet are ready."

✪ ✪ ✪

When our meals arrived, we all began eating in silence. Although there were no words spoken, I could just barely perceive hit-and-miss thought-forms in my mind. These perceptions went on for several minutes. They were not linear sentences but complete whole sentences and sometimes entire paragraphs. The more I focused on receiving these thought-forms, the stronger they became.

"You've been here a long time, Tony. Have we made any progress with respect to evolution?" John telepathed.

"There are pockets of real progress here and there around this planet, but those who control the resources resist change," Tony replied. "Some even want to return to primitive times."

"Do you still feel our strategy of focusing on the average person is the best way to create an evolutionary movement?"

"I think that is our *only* hope. Throughout their history most revolutionary changes have come from the efforts of ordinary people, mostly fueled by dissatisfaction. Too bad most of the changes eventually made were external conditions rather than internal transformation in their thinking."

"What's your progress been with Bill, so far?" Tony telepathed to John.

"Even before appearing here, we all liked Bill's focus on personal transformation as the *source* for change of external conditions. That's one of the main reasons we began our work with him 10 years ago," John replied.

"Do you think his writings might have a chance of going

viral?"

"If the populous is ready, they will. If not, then we keep trying until time runs out. At that point, we return home and hope for the best."

I pretended I didn't know what was going on between the two of them. So I focused on people passing by as a diversionary tactic. It didn't work.

"What do you think, Bill?" Tony telepathed.

At first, I wasn't sure that they had discovered my subterfuge. But they were both staring at me and smiling. Game's up! They both knew.

So I projected the thought, "We have a history of changing primarily in response to crisis. I don't know of any real change that's resulted from a motivation to get along better as people." And I emphasized, "*I* simply don't know if we have capacity to change from such a motivation. Especially the kind of evolutionary change you're talking about." We all paused in silence for a minute or so after my last statement.

Then, John telepathed, "Congratulations! It's about time you joined our silent conversations. You actually mastered this ability many years ago with one of your Earth teachers. You and I routinely used it in our sleep-state conversations. Like staying current in any language, you've simply had no one to practice with in the wake state?" His smile broadened. "Now you have me."

Again, Tony extended his hand to me with a firm shake, smiled broadly, and in the next instant, he was gone.

John said, "Tony had pressing business in Southern France. He's beginning a new mentoring relationship in the province of Provence. He indicated that he would be following your progress."

❂ ❂ ❂

After dinner that evening at our five-star Hôtel de Crillion, I thought it might be a good time to learn more about the Network of Pleiadians. When we were relaxing in the lobby, I asked John, "Where are the other Pleiadians located besides you and Tony?"

"In addition to the United States and France, we have Pleiadians in South America, China, India, Japan, and the Middle East. We are all working together to bring about the change Tony described."

"How successful have you been so far?" I asked.

"You can answer that question as well as I can. You've had 10,000 wars in 5,000 years, with no apparent end in sight. Even to the present day."

"What's been your approach to changing things?"

"When Tony first arrived, he focused on leaders from around the world. Those he felt might be receptive to change. Unfortunately, most of them were only interested in the welfare of their own country. They had little concern for others; especially, those they opposed."

"Didn't Tony have success with *any* leaders? After all, he said he's been here about sixty years."

"A few. But every time he was successful and a leader began making changes, he was assassinated by those in opposition. Then, everything went back to the way it's always been for centuries. You tend to kill anyone who becomes influential in proposing a more equitable way of living."

"What makes you think you can be successful now?" Given our track record."

"We've been trying a different approach over the past ten years."

"You mean the stuff Tony said about focusing on ordinary people?"

"Yes, focusing on ordinary people in selected places around the planet."

"Where do the protégés come in to this strategy?"

"Since we can't intervene directly, the protégés are the ones who must provide the spark I spoke of. They are the key to our new approach." John said.

"What did Tony mean when he said, "You will keep trying until time runs out?" I asked. I had not been able to let go of that offhand comment since it seemed like there was a serious consequence associated with it.

"He means, until You create an event that will probably lead to an all-out nuclear exchange. Then our attempts to help You will be over. And we will return to our home."

Just for an instant, I sensed that John wanted to say more. But instead, he stopped himself and asked, "Do you have any more questions?"

"Yes. Why do you want to help us so much, when we don't seem to want to help ourselves?"

"That's a good question," John said. He reflected for a moment and replied, "You are really an extension of us. We are connected more than you realize. We are simply at a more evolved state than You are. Our fates are tied to each other, so it's only natural we would want to help you." John paused, and asked again, "Anything else?"

"No," I replied. "I think I understand. I just need to sleep on it." Although John may not have realized it, his last few statements had the greatest impact on me since his arrival.

"Okay, let's do some more of Paris tomorrow!" he said in a light-hearted manner.

I got a telephone call in the middle of the night at 1:39 am. It was John. He said he needed to talk with me immediately. I asked could if it could wait until morning since we still had so much to see in Paris.

"I think we need to meet now. It would probably be more difficult in the morning. Why don't I come to your room and explain," John said.

Before I could respond, he hung up. I assumed that meant he would be knocking on my door in five minutes or so. Assuming he saw no reason to teleport around the hotel.

So I got out of bed and quickly began dressing and getting the sleep out of my eyes. Quicker than I thought, John was knocking softly on my door. When I opened it, he entered and sat on the couch chair. He had a serious look. Not the fun-loving John I had experienced walking around Paris.

"There's something I think you ought to know about our Network of Pleiadians. As I informed you, there are seven of us, all doing work involving the transformation of planet Earth."

"And?" I asked with increasing anxiety.

John explained that an alliance of very powerful and influential individuals had learned of the Pleiadian Network and its work to further the evolution of planet Earth. The alliance calls itself the Guardian Angels. "As you know, the Guardian Angel concept is to guide and intercede in behalf of those requiring protection. Their objective is to preserve your present way of life."

"What's the problem with our present way of life?" I asked. "We aren't perfect, but it's responsible for most of the progress we have made so far," I ended with a confused look.

John looked disappointed by my reply. Then he said, "I thought we discussed this subject in Salt Lake City. Your present way of life is leading to increased armed conflict and more countries with nuclear capability. These trends increase the chances of your global self-destruction."

He looked as though he was pleading for my understanding. "Suppose we drastically change the way we live with each other. You know, greater understanding, respect, and the acceptance of differences between us?" I appealed.

"These measures would only work on a permanent basis if they resulted in a transformation in your thinking. If the most important factors driving your way of life are domination, control, and power over each other, then those measures would make no difference in the long run. Don't you see that?" he asked again.

"How does this relate to the Guardian Angels?" I asked.

"The Guardian Angels view planetary evolution as an erosion of their power, control, and wealth."

"Why are we worried about them?" I asked.

"Because they see our work as a serious threat to most of the wealth being in the hands of a few. With evolution, there would probably be greater emphasis on working together to ensure the welfare of everyone, globally."

"I think I'm beginning to see this whole Quest thing in a bigger perspective than before. What do you expect the Guardian Angels to do about *your* activities?" I asked naïvely, as though I wasn't yet part of John's agenda.

"I expect them to try to discredit us at the very least and possibly destroy us if what we do begins to catch on," he said with a look of seriousness.

A light came on in my head and I asked, "Do they consider *me* part of *your* Network?"

"I'm not sure, since they are probably not aware of my arrival or our association. I'm certain that if you returned to Salt Lake and lived your normal life, you'd be okay." He paused. "But you have to decide fairly soon, I would guess."

"I guess I *do* have a decision to make," I said with a newfound seriousness in our relationship.

❂ ❂ ❂

"Just for my information, how did the Guardian Angels learn about the Network of Pleiadians?" I asked John.

"When selecting some of our initial protégés, we were not very careful in ensuring their commitment to the secrecy of our intentions. We chose them over shorter periods of observation and subsequently learned they were less committed to resolving the challenges they would face in preparation for the Quest. The same types of challenges you have been experiencing."

"So what did they do?" I asked.

"Several of them chose to discontinue their association with us. A few continued to write blogs in support of planetary evolution on their own. Some did so as business ventures." He smiled and said, "We are no longer a secret."

He added, "Our guess is that the Guardian Angels was organized in response to the network of blogs that started to appear around the world; including yours as *The Voice*. None written by our network of protégés have gone viral as yet, even with reinforcing messages from other protégés from around the world."

"So what do we do now?" I asked.

"Regrettably, we must leave Paris, probably tonight."

"Leave, Paris! Why?"

"I have just learned of an imminent threat to us. I am not certain of their motives, but you and I are targets of their search."

"Why are we targets? We haven't broken any laws" I looked at John and asked, "Have we?"

"No, we have not, Bill. But the Guardian Angels operate separate from the law. They are a law unto themselves. In any case, I think we need to leave Paris tonight. Then you can decide if the Quest is right for you."

Another light came on. "In truth, the protégés are the vulnerable ones, since the Network can teleport at will," I said.

"I will do all in my power to protect you and provide assistance in preparing you for the Quest. Should you decide to pursue it," John stated with complete sincerity.

"I would guess it's just a matter of time. If I don't return home very soon, they will naturally assume I'm part of your Network," I stated, mostly to myself.

"It's your planet, not ours," replied John. "Since we have no aggressive motivations, we cannot play any direct intervention role. You have to save yourselves as a planet. That's Your responsibility."

Chapter**Seven**—The Guardian Angels

Robert Stewart Ellington was deeply disturbed by reports of the increasing popularity of the Blog Site *"The Voice."* He was an avid surfer of the Web. As an investment banker, it was one way of keeping pace with the trends of society, people, and world events. All critical dimensions of information that was key to his continuing success.

Ellington was also aware of the power of social networking in *reflecting* people's opinions as well as *shaping* them. What concerned him most was The Three Degree Rule. Which, in essence, states that we influence others who are three friendships removed from ourselves—with decreasing impact. What we say within network groups has an impact on our friends (one degree), our friend's friends (two degrees), and our friends' friends' friends (three degrees).

What disturbed him most were the major characteristics of such groups: *connection*, *contagion*, and a *lack of control*. Each of these characteristics was presently playing out with respect to *The Voice*. During the past year, its popularity had increased to more than 4,000 individual visitors per month. Ellington was not interested in those one-time personal scandals that drew millions for a couple of days or even weeks if the person was sufficiently successful. People loved tearing down their heroes to the delight of the news media. That's why they built them up in the first place. He was more interested in those that consistently grew in size and drew a large following. They represented *connection*.

His next concern was, "what the site was saying." Anything that could pose a possible threat to his personal or professional empire was considered to be *contagion*. A threat directly related to the erosion of his power, control, and wealth. So far, *The Voice* qualified for the first two—connection and contagion. And the third was a given. The Internet was not only uncontrolled, it was "out of control" as far as Robert Ellington was concerned.

Although the guy running the Blog Site attempted to fly under the radar, Ellington's IT Team was able to identify him as Dr. William Bradley, former Professor of Chemistry at a fairly prestigious university. His blogs suggested that the world should be prepared for a major shift in economic power and political influence from the present dominant western powers to eastern powers, anchored by China, India, and Japan. Furthermore, he suggested that our only hope was greater interdependence, collaboration, and equalization of wealth. 'Socialism bordering on communism,' thought Ellington.

The *real* issue in Ellington's mind was the growing popularity of the Blog Site. Anyone could make the Three Degree calculation: 4,000 x 4,000 x 4,000 equaled 64 billion people. Ten times more than the number of people on the planet!

Robert Ellington was snapped from his reverie when his

butler informed him that his weekend guests were arriving. "Sir, several of your guests have begun arriving, I thought I would inform you in the event you wanted to greet them."

"Yes. Thank you, Willard. I will be joining them shortly," Ellington replied.

This was the Guardian Angels' second meeting. Robert Ellington had devoted a full six months to acquiring the membership of the Guardian Angels. He selected six exceptional individuals with a firm commitment to preserving the dominance of the western world. One of the utmost requirements for membership was a strict code of secrecy. A secret of their involvement each would be willing to take to the grave. They all, of course, swore an oath.

The weekend gathering was being held at Robert Ellington's country home in upstate New York. The estate had been in his family since the early 1900s. Robert Ellington was a descendant of investment bankers who had transitioned from multimillionaires in the first part of the 20th century to multibillionaires in the latter. He realized that the blogs written by *The Voice* were proposing a new world order in terms of governance, the distribution of wealth, and accordingly, the exercise of power. To all of which, he was firmly opposed.

His background selection of each member included in-depth research and even personal background checks. The background checks served as an additional measure of control in the event any of them had second thoughts about their involvement or considered breaking the oath of secrecy. Fortunately, all of them had skeletons in their closets that he could use in the event of a betrayal.

For the time being, Ellington decided to set aside his concerns about the blogs as he walked to the foyer to greet his guests for the weekend. He had already concluded it was time for decisive action to be taken. Tonight, he would simply enjoy a relaxed dinner and stimulating conversation.

✪ ✪ ✪

Promptly at 7:00 pm, each of the Guardian Angels assembled in the spacious library for drinks. The group no longer required a schedule or needed to be called. On the previous occasion, Robert Ellington had made it perfectly clear that he would not tolerate lateness or gaudy attire. Formal dress was required. He wanted to establish a clear code of discipline and professionalism. This code particularly applied to their casual academic member.

One of the first to arrive in the library was Sir Noel Elliott Kensington. Like Ellington, Sir Kensington was descended from several centuries of British bankers. His ancestors had played a key role in bankrolling the Union during the Civil War. He and Robert Ellington had done several business transactions over the years. They were perhaps closest of the six group members. In fact, Sir Kensington was Ellington's first choice to become part of the group and required the least background check.

The remainder of the group consisted of Dr. Margret Summers, an economist with the World Bank; John Carson, senior senator from California and chairman of the powerful Senate Oversight Committee on Homeland Security; Dr. Richard Kinsey Moore, world-renown astrophysicist from California Institute of Technology; and the Reverend Jonathan Sterling Littleton, a Christian evangelist from Dallas, Texas. Although Reverend Littleton was based in Dallas, he had a huge following in Europe as well as parts of Asia receptive to the Christian message.

Dr. Moore, the astrophysicist, and Senator Carson had become fast friends at the first group meeting. Both lived in southern California and enjoyed its "laid back" lifestyle. They were both a bit irritated by the formality and time-consciousness of Robert Ellington. But they were equally concerned about the influence of any secret group, like the Network, on American soil.

The main reason Dr. Moore joined the group was because he felt his association with the Guardian Angels might provide him an opportunity to encounter one of the aliens that Ellington had suggested was here on Earth. He had as deep an interest in their extrasensory skills as he had in learning how scientifically advanced they were.

Although he had read the blogs posted by *The Voice*, he wasn't a zealot when it came to the preservation of America as *the* world power. A simple study of history showed that all civilizations had a rise and fall. They declined mostly by their own devices connected to greed, ethnocentrism, and resistance to change.

Senator Carson had a different motivation. His commitment was to preserving the American way of life. There were some people who were born to be led. And that applied to the overwhelming majority of people on the planet. Hell, if you started the whole thing over again with a pot of money and no one owning any, within five to ten years the distribution of wealth and power would be exactly as it is today, he reasoned. When it's all said and done, the cream rises to the top. That's the nature of this planet, clear and simple. Darwin got it right over 150 years ago.

At precisely 7:30 pm, Willard announced, "Dinner is served in the dining room, to your right as you exit and on your left two rooms down." Although everyone knew exactly where the dining room was located, protocol required that Willard make this announcement every time they met for a meal or a meeting. Most of the group found this practice amusing, but not Robert Ellington or Sir Kensington.

When the group was seated in pre-assigned places, in the spacious dining room, Robert Ellington tapped his water glass and thanked everyone for their attendance. 'As if anyone had a choice,' thought Margret Summers. He proceeded to offer a toast to the success of their venture, since everyone had both a glass of red and white wine already served at their respective places. Reverend Littleton chose to toast with his glass of water.

After the plates from the main course had been removed, Ellington posed a question to the group, although his attention was focused on Dr. Margret Summers. "What's your analysis of the present world economic situation?" he asked.

Although Margret felt imposed upon by Ellington, everyone also looked at her in anticipation of an answer. After all, they all knew of her brilliant career as a Wellesley undergraduate and a combined Harvard Ph.D. in economics and business. Then working at The London School of Business and Finance for ten years before being offered a position with the World Bank that she couldn't refuse. She was known as a fiscal conservative who pronounced that large debt combined with market saturation and uncontrolled financial regulation was a formula for impending disaster. She had written about many historical precedents where this combination signaled the fall of powerful economies in the past—some temporarily and some permanently.

Margret stated somewhat timidly, "I worry about the increasing debt the U.S. is taking on. I realize much of it was to save our financial institutions, and by implication, the economy. But I don't think our financial institutions learned anything new. They believe themselves to be above the rules of fiscal responsibility; even with the recently passed financial reform legislation," she ended.

Then Sir Kensington asked, "What would you have done? Let them go down the drain?"

This question set off a spark in Margret Summers, and she dropped her timidity. "I would have let them experience greater loss so they would feel what the rest of the country was going through. Something like what the automotive industry experienced. It appears that industry has undergone a transformation and will probably emerge more globally competitive in the future." Her eyes burned into those of Sir Kensington until he dropped his stare.

It was clear Margret was apolitical—that is, she was not only neutral, but almost disinterested in politics. She felt politicians were more or less the same. After being elected, their number one objective was to remain in office regardless of whether the country suffered or not. The real tragedy was when one was voted out of office they were commonly replaced by someone with a different philosophy, but the same primary motivation.

Senator Carson, who was known as the great compromiser, picked up what he considered to be cynicism on Margret's part and posed the question to Reverend Littleton. "What's your take on the economic situation, Reverend Littleton? I do realize that it's easy to be a 'Monday morning' quarterback after the horses are out of the barn." Everybody laughed in reference to the fact that Littleton was from a ranching area of Texas. It also lightened the mood of the conversation which had become tense with Sir Kensington's question.

Reverend Littleton took an introspective moment before replying and stated, "In a phrase, 'this too shall pass.' What I mean is I tend to take the long view. Countries, like people, are tested. If we stick to our well-known Christian principles, we will come out okay," he ended, smiling.

Dr. Moore was clearly dissatisfied with Littleton's Christian mumbo jumbo. It's like no matter what the outcome, he's covered. So, he asked, "Do you believe our financial institutions should have 'experienced greater loss,' as Margret stated?"

Reverend Littleton was taken aback by the directness of Dr. Moore. 'He was obviously a heathen, given his impudence to a respected man of the cloth,' he thought. However, he continued smiling broadly, as he had learned to do when dealing with lost souls, and replied, "I believe we should not wish loss on anyone or any institution. If we are counseled by the words of the Bible, we will make the best decisions. I also think we too often underestimate the power of prayer in dealing with situations we as humans do not have the wisdom to resolve. As I stated earlier, 'this too shall pass,' and in retrospect, we will look back and conclude that things were not as bad as they appeared. The key is that we stick to our well-tested Christian principles," he concluded, with a broad smile.

Dr. Moore replied, "I don't think the boys on Wall Street are into prayer when it comes to making a buck. Do you?"

Before Reverend Littleton could reply, Senator Carson said, "I think we're all probably saying the same thing, but in different ways. We need to ensure our free enterprise system based on Christian principles." An as an afterthought, he added, "with the proper checks and balances, of course."

It was clear that the conversation was over. The mood of the room consisted of stillness, reflection, and frustration. Robert Ellington thought to himself, 'I've chosen the perfect team. All were *rugged individualists* in their own unique way. Ayn Ryand would be proud of him.'

❂ ❂ ❂

After breakfast the following morning, the Guardian Angels assembled in the study, a state-of-the-art meeting facility. It was spacious with high ceilings and had a large conference table that could comfortably accommodate 12 seatings. The outer wall consisted of two large windows that featured the enclosed wooded perimeter of the 30-acre estate.

Coffee, tea, juices, and a variety of condiments were arranged on a side table. After conferring with Robert Ellington, Willard left the room. Ellington tapped on his water glass to get everyone's attention, and then stated, "We have much to cover before parting tomorrow at noon. I have provided an agenda that's in front of each of you. I'd first like to have us agree on the items and perhaps what we would like to decide by midmorning tomorrow. Does that sound like a good start?"

Dr. Moore stated in response, "These all appear to be 'action' items or more precisely 'reaction' items. Have we established the fact that the Network is a hostile group?" he asked. "More to the point, has anyone made contact with our visitors?" he smiled.

Ellington responded, "We have established that they have been here for some time, maybe ten years or probably more. They arrived here in varying numbers over that time frame."

"Why do we consider them to be a threat? I think that is what Dr. Moore is asking," Margret Summers asked. "We agreed at the first meeting to gather as much information about their activities as possible as a basis for what we might do," she concluded.

"We have limited confirmed information. Some of what we know has come from their former protégés who left the Network or private sources. The protégés suggested the recent arrival of a new Pleiadian. We suspect a connection between this new Network member and the Blog Site called *The Voice*. As you know, the blogger has remained anonymous and refused to communicate with anyone directly," replied Ellington. "Although he tries to mask his true identity and the source of his web transmissions, we know who he is and where he is located. I'm certain the government is also monitoring his blogs by now."

"So, what has this so-called Network done that is of concern?" Margret asked again. "You stated at our first meeting the existence of a powerful subversive group that was a threat to the American way of life as well as possibly to the safety of the planet. That's why I am here."

Ellington paused a minute to organize his thoughts. Then he proceeded. "As you know, at the first meeting we only had preliminary evidence of an extraterrestrial Network of aliens. There is no way of confirming such a Network without direct contact. The blogs on *The Voice* website are presently of equal concern. Particularly, their increasing popularity and possible connection to the alien Network." Ellington was trying to get the group to realize they needed to take action to shut down *The Voice* and its socialistic ideas that were becoming increasingly popular.

"So what do we know for sure?" asked Dr. Moore again.

"First, the aliens have made no attempt to contact any world leaders. Second, they have formed so-called mentor-protégé relationships with selected individuals around the planet. Presumably, those who are highly receptive to a change in the world order from west to east. And third, the aliens appear to have extrasensory abilities."

"What do you make of these observations?" asked Senator Carson.

"I personally believe they are trying to brainwash those they form relationships with and use them as pawns. If they do have extrasensory abilities, they can be used for eavesdropping and surveillance; possibly to gain information for an attack by others of their kind." Ellington ended, becoming a bit frustrated that the others couldn't see the possible dangers posed by the alien Network.

Since things were getting off to a rocky start, Ellington concluded the group needed time for reflection so his comments could sink in. He politely suggested they take a break so everyone could attend their personal needs.

❂ ❂ ❂

After reassembling from the midmorning break, Ellington resumed his briefing to the group with a slight grin of someone having insider information. He opened the session in a more relaxed fashion and asked, "Are there additional questions before we consider the agenda items I have proposed?" He realized the group consisted of people sufficiently confident in their own opinions that they could not be railroaded into making decisions he wanted.

Senator Carson nodded and asked, "If it's been more than ten years since the arrival of these so-called aliens, why don't we know more about them and their intentions? I've heard nothing of such a group from my position as head of the Homeland Security Oversight Committee. Believe me, I discreetly asked around since our first meeting."

Ellington replied, with a smug look, "Actually my IT guys have gathered information by *researching* a woman who was a close associate of Dr. Bradley. As you know, I began a dossier on Bradley and his associations more than a year ago after reading his Blog Site. I informed you of his background at our first meeting.

In any case, she was involved in the highly confidential Defense Department program to use extrasensory abilities for surveillance gathering using *remote viewing*. It was called Project Star Gate and was discontinued in the mid-1990s for lack of definitive results."

Everyone knew that "researching" probably meant hacking into her website; particularly, with his highly experienced IT Team. But no one wanted to be part of a discussion involving illegal actions which could be prosecuted. So, no specific details were asked about how the information was obtained.

"So what does she have to do with the Network of aliens?" Dr. Moore asked, impatiently. He was obviously not impressed with Ellington's smugness. "Is she one of them?" he asked.

Ellington's eyes flashed momentarily and then he calmly replied, "As I just said, she was one of the stars of the Star Gate program. In fact, she was the most impressive one in the development of telepathy and remote viewing for surveillance. From the information we've been able to gather, it's suggested that at least one member of the alien Network has been here for an extended period of time. Probably gathering information about our defense weaknesses."

"How'd you come to that conclusion?" Carson asked.

"It's just an assumption at this point, Senator. Our private sources suggested this possibility based upon the messages she intercepted between the aliens," he lied.

"What did the messages say? asked the Senator.

"The messages discussed several mentor-protégé relationships and the progress made by the various protégés here on Earth. They were discouraged that none had been able to find a way to change the thinking of people. Probably, to make us more submissive to their motives."

Ellington smiled, like the cat that had caught the mouse, "Now, the most interesting part of her intercepted communications. Just recently, a new alien came to Earth to start a mentoring relationship. This confirms information we've gotten from other ex-protégés."

"So what?" asked Dr. Moore, who had risen from his seat and leaned against the wall. "What's so special about the new relationship?" As an academic and prominently respected by his peers, Dr. Moore was naturally combative. That was the nature of healthy scientific dialogue.

Ellington ignored Dr. Moore's skepticism and proceeded. "The new mentoring relationship is with her former prize student who lives in Salt Lake City; none other than Dr. William Bradley. Who is one and the same with *The Voice*. We believe their plan is to use the popularity of his blogs to achieve the change they want. When his name was telepathed between the aliens, she projected a strong emotional response, which they detected. Since that time, she has not been able to pick up on their conversations."

"Why didn't she report their communications to the authorities?" Senator Carson asked.

"Our source could only guess about that question. If she

reported intercepting telepathic messages between aliens, would anyone believe her? Furthermore, if the military did, where would she be now and for the rest of her life? She said she's happy she can no longer pick up any messages and hopes it stays that way." Ellington didn't mention that all of this information came from hacking into her personal computer diary; and no one wanted to know his source.

"I assume you've had this Dr. Bradley under surveillance?" asked Sir Kensington.

"Well, that's the bad news. He seems to have disappeared the day before we sent a team to his home to begin watching his movements," replied Ellington. "I wanted to know his whereabouts based upon whatever actions we decide to take at this meeting."

"What are we doing to locate him?"

We're monitoring the phones and emails of his business associates in order to get some idea where he is. We've even researched the website of the CEO, but we've found nothing as yet. It's just a matter of time," he smiled broadly."

"What do you suggest we do at this point?" asked Sir Kensington.

"If his intent is to promote his socialistic ideas in conjunction with the aid of the alien Network, then his blogs need to be stopped. Their popularity is already approaching the 'tipping point' to go viral."

The conference room was totally silent. No one wanted to ask if stopping Dr. Bradley's blogs also meant stopping him!

Finally, Sir Kensington spoke up, "I think you've done some extraordinary investigative work under very difficult circumstances, Robert." Sir Kensington was the only member of the group who referred to Ellington as Robert. "I think we're all agreed with your suggestion of stopping the blogs of Dr. Bradley. We also trust that you'll take *whatever actions* you need to, within legal boundaries, to accomplish this objective."

With the legal phrase added, the others nodded their approval.

Sir Kensington thought, 'It's too bad Ellington had to reveal so much in order to convince them of the urgency we are facing. It's still a mystery to me why General Cornwallis lost the decisive battle of the Revolutionary War to the Americans. If the British had prevailed, the Empire would still be intact.'

ChapterEight—The Empath

Patricia Christensen lived alone in the remote town of Coalville, Utah; not far from Park City, the famous ski resort. She was an attractive, medium-height woman who lived a simple life. She wore little or no make-up. At present, she was in her early sixties. Her innocent-looking face masked her unusual psychic abilities, unless you were perceptive enough to detect the wisdom in her eyes. Around the age of 4, she discovered she could read people's thoughts. At first, this ability seemed to be fun. Then, as she began to understand the thoughts of adults she encountered, she decided to shut down this extrasensory skill.

She was married at 18 years of age at the strong urging of her family and relatives. Shortly thereafter, the inner portal opened again. She could not only read people's thoughts, but also experience their emotions. Such a person is called an Empath. It was an ability she had little skill in managing at the time. The more she could read her husband's feelings and emotions, the more removed he became. Pat knew, well before he expressed it, that he considered their marriage to be a mistake. They were divorced, by mutual consent, after three years together. She never married again.

After her divorce, Pat had never felt so free in her life. She loved living alone, which provided the opportunity for her to explore, learn, and fully develop her natural extrasensory skills. In her small hometown of Coalville she was readily accepted and supported by her relatives and friends. As word of her ability to "help" people began to spread, she built a steady clientele of people wanting psychic readings; many from neighboring Park City.

Pat acquired her real estate license two years after starting her thriving private business. Although not driven by money, she was very successful in selling homes because she could "read" people and their preferences. Her interest was simply to make enough money to live comfortably.

During her early thirties, she was visited by the wife of a Washington, D.C. governmental official. The couple was vacationing in nearby Park City. He worked for the Defense Department. Pat performed several readings for his wife, Nancy Crenshaw, over a three-year period every time the couple visited Park City. Pat travelled to Washington on one occasion to assist Nancy through a difficult marital period. Nancy credited Pat with saving her marriage with Mitchell.

During the early 1980s Mitchell Crenshaw was assigned to head up a highly secret Defense Department program: The Star Gate Project. The program was, in part, a response to a similar effort in the Soviet Union to use psychic powers for remote surveillance and information gathering. Nancy recommended that Mitch interview Pat as a possible member of his psychic team. She easily passed the tests the program facilitators administered.

Pat and Mitch became fast friends. She soon trusted him without reservation given her naïvety regarding the work she began performing. She was more than 70% accurate in terms of her clairvoyant visuals and 90% accurate in her emotional perceptions—or empathic readings, as they were called. She would often be used in diplomatic situations to sit in an adjacent room and read the thoughts and feelings of those involved in negotiation processes.

Pat was convinced that remote viewing could be used to complement other methods of information gathering. And in cases of no information at all, this form of intelligence gathering was better than nothing. However, the traditional scientists who were hired as "consultants," totally undermined the program. They described it as "pseudoscience," with no basis of provable theory or predictable observations.

This was not the way the space program progressed in the initial stages, Mitch argued. Their failures were considered to be learning opportunities. In the Star Gate Project, it was expected that they "prove" they were 95-100% accurate in the initial experiments. Mitch was under such pressure to produce immediate results that a learning curve was not possible. Well, that was history now, "C'est la vie,"—that's life, Pat often reminded herself.

When the Star Gate Project was declared "unsuccessful" and gradually replaced with satellite spy systems, she retired from government work and moved back to Coalville. Her intention was to live a quiet and rather uneventful life in the place where she grew up. That is, until she began picking up strange telepathic messages.

✪ ✪ ✪

Pat felt an obligation to inform someone of the intercepted messages she began receiving between the Pleiadians. The only person who would understand and possibly believe her was Mitchell Crenshaw—her former mentor and Control at the Defense Department. She had first informed him of the messages shortly after she accidentally intercepted the first two or three, almost ten years ago; both from *The Pleiades* and on Earth.

More recently, she revealed to Mitch that the exchanges indicated a stepped-up effort of Pleiadians coming to Planet Earth. Their objective was to form mentoring relationships in selected areas of the world. The areas were selected on the basis of *both* their potential to influence global change *and* receptivity to widespread spiritual awakening. These were the areas they were most likely to find protégés who were willing to be part of the Quest. Exactly what the Quest was she did not know.

Over a ten-year period, six additional Pleiadians teleported to Planet Earth; in addition to Antonio in the 1940s. Each proceeded to set up a Resource Center in their area of the world for functioning on Earth. Resource Centers consisted of currency, clothing, identification, and anything necessary for easily navigating the differing systems of the planet. A major advantage was that each Network member also retained his or her natural extrasensory abilities learned on Pleiades.

Antonio, aka Tony, was head of the Quest program. His first forty-five years on Earth had been devoted to understanding the major cultures and systems of operation. It also involved deciding what areas of the Earth best met the two criteria for the Quest. Most of all, he was assigned to determine if the Quest could be avoided by the natural evolution of the people of planet Earth, without the influence of the Pleiadian Network. After forty-five years of observation, Tony concluded that not only was there no possibility of widespread evolution, but the situation on planet Earth had gotten worse.

Pat finally informed Mitch of her most recent intercepted communication involving Bill Bradley, her former student. She described how quickly Bill learned clairvoyance and telepathy. Most of all, she informed him of the opening of his crown chakra and the permanent impact it would probably have on his life.

Since that last transmission she had not intercepted any further communications among the Pleiadians. She was certain the communication frequency had been readjusted because of her emotional reaction to Bill's name being discussed. Quite frankly, she was relieved. That is, until her latest communication from Mitch over their secure email line. There was an excellent lead on the head operative, Antonio, as well as the newest arrival from *The Pleiades*. The new arrival could be located through his association with Bill. Throughout their transmissions Mitch had used a code name for the alien Network coined by his boss, *The Seven Sisters*. The name was derived from *The Pleiades* cluster of the seven major stars in the Taurus constellation.

Reflecting on her relationship with Bill, she decided to set aside her loyalty to Mitch and focus her attention on the newest Pleiadian Network member and Antonio. She telepathed to them, 'Bill is in great danger. Government sources want to know the details of your influence on him. Tell him the truth about what he's getting into.' She hoped the communication would be received by these Network members—who would, in turn, inform Bill of his situation. That was the least she could do for him.

Considering his senior status and the DoD retirement pension, Mitch had informed his boss from the very beginning of Pat's emails. His boss was head of the Defense Intelligence Agency (DIA) of the DoD. The agency was established in 1961 to consolidate and integrate all military intelligence of the DoD. Mitch wanted to be sure he was covered in the event this situation turned into a full-fledged crisis—as situations of this nature often did in Washington, D.C. Their focus was actually on gathering intelligence about the Network of aliens. Dr. Bradley was simply a loose end that could be easily "handled," if necessary. Presently, he served as one of the best leads in identifying and locating the newly arrived Pleiadian.

✪ ✪ ✪

I met Pat at an off-beat Salt Lake party shortly after my divorce. A good friend of mind thought I needed to meet new people. In truth, I was bored to death and about to leave the party. Suddenly, I could feel someone boring into my consciousness. The unmistakable feeling that someone was staring at me.

At that instant, I looked over at Pat, and our eyes locked. I walked over and introduced myself as if I had found my reason for being there. That introduction began one of the most rewarding relationships in my life. I experienced an immediate level of comfort. So I asked, "What do you do for a living?"

"I'm a psychic reader, and I sell real estate as my day job," she replied. I think she thought the psychic stuff would chase me away. On the contrary, I began asking questions about the validity of psychic readings. If I only knew, at the time, of her past work for the DIA, I'm not sure what I might have done.

"How good are you at psychic readings?"

"I think I'm pretty good. At least, that's what most of my clients say," she replied, smiling. "Why do you ask?"

I immediately felt a comfort level with Pat, similar to my first experience with Weldon. So, I decided to let it all hang out. After all, she'd opened the door with her admission of psychic readings. "Some years ago, I began to spontaneously channel stuff. At first, I didn't understand what I was writing. Then, I met a guy who ran a metaphysical bookstore. He was the first person to open my eyes to the meaning of what I had written. I use the phrase 'I had written' very loosely," I smiled. "Since what

I actually do is write the thoughts that are planted in my mind."

She smiled knowingly, and said, "I think I understand."

"Have you written anything about the readings you do?" I asked.

"No, I haven't written much at all. I'm more hands-on in terms of what I do," she said. "Maybe you could let me see some of your writings. I have an interest in channeled materials."

Pat gave me her business card and I promised to give her a call. That was the beginning of my relationship with Pat Christensen.

The next day, I called Pat to set up an appointment for a reading. Once I have an interest in something new I don't usually waste time in pursing it. Fortunately, she had a cancellation for the following day and was able to schedule me for that time slot. 'There are no accidents,' I thought.

When we met the next day, she asked, "Where would you like to begin?"

"Ask your crystal ball where all this channeling is taking me. And why have I been chosen to write stuff I don't understand nor necessarily believe. How's that for a start?"

"I'd say several sessions," she smiled. "And for the record, I don't use a crystal ball. You've seen too many movies."

"Good," I replied. "What do you need to know?" I wanted to get right to the point to see how much she knew about me and my life. I was surprised to discover she knew more than I would have imagined.

"First, I should explain psychic readings are based upon the date and time you were born. Certain general characteristics are associated with time periods throughout the year. What month and day were you born?" she asked.

"December 4th."

"Okay, you're a Sagittarian." She opened a small book and

located the page she was looking for. She read from the book, "Presumably, you love your freedom and independence. You are straight forward, sometimes to a fault. You are introspective with abandon. And, you strive for lofty goals. Right, so far?"

"Perfect. What about the writings?" I asked impatiently.

"It isn't surprising that you'd be a perfect candidate for channeled transmissions. These things are never by accident. Are you aware of that?"

"I could have guessed as much." I smiled, thinking of my thought about this meeting. "I've always been interested in personal introspection."

"Why is that?"

"That's where I usually get answers to what I'm going do next."

"And what is that?" Pat asked.

"I still don't know what it is as yet. But I have feeling I'm getting close. I think the transmissions have a lot to do with guiding me. That's why I'm so interested in your readings."

"Give yourself some time. Your answers may come quicker than you think."

I was becoming more comfortable with Pat. I had an intuitive feeling she knew much more than she revealed.

"Okay, let's start with your first question, 'Where is your channeling taking you?' If we can answer that question, maybe we can discover why you've been chosen."

"That sounds like a good start."

"As you move to more advanced Guides, you will need to develop the skills they communicate with. As a start, you will need to learn more advanced forms of clairvoyance and telepathy. Their communications are holistic and multidimensional, not linear and three-dimensional as you use for your five senses communications."

"What exactly does that mean?" I asked.

"If you're writing a book, you may get whole paragraphs

or even the entire book in one download. Sometimes several chapters are transmitted simultaneously, like different radio stations broadcasting at the same time. You can only receive such transmissions using advanced extrasensory skills, not those easily transcribed by receiving sentence after sentence. Although you may write this way, that's not how you receive them."

"I've already had those experiences and they've mostly resulted in frustration when I try to write them," I responded.

"The same is obviously true of visuals. Initially, they are three-dimensional. Later, you will probably receive multidimensional visuals, similar to what you experience when you're dreaming. It all depends on how fast you learn."

"Again, where do we start?" I asked impatiently.

Pat began by slowly taking me through a relaxation process. Then she asked me to state what I was thinking. After I responded, she instructed me to continue describing my thoughts for as long as they surfaced from my subconscious mind. After fifteen minutes of continual talking, Pat asked me to stop. She had made her point.

"What did you learn?" she asked.

"That my mind never stops. It runs continually, even when I am not consciously aware of it."

"I'm going to replay part of your taped response." She had informed me we would be taping selected parts of our sessions for homework. She pushed the repeat button on the digital recorder.

After listening for ten minutes, Pat stopped the replay and asked, "What do you think?"

"It's mostly nonsense, filled with judgments about everything and everyone I know."

"Right. At least, we give ourselves a break while sleeping. So, the first step is learning to stop the continual conversation with ourselves, both conscious and unconscious, while we are awake."

"That might be a challenge," I responded.

"You've already learned to do it while sleeping. That's the main reason you presently channel. You're simply going to learn how to quiet your mind in the wake state. This will allow you to pick up projected thought-forms, no matter how weak they are," she said. "Are you ready to take the next step?"

"Sure," I responded, a bit more tentatively. I was starting to feel like I was crossing into a whole new dimension of my life, for which there would probably be no return.

"Okay," Pat said quietly. "Close your eyes again...., quiet your mind...., and listen with your inner ear. The thought-forms will be faint, at first." We repeated this process until I became frustrated and wanted to stop. Pat patiently urged me to keep listening. She knew that frustration was an essential part of letting go; particularly, for people who had an issue with control.

I sat there listening. Eventually, I completely lost track of time or where I was. Then a very faint thought-form "popped" into my mind. It was totally different from the gibberish I had repeated earlier. This thought-form was of the noon day sun on a meadow. I opened my eyes, and saw Pat smiling at me.

"Tell me what you got?" she instructed.

"The noon day sun on a meadow."

"Perfect. Although, I also sent you several other scenes and messages. Let's try a few others and we'll stop for today. You can practice at home what you've learned so far."

"Can I come back tomorrow?" Once I learn something I usually want to go as fast as I can.

"No. I think you should process what we have done so far for a few days. As you learn to open your inner ear, you will also have to learn how to keep it closed most of the time; for your own protection," she ended.

The way she stated this warning led me to think she was

recalling something personal.

◎ ◎ ◎

Over the following months, I became highly skilled in telepathic communication. I also learned to keep my inner ear closed most of the time. Since the channel to my "inner senses" had been opened, Pat suggested we extend it to my "inner eyes"—clairvoyance.

We began by simple recollection of visual scenes in her home, where she held the sessions. Then the projections were extended to my home and other locations I had recently visited. I found the recollection of visuals much easier than telepathy since I was already an 80% visual person in terms of my learning style.

Pat explained that the inner senses were simply a *natural extension* of the outer senses that came with an evolution in consciousness. "People we describe as gifted or brilliant have simply learned how to tap into a creative consciousness that's available to all of us. Unfortunately, most do not choose to use it."

"Why is that?" I asked. "Everyone wants to be more creative."

"Because of the fear associated with change. Every time we get a creative idea, we also change something about what we already believe."

"I never thought about creativity that way. I just thought it was simply adding more to my basket of ideas."

"This is the important point. Creativity is *not* reserved for a few privileged people. All it takes is the *courage* for inner exploration to be as creative as you choose. Now, with that short lecture, let's begin today's session."

"We're going to do something very different today," Pat said, as we began.

"Oh? Different how?" I asked skeptically. I knew that when Pat said "something different," it was probably a major step from what we were already doing.

"Just trust me. I'm not going to let you know what I have in mind. If I tell you in advance your conscious mind will immediately create diversions and resistance to where I want to take you. So, you'll have to trust me on this one."

"What should I do to avoid diversions?" I asked.

"Let your mind go where I instruct it and perceive whatever you 'hear' and 'see' with your inner senses. Are you willing to let me have total control of guiding you?" she asked.

"Yes. I think so," I replied hesitantly. Somehow, I knew this trust thing was going to come up. Up to this point, I'd been able to avoid it.

"You have to be absolutely sure," she said. "Or we won't do this exercise. You have to be willing to let go completely. I assure you, whatever happens will ultimately be controlled by you."

I wasn't quite sure what Pat meant by this last statement. Allowing myself to be totally controlled by another person was something I had never done before, and she knew it. It was the same as putting my *life* into someone else's hands. A quick memory flashed of the time a female massage therapist had asked me to let her have control of relaxing the tension in my body. My body responded, "Not totally." Now Pat was asking the same question.

"Let's not do this exercise. You're obviously not ready," she said, somewhat impatiently and stood to end the session.

I was quick to respond. "Yes! I am willing. I *am* ready." Another memory: jumping into a pool of water over my head when learning how to swim for the first time. Just do it! Don't think about it.

For the next two hours Pat led me through an intense process of moving through the seven chakras, culminating with the opening of my *crown chakra*—a visual opening at the top of my head for energy to flow through. The chakras—a Sanskrit word—are a series of energy spheres located along the spine culminating at the top of the head. They are connected energy vortexes vibrating at different frequencies.

In the weeks following that session, I came to realize that something had permanently changed about my life. A door had been opened that never previously existed. I felt I was just beginning to learn what it meant to be a human being. But most of all, the old Bill was gone and would probably never return.

William A. Guillory

Chapter**Nine**—The Flight

John calmly informed me that he called my room when he was abruptly awakened by two men making inquiries about us at the front desk. He was awakened by a *clairvoyant premonition*, an extrasensory skill which warns him of impending danger. Fortunately, we checked in separately using false names. They matched perfectly our expertly designed passports; courtesy of the U.S. Resource Center.

The two men had a picture of me which the night attendant did not recognize. He suggested they return in the morning when the daytime check-in attendant would be there at 7:00 am. They thanked him and indicated they would return at that time.

"How did they know we were here in Paris, at the Crillion?" I asked, as we used the stairway for gaining access to the ground floor.

"My friend, you truly are naïve. You can be tracked by practically any means associated with your personal identifications. Starting with your credit cards, cell phone, laptop computer, and most of all video surveillance networks on practically every street in most major cities. Both governments as well as global organizations have such resources. Do you have any idea of the number of active orbiting satellites that are used for planetary surveillance?"

"No, I don't," I replied.

"There are about 300 to 400 that are active. And, they are monitored twenty-four, seven, three-hundred and sixty-five point four; taking into account leap year."

We exited the hotel by the side door onto rue Boissy d'Anglais. We walked north a few blocks until we flagged a cab near Place de Madeliene for Airport Charles De Gaulle. John suggested we should go to Israel, Tel Aviv in fact.

"Why go to Israel?" I asked.

"It's a western-friendly country," he stated. "But one that does not easily lend its surveillance system to United States intelligence or resources.

"Can we get reservations this quickly?" I asked.

"I've already made reservations using a *telepathic wire*." Then he paused and said, "I don't think we should travel together. I'll teleport to Tel Aviv and set up everything and meet you at the airport when you arrive."

"Do you think that's a good idea, John?" I asked. He could clearly see my fear coming through. I had gradually adopted a sense of safety in the company of John. Now that I was about to become a "fugitive," I felt as though I was getting into a situation I'd only read about in novels and seen in the movies.

"Yes, I do, Bill" he replied. "They are looking for two people traveling together; one middle-aged male and one of unknown origin. After all, I am an alien," John said laughingly.

"This is no time for jokes, John. I'm acting like a fugitive and I haven't done anything! Why the hell are we going to Israel? I don't know anybody there, except for a guy I knew who was a postdoctoral fellow at Stanford."

"Would you prefer talking with the two gentlemen at the hotel?" John asked.

"What do you think they want with us?" I asked. "I thought you said no one knew about you or our relationship."

"That's what I thought, too. But obviously that's not the case now. Apparently 'they're on to us.'" John laughed again as he recounted a movie having that line. He also made a mental note to discuss with Tony other sources of intelligence about their presence and activities; particularly, after receiving the telepathic message from Pat about Bill's safety.

"Nobody's going to really believe that I'm not your protégé. And now we're leaving the hotel in the dead of night and catching a plane to Tel Aviv," I said.

"Look, we can discuss this later. Right now, I suggest you get on the plane with your overnight bag and get off in Tel Aviv and 'I'll be there.' You know, like the song," John laughed again.

"This is not funny, John," I stated defiantly. But underneath, I was scared shitless.

"Yes, I know," he replied. "It is getting quite serious. But what other choice do we have at this point?"

❂ ❂ ❂

When John met me at the Tel Aviv airport, he told me everything was set up and ready to go. He said he had gotten us a rental outside of the city in an area overlooking the sea.

"I need some rest and time to think about where my life is headed" I said. I was exhausted after the red-eye flight from Paris. "I have a sinking feeling in my stomach that I've crossed the line."

"I understand. But, I'm excited about your decision. Tony and I were depending on you to have a great impact on the movement.

"What decision?" I asked.

"The Quest, of course," he replied. "You just said that you had crossed the line."

"I said I had a *feeling*, not made a decision. And, what movement are you talking about? How is the Quest related to a movement?" I asked, still exhausted from my long flight from Paris.

"They are one and the same. The movement is the *process* of achieving the Quest."

"How does the movement involve me?" I asked, with a confused look.

"It's the process you will use to begin transforming the consciousness of the planet," John smiled, as if I had been awarded the grand prize at a county fair.

"I don't have any process for transforming anyone or anything," I stated, emphatically. "I told you that before."

"Yes, you do. You just don't know what *form* it will take at present. That's the creative pattern you've been using for years. You create the solution in a type of 'holding pattern,' and then you let the actual process take form over the following days. Presto! There it is," John exclaimed, with a smile of satisfaction.

"You've really become a comedian lately. I didn't really know how much being human was part of your Pleiadian personality. Actually, it helps to keep this whole process in some perspective."

"At least you won't have to worry about resources. We can either manufacture or get anything you need from our Resource Center here in the Middle East."

"I was wondering how you 'make arrangements,' like hotel reservations, plane tickets, seat assignments in first class, and most of all, manufacturing local currency."

"Reservations are rather easy using a *telepathic wire*. It's just like wiring reservations, but we use a telepathic thread. The message goes directly into the mental processing of an agent's mind."

"What about money?"

Money is relatively easy to duplicate as well as any official documentation, like we used in Paris. It is obviously the easiest way to get the things we need without being traced. That's why I said, you don't have to worry about resources. Our training for Earth was quite thorough."

"So, that makes us counterfeiters, too," I said seriously.

"I guess it does," John replied. "It's a cheap price to pay for what we're trying to do for this planet. Don't you think?"

I didn't reply.

✪ ✪ ✪

The rental that John referred to was a villa overlooking the Mediterranean Sea. It had high walls for privacy and all the luxuries one could imagine. John referred to it as 'hiding in plain sight.'

He had already obtained all the clothing and sportswear I needed. I had the entire 2nd floor to myself, which was like a mini-apartment. John had set up an extensive communications center with the latest support equipment and fastest laptop. From his perspective, everything was set and ready for me to get started.

All I knew is that I needed to sleep. Which I did until evening had set in, at which time I felt functional again. Actually, I felt refreshed by the beauty of the surroundings. The calming feeling that is the prelude to my inspired writings began to set in. So I booted up the laptop and allowed the inspiration to move through me. I named the Blog Site *The Messenger* and began typing.

> *These are difficult times for us all. We are experiencing change in the world order of economic and political power comparable to Galileo's pronouncement that the Earth was not*

the center of the universe. Adaptation to change of this magnitude requires a transformation in human consciousness—particularly by those who have traditionally been most powerful. This change begins with the acknowledgement that we are all creating a more dangerous, chaotic world driven by fear. There are two key factors in bringing about this transformation to create human compatibility, and both center on the word responsibility. First is responsible leadership that focuses on interdependence and unity rather than dissension and separation. The second is personal responsibility by each of us for creating greater human understanding, tolerance, and acceptance of the differences in the ways we are and what we value. The second is, by far, the more powerful in transforming human consciousness because it involves the everyday interactions that shape our basic nature as people.

The Messenger

When I completed the blog, I asked John to assist me in setting up worldwide distribution. Not surprisingly, each of the other six Network protégés translated the blog and distributed it throughout their spoken language areas of the world. The blog was also placed on Facebook, Twitter, LinkedIn, Google, and other social networking sites in addition to *The Messenger* Blog Site. The objective was to send the missive into cyberspace and begin to create global conversations.

For me, this was my first irreversible step into fully committing to the Quest. In retrospect, I could see that this action was really a culmination of a journey started more than ten years ago when I resigned from the university. The journey actually began with the first channeled messages I received from literally "out of the blue."

❁ ❁ ❁

Later that evening when John and I were having a leisurely dinner, he said, "I've invited Gala to join us here in Tel Aviv."

"You did what?" I asked.

"I asked Gala to join us. There is support she can provide you that I can't; particularly, when things get difficult," he replied, calmly.

"Why didn't you ask my permission? I don't want her to get involved in what I'm doing. I have a feeling this whole Quest thing is going to become a dangerous affair. I'm not as naïve as I might look."

"I am fully aware that you are not naïve at all. I knew that if I discussed her joining us, you would have been against it," John said calmly. "That's why I didn't ask your opinion."

"You're damn right about that!" I replied.

"I felt it was really her decision once we explained the situation we are dealing with. As I said, she can support you in ways I can't. You obviously trust her."

"I still think you should have asked me first. This situation is getting more dangerous by the moment. Why put her life in danger?"

"I was really thinking about you, Bill. She can also be helpful in the event we need to move to another location. The two of you can travel as a married couple, since they are probably still looking for two adult males travelling together. In any case, she'll be arriving tomorrow afternoon. We can explain the whole situation then and let her decide."

John simply sat there while allowing me time to cool off from a fait d'accompli—a done deal. In fact, if there was anyone I would want to be near me, it was Gala. I knew I could depend on her opinion of the subtleties of my blogs that John or the Network members couldn't understand. I had revised my writings in the past based on her comments about my sometimes being out of touch with reality. I wished I had had her input into my first blog, but now it was travelling throughout the "blue infinity"— cyberspace.

❂ ❂ ❂

The first indication that the blog had hit the mark was strong divergent views regarding a "change in the world order," "*who* was creating a more dangerous world," and "*whose* responsibility it was to create a more peaceful world."

Predictably, many indicated that they didn't understand what was meant by "transforming human consciousness." This was clearly an idea we would have to learn together over time. If I'd written, "change the way we live," most readers would have probably yawned. The Internet was buzzing about each of the comments. Fortunately, this means of communication was still relatively unregulated and uncontrolled.

The conversations involving a change in world order seemed to be more focused in an older demographic. It was pointed out over and over again, that the heart of economic power was creativity and innovation. The U.S. and other western countries still dominated new scientific and technological breakthroughs. Some even mentioned that the U.S. was still the most powerful military force on the planet; although, no mention had been made on the blog about military power or weaponry, by intention.

There was discussion about China being the source of money used for "bailing out" American financial institutions during the 2009 economic crisis. Support for a shift in world order was strongest in Asia where it was pointed out that the continuing shift of manufacturing and technology to southeast and southern Asia were key indicators of a shift in economic power.

The discussion of terrorism was at center stage in terms of global fear. One dimension of the conversation was why not use diplomatic means of achieving peace and prosperity. The other was that such means had never brought about any lasting change for the "have-nots;" hence, the resort to violence. One common theme that seemed to emerge throughout the world was the continual erosion of civil and private liberties in the name of national security.

The suggestion that each individual is far more powerful than what she or he thinks in bringing about change was of great interest, particularly by a younger demographic. This suggestion made sense to most of them, consistent with their belief that they had the power to change the world. I was reminded of the quote by Ryunosuke Satoro, the Japanese poet, who wrote,

"Individually, we are one drop.
Together, we are an ocean."

One comment pointed out the power of social networking as a means of expressing the influence of a collection of individuals. There were an equal number of comments regarding the fact that our political and business leaders, worldwide, were responsible for the state of the world. That our job was to ensure that they serve our needs or be voted out of office.

By far, the most perplexing comments involved the idea of *transforming human consciousness*. As I previously pointed out, this concept was confusing to most. They asked, "What exactly *is* human consciousness and how does transforming it have anything to do with the state of the world?" I'd thought long and hard about using more familiar terminology like changing our way of life. Terms that we could easily relate to even though they were also somewhat vague and certainly *not* what I had in mind.

Then there was the question, "How does transformation differ from change or are they both the same?" The jury was still out as to whether the public would lose interest because of accurate, but perplexing, terminology. After all, in the cyber world, people don't want to work too hard at understanding what is being said, or not at all!

For the moment, I felt I had accomplished my first major objective: initiate a worldwide conversation. The responses had proven that this objective had been accomplished.

Gala arrived the following morning on the same flight I'd taken from Paris. John felt it best that I remain at the villa, away from any form of surveillance, particularly, in Tel Aviv.

After checking through customs, she was delighted to meet John, *in person*. It was like two old friends reconnecting. From Gala's perspective, she was on vacation. She thanked John for the invitation to join us. Fortunately, or unfortunately, she had no idea what she was getting into as yet. On the other hand, maybe Gala knew more than she revealed.

"Where's Bill?" she asked excitedly.

"He is back at the rental. As usual, he's working on a new project."

"What new project?" Gala asked.

"Oh stuff. You know Bill. He has a compulsion to write about whatever is on his mind." In order to divert the conversation, John asked, "How was your flight? You look refreshed and cheerful."

"I slept on the flight from Paris. And first class wasn't bad," Gala said, smiling. "I've never been to this part of the world."

John had informed Gala to pack lightly since everything she needed could be obtained in Tel Aviv. And off they proceeded to the "rental." The weather was beautiful as usual, in the low 80s. The day was sunny. The kind of conditions that ensured one shouldn't have a care in the world.

But powerful forces were at work, attempting to find the location of one Dr. Bill Bradley and anyone associated with him. In fact, Gala's customs clearance had already been relayed to Washington, D.C. Greater interest was being directed to Dr. Bradley, since government intelligence sources also knew exactly who The Messenger was.

❂ ❂ ❂

When Gala arrived at the villa, she was astonished at the accommodations. "I thought you said this was a rental, John?"

"Yes. It is a rental villa," he replied. "We're hiding in plain sight."

"Why are you hiding?" Gala asked curiously.

"I'm only kidding," was John's reply. "I really meant we want privacy."

'Good catch,' I thought, as I approached them. "Hey, Babe, how was your flight?"

"It was wonderful. Thanks for inviting me to join you here," she replied, cheerfully.

As we embraced, I could feel that charge that goes through my body when we touch. In truth, I had not realized how much I missed being with her. Besides the calming effect she has on me, I feel complete as a person. Then, John's comment popped into my mind, "She can provide support for you that I can't."

"Well, we can thank John for thinking of you," as I eyed him with a snide look. "Let's walk around the grounds, if you're up to it?" I said, smiling.

"Love to," Gala said, excitedly.

When Gala and I had wandered away and John went into the villa, I took her aside and began to explain my situation. In particular, I told about the Guardian Angels and their reaction to my blogs. When I finished, her excitement had disappeared.

"What I want you to realize is that things are getting out of my control," I explained. "I've taken a major step by publishing a blog on a change in world order." Then I explained to her the details of her invitation.

"It was John's idea to invite you here, without my knowledge," I stated, with a look of seriousness.

"Do you want me to leave?" she asked, in her direct way.

"Yes. That would be best for you." I replied.

"What about you?" she asked. "Will you be okay without me?"

"I think I've stepped over a line. I don't think I can return to my life as it used to be. But what's most frightening is I have no idea where *I'm* headed. That's why I want you to go back to the U.S. At least you'll be out of harm's way"

"Okay. I'll think about it," she replied. She was on the verge of tears.

When she started to say something in protest, I took her hand and we resumed our leisurely walk around the grounds of the villa.

Chapter**Ten**—The Surveillance

"Looks like we can no longer protect your prized student anymore, Pat," Mitch Crenshaw stated over their secure communications line. "Doesn't matter what name he goes by, when he stirs up public attention like the recent *Messenger* blog, it's out of my hands or anyone else's."

"I guess I knew it was inevitable," she replied. "There's no brainwashing going on. He's simply writing what he believes. Actually, it goes beyond what he believes. It's probably what he feels his life is all about at this point; whether he's aware of it or not."

"I've already turned over all of our communications about the *Seven Sisters* to my boss. He passed the information to the CIA and Homeland Security. They were not pleased that we didn't inform them years ago, given what we suspected," Mitch said, appearing to be innocent of violating her trust in him. His boss had been receiving her emails from the very beginning.

"There was nothing substantive we had to prove the existence of extraterrestrials," Pat responded, defensively.

"Yeah, I know. But they believe they have a right to know anything in the name of national security," Mitch replied. "I told them we didn't believe there was any threat to national security. Plus, we had nothing tangible as proof; just your emails of their intercepted conversations. The only other stuff was about Dr. Bradley, which I'm sure they already know, anyway."

"I hardly see Bill as a threat. All he's doing is writing about stuff that'll never happen in our lifetime," Pat laughed, in an attempt to make Bill appear to be another harmless voice in the wilderness of change for the better. But she knew how government intelligence agencies worked. They left no stones unturned. If there was a *suspected* threat, better to eliminate it than have it come back as a future oversight.

"That's not what the Secretary of Homeland Security thinks. She blew a gasket when I suggested the same thing. She asked me in a scalding tone, 'Who are you to determine what a threat is? We apparently have an American citizen in the company of an alien with no idea why the alien is here. And you think there is no reason for concern?'"

"What would she do if she caught one of the aliens?" Pat asked, laughingly.

"I'm not quite sure. I assume she understands what teleportation is. She *is* a very bright person," replied Mitch, laughing.

"Maybe something will eventually get to the President or someone who can act responsibly in discovering what their real objective is. It has to be something quite serious given the time and resources they have committed."

"I think before this whole affair is over, they're going to need you to try to make contact with the Network. Ultimately, we will need a direct line of communication to discover their real purpose for being here. Not some message delivered through Bill's blogs."

"I have no interest whatsoever in *serving* the government again. Not after the way they discredited everything we accomplished. I was young and naïve when I joined Star Gate. That's all behind me now. It's a door I have closed on my past," Pat said, with finality.

"I understand, Pat," Mitch replied.

"In any case, they'll probably go through surveillance, threats, and a show of force first, before discovering that none of those approaches will work. Then they'll begin to look for alternatives," she said. "I just want you and them to know that I am absolutely not available."

Mitch had a thought about Shakespeare's Hamlet, where Hamlet questions his mother's commitment to her slain husband, "The lady doth protest too much, methinks." Then Mitch said, "Well, hang in there. Just thought I'd update you on what's going on here in D.C. Wish I were there with you in Utah. I think things are about to 'hit the fan' here in Washington."

❂ ❂ ❂

"You missed Bradley in Salt Lake City by one day. You missed him again in Paris by six hours. At least you're closing the gap." Robert Ellington stated coldly to his two "contracted associates"—Ryan Doyle and Peter Cook. They were assigned to locate Dr. Bradley, report his activities and associations, and receive further instructions. So far, they had only been able to locate his trail. And that was accomplished through the efforts of Ellington's IT Team.

Doyle and Cook were unaccustomed to missing their target *or* being berated by a client. Cook was fuming. Doyle was more in control. He assumed Ellington was a pompous aristocrat who had spent most of his life demanding performance from others of which he was not capable. After catching his breath, Doyle responded, "Sorry again about missing him. When we make contact, I promise you we won't lose him again."

Ellington sensed the voice of a professional. It was almost, but not quite, an apology. "Let me talk with my IT guys. I'll get back to you and Cook with updated information of their whereabouts," Ellington replied in a clipped tone. Then he disconnected.

Shortly after Ellington began following the blogs on *The Voice*, he set up a sophisticated intelligence unit. The unit consisted of three highly-trained individuals with extensive knowledge of information technology. The team was headed by Jeremy Lieberman. Ellington referred to them as his "IT Team."

The team combined their knowledge of information technology with unusual human instinct to obtain practically any information they desired. Hacking into Pat Christensen's website and her email file, without her knowledge, was a no-brainer. On the other hand, if Jeremy had known they were one click away from the Defense Intelligence Agency (DIA) portal, he would have needed a diaper!

Ellington exited his office at the New York estate and descended to the basement where his IT Team was busily tracking Dr. Bradley. He called his subterranean facility Central Control.

"They were in Paris last night at the Crillion Hotel. Where are they now?" Ellington asked Jeremy. Ellington wasted little time with small talk and commonly got to the point immediately. The IT Team found Ellington more amusing than insulting and was not offended by his insensitivity. They were paid extremely well and learned long ago not to take their clients' behaviors, personally.

Jeremy responded. "We know they have split up as a diversionary tactic. We have to decipher the authenticity of 200 passports before we can confirm that, at least, one of them took the early morning El Al flight to Tel Aviv. Right now, that's about a 70% probability. We can never reach 100% without visual confirmation." Jeremy interpreted the information and data they collected. His ability to process information bordered on the extrasensory.

"So, what are you saying?" Ellington asked, impatiently.

After taking a look at the refreshed computer screen, Jeremy turned to Ellington and stated, "There is *now* an 80% probability one of them flew to Tel Aviv on the early morning flight two days ago." Then he smiled at Ellington with a laid-back look of satisfaction.

⊗ ⊗ ⊗

Dana Hartman was a product of the heartland of America, Davenport, Iowa, one of the "Quad Cities" including Bettendorf, Rock Island, and Moline across the Mississippi River in Illinois. She was a tall, attractive brunette, about five-nine without heels. Dana was not intimidated by men, even aggressive ones. In fact, it was more often the opposite.

She was the eldest of four children which included three younger brothers. She grew up on her family's farm just outside of Davenport. Her family nearly lost the farm during the Farm Crisis of the 1980s. Their homestead was saved when her mother got an industrial job in nearby Davenport.

At 45 years old, Dana Hartman was head of Homeland Security. Her professional successes had been meteoric. Some referred to her as the "golden girl" in spite of her brown hair. She attributed her success to hard work and unusual responsibilities as an adolescent. When her mother worked in Davenport, she had the responsibility of caring for her three younger brothers as well as overseeing the upkeep of their home.

In truth, Dana could understand why Crenshaw and his boss had not reported the intercepted transmissions—particularly with the previous administration's appointee as head of Homeland Security. After all, the Star Gate Project had been all but discredited and a forgotten memory in DIA. Anyone with any sense would know he or she would be transferred to a lost outpost if there was an unsubstantiated report about aliens.

However, she felt it important to impress the DIA with the far-reaching power of her agency. If there were any secrets involving national security, it was theirs to hoard—even from the President, if it weren't important for him to know. It surprised Dana sometimes how addicted she had become to power. She rationalized that if you didn't have and exude power in D.C., you'd be quickly overrun or manipulated by the agenda of others.

Besides Pat Christensen, Dana had to keep a close eye on that idiot vigilante group, led by Robert Ellington. It was always rag-tag operations like his that created government embarrassment and exposed much more than the public needed to know. The problem was there was no tangible evidence of anything alien. How could she bring something to the President claiming that extraterrestrials were running around the planet recruiting unsuspecting humans to do their bidding? She would probably be out of a job when he asked, "What proof do you have?"

As she reflected on how she got here, everyone assured her how successful she had been: four-year scholarship to the University of Chicago, Yale Law School, and Assistant District Attorney in Davenport, Iowa. Then followed by her move to the nearby Chicago District Attorney's office where she gained national recognition because of her exceptional success in courtroom prosecutions. They referred to her as having the "Medici touch"—in reference to the most influential Florentine family during the Italian Renaissance. No matter what challenge the family encountered, they turned it to their advantage. In the present situation, she wondered if her magic touch had finally met its ultimate match.

Dana was smart enough to know that traditional methods were not going to work in the present case of the *Seven Sisters*. Since taking office with the new administration two years ago, she had taken the meager file concerning aliens more seriously than her older predecessor. Her surveillance information was the result of an enterprising Gen Xer, Don Caldwell. He put together the Network of Protégés using the agency's extensive surveillance system as well as the members of the Guardian Angels. Dana referred to Don as her "go to" guy in vital projects involving "IT intelligence gathering"—an official-sounding phrase for domestic and international hacking and eavesdropping.

Don began piecing together the protégé membership using keywords in the same email documents, blogs, or other communication formats. The keywords he used were "network", "transformation", "compatibility", "spirituality", and "extrasensory". He also noted that participation in the Network occurred over a ten-year period and appeared to be complete with seven members. The latest member to join was Dr. William Bradley. Don and Dana conferred about what they knew and what was conjecture based upon their only direct observables— the protégés.

First, the protégé network appeared to consist of seven members. Second, the identified locations around the world were the Middle East, France, South America, China, India, Japan, and the U.S. Third, the exchanged messages among the protégés seemed to focus on something they described as planetary transformation. Presumably, this activity involved ways of influencing change in people. They referred to this process as the Quest. The email exchanges appeared to contain nothing about conquering the Earth or anything threatening to people or property—unless they were using coded language or hidden messages.

In terms of conjecture, each protégé was assumed to be associated with a specific Pleiadian—which meant there were seven in all located around the world. Keeping track of each protégé was Homeland Security's best way of tracking the movements of the aliens. For the time being, it was also assumed by Dana and Don that the messages from the protégés were being orchestrated by the assigned Pleiadian. The questions that kept her awake at night were "What did the Pleiadians want?" and "Why were they here?"

Given what they knew and could guess, it did not appear that they had an aggressive agenda. However, her job was to assume that was the case in the absence of corroborating information to the contrary. Her overriding question was, "How could she establish direct contact with the aliens to have these questions answered?"

That piece of the puzzle was beginning to take shape in her mind based upon Pat's emails she received from the DIA people. If one were to believe it, this Pat Christensen appeared to be the only person who had "received communication between the Pleiadian Network." That is, until they discovered her interception. Dana wondered if it were possible for Pat to *initiate* contact with them directly. She would have to think through this possibility very carefully. In the meantime, she would restrict the knowledge of this project to her and Don as she prepared to leave for yet another of the innumerable meetings in Washington, D.C. Just before leaving, she called Don on her secure phone and gave him a special assignment.

Doyle answered his phone on the third ring since he knew it would annoy Robert Ellington. Finally, he said, "Hello, Doyle here."

"Doyle! This is Robert Ellington," Ellington said excitedly.

"Yes," Doyle replied, dryly.

"Bradley definitely flew to Tel Aviv. That's where you should pick up his trail. By the time you and Cook arrive there, I should have more information for you. My IT guys have already made reservations for your flight from Charles De Gaulle Airport late this afternoon. They have also arranged hotel reservations in Tel Aviv. Contact me as soon as you arrive," Without waiting for a reply or saying goodbye, Ellington clicked off.

Doyle said to himself, "asshole." Then he turned to his partner and said, "We're off to Tel Aviv; the excitement capitol of the world. At least the weather is great."

Dana abruptly awakened from a dream in a highly emotional state. The dream was as vivid as though it had actually happened to her. She laid in bed and recalled the sequence of events she experienced.

> *A maiden from Greek mythology appears to her. She tells Dana her name is Maia. During the dream the Greek maiden offers her a bouquet of yellow roses. She takes Dana's hand and leads her along a garden path. Dana stops to take off her shoes to feel the ground beneath her feet. With each step she gains more confidence. Then she comes to a point where the path ends and there is a gap to the other side. She has no assurance of what will occur as a result of stepping off into the gap. Maia takes the bouquet of yellow roses and gives Dana a bouquet of "lilies of the valley" and tells her to step off. Dana hesitates, her heart pounding,*

and then steps off. Like magic, a new paved road
appears beneath her feet. She walks to the other
side. Maia meets her there with a new "bouquet of
palm leaves" and tells Dana to go on her way.

The dream had stirred such emotions that she proceeded to
write every detail.

The next day she cancelled all her morning appointments.
She called her mother in Davenport to enquire if her high school
friend, Julie Preston, still had her flower shop. Her mother
assured her that Julie's business was still thriving. She gave
Dana Julie's phone number. Julie had majored in fine arts at
Iowa State after both graduated from high school and went their
separate ways. Julie returned to Davenport to start her flower
business.

"Julie! I bet you can't guess who this is after all these years,"
Dana said, in a girl-to-girl tone.

"Please give me a minute," Julie said, "while I finish with a
customer I'm serving."

Dana was momentarily taken aback. She was not accustomed
to anyone putting her on hold. On the other hand, this was a
personal call to someone who probably could care less about the
Washington D.C. protocol.

Julie returned to Dana's call and said, "Give me a significant
event and I'll guess."

Dana replied, "I was selected as most likely to succeed in our
high school graduating class." Then she added as an afterthought
to herself, "because I intimidated boys."

"Dana! Dana Hartman!" Julie cried out. "How are you?"

"I'm fine. Sometimes I wish I could give this job to someone
else, like Lloyd Richardson. Remember him?" Dana asked.

"Of course I do. He's been our mayor for two terms now. What
can I do for you?" Julie laughed and said, "Sorry to put you on
hold. That phrase just comes out automatically when I'm with a

customer."

"Well, in truth you *can* do something for me. I'm giving a friend an array of flowers for a special occasion and I thought you might help me with my selections. I already have a few choices in mind. I thought you might tell me what they mean."

"Okay," said Julie, "shoot!"

"The first one is yellow roses."

"Yellow roses signify friendship and devotion to others," replied Julie.

"Lilies of the valley," Dana said.

"Lilies of the valley signify trust or, most often, trustworthiness."

"Palm leaves," said Dana.

"Palm leaves signify victory or, depending on the situation, they can also mean success."

"My last question is weren't you a fine arts major at Iowa State?" which Dana already knew. She rarely engaged a conversation where she didn't have the complete background of a person—even informal ones.

"Yes, but I've forgotten pretty much everything about it," Julie said.

"Well, you might remember this one as a long shot. Who is Princess Maia?"

"Oh, her I'll never forget. She was the eldest daughter of Atlas and Pleione in Greek mythology. She was known for her compassion and wisdom. Another piece of trivia you might add for the fun of your gift, *The Pleiades Star Cluster* is named after the *Seven Sisters* and Maia, one of the sisters, is the largest star."

"Thanks, Julie. You've been a great help. I'll look you up the next time I visit mom and dad." Dana clicked off her secure cell phone.

If her dream hadn't been so real, she would have simply ignored it, like she did most of them. But the apparent message from Maia was *friendship*, *trust*, and *success*. What did it all mean? And were Pleiades and the *Seven Sisters* connection coincidental? She decided to think on it for a couple of days, although she didn't believe in coincidence, particularly in her present job.

Chapter**Eleven**—The Decision

The following morning Gala and I awakened refreshed. It was like a new chapter in our lives had begun. Although I felt I had made a decision about my own future, her decision would play a critical role in our future together. In spite of the situation we faced, as far as Gala was concerned we were on vacation. Her first thoughts were about sand, sea, and shopping in Tel Aviv.

As I reflected on the five years we had known each other, I thought about how a close friendship had evolved into a committed relationship. We had both experienced marriages that ended in divorce. Neither of us wanted to experience again the discord that is a prelude to separation. We had built a relationship with a solid foundation, brick by brick.

I was snapped back to reality when Gala asked, "Okay, what's the plan for today?" Which was code for 'I have it all planned, but I'm giving you a chance to see if you've figured out what we are going to do.'

We had adopted a new approach to touring in our recent

travels. Our approach was to "experience" the people, the culture, and the cuisine. We had become less interested in historical sites and symbols. You might say our focus was on our experience of the present—rather than the past—and making the most of each moment life provided to us.

After breakfast on the patio, we bid John goodbye. He said, "Keep an eye out for our friends from Paris."

I said I would and headed for the white sand beach. I sat and read while Gala swam in the warm Mediterranean water for an hour or so. I kept a close eye on her as was my habit. I also had an uncanny feeling of lurking danger. I can't explain it. It's like a signal goes off in my stomach that something is not favorable to my well-being.

I wondered if this signal was similar to the inner sense that John had experienced in the hotel relating to the two men following us. "Hold that thought," Gala exclaimed, as she came up to our umbrella on the beach. "Now, put it in my hands." She offered me cupped hands.

So I pretended to deposit my "thought of danger" into her cupped hands. Off she ran back to the water and allowed it to be washed away. She returned and plopped down next to me as though she didn't have a care in the world. Who knows? Maybe she didn't.

"Now," she said, "a penny for your remaining thoughts."

I just don't have the ability to fake anything when there is danger in my stomach, so I said, "I was just feeling anxiety about our future."

"Why should you feel anxiety when we both know what we are going to do?" she replied, with a carefree smile.

"It's not that simple, G-Baby," I replied. G-Baby was my special name for Gala.

"What's complicated about it?" she asked.

"I'm getting clear about the implications of *my* life, but that doesn't mean you have to follow me."

"Follow you! What makes you think I'm following you? Don't you think I'm perfectly capable of making my own decisions?" Calmness gone. Eyes flashing. Hands on hips for emphasis.

"I didn't mean it like 'following me.' I know how independent you are. I just meant that I think you ought to return home before you get too involved in this whole affair. Quite frankly, I'm concerned about where it appears to be heading."

"And where is that?" she asked.

"To a place where there is no return to what your life is like now," I replied.

"Except for you, my life isn't that great. I go to work early, come home late, play in my garden, and go to bed. The next morning, I repeat the same routine."

"You might find you like that routine more than you think. At least it's predictable. And you also have your friends from Eastern Europe."

"You don't seem to understand. My life has changed dramatically since I met you. I'm not as dependent on people from my home since we've been together."

"What about your son?" I asked. Her son was unmarried and stayed pretty close to home. It was a tradition. They were more like roommates unless she wanted to exert her authority over something she really wanted.

"He's thirty-two for God's sake! He has his own interests, friends, and lifestyle. I'm sure he'll do just fine."

"There's no need to solve anything right now," I said reassuringly. "Let's just keep talking to each other honestly about our concerns. I'm sure when the time comes, we'll know what to do."

"Okay. You got a deal," Gala smiled. "Let's just enjoy our vacation." She was back to where she was before I suggested she should not "follow" me.

While Doyle and Cook were en route to Tel Aviv, Ellington's IT Team was busily attempting to locate Bill Bradley and his "traveling companion." This was about the time that Jeremy Lieberman hit upon a brilliant idea. He surmised that most people who rented cars used credit cards—either on file or at the time they purchased a rental agreement. Only a small percentage used cash transactions. Bill and his buddy had been very careful to avoid a paper trail of credit purchases. So the obvious conclusion was to focus on car rentals that were cash transactions over the last few days in Tel Aviv—starting with the airport.

They got a hit on a Mercedes rental. This rental also fit the pattern of using high-end services, as in Paris. They were beginning to build a profile of either Bill or his companion. The next obvious step was to find out if the rental had a built-in GPS system. That was a no-brainer. A Mercedes. Of course it did. The new GPS system in high-end rentals could broadcast their location 24/7/365, whether in motion or stationary—making it easy for Jeremy's team to locate their target.

The location of the Mercedes was sent to Doyle and Cook. They had arrived in the early morning hours, picked up their rental car, and got a precious three hours of sleep.

Now they were visually scanning the beach where the Mercedes was parked. No luck. They didn't spot any couple of two men together. Then they spotted a person matching the picture they had of Bill Bradley. He was a bit older, but it was definitely him.

Instead of being with a male companion, he was with a female. Doyle used his 20x mini camera to focus on Gala and took her picture. He sent the photo back to the IT team in upstate New York to confirm she was Bradley's female companion from the dossier. Then he took out his satellite phone and called Robert Ellington.

Ellington retrieved his phone on the second ring. "Yes?

Ellington here," he said, after being awakened from a sound sleep.

"Doyle. You told us to call you when we made contact with Bradley. We have him in visual contact on a beach in Tel Aviv. He is in the company of his female companion. Repeat. His female companion from the dossier we compiled. There is no male companion present. What would you like us to do?" he asked.

"Maintain visual contact and follow him and his companion to where they are staying. Attempt to confirm his other male companion and contact me again for further instructions."

"Is that it?" Doyle asked. He was expecting instructions of more definitive action to be taken.

"*Her* presence complicates matters for the present." Ellington paused, and then stated, "Just in case we need to take further action, use our contacts there to make sure the two of you are armed. That's it for now." As usual, Ellington clicked off without further comment.

❂ ❂ ❂

Gala and I gathered our belongings and returned to the parking lot where the Mercedes was parked. We both slipped on a pair of shorts over our swimsuits and prepared to drive away.

Doyle and Cook were several parking spaces from the Mercedes. The Mercedes backed out and began moving away. Cook pushed the button for the ignition on their rental car, but the starter only whined. Doyle looked at him as if he didn't know how to drive. They both began to panic as the Mercedes drove away with their engine continuing to whine.

Finally, Doyle concluded that they had lost their target, yet again. He got out of the car and told Cook to pop the hood. Cook reached under the dashboard and pulled the lever to dislodge the hood latch. Doyle inspected the various connections and noted the leads exiting the battery were dislodged. He reattached them and decided it was definitely time to connect with Ellington's local contact. It was clear there were local assets overseeing the security of Bradley and his female companion.

After acquiring the hardware for serious business from Ellington's local contact, Doyle phoned Ellington again.

"Ellington, here," he said after connecting on the first ring.

"Doyle. We have a problem."

"Don't tell me. You've lost him again."

"More than that. When we started to follow them, our car wouldn't start. We either had a loose battery connection or it was sabotaged. I don't believe in coincidences. Someone must have been watching us while we were watching them."

"Are you armed?" Ellington asked.

"Yes. We connected with your local contact here in Tel Aviv," Doyle responded.

"From now on, *protect* yourself. Do you understand?" Ellington was being very careful not to give any instructions to harm Bill Bradley or his companions in any way—especially over the telephone.

"I'm not sure," Doyle replied. He was clear they could protect themselves. He wanted specific instructions about Bradley, and possibly his associates.

Ellington wanted to be very careful here, since he had given his word to the Guardian Angels that he would not take any illegal action that could implicate them. "I'll get back to you when my IT guys discover where the Mercedes is. I'll give you clear instructions at that time," he said.

"Got it," replied Doyle, and he clicked off. As a professional he had no problem eliminating Bradley or any of his friends, he just wanted be sure that was what Ellington was requesting.

Gala and I drove from the beach to the outdoor Carmel Market. The Market had practically anything one could think of, mostly things we didn't need. Gala particularly enjoyed bargaining. It was like being home again in a Ukrainian marketplace.

Again, I had the uneasy feeling that something was not quite right. I began to scan the crowd more carefully. I had mastered this instinct as a teenager growing up in the New Orleans housing projects. If you didn't master the instinct, you had a very difficult adolescence; if, in fact, you survived adolescence. For just a split second, I noticed two men who pretended to be separate. They were both obviously faking the shopping process. The stall owners also recognized the façade and asked the pair to move on.

I walked over to Gala and whispered for her to follow me with no questions asked. I took her hand firmly and navigated several twists and turns through the market. We finally ended up out of sight at the back of a small restaurant.

"What's going on?" Gala asked. Obviously upset after being dragged away from her shopping feast. The look I got was, 'this better be good.'

"I think we are being followed," I whispered.

"By whom?" she asked, as though I was supposed to know the answer to that question. I've often thought that her mind works in a logical, sequential manner, even when a series of questions has huge gaps of missing information. So, I assumed an attitude of, 'It is not mine to judge, but simply to serve.'

"I have no idea. There were two men who were asking about us in Paris. That's why we left in the middle of the night."

"Are they the same ones?" she asked. Same type of question again, I smiled, in spite of our situation.

"How would I know? I didn't see them there and I hope we don't see them here. I just hope I'm just being paranoid."

"Perhaps you should have listened to John about the people from Paris," she said.

My first thought was, now it's about *me*, not *we* should have listened to John. I let that thought pass without replying. We needed to be "one" in the present situation. So I said, "You're right. *I* should have taken his warning more seriously. But we are more than 3,000 miles from Paris and we're in the southern hemisphere. How could they find us?" I realized my question to her was as ridiculous as hers to me a minute ago.

Our conversation abruptly stopped when the two men who I had noticed walked into the restaurant. They could not see us in our little "coffin corner" of the restaurant. They asked a passing waiter something and he pointed to our little hide-away.

"Aw, shit," I said to myself, "not like this."

Gala asked, "Are we in trouble?"

"Have you ever heard the story about the alligators in the swamp?"

"What alligators?" she asked.

Just then, the two guys approached our table. I was about to scream for help, when one of them smiled and said, "Bill and Gala, I am Bin," and pointing to the other guy, "this is Anwar."

In the midst of my excitement I hadn't realized one of the guys had begun telepathing. "I am one of the seven Pleiadians. Anwar is my protégé, a Palestinian," and then he smiled broadly.

When they were seated, Bin began, "We were asked by John to make sure you were safe during your sight-seeing of Tel Aviv."

"We were actually afraid that the two of you might be the two men who were looking for us in Paris. That's why we were trying to escape and hide," I replied.

"That was probably a good idea. There were two men who were watching you at the beach. They took photos of both of you. One of them must have known who you were already because he pointed to you," Bin said.

"That's why I had the uneasy feeling," I replied.

"Where are they now?" Gala asked.

"We disabled their auto," replied Anwar, smiling. "That's why you were able to drive here without an incident. We followed you."

"We think they must have some type of tracking device on your car. Does it have a built-in GPS?" asked Bin.

"It's a Mercedes. It probably does. Particularly, since it's a rental. GPSs with tracking devices are pretty standard now," I said, "especially on high-end vehicles."

"Then we need to finish your shopping using our car for transportation. We can still watch over you, but I do suggest we move to another tourist site," Bin said. "They're probably trying to locate your new position."

"Meanwhile, I'll get an enterprising taxi driver to drive your Mercedes to Jerusalem and other points of interest in Israel," smiled Anwar. "I'll hook up with the three of you at the other venue."

Bin said, "Next stop, the Nachalat Binyamin pedestrian walkway. If you like to shop Gala, I guarantee you, you won't be disappointed. Courtesy of the Middle East Resource Center."

Gala's smile returned as well as her carefree attitude as she whispered to me "Hakuna Matata," which is a Swahili phrase that means, "There are no worries."

❂ ❂ ❂

Doyle and Cook decided to have lunch while waiting for the new coordinates from Ellington's IT Team. They hadn't gotten much sleep. They were still tired from the flight from Paris. And they had lost their target again. All in all, it was a pretty lousy day, so far. Just then, Doyle's satellite phone began ringing. He knew it could only be the "man" and they hadn't even eaten yet.

"Ellington here," was the reply after Doyle said, "Doyle here."

"I have the new coordinates for you. It looks like our couple is on the move again. The heading appears to be Jerusalem. Head in that direction ASAP. I will keep you informed when we have a stationary reading." As usual, Ellington simply clicked off.

Doyle related Ellington's instructions to Cook. Cook's pupils expanded as though he was trying to adjust to a darken room. "He said what?" Cook asked.

Doyle tried to remain calm because he knew Cook had a short fuse. He didn't want it to go off, so he asked, "What do you think we should do, Peter?"

"I think we should *at least* eat something. And I don't mean a take out!" Cook responded.

"If they are going to Jerusalem, then any pilgrimage they take will be hours," reassured Doyle.

"Okay," said Cook. "Are we agreed?"

"That's a Roger," said Doyle as they did a 'high five' and both fell out laughing.

The waitress arrived with their order. She had six plates of food, four for Cook and two for Doyle. She wondered how two human beings could consume so much food, if in fact, that's what they were, she thought to herself.

Their satellite phone began ringing again. Unfortunately, it was stored securely in the glove box of their rental. They felt it unnecessary to have it in the restaurant since they knew the destination of their targets. They had both decided to have breakfast without interruption.

They completed their meal and felt almost human again. Cook patted his stomach with a look of satisfaction. Doyle felt the same as Cook but considered himself to be more cultured and sophisticated. So he simply belched with his fist to his mouth.

They got into their rental and headed for Jerusalem, the Holy City. Upon arrival they began looking for the parking places of private cars.

It was time to hook-up with the "man" again, so Doyle dialed Ellington. He connected after the first ring, "Ellington here."

"Doyle here." And he almost laughed.

Ellington said, "Are you at the Dead Sea Resort?"

"What?" Doyle asked.

"The Dead Sea Resort. I left a message on your phone. Somehow, they changed their minds and headed for the Dead Sea."

"It sounds to me like they've decided to tour the whole damn country in one day," shouted Doyle, losing his cool.

"Where are you now?" demanded Ellington.

"We're in the Holy City," responded Doyle.

"What Holy City?" asked Ellington. "There are hundreds of Holy Cities in the Middle East."

"Jerusalem," replied Doyle.

"Well head to the Dead Sea, damn it!"

Doyle sensed that Ellington was beginning to lose it. He wasn't quite sure he wanted to be around when that happened. After all, he and Cook were professionals. It would be so much simpler to eliminate their targets and be done. Ellington had no idea of the difficulties involved in surveillance with no definitive plan. Finally he asked, "Is that a stationery reading or a moving one?"

"I don't know," shouted Ellington. "Just head for the Dead Sea and I'll be in touch." Then he clicked off, obviously without saying goodbye.

Doyle said, "Prick." He realized he was running out of male body parts to call Ellington. Soon he would have to resort to female parts again.

❂ ❂ ❂

Meanwhile Gala was having the time of her life. Arts, crafts, jewelry, ceramics, and gifts for anyone she could think of. Money was no object with the Middle East Resource Center providing as much inflation as she desired. Bin had promised her that all the gifts she bought would be mailed to each person on her list.

Bin and I carried on a continual telepathic conversation. He explained the complexities of the Middle Eastern situation and suggested that simply having a stalemate was winning. There was so much history of cultural and religious conflict that it seemed to be a way of life.

Gala was exhausted after only two hours of shopping at the pedestrian walkway with no spending limit. Normally, her greatest bargaining efforts would be with me about money for an item, not the store owners. Once she saw what she wanted, price was a secondary issue. She still refused to pay the advertised price since bargaining was such an important part of the shopping experience.

Anwar had returned, but he had not joined us. Instead he continued to ensure there were no other sources of danger. Both he and Bin were pleased, so far, that there was no interest by the local or national authorities of Israel. It was vital in this part of the world that their work keep a low profile.

The four of us assembled shortly after Gala declared she was done. She commented that it was more fun to bargain with me about purchases than with the store owners. But it did feel good to have a no-limit spending spree for once.

We returned to the villa in Bin's car. John had prepared for an evening dinner on the spacious patio overlooking the sea. We brought him up-to-date on our morning adventures in Tel Aviv. Anwar related how he had employed a bored taxi driver to tour as much of Israel as possible before returning the rental to the local airport—for a generous fee, of course.

When we assembled for light drinks before dinner, the conversation turned serious.

"They were able to identify and locate your Mercedes rental. They're probably also attempting to locate this villa," said Bin.

"It's obvious they have a fairly sophisticated information gathering system and can probably hack into private websites with ease. But locating your rental requires more than just computer proficiency. It also requires someone who has unusual intuitive abilities," added Anwar.

"They must have established some pattern or profile of our movements," I added.

Then Gala almost shouted, "Duh! Look at the place that we are staying. And the rental we're driving. And the unrestricted shopping I had. I'm sure the store owners passed the word as we moved from store to store. What do they all have in common?"

John chimed in, "expensive taste! That includes the Crillion Hotel in Paris and Bill's first-class flight to Tel Aviv."

"And who are 'they'," Gala asked?

"*They* are a group of powerful individuals who are dedicated to preventing the Quest here on Earth," he stated, neutrally.

"Bill told me about the group. What exactly is the Quest?" she asked.

Gala had a general idea of the answer to her question, but it was time she understood the details of my anxieties and fears. And what she was getting herself in to.

We all spent the next half-hour explaining the entire sequence of events to Gala. She interrupted often to either ask questions or fill in the gaps of what she already knew.

Although she hadn't thought about it, the more she knew the less chance she had to return to her life in the U.S. It's like side stepping down a steep ski slope. The further you side-step downwards, the closer you come to a point of no return. The only choice at such a point is to aim your skis down the mountain and go for it!

By the time Gala had all her questions answered, the only thing left was her decision. Silence again. She looked almost lost as she began to think of her mother, her son, and all she had gone through to finally become an American citizen—something I took for granted.

After what appeared to be an eternity, she said, "I'm in." Silence again.

Then John smiled and said, "Let's eat."

❂ ❂ ❂

Before going to bed after dinner, I had that inner stirring to write. I informed John that I needed to spend time in the office. He understood perfectly.

Bin and Anwar bid us their parting goodbyes, stating that there were contingencies they had to take care of for our continued safety. They both commented that it had been an exciting day and were looking forward to what tomorrow might bring. Bin said again that he hoped our adventures would stay under the Israeli Security radar.

When I arrived in the second floor office, my thoughts were already a flowing stream of consciousness. I immediately began writing.

> *In this blog, I have some very difficult things to say. It is a continuation of our discussion about responsibility. Speaking bluntly, we are each 100% responsible for most, if not all, of the problems we experience in our world today. Either by abdicating responsibility or hoping our leaders will solve our problems for us. Even when it is evident they have no desire or capacity to do so. For example, there would be no "drug problem" if there were few, if any, drug users—both rich and poor. We would have very little deficit if we didn't individually borrow and spend beyond our means. We would have enough monetary resources for healthcare, education, and job opportunities for everyone if we were not driven by greed to accumulate, individually, far beyond our necessities for a comfortable life. So when things go against us, we look for a scapegoat or the government to blame. If we begin to take 100% responsibility for the conditions in our lives, we*

*would experience a transformation in our ability to create a global movement for change. However, this change has to originate **within** each of us. This is the essence of what it means to be empowered. This is the fundamental nature of the human spirit that is inherent in each of us. We simply need to recapture that spirit and take action in behalf of our collective welfare.*

The Messenger

After worldwide distribution of my second blog, reaction was swift and divided. The number of visitors to the Web Site doubled as compared to the first blog.

The suggestion that we were each 100% responsible for the things that happen in the world today was overwhelmingly rejected. History had shown that special interests groups significantly influenced world events. In some cases, they actually controlled them. How could the Messenger accuse hard-working citizens of causing the problems in the world? In most cases they were victims.

Others pointed out that Western nations, based upon capitalism, depended on large-scale consumerism as the basis of a healthy economy. Consumer spending and acquiring more goods and services would create more jobs, even if the result was large-scale personal and societal debt. Not to mention the accumulation of totally unnecessary objects that made no contribution to the quality of life.

There was a sizeable group of comments that stated that the blog was a breath of common sense. And maybe a society that depended on out-of-control spending, driven by greed, deserved whatever fate that resulted. They suggested that some kind of major crisis was the only hope we had for eventually learning how to sensibly live within our means.

Taking 100% responsibility for change was a theme that resonated with a majority. Not 100% responsibility for the present conditions. That was the fault of governments worldwide. The disagreements centered on what to *do* in bringing about change. The suggestions ranged from electing individuals with the direct opposite philosophies of those in office to a global revolution against those in power everywhere.

I was extremely pleased with the response from such a global audience. I also knew that *anger* was an essential part of the transformation process. Agreement was not the objective at this point. People were truly on the verge of desperately wanting something different. The second theme that gave me confidence was the acceptance of 100% responsibility for creating change. The crucial questions were, "What form would the change process take?" and "What were the intended results?"

✪ ✪ ✪

"Dana, I have a call from someone who claims to be Head of Israeli Internal Security. I asked him to leave a message and you would get back to him. But he insists on talking with you now. And for clinchers, he says he went to school with you at the University of Chicago. What should I do?"

"Who is he, Cheryl?" Dana asked.

"That's the problem. He won't give me his name. He says in his position, it is best not to advertise who he is."

"You said the call was from Israel?"

"Yes. That's a confirmation. I have the country code here on my phone," Cheryl replied.

"Okay, put him through. I'll handle it," Dana stated with an air of authority. She was accustomed to security forces around the world wanting direct access to her. Rarely did these requests originate from Israel unless it was the Israeli Intelligence Agency—IIS—the intelligence agency comparable to the CIA.

"Dana. This is Saul Wiseman. You might remember me from our classes in political science at the University of Chicago," Saul said.

Dana searched her memory momentarily, and then replied, "Of course I remember you, Saul. You are *not* a forgettable person. I also remember our debates about the Middle East," Dana replied, with a smile of fond memories.

"I am head of Israeli Internal Security."

"I am not surprised. It was obvious you would go far in whatever you chose. What can I do for you, Saul?" Dana asked. She regretted that she made it so difficult for him to talk with her directly.

Saul got straight to the point. "There are two American private detectives here in Tel Aviv. It was reported to us that they have secured handguns for personal use. They have the proper permits," he quickly added, "or the guns would not have been issued." Saul didn't add that there was little involving firearms that the Israeli Internal Security wasn't aware of.

"How does that concern my office, Saul? Isn't that a simple local matter you can handle?"

"Maybe. Maybe not. They have apparently been surveilling two other Americans for reasons we are not aware of. I just thought we ought to touch base with you in case this turns into an international incident on Israeli soil," Saul said. "Something unpleasant for us both."

"Who are they?" she asked.

"They identified themselves as Ryan Doyle and Peter Cook. As you know, we are made aware of any firearms dispersed in our country. They claimed the guns were for protection. Apparently, their vehicle was tampered with from unknown sources."

The two names immediately aroused Dana's attention. She was now forced to do something about these two emissaries of Robert Ellington, without creating a media incident. "Saul, I would appreciate it if you could keep an eye on the two of them.

And the moment they do something that even looks like it is illegal, call me immediately; anytime, day or night." She gave him the number of her private secure phone, which she changed every six months.

"Okay, we'll keep an eye on them and send you daily reports. By the way, congratulations on your appointment as Secretary of Homeland Security. And I return the compliment. I was confident you would go far in your career," he stated, without fanfare.

"Thanks, Saul. Call me directly if you feel we can assist you." Then she clicked off.

✪ ✪ ✪

As Dana was preparing to leave for the day, her secure line rang.

"Dana. This is Don Caldwell."

"Yes, Don? What have you got for me?" Don didn't call her secure line unless he had something important to inform her of.

"You remember that special assignment you gave me?" he asked, attempting to create a bit of drama.

"Yes, I do" she replied, impatiently.

"I discovered more than what the DIA gave us. The emails of the Pleiadian communications are exactly as we have on file."

"And?" Dana asked with a bit of annoyance.

"Patricia Christensen was indeed the prized student of the Star Gate Project and was quite upset when the program was cancelled. She felt they were on the verge of a breakthrough in the development of extrasensory reconnaissance abilities."

"Don!" Dana stated, clearly out of patience. Don loved to bait her when he had something special to tell her.

"I also discovered that an IT surveillance of Pat Christensen's web site was made. I traced the source of the hacker. Guess where it is?" Don teased.

"Just tell me, Don," Dana demanded.

"None other than Robert Stewart Ellington's estate in upstate New York!" he ended, proud of himself.

Dana smiled and said, "Gotcha!"

William A. Guillory

Chapter**Twelve**—The Pursuit

Robert Ellington's original plan was to discredit Bill Bradley through character assassination. Doyle and Cook had compiled considerable information about Bradley's personal life from a variety of sources. Some knew Bradley very well, some only peripherally, and some not at all. Most had strong opinions one way or the other.

If Bradley were running for public office, his opponents would have a field day with the stuff they collected, most of it untrue. There would be a feeding frenzy. The frenzy would probably last for a week or so. The branding, however, would be permanent. Ellington always found it amusing how the public adhered to a standard that very few individuals, if any, could meet.

Well that wasn't his problem. He had a financial empire to protect. And as far as he was concerned, "All's fair in empire preservation." The problem he faced was he seriously began to doubt whether the personal information would be enough to discredit Bradley's influence. The second blog from the Messenger had resulted in a doubling of the site's popularity, or more precisely, the visitation rate. The visitation rate represented only the primary effect. What about the secondary and tertiary effects—friends of friend, friends of friends' friends?

The reason for organizing the Guardian Angels was to have a solid front of successful, respected individuals aligned with him when the personal revelations were made public. His plan involved the planting of anonymous information about Bradley's life on Facebook, Twitter, and MySpace where no one cared if the rumors were true or not. That was just the nature of people. Since his blogs had created pros and cons, the cons would ensure rapid dissemination of any damaging innuendo around the globe, at lightning speed.

The next step would be public condemnation by respected members of the Guardian Angels—starting with Senator Carson. He was skilled at "implying" but not explicitly stating that anything that hinted at the welfare of the masses bordered on *socialism*. Once that word was stated, the conservatives would begin circling. Confirming his earlier assumption, social networks were ideal for *reflecting*, but more importantly, *shaping* public opinion. Most people didn't have the luxury or interest to think for themselves. That's why the Guardian Angels were such a necessity, he reasoned.

With that strategy all but useless, at this point, 'what would be an alternative plan?' he asked himself. Quite unconsciously, he had been moving toward the decision that Bill Bradley must be stopped. Once and for all! 'That's the only way to silence his blogs,' he concluded. Surveillance had become a nightmare, which Doyle had informed him. He had instructed them to arm themselves. Why? Not for their own protection. *They* didn't need protection.

If it all happened in another country with no direct ties to him and the Guardian Angels, it just might work. After all, none of the other protégés' blogs had achieved the same level of success as the visitation rate of Bradley's. He seemed to be the major influence in the so-called Quest at present. The age-old strategy might just be the answer—cut off the head and the body dies. His final instruction to Doyle and Cook was Bradley must be eliminated.

❂ ❂ ❂

I abruptly awakened from a restless sleep. I looked over at Gala, who was soundly asleep. Somehow I felt a strong sense of imminent danger—that feeling in my stomach again, which I assumed was *clairvoyant premonition*. As John had informed me.

I'd begun to imagine I could actually visualize the source of this feeling if I concentrated hard enough. I was also frightened to "see" any harm that might come to me or Gala. And if I did visualize an undesirable event, would I have the power to change the outcome? All these thoughts created sufficient confusion that visualization was completely blocked, even if I wanted the experience.

I got out of bed and slipped on my pants and a T-shirt. Just as I wandered out of our upstairs bedroom, I saw a shadow coming up the stairway. I stopped and stood as flat as possible against the hallway wall. 'Good thing my pants and T-shirt were a dark color,' I thought. I felt ridiculous standing there as though I would be unnoticed by a stalker.

I held my breath as the shadow slowly made its way to the top of the stairs. The only possible weapon in the hallway was a magnificent picture of a sunset on the Mediterranean Sea on the wall. I slipped inside the doorway to the office adjacent to the bedroom, so that I wasn't totally exposed. The thought made me feel even more ridiculous.

As the shadow began making its way toward me, I was trying to figure out how I could use the picture to protect myself. Maybe

I could pretend to be part of it looking at the sunset. I finally reasoned the only real weapon I had was surprise—particularly if I was confronted with a gun. My plan was to charge the gunman and then make it up from there, either using the dislodged gun or the picture on the wall as backup. Brilliant! What a stupid plan. But what other choices did I have?

Just when I was ready to spring into action, a familiar voice whispered, "Bill? Is that you?"

I let out a deep sigh of relief and replied, "Of course it's me, John." I could feel my heart go from 200 to 180 beats per minute.

"Why are you standing here in the hallway?" John asked, somewhat amused.

I just looked at him with unfocused eyes; thankful for the reprieve I'd been given. "I just woke up and felt there was imminent danger. In fact, I still feel it, in spite of the fact that it's you sneaking up the stairs."

"I had the same feeling. That's why I was quietly making my way to your room," John whispered.

We both stopped talking when we heard a soft noise from the back patio door. "Wake Gala and have her dress for a quick departure," John whispered to Bill.

That's the thing about reprieves, they have no permanency. I started to ask John the obvious question. Departure? How? We were trapped upstairs. I wondered if he had some extrasensory powers in defense of guns. Maybe he could do an energy thing and have them melt in our stalker's hand. I had forgotten he could read everything I was thinking.

John put his finger to his lips for me to be silent and pointed to our bedroom where Gala was asleep.

I entered our bedroom only to see Gala putting on her jeans and a long-sleeve T-shirt she had bought that afternoon in Tel Aviv. "What's going on?" she asked, with concern on her face.

I wanted to tell her everything was fine. I was armed with a painting of the sunset on the Mediterranean. "John and I thought we heard something at the back patio door. We may have to make a quick exit," I replied. I realized I had just made the same stupid statement to Gala that John had made to me. Exit? How? Her puzzled look indicated she had also become telepathic.

John met us as we exited the bedroom and whispered, "Go to the end of the hallway to the alcove. There's a window there. Jump to the back porch. Then run to the quay at the back of the property. I'll meet you there. Meanwhile, I'll create a diversion with the intruders. I'm, sure this isn't a social call at this time of night," John smiled and was gone.

We made our way to the alcove. Just then, we heard two "poofs" and two bullet holes in the wall where we stood. Gala was fumbling with the window as I stood there unarmed pretending to protect her, which meant I was willing to die first. Another two poofs. This time I felt debris from the edge of the wall singe my arm.

The two intruders stopped abruptly when they heard a voice behind them shout, "Okay, we've got you trapped! Come down the stairs and throw your guns down first!" It was John buying time for us. I have no idea how he could imply they were trapped. My sunset weapon was out of reach and I knew I was going to die. I pushed Gala aside and quickly opened the window. She jumped to the porch and landed softly in her sneakers. I followed somewhat less athletically, but safely. We both sprinted to the quay.

The two gunmen decided they heard only one voice from below, so throwing down their weapons, in a foreign country with breaking and entering, was not an option. They turned and made their way to the stairway, anticipating an exchange of gunfire. None came. Then Cook looked at Doyle as if to ask, 'Are we crazy or what?' And then he asked, "We *did* hear a voice, didn't we?"

They just looked at each other, not knowing whether they

should proceed up the stairway again or try to locate the voice. Just when they decided to split up and pursue each, a loud security alarm went off. Immediately afterwards, the house was covered with blinding light. "Throw your weapons out of the doorway and exit the house with your hands behind your head. This is the Israeli Security Force!"

"Aw shit!" said Cook.

❂ ❂ ❂

Gala and I made our way to the quay at the water's edge. John was there waiting. He had a small motorboat waiting for a quick get-away. Quite a commotion was going on at the villa, with bright lights and the security alarm he had set off. Predictably, the response of the Israeli Security Force was instantaneous.

Gala asked, "Where did they come from?"

"They were probably more aware of what is going on than I thought," John replied.

"You may have extrasensory abilities and unlimited resources, John. But you still have a lot to learn about how the channels of information operate on this planet," I said. "Particularly, information involving national security."

John began navigating the boat out into the open water with a paddle. He had no intention of attracting attention to our watery escape.

"I guess it's obvious how our two friends located us," John said, smiling as he looked at Gala.

"A gorgeous villa. Obviously," she replied.

"I thought we had more time, at least until the morning. But how did the Israeli Security Force become involved?" I asked.

"My guess is somehow the U.S. security agencies have become involved in our little escapade," John replied, with a guilty look on his face.

"What's up, John?" I asked.

"I forgot to mention, Tony and I received a message from Pat. She wanted you to know that certain government agencies had become involved in this affair. And, that you may be in danger."

"Why didn't you tell me about this earlier?" I could feel the anger bubbling in my stomach. Not so much for my safety, but for Gala, who had committed to this whole affair with incomplete information about the danger involved.

"Tony and I decided you were not really in danger from the government agencies. They wanted to use you to locate us. We decided to let you know about her message at the right time; which is now."

It finally occurred to me that both Tony and John were more committed to my involvement in the Quest than my safety; or Gala's by association. I guess at some level I always knew this by the way John seemed to be pushing me along at a faster rate than I could decide about my commitment. I really couldn't blame them for the decisions I'd made so far. But from here on out, I decided to take control of where this whole thing was headed as well as my involvement.

Hell, the government *had* to become involved at some point. To assume otherwise was being naïve. If nothing else, the response to my last blog probably also attracted *their* interest. The truth was, at some level, I was holding on to the hope that I could return to how my life had been before John showed up. Now I could see clearly that life was gone, forever. All I had was what I made of the future.

When I became conscious again, everyone was staring at me. It was like they had followed me through my mental exploration. Surprisingly, I felt quite calm and at peace with myself. I had finally closed the door on my past life.

"The two guys tonight are probably the same ones from Paris and today at the beach," John said.

"I think it's time we figure out what's going on. It doesn't appear that time is on our side," I said. At least two groups are trying to apprehend or eliminate us."

Just then, a helicopter with a spot light began a slow circular reconnaissance of the property around the villa. It was attempting to locate the whereabouts of its recent occupants.

❂ ❂ ❂

"May I see some identification from both of you?" asked Saul Wiseman, rather sternly. "We already know you are Americans."

"We are retained as private investigators for a very influential American businessman," Doyle said formally.

"Before you take any action, I would suggest you give him a call," Cook blurted out before Doyle could restrain him. "It may have serious repercussions with respect to your future."

Wiseman's eyes flashed momentarily. Then he regained control and replied, "I am quite comfortable with my future with or without the knowledge of your influential businessman. I think you ought to be more concerned about *your* immediate future."

Doyle and Cook reluctantly handed over their credentials as private investigators.

"Ryan Doyle and Peter Cook, private investigators," Wiseman read. "And just who is your American businessman who has the power to reach here into Israel and influence my career?" asked Wiseman, amusingly, but not smiling.

Doyle indicated to Cook to "shut up" and let him do the talking. "I'm sorry we seem to be uncooperative. I guess it's because we were just in a life-threatening situation. You see someone in the house shouted they had us surrounded. And we simply fired shots in self-defense."

"What were you doing on the premises in the first place? You are not the registered occupants, are you?" Wiseman asked.

"That question goes back to our assignment. We were

retained to surveil the occupants of this house and report back to our client."

"Does surveillance include breaking and entering?" asked Wiseman.

"Well, that's just it. We thought we heard a cry for help and decided to enter the premises in an effort to provide assistance. The welfare of the individuals under surveillance are very important to my client," Doyle responded confidently. He often surprised himself at how easily lying came to him. Cook was equally impressed.

"Why were you inside the property boundaries in conducting your so-called surveillance?" Saul Wiseman asked.

"We couldn't do much in the way of surveillance for their protection outside the walls, now could we?" Doyle replied, with a wry smile.

"Regardless of what your motivations were, we take the possession and use of firearms very seriously in this country. You will have to come to our offices and file a full report."

In a final effort to "fish," Wiseman asked, "What exactly are the reasons these individuals are under surveillance?"

With a thin smile of 'nice try, Wiseman,' Doyle said, "That information is confidential, of course."

After Doyle and Cook were taken away, Saul Wiseman pulled out his SAT phone and dialed Dana Hartman's secure line. Dana responded on the second ring, although she was awakened from a sound sleep. She had mastered this skill since becoming Secretary of Homeland Security. "Yes?" she asked in clipped tone, now fully awake.

"Sorry to call at this time of the morning," Saul apologized. "But you told me to call you any time something happened involving Doyle and Cook."

"What is it?" Dana asked, getting straight to the point of Saul's call. She'd learned early in her job that no one called in the middle of the night with good news.

"We have trespassing, breaking and entering, and possibly illegal use of firearms. However, the occupants of the rented residence are nowhere to be found to press charges."

"What does that mean, Saul?" Dana asked.

"We have no basis to hold them for more than twenty-four hours. The assumption is the residents will show up to press charges. My question is 'What do you want me to do with them Dana?"

"What are my options, according to Israeli law?" Dana asked, her background as District Attorney kicking in.

"As I said, we can keep them for twenty-four hours and release them or politely ask them to leave the country for any destination they choose. The latter option will happen in any case."

"Can I have both, Saul?" Dana asked.

"It will be my pleasure, Dana." Saul was about the click off when he said, "Oh, I almost forgot. They informed me that my future might be jeopardized by a very influential American businessman if we pressed charges. Do you have any idea who they were referring to?"

"No, I don't," Dana lied, without hesitation. "If I find out, I will let you know." She decided it was time to take care of those idiots, once and for all. Within five minutes, she was sleeping peacefully again.

Saul smiled to himself. He could detect a lie as easily as he could read the emotions of his children. It was an instinct, from his part of the world, which was necessary for survival. "Okay," he said. "I'll let you know when we release them and what their initial destination is. Then, they're all yours."

✪ ✪ ✪

As the helicopter overhead made larger and larger circles around the villa, John started the small motor and began moving away at a more rapid rate. Within minutes, he felt secure they were out of the reach of the Israeli Security reconnaissance.

"Where are we headed?" I asked.

"A rendezvous," John replied.

"With whom?"

"Friends of yours, at this point," John smiled. It still amazed me how calm John was in these situations. Perhaps, it was because he *knew* he couldn't die or perhaps he knew the most probable outcome of short term events. We hadn't explored the subject of whether he could see into the future; or how far?

"And then what?" I asked, getting a little tired of John's smile *and* word games.

He turned to me and said, "That depends on you and Gala; India, China, or Japan. We have Pleiadians and Resource Centers in all three regions."

I looked at Gala, who simply hunched her shoulders as if to say, "How would I know which is better?"

We rode in silence for another ten minutes or so. Then just ahead a lone, non-descript boat emerged. Along the starboard side was a fading name, *Red Star*. It could accommodate both fishing and cruising. Bin and Anwar were there to greet us.

"We are glad you made it out okay," Bin said. He and Anwar helped Gala and I aboard. "We expected to see you later this morning. Good thing we put the contingencies into place tonight."

"By contingencies, they mean the motor boat for our escape and this vessel for our exit of Israel," John said. He turned to Gala and smiled. "I'm glad you got your shopping done, Gala, before our hasty exit."

Anwar started the powerful vessel as we headed south outside of the waters of the Israeli coastline. The rest of us assembled in a hastily devised conference room below deck.

John began. "No matter which destination we choose, India, China, or Japan, we have to proceed through Port Said, through the Suez Canal, and into the Red Sea. Bin and Anwar have made arrangements for our safe travels through those Ports. Right now, we need to decide on our next destination."

"I've given it some thought." I said. "And I think it's India. The security system is not as extensively developed as China or Japan. There are also easily accessed rural regions for setting up our post. I think we should also rely on the recommendations of the regional Pleiadian and his protégé.

John could sense me taking greater control of decisions involving the Quest. So he decided to step back and focus his role on the safety and security of Gala and I.

I turned to Bin and asked, "Okay, what's the best way to get to India? And how?"

Bin replied, "We can take a water route across the Arabian Sea, stopping at the small Yemen island of Socotra, and on to Mumbai; formerly known as Bombay under British rule. That route has several hazards including satellite surveillance and piracy on the high seas."

"What's the alternative you have in mind?" I asked Bin.

The other is a land route. We dock at the port of Jeddah and travel across Saudi Arabia to Riyadh and then to Dubai, where you can take a private plane to Mumbai. That's the route I recommend," Bin replied.

"Why?" I asked. My thoughts were travelling across Middle East countries *always* involved unpredictable hazards, especially for outsiders. Once imprisoned, you might never see daylight again.

Bin replied, "Saudi Arabia and the United Arab Emirates—UAE—where Dubai is located are among the friendliest countries to the U.S. in the Middle East; besides Israel, of course. Travelling across those countries should be easy for Gala with her Asian features and you with your bronzed complexion. And, of course, we all know, John is nondescript."

Everyone laughed, except Gala. I related the story of describing John as nondescript. Although she understood the story, the telling of it was not near as amusing as the experience.

"Land and air it is," I stated, gaining greater confidence in my new role.

Later, that evening, under the stars of the Red Sea, I wrote my third blog.

> *When I think about my capacity to change the world I feel dwarfed by the forces that resist change. When I reduce "the" world to "my" world, the task does not appear to be as formidable—particularly in light of the Three Degrees of Influence Rule. If we each decide to change our world of relationships we could change the world, with or without the assistance of those in power. We do so by small acts of support in behalf of the welfare of others. This suggestion sounds simplistic, and to some extent naïve, on the surface. And it is for those we already love and care for. However, this way living becomes more challenging, in practice, for those we don't like or have biases against. To treat them with kindness triggers the humbling act of transformation. The result is an incremental evolution to a higher state of consciousness. Not only are we changed as human beings but our capacity for creativity, innovation, and imagination increases by a quantum jump. This is the opportunity presented to us. The question is, do we have the courage to take it!*

The Messenger

The blog was disseminated throughout the world at lightning speed with the assistance of the other six protégés.

Again, response to the blog was swift, as if most had been waiting for my next missive. Most agreed they had the capacity to influence their world of relationship. They questioned whether there would be sufficient interest by most to cause a wave of change.

They unanimously agreed that influencing those closest to them made sense. This approach was also easiest to put into practice. Being kind to people they disliked was considered the critical step. Most of those who responded wanted to know "What's in it for me? My efforts might be rejected or worse, I might be considered as weak!"

What most did promise was that they would forward the blog to a long list of people they knew that *needed* to hear this message. The result was an overwhelming number of secondary and tertiary people exposed to the blog.

Interestingly, when small acts of support were connected to transformation, a considerable number stated they were now beginning to understand the meaning of the phrase, *an evolution in consciousness*, discussed as a key element in the first blog.

❂ ❂ ❂

With Saul's call and his interest in the influential American businessman, Dana began to feel the whole thing was getting out of control. She knew Saul would also report the incident to the Israeli Intelligence Agency—IIA—as a matter of procedure. It was time for her to bring in the Central Intelligence Agency (CIA) and the National Security Agency (NSA).

When she called Lloyd Pierson, the Director of Central Intelligence (DCI) of the CIA, the following morning, he was already referring to what happened at the villa as the "Israeli Incident." She should have known by now that there were no secrets among the intelligence agencies when none of them had the facts of something they didn't control.

"Lloyd, this is Dana. Thanks for returning my call. I wanted to update you on a situation we've been following. Since it has moved beyond the U.S. border, I thought you should know what we know," Dana began.

"Are you referring to the *Israeli Incident* or something else?" He wanted her to know that the CIA had eyes and ears in places she hadn't even begun to discover, whether domestic or foreign. What she wasn't aware of was that he had also received the report from the DIA when they officially informed her of the extraterrestrials. At the time, Lloyd wanted no part of running it without solid proof. His excuse was, it was a domestic target, not foreign. Now things had changed.

"We've been following two situations we believe are connected. One involves a Dr. William Bradley, who has apparently been under surveillance by two private investigators named Ryan Doyle and Peter Cook." She paused, apparently giving time for the DCI to write their names.

"Go on," he replied.

She continued, realizing that their call was probably being recorded anyway. "The two private investigators were apprehended by the Israeli Security Force in Tel Aviv for a variety of minor charges." She paused, again.

"What's the connection to us?" he pressed, extremely amused as he sensed her irritation.

"Apparently, Dr. Bradley is being accompanied by someone who has not been identified." She paused, trying to figure out how to describe Dr. Bradley's companion from Pleiades.

Complete silence on the other line. So she continued. "We have reason to believe the unidentified individual may be from a source outside of our solar system. I don't know any other way to say it." Silence again. "Before you respond allow me to send you the report the DIA sent us a week ago."

"Why are you bringing us in at this point?" Lloyd asked, applying the full press of federal agencies withholding information from each other.

Dana was becoming increasingly agitated with Lloyd's

smugness and lack of cooperation, since the situation had gone beyond Homeland Security with the so-called *Israeli Incident*. He probably didn't realize that she had little or no interest in trying to outdo the intelligence-gathering of the CIA in order to gain favor by the President. So, she finally said, "I will also be informing the NSA after our conversation." Out of instinct, she decided to withhold the information from Lloyd about the Pleiadian Network and the *Guardian Angels*.

"You know Ken will have to brief the President." Lloyd was referring to Kenneth Clarke, head of the NSA—National Security Agency. "Meanwhile, I'll see what our sources can uncover about Dr. Bradley's whereabouts in the Middle East. And his associate, of course." They both clicked off.

The call to Kenneth Clarke was equally frustrating for Dana. He wanted details and specifics. And most of all, he wanted proof. He indicated the President was going to ask him questions that he couldn't possibly answer.

Dana suggested he talk with Mitch Crenshaw over at the DIA to get the best answers to the extraterrestrial thing and the intercepted communications of Pat Christensen. In the meantime, she would send the DIA report to his office and wait for further instructions. In essence, she was passing the ball to the NSA that was passed to her by Mitch Crenshaw. The same ball the CIA wanted no "official" part of!

ChapterThirteen—The Escape

The CIA had now unofficially taken up the charge of locating and possibly apprehending Dr. Bradley. They didn't know what to expect of his alien companion. This decision required some degree of information sharing with the Israeli Intelligence Agency (IIA) because of the necessity of their assistance. They had an extensive intelligence network in the Middle East.

Lloyd Pierson put in a call to the head of the IIA, Ariel Levin, to discuss the *Israeli Incident*. "Hi Ari, I just wanted to follow up on the *incident* we seemed to have dumped into your lap. What's the disposition with respect to Doyle and Cook?"

"We released them after twenty-four hours. They made a cell phone call to their influential American businessman. Then boarded a flight for Paris," Ari replied.

"Who is he?" Lloyd asked, fishing to discover how much the Israelis knew about the *Seven Sisters*.

"Come on Lloyd, I haven't told you anything you don't already know. Is this thing more serious than we realize?" Ari asked, becoming more businesslike. Ari and Lloyd had a long history of working together in preemptive activities involving terrorists. In spite of these joint ventures, both revealed only what was necessary to achieve their common objectives.

"Maybe. Quite frankly, we honestly don't know."

"What does that mean?" Ari asked.

"Look. Can I be frank with you without any wisecracks or laughter?"

"Try me," Ari replied.

Lloyd related the contents of the DIA report and the surveillance of Doyle and Cook.

"What's the surveillance all about?" asked Ari.

"We're not sure. We do know that Ellington is an ultraconservative investment banker. The stuff on Dr. Bradley's secret Blog Site is not necessarily in alignment with Ellington's philosophy. And that's putting it mildly. From there, your guess is as good as mine."

"What do you plan to do about Ellington?" Ari asked.

"Since he's domestic, I think Dana over at Homeland Security will shut him down. That should put a leach on Doyle and Cook. However they conceal their return to the U.S. should be irrelevant," Lloyd replied.

"What do you need from us?" Ari asked.

"We need to locate Dr. Bradley and bring him in for questioning. As I mentioned, his travelling companion from Pleiades is alleged to have extrasensory abilities."

"Like what?"

"Look, I can't confirm any of this stuff. So, I'm telling you what others have reported to me."

"I understand, Lloyd. I assure you I'm listening seriously. We've also read Dr. Bradley's two blogs and have monitored the responses, both here in the Middle East and from around the world. There appears to be an evolving rebellion against conflict and killing. Particularly, where most of the people dying are civilians."

"Okay. He is apparently telepathic, clairvoyant, and can teleport. Most of all, he's not really human although he uses a human body."

Silence on the other end.

"Are you still there?"

"Yes, I'm still here," Ari replied, deep in thought.

"I told you this is what we have been able to gather from others."

"What does he want? The alien that is? Have any of your agencies made contact?"

"I don't know what he wants and no, we haven't made contact. We believe if we locate Dr. Bradley, we locate him. And I'll set you up with a personal interview," Lloyd laughed.

"Okay, Lloyd. I'll see what we can find out. After all, the only options for Dr. Bradley are by land, by air, or by sea. Apparently, the other fellow has a fourth option," Ari also laughed.

"By the way, I'm assigning my best field agent in the Middle East to work with your people. Brian Carlson. He's been around more than 18 years."

"Good choice," said Ari. "We know him well. We'll make contact and keep you informed."

Then Ari clicked off.

✪ ✪ ✪

While sailing south on the Red Sea to Jeddah, Saudi Arabia, Gala and I began to seriously discuss our future.

"It seems my life has been a whirlwind since John appeared. I haven't really thought about anything else," I said to Gala.

"I always knew you were being prepared for something. I just didn't know what," she replied.

"It appears the Quest is it. It scares me just to say it. Somehow, my picture is, it should be someone with a more puritanical background; someone who has lived a life of goodness. That's certainly not me."

"I don't think that person exists on this planet. If he or she does, they have not revealed themselves, as yet. After all, even Gandhi and King were not puritanical as I understand their history."

"One thing for certain, I can't do it alone."

"You have John," she replied, shyly, testing my reaction.

"That's not what I mean," I replied, with a knowing smile.

"What *do* you mean?" She asked, pretending a lack of understanding of my meaning.

"I think I need you."

"You *think*?" she asked. Her eyes flashing, as usual when she's upset. She was thinking, 'after all this time, you *think* you need me.'

"Look. I have always prided myself on never *needing* anyone. I've always believed that need creates dependency. That's not what I believe love is all about."

"What *do* you believe it's all about?" Gala asked, with that invasive look into my synapses.

"It's a *commitment*; particularly during the difficult times when a relationship is tested most."

She just remained silent, knowing that I had more to say; which was a minor miracle for her.

"There have been times when *I* didn't commit. I ran. And there have been times I did commit and the other person ran—in one way or another. It isn't always clear to others or to me how we set flight into motion or for what reasons."

"What does all of this have to do with us?" she asked, anxious to get to the point.

"I'm asking you to be with me in the Quest. I'm asking you to be a permanent part of my life. I am letting you know that I'm committed to you." Then after a pause, I said, "And, I'm afraid of marriage." I felt a sense of relief having said exactly where I was in our relationship. I had promised Gala that I would be honest in our relationship. If it could not survive honesty from us both, then marriage was certainly out of the question.

"Everything you've asked has already been answered. Or haven't you noticed."

"I guess I never formally asked you. Now, I am."

"Okay. Yes, I am with you in the Quest. Yes, I am here to stay. And yes, I'm committed to our relationship. I will not run. However, the marriage thing is still on the table. But I promise not to press you; in spite of the fact we are not getting any younger during uncertain times."

At that point, John conveniently wandered onto the deck. "We should soon be docking in Jeddah. Both of you will have to put on the proper attire for a Muslim country."

"That should be interesting," Gala said, amusingly.

"Oh, one other thing I want to caution you about," John said to Gala. "You will have to act submissive in public. Don't look at anyone directly in the eyes, particularly men. Can you do that, Gala?"

She hesitated momentarily. Then responded with an amusingly meek, "Yes," and batted her eyes coquettishly.

John said, "That's not quite what I meant."

"I know exactly what you meant. I am originally from that part of the world," she responded, eyes flashing.

"This response didn't surprise me, since my nickname for Gala was "Fire."

✿ ✿ ✿

May I speak with Robert Stewart Ellington," Dana stated formally, after having him hold for several minutes.

He had expected her call after the *Israeli Incident* had made the news. Fortunately, his name had not been mentioned as a connection. Little did he know, the suppression of his name was the price the intelligence agencies had agreed upon for the dissolution of the Guardian Angels and his activities against Bill Bradley.

"This is Robert Ellington," he replied. Although he tried to retain his air of importance, he knew the call he was about to engage could be disastrous. He only hoped for the best.

"Mr. Ellington, it has come to our attention that you have organized a group of American citizens and a British national to discredit the reputation of one Dr. William Bradley. Is this accurate?" Dana asked using her courtroom voice.

"Not exactly," he replied. "My group opposes the statements Dr. Bradley has posted on his Blog Site," he responded, in defense.

"That's not my question. We'll get to your identifying his Blog Site in a minute. But now, I want to know if you have hired private investigators to solicit personal information about Dr. Bradley's life, with the intent of using it to discredit him personally. That is what we have been told by your private investigators," she lied for emphasis. She could sense his defensiveness from her courtroom experience.

"I'm not certain of the details of what you have been told. But my group has a perfect right to research individuals with differing opinions. We try to understand their point of view when it differs from ours."

"Would you call investigating personal relationships he has had part of your research involving a differing opinion?" she asked.

"No, I would not."

"Good, we agree on one point of your so-called research. Did you hire the private investigators, Ryan Doyle and Peter Cook to surveil and possibly harm Dr. Bradley?" she pressed more forcefully. "They were involved in a shooting incident in Tel Aviv. They indicated they were hired by you," she lied again. After all, this was not a court of law. Nothing she said required proof. Just free-for–all interrogation.

"Absolutely not!" he responded, almost losing his composure. Good thing this wasn't a courtroom questioning, he thought. "I hired them to keep me informed of others who might have similar viewpoints as his. Again, solely for our data gathering." Since he assumed, at this point, she had most of the facts, his only thought was what his fate might be.

"Data gathering," she stated. "That brings me to my third point. Did you hire information technology specialists to hack into the website of a Ms. Patricia Christensen? As well as for the identification of Dr. Bradley's anonymous websites, *The Voice* and *The Messenger?*"

"What?" he stammered, being caught off guard about his IT adventures. Jeremy had assured him that the hacking they did was untraceable. Apparently, such assurance didn't apply where the federal government was concerned.

"You do realize such actions are considered to be an invasion of privacy. Not that it would result in jail time for someone like you. But your reputation as an upstanding investment banker could suffer immensely," Dana ended.

Robert Ellington remained silent, relieved that she did not mention any felony charges, or worse, incarceration.

She continued with the denouement—the dagger. "Your IT specialists' invasion into Ms. Christensen's website was discovered by the Defense Intelligence Agency. They reported it to us and asked our recommendation, since we handle Homeland Security for *all* citizens."

His response was continued absolute silence accompanied by a deep sense of fear. "What would you recommend, Ms. Hartman? I am just an American citizen trying to protect the American way of life."

"And your private investments and wealth," she added.

"Yes, that is true," he said meekly.

"I recommend you disband your group. Tell them they are

fortunate not to be prosecuted or exposed. You disengage your private investigators before we take them into custody. Warn them, that if any action is taken against Dr. Bradley or his associates, they will never see the light of day again. I assume you do realize the latitude we have when we *suspect* a threat to national security. Finally, I strongly suggest you quietly watch, from the sidelines, as governmental sources work to preserve and protect the American way of life. And that's being generous," Dana ended.

"You've got a deal," he responded. Before he could say thank you, Dana had disconnected.

❁ ❁ ❁

We docked into Jeddah in the early morning hours after midnight. We were met by a cousin of Anwar who provided us a somewhat dated Range Rover that ran like new. He asked no questions, made no comments, but simply provided us with the keys to the kingdom. And then he vanished into the night.

Off we proceeded eastward on Highway 40W toward Riyadh. When dawn was breaking, we encountered our first military stop along the highway near Makkah. Both John and Bin *went ahead* to meet us on the other side of the checkpoint.

We were asked for identification and the purpose of our travels. Anwar smiled broadly and told them that Gala and I were a married couple being transported to Riyadh for employment by an important government official, and he was hired to provide transport.

The military guards asked for our papers and identification. Anwar handed them over, including the document from the government official. One of the guards walked over to a small hut and presented them to the officer in charge. The officer looked them over, then scanned our Range Rover and initialed the papers for passage through the checkpoint.

While we were receiving the initialed clearance, the other guard pulled out a flashlight and focused it on each of our faces. My bronze skin and eyes were native to Saudi Arabia and Gala's dark skin and East European features aroused no suspicion. Fortunately, she kept her eyes lowered and appeared submissive; a minor miracle. Our papers were, of course, perfect forgeries from the Middle East Resource Center.

When we exited the checkpoint, we felt confident that the rest of our trip across Saudi Arabia would be easy. That turned out to be an incorrect assumption.

Using the combined resources of the CIA in the Middle East and the Israeli Intelligence Agency travel by air and land from Israel were quickly ruled out. Satellite surveillance focused on a watery escape probably south via the Suez Canal. Most of the vessels on the Red Sea were accounted for and identified except for a lazy tourist fishing boat. It was heading south along the Saudi Arabian coastline, but outside of their territorial waters.

The boat was not unusual since such trawling ventures were not required to register with any port, unless they chose to. When satellite scanning was conducted over several passes, it was noted that the fishing poles were in same positions and appeared to be untouched. Furthermore only two occupants appeared to be visible on all the passes made; a small number for such a venture. Upon tighter focusing, neither of the occupants seemed to fit the identity of Dr. Bradley.

The clincher came the following day when the boat was no longer on the Red Sea. It should have been south of the Port of Jeddah. It was assumed by Carlson's team that the boat must have docked in Jeddah during the night. The question was, with whom and what mode of transportation would be used from there—air or land?

❂ ❂ ❂

Retired General Kenneth Clarke, head of the National Security Agency, routinely met with the President to update him of present and evolving threats to the U.S. Today, however, he felt a pronounced sense of anxiety about relating his report from the DIA and Homeland Security. His first impulse was to have both Mitch Crenshaw and Dana Hartman accompany him. But their presence would be premature at this point.

He sat down across from the President and they began the briefing. "What have you got, Ken?" the President asked. "Today is going to be one of those days. I can feel it."

Ken thought, 'You're right about that, Mr. President,' and he decided to just plunge into the *Seven Sisters*.

"Mr. President, there has been a series of blogs by a fellow who calls himself *The Messenger*. The blogs have attracted an unusual amount of worldwide attention. The messages could potentially become a problem."

"What do you mean?" the President asked.

"For example, he suggests that ordinary people have the power to change the conditions of their lives, with or without those in power."

"Isn't that a good thing, Ken?" the President asked. "It certainly reduces our responsibility for the miracles we've promised them."

"It goes further than that, Mr. President. The blogs also suggest that a transformation in human consciousness is necessary for this change to occur."

"What does that mean?" the President asked. He was clearly confused, but also smiling. "Sounds like something I heard in one of my psychology courses in college."

"Apparently, it means a change from focusing on personal gain to helping others succeed. At least, that's my best interpretation from his blogs," Ken stated.

"How is that message a problem?" the President asked, looking even more confused.

"He goes on to suggest that those in power have shown little intent or capacity to lead such a process—including government."

The President put two right fingers to his temple in an introspective way and said, "Continue. Somehow, I have a feeling you haven't told me everything."

"This person, whose real name is Dr. William Bradley, has a companion who we believe is strongly influencing his blogs," Ken stated, with reluctance.

"So?"

"His companion is believed to be from a distant star system called Pleiades. In other words, Mr. President, he's an extraterrestrial." There, Ken thought to himself, it's out.

The President just stared at Ken. Wondering when he would burst out laughing. But Ken looked dead serious.

"Let me get this straight," the President said. "You're telling me there's an extraterrestrial running around this planet that's influencing one of the most popular blogs on the Internet?"

"Yes, Mr. President. There may actually be seven in all."

"Seven what?" asked the President.

"Seven extraterrestrials from Pleiades," Ken replied.

The President stared harder at Ken with a deeper wrinkle between his eyes, trying to absorb that what he was being told was, in fact, reality. "What do they want? Why are they here, Ken?"

"At this point, we don't know, Mr. President. But the only person who appears to be able to communicate with them is a Patricia Christensen. She was the most advanced person in extrasensory abilities in the Star Gate Program. The program was discontinued during the mid-1990s."

"So, what do you suggest we do? Where do we go from here?" the President asked.

"I suggest we locate Dr. Bradley and bring him in for a 'conversation' regarding his blogs and what he knows about the extraterrestrials."

"What about the extraterrestrials? How do we make direct contact with them? We have to face this situation sooner or later. Don't we? The sooner, the better."

"I suggest we contact Pat Christensen to help us there. But it has to be very delicate. She's still very upset about the way the Star Gate Program was discontinued. The scientists we hired as consultants to evaluate the program labeled it 'pseudoscience.' They discredited practically all the work that was done during the program. She holds the government responsible even though it was another administration in office at the time."

"Okay, let's see if we can convince her to help us make direct contact with these so-called Pleiadians." The President was about to leave when he turned to Ken and asked, "Who else knows about this whole thing?"

"The DIA, CIA, and Dana Hartman over at Homeland Security are all aware of the situation. In fact, Dana was the only one with enough guts to let me know what was going on."

"Good. Let's keep a tight lid on this situation."

"I will, Mr. President." Ken responded, confidently. In spite of his confirmation of secrecy to the President, Ken knew from long experience in Washington that this situation was probably one of the main topics of discussion at Washington's power lunches. Fortunately, no one had any proof, as yet. Not even them.

"And Ken," the President said as an afterthought, "Have Dana make contact with Pat Christensen. She has a way of accomplishing difficult tasks using all the resources around her. There must be something we can do for Pat to make up for how we embarrassed her."

"Will do, Mr. President."

"And have Dana call me directly for updates. I'll tell my Chief of Staff to keep an open line of communication for her. Anything else I need to know, Ken?" the president said with a questioning look of 'You have told me everything. Haven't you?'

"No, Mr. President," Ken said. And the President departed.

✪ ✪ ✪

As the Range Rover caravan made their way across Saudi Arabia to Riyadh, everyone appeared to be with their own thoughts; particularly, me. I wondered if this was a 'fool's errand.' 'People on Planet Earth had *no intention* of changing,' I thought to myself. The basic instinct of confrontation seemed to rule the day when faced with conflict. My blogs were probably a waste of time.

Perhaps I should forget about my attempts at human compatibility and let the whole thing proceed to its inevitable conclusion—the same as *Lemuria* and *Atlantis*. The forces opposing change in human beings were just too strong. Like the Beatles' song, just *"Let it Be."*

From there, I fell into the recesses of sleep—and the landscape of dreaming; except, it did not appear to be a dream. It appeared I was also awake—somewhere between the two.

> *After leaving my physical body behind, I was transported through time and space at such a velocity that the two eventually merged into one, as described by Einstein—the time-space continuum. I had a feeling of being accompanied by someone on this journey, although I could not see a companion. We arrived at a portal where intersecting colors transformed into a colorless transparency vibrating at an incredibly high frequency on the other side. After I crossed the portal, I could feel the presence of others, but I could not see them. Then I received a telepathic message: 'This Council is a forum for*

all evolved life forms of this galaxy.' I telepathed in return: 'Why am I here?' The reply: 'You have been summoned to learn of a grave situation that Planet Earth will face if you do not radically change the ways you govern.' I replied: 'What is the grave situation?' Before I received an answer, I began to feel being pulled back through the portal and eventually into my physical body. I was struggling to learn of the grave situation, but all I could sense was an echo. Then I abruptly awakened—trembling, frightened, and on the verge of tears.

We eventually stopped to stretch our legs and take a break from the long drive. John and I wandered off together without the necessity of comment.

"What do you think of your dream?" John asked, smiling.

"I don't understand most of it." I'd stopped asking questions of John like, 'How'd you know of my dream?' "Although it was a dream, everything felt so real. Where is this place?"

"It's not really a location, as much as it is a dimension in the time-space continuum. It's a dimension where all intelligent life forms meet to decide the evolution of the Milky Way Galaxy."

"Why is that necessary? Everything is so far apart and changes are happening all the time."

"Even considering the distances between heavenly bodies, we're all connected. Right down to a small planet like Earth. Whatever you do on this planet affects us all. It's the Council's responsibility to make sure others of this galaxy are not adversely affected by your actions here on Earth."

I just looked at John, trying to grasp the implications of the comments that he related in such a casual way. His description was like a science fiction episode from Star Trek. "Something *happened* to me, John. I don't *feel* the same." The tingle at the top of my head had been activated again. For just a fleeting moment, I felt like a stranger to my surroundings, as if playing a role in a staged play.

"Once you have crossed the portal, most of what you experience in everyday living appears to be less important. This awareness allows you to focus on those things that are truly important in your life. There are many humans who have crossed the portal. Many associate the experience with their religious beliefs."

"Then, is crossing the portal a religious experience?" I asked.

"It really doesn't matter what you call it. The point is it's a life-changing experience. Most people have this experience as a result of a traumatic event in their lives. Such as a divorce, loss of a loved one, or commonly a near-death experience; like an automobile accident or a serious operation. What's important is the transformation to greater understanding and acceptance of others, as a result of greater detachment. This is the evolution we are attempting to achieve here on Earth, without the necessity of a personal or worldwide crisis." John ended.

"How do I return? There was a grave situation they wanted me to know about."

"You simply request it. Before you go to sleep, you make a request that your dream state companion take you back. Your companion will accompany you through the portal until you can cross the entryway alone."

William A. Guillory

Chapter**Fourteen**—The Destination

O nce the CIA-IIA operatives in Saudi Arabia concluded they didn't have the freedom or the resources to conduct a widespread search on their own, they decided to do the next best thing. Use internal resources. They determined that the fugitives were almost certainly travelling by ground.

Considering the number of military checkpoints throughout Saudi Arabia, they planted a story with the Saudi Security Agency—SSA—that a clandestine group had penetrated the country. Their intentions were unknown, and none were Saudi nationals. If the tip was ever traced back to them, everything planted was truthful.

The SSA picked up on the story with lightning speed. By dawn, an all points alert went out to all military checkpoints. They were instructed to be on the lookout for a small band of non-Saudis. They were to be apprehended and questioned about their business in the country. If they appeared suspicious, in any way, they were to be brought to Riyadh for further questioning.

The Network team, Gala, and I were feeling good about passing Riyadh without incident. We expected no further problems as we headed northwest toward the UAE border en route to Dubai. Particularly, since the first sign-off on our travel made it easier to move through subsequent checkpoints.

As we neared the last military checkpoint, prior to the border, we encountered a line of motorcars in front of us. Passengers were ordered to exit their vehicles. They were questioned, and their autos were being thoroughly searched. Everything was done with military precision. One passenger who protested the search of his private dossier containing a sensitive business merger was promptly taken away to be sent to Riyadh for questioning.

"This is not looking good," I volunteered.

"What do we do now?" Gala asked, with a frightened look on her face.

"We'd better do something soon," Anwar said. We're only a few cars from the checkpoint.

John and Bin conferred and decided that something urgent needed to be done. The original story about Gala and I travelling for employment could no longer be used. After all, we were now *leaving* the country. John amusingly said, "You could say you were fired before you were hired." None of the others found his comment amusing.

John continued, "Anwar, when you get the sign to move past the checkpoint, don't hesitate." Then he said to Gala and I, "And most of all, when you and Gala pass the checkpoint don't look at the guards. Just look straight ahead as if you are interested in what is happening on the other side of the checkpoint."

We both responded, "Okay."

John said, "And don't look scared," with his usual smile whenever there was danger. Then he and Bin were gone.

As we neared the checkpoint, about two cars away from the search, we heard several explosions followed by gunfire. The soldiers who were conducting the "stop and search" were ordered to mount their jeeps and head for the commotion, leaving one behind to monitor traffic. Shortly afterwards, the remaining soldier received orders by walkie-talkie. He began instructing the line of autos to move through the checkpoint as quickly as possible.

Anwar put the Range Rover into gear and shot through the checkpoint. Just on the other side, up ahead of us, we saw detonations along the highway of roadside bombs. A soldier moving traffic along cautioned everyone to stay calm and move quickly down the highway; as if moving quickly would avoid a bomb going off.

Drivers ahead of us were reluctant to do so since they feared someone had planted bombs all along the highway. The lead driver simply stopped and refused to proceed. He feared he was simply being used to detonate any other planted roadside bombs—which was true.

The officer directing traffic came up to him, pointed a gun to his head, and said, "You either die here or take your chances along the road. Which would you like?"

✪ ✪ ✪

Dana was actually excited about the President choosing her to make contact with the extraterrestrials. Her agency's focus had always been on them as a potential threat to U.S. security. She could discern no threat to the U.S. in Bill Bradley's blogs. Ellington's agenda had been personal. In fact, he and his band of renegades posed a greater threat to public panic than Bill Bradley's blogs, she reasoned.

Dana wondered what might be the best approach to soliciting the help of Pat Christensen. She knew a "service to your country" appeal would be useless. And Pat certainly couldn't be coerced. After the way the Star Gate program was discontinued, she probably couldn't conceive of the government having the audacity to ask for her help. Then the words of her recent dream popped into her mind: *friendship*, *trust*, and *success*. Those words applied to any hope of her convincing Pat to help them make contact with the Pleiadians. There was only one person she could think of that related to Pat in this way.

Dana picked up the phone and called Mitch Crenshaw. "Mitch, this is Dana over at Homeland Security," she stated, with the least amount of formality as possible.

"Hi Dana. What can I do for you?" he replied, somewhat cautiously.

"I've been instructed by the President to contact Pat Christensen. He wants me to convince her to try and make contact with the alien network. I don't even know how I would begin such a task. So I'm calling to ask your advice."

"Why do you feel I would know how to convince her?" he asked.

"I know you were her mentor in the Star Gate program. I know you believe in her extrasensory abilities. And I believe she *trusts* you," Dana replied.

"All that is probably true, but I doubt I could convince her to participate in this *Seven Sisters* episode. She would know making contact, if it *were* possible, would lead to greater involvement on her part. And I don't think she wants any part of this."

"Mitch, she's our only hope to deal with this whole situation in some sensible way. You know our government's approach is to assume hostile intentions until proven otherwise."

"Of course I am aware of our government's approach, in spite of Dr. Bradley's blogs about peace and love. But getting Pat to come out of retirement after the way she was treated is no small request."

"What about a call from the President?" Dana asked.

"That would be even worse," he responded emphatically.

Dana could sense Mitch wearing down in spite of his verbal resistance. She knew that somewhere in his thinking this could be an opportunity to actually vindicate the efforts of the Star Gate program; especially if Pat could engage the Pleiadians telepathically to begin a two-way exchange.

"What other alternatives do *we* have, Mitch?" she asked. "How can *we* make up for the Star Gate fiasco?"

Dana had worked the conversation to an alliance between her and Mitch. And now she had placed the ball firmly in his court for *him* to resolve *her* situation. She decided he was the key to their *success* in enlisting Pat. After a long pause, he responded, "Let me give Pat a call and see what I can do. But I can't make any promises," he stated.

"All I can ask is that you do your best." She was about to hang up when a final thought popped into her head. "And Mitch?"

"Yes, Dana."

"I want this conversation and any actions you take to *absolutely* remain between you and me only," Dana stated, now sounding official. "Do you understand what I mean?"

"Yes, I understand," he replied, feeling somewhat chastised.

Dana had determined that Lloyd Pierson, the DCI, was so smug in his conversation with her because he already knew practically everything she was informing him of. And the only source of that information was the DIA.

✪ ✪ ✪

Worldwide concern began to evolve as unsubstantiated stories on the Internet began to circulate involving "aliens among us." No one knew where they originated or who was the source. But there was a growing interest in the suspicion that "something" was going on.

The President of the U.S. got a call from the Prime Minister of Israel. After few minutes of debrief about the Middle East situation, the Prime Minister finally came to the point of his call and asked, "What's the situation with this alien story? It's even on the Internet. Does it have any validity?" he asked.

The President was momentarily taken aback, but quickly recovered. "We've had reports from some of our personnel about aliens," the President replied, cautiously. 'How the hell does he know to contact me about this situation?' the President asked himself. Then he continued, "We're trying to get more information to confirm what we've been told."

"Mr. President, we've had reports of an American, Dr. William Bradley, being tied to this incident. Do you have any information regarding his involvement?" The Prime Minister asked. The reports of both the *Israeli Incident* and the DCI's conversation with Ari Levin had rapidly travelled up the Israeli intelligence chain; ultimately to the Prime Minister.

The President was at a loss for words. His relationship with the Prime Minister was too important to continue withholding information. So the President replied, "Look, I hesitate to tell you information for which we have no factual basis. And that's what we're dealing with here."

"I understand, Mr. President. What can you tell me?"

The President related most of what he had been briefed upon by Kenneth Clarke. He left out his instructions to have Pat Christensen attempt to contact the Pleiadian Network.

"Thank you, Mr. President. I understand the necessity for proof in what you reveal in a situation such as this. I hope you will keep us in mind if we can be of assistance to you."

"I can assure you we will," the President replied.

The Prime Minister was about to disconnect when he said, "Oh, I forgot to mention, we will use all of our intelligence resources in Saudi Arabia to assist your CIA operatives there."

After a pause, the President said, "Thanks for your cooperation." Then he disconnected.

The President informed his private secretary to have Kenneth Clarke, the head of the NSA, come back to his office immediately. When Clarke arrived, the President said, "I just got off the phone with the Prime Minister of Israel. He seems to know as much about the *Seven Sisters* as I do. How's that possible, Ken?"

"I don't know, Mr. President. But I'll certainly find out and let you know." Kenneth Clarke was a retired four-star General. Although polite, there was a plate of steel just beneath the surface. He disliked intrigue used for political purposes and was visibly embarrassed at what he had just learned from the President.

Clarke was stirred from his mental examination of possible leaks when the President asked, "Where do you plan to begin?"

"Although I was briefed by Dana Hartman, there are at least three other sources who had the information I shared with you: Lloyd Pierson, Mitch Crenshaw, and Mitch's boss at the DIA."

"What about this Ellington guy?" the President asked.

"We don't know how much he knows, but we think Dana has put a stop to his activities. His focus was mostly on quieting the 'voice' of Dr. Bradley. He's mostly concerned about how the blogs will influence the financial markets; and his investments."

"The Prime Minister also informed me we have CIA operatives in Saudi Arabia. Does their presence have anything to do with the *Seven Sisters*, Ken?" the President persisted.

"I really don't know, Mr. President," Ken replied, further embarrassed.

"Okay, Ken. Do whatever you have to do to find out what's going on and who is involved." The President stood to indicate that the meeting was over. The he added, "And keep me informed."

"I will, Mr. President. Next time we meet, I promise you, I'll have answers."

✿ ✿ ✿

Bin and John "reappeared" in the Range Rover as they continued east to the United Arab Emirates border. They were

both laughing like kids who had experienced their first childhood prank.

"How did you do it?" I asked, trying to get their attention.

"It was really Bin's idea," John said, trying to control his excitement. "The checkpoint magazine contained several roadside bombs and automatic weapons. We simply borrowed them for our little diversion."

Bin cut in and explained, "We used a timing device to set them off in sequence, on each side of the road, when there was a significant gap in the traffic entering and exiting the checkpoint. Then we began firing the automatic weapons further along the highway. You can imagine their reaction when they discovered there was no one there to arrest."

John took over again, excitedly. "They were totally confused by the bombs going off. The only response they could think of was to cautiously approach the site of the explosions, armed and ready to fire."

Bin again, "Then the officer in charge came up with the brilliant idea of letting traffic proceed as a way of setting off any remaining bombs. He instructed his troops to allow the flow of autos to proceed until there were no further explosions for a mile or so."

"We timed the explosions for when you were second or third in line to create a little anxiety and to ensure there would be an "incident" on the other side of the checkpoint." John said, smiling. "We didn't know exactly what their response would be, but we were confident that the 'stop and search' would be of secondary importance. Everything worked perfectly!" He ended.

I asked somewhat seriously, "And just who was the anxiety intended for?"

John replied, "For you and Gala, of course."

"John, I don't think you realize the seriousness of what we are dealing with here in the Middle East. These people take security situations as a 'life and death' threat. I'm not sure I appreciate the amusement of what we just experienced."

Then Gala said, "Don't you think you're being a bit anal, Bill? We're safe aren't we? What's the problem?"

Of all the people, I expected Gala would support what I had just said. However, she referred to me as being anal. I just hoped it was the language thing again and that she wasn't really expressing what that word implied. From the look on her face I concluded there was probably no mistake!

❂ ❂ ❂

The team of CIA and IIA agents from Israel had set up operations in Riyadh. It was the obvious location to intercept reports from the various checkpoints. The Israeli intelligence network in Saudi Arabia was much more extensive than the CIA. Their network gathered information from various checkpoints along Highway 40W—the main highway—from west to east across Saudi Arabia.

Using counteragents and bribes, they learned that several vehicles with non-Saudi nationals had travelled easterly across the country during the last twelve hours. Most of them were military personnel on official service to the Saudi government.

There were also other civilian vehicles that had passed several checkpoints. One that stood out was an older model Range Rover containing three occupants—two men and one woman.

The CIA-IIA team concluded that this vehicle was their best bet, particularly if it circumvented Riyadh and continued to the Saudi-UAE border. They immediately contacted Langley for satellite surveillance of the Range Rover near the Saudi-UAE border.

They were informed that satellite scanning of the region would not be possible for another four to six hours, depending on other protocols.

Carlson immediately contacted the DCI, Lloyd Pierson, and

informed him of the situation. Fifteen minutes later, Carlson was informed that surveillance would begin within a half-hour.

When the CIS-IIA team intercepted the report from the checkpoint nearest the border, they suspected the Pleiadian Network group. They decided that Dr. Bradley and his companions were headed for the UAE. What they did not know was their destination and plans once they got there.

They were equally unsure of what action they should take if an encounter occurred. Apprehending Bradley and any other human companions was a no-brainer. Still, that didn't ensure capturing any aliens, whatever that meant.

The CIA team informed Lloyd Pierson of the incident near the border. Then Carlson asked, "What should we do when we locate Dr. Bradley and his companions? We definitely know he's headed for the UAE and possibly Dubai."

Lloyd's reply was to proceed to Abu Dhabi—the centrally located capitol of the UAE—using the fastest form of transportation available from the SSA. From there, they would be informed of the whereabouts of the SUV using satellite surveillance. Then a determination could be made for apprehending the entire group and transporting them back to the U.S.

Lloyd Pierson felt for the first time they were possibly ahead of the game, instead of playing catch-up. He thought to himself, 'If they had left it to the professionals in the first place, this *Seven Sisters* affair would have been resolved by now.'

Then Carlson asked, "Apprehending the human team members may be easy, but what about the aliens?"

Pierson replied, "I suggest you use a diplomatic approach. Make it clear we're not arresting Dr. Bradley. Hopefully, Bradley will convince the others to come along." The more Lloyd explained what should be done, the more he felt he had no sensible answer for Carlson. Perhaps, his thoughts about resolution were a bit premature. Maybe even a lot premature.

Carlson's last reply was, "We'll contact you for further instructions once we locate them."

❂ ❂ ❂

Mitch Crenshaw sat in his office trying to reconcile his personal dilemma. On one hand, he wanted to protect Pat from what he could only imagine to be a situation of such magnitude that ordinary citizens were easily expendable. Particularly, after the government got what it wanted. On the other hand, he honestly believed that Pat was the only hope for making constructive contact with the Network of Pleiadians.

Such contact was crucial to begin answering the questions relating to national and possibly global security—"Why were they here?" and "What was their objective?" Somehow, this claim of evolutionary transformation, whatever that meant, did not seem to be the whole story.

Finally, he picked up his phone and called Pat. He got her answering machine and felt relieved. The feeling of relief was quickly extinguished when she picked up during the message recording and said, "Hello, Mitch."

❂ ❂ ❂

Carlson put in a call to his contact at the SSA shortly after his instructions from the DCI in Langley. He delicately requested air transport to Dubai. Predictably, his contact wanted to know the details of such a request. The CIA and the SSA had a good working relationship. Saudi Arabia was one of the major suppliers of oil to the U.S. from the Middle East. Security was vital in protecting their mutual interests.

Carlson stated to his contact in the SSA, "We've identified the small group of fugitives traveling across your country as

Americans." He felt at this point, he had to offer him something in the way of justification for such a sudden request. But no way did he intend to go anywhere near the true nature of his assignment. "We've been instructed to apprehend and return them to the U.S."

"Why do you want to apprehend them?" his contact asked.

Carlson replied, "We want to question them about a situation that occurred a few days ago here in the Middle East," attempting to make his explanation sound routine.

"You mean the *Israeli Incident*?" his contact asked. Anyone familiar with the Middle East knew that the communication system in the region was instantaneous; even if most of it was only partially accurate. Security surveillance went both ways.

"Yes," Carlson replied. "We just want to return them to the U.S. to avoid another possible embarrassing situation. Apparently, it started out as a domestic dispute that went international."

"Let me check with our Head of Security here in Riyadh. You know I don't have the authority to grant your request. I'll get back to you as soon as I get a reply."

Feeling a sense of anxiety, Carlson pressed, "When do you think you might know something?"

Silence on the other end indicated that Carlson had overstepped his privilege. So he backed off and stated, "I'm sorry if I appear to be pressing. This situation appears to have a high priority in my country. We simply want to avoid another international incident. I appreciate anything you can do in behalf of my request."

The SSA contact had now elevated his level of interest in Carlson's request to "code red." He began to piece together information from the checkpoints regarding the identities of the Range Rover occupants and the incident at the last Saudi checkpoint prior to entering the UAE. The incident was sufficiently embarrassing that steps had been taken to suppress it. "How could their own roadside bombs and automatic weapons go off with no one there?" he asked himself.

The papers of the occupants of the Range Rover had not indicated they were Americans. Yet the *Israeli Incident* was reported as an American domestic dispute. The usual "love triangle" and private surveillance to gain an advantage in a property settlement. No names or other forms of identification were given by the Israeli Internal Security. It was confusing why Americans allowed scorned wives the privilege of property in the first place. Rejected wives were lucky to have the freedom of serving another husband, the contact thought to himself.

Now he had an excellent reason to make the request of his agency Head. Something was going on here that involved the CIA. It was happening on Saudi soil. And now there was a request for Saudi air transport. The explanations were full of inconsistencies and unanswered questions.

He made the call to his agency Head. He was told he would be contacted after his request was processed.

The contact indicated that the agency Head might want to review his request ASAP. That it might be related to the "Border Incident." Now he felt he was covered in the event the situation turned out to be a *Saudi Incident*.

✿ ✿ ✿

We crossed the northern border into the UAE without further incident. The scenery was magnificent as we travelled along the southern shoreline of the Persian Gulf. Particularly, after the trip across Saudi Arabia had been sand, and more sand. We decided to stop at the Marina in Abu Dhabi for lunch.

Before entering a Marina restaurant, Anwar suggested that Gala cover her face completely except for her eyes. He also asked, smilingly, if she wouldn't mind walking behind the three men.

She flashed her coquettish smile again and replied, "I don't mind at all."

We were seated at a table overlooking the water and given menus. John and Bin did a quick scan of the restaurant for anyone who might be associated with UAE security; including the local police. None were noticed. They also located two exits other than the front entrance: one, a back door to the Marina walkway; and the other through the kitchen.

We were all famished and tired after the excitement of escaping Saudi Arabia. We each scanned the menu, which was written in both Arabic and English. The waiter returned and everyone ordered.

When the waiter left our table, Bin said, "I think we need to consider changing our means of transportation. It is highly likely that the roadblock at the last checkpoint was set up for us."

Anwar said, "I agree completely. They must have learned we were travelling in the Range Rover. Fortunately, I'm fairly certain it cannot be traced back to my cousin."

"Nevertheless," Bin stated, "We've probably extended the use of the Range Rover to the maximum without an all points alert. Even here in the UAE."

The waiter returned with our meals. He smiled broadly and asked, "Where are you from?"

Anwar replied with a clipped answer that indicated we were not interested in questions and answers, "Saudi Arabia."

The waiter's eyes flashed momentarily and faded into a broad smile, "Welcome to Abu Dhabi, enjoy your meal." He turned and abruptly left our table. Not a good sign, I thought.

"We should bypass Dubai," I said. "

That's probably where they think we are headed."

Anwar said, "There is an airport in Ras al-Khaimah, in the northeastern part of the country, west of Dubai. It could provide the perfect exit to Mumbai."

"Let's discuss this matter later," Anwar said. "I don't trust our waiter." We proceeded to eat our meals engaging in small talk about visiting Dubai.

The waiter returned and began removing our plates. He smiled again as though he knew something we didn't. Then he asked if we would like something more from the menu. John ordered a serving of tea and biscuits for two.

The waiter was perplexed at first. Then he departed to fulfill John's order.

"We still have to find ground transportation in the meantime," Bin said.

John suddenly stood and walked toward the entrance of the restaurant. The feeling in his stomach had been stimulated by a sense of danger. He looked through the small fog-covered window. Then he quickly returned, smiled, and said in his low-keyed way, "I think we need to make a quick exit. Our extended use of the SUV just ended. The local police are examining it in the parking lot."

Just then the waiter returned with the tea and biscuits. As he departed, we were all aware of what the waiter knew that we didn't.

We looked over at him and saw he was smiling broadly.

John smiled in return.

William A. Guillory

Chapter**Fifteen**—The Enlistment

"Hello, Pat," Mitch responded, soberly. "I guess you know why I'm calling." He wondered how he had gotten roped into this position.

"I have an idea," replied Pat. "Why don't you tell me and make it official." She had no intention of making his request easy.

"I'm actually calling in behalf of the President. He wants your help in making contact with the Pleiadians." Mitch was attempting to position himself as being on Pat's side.

"What makes you think I can contact them? I told you I only intercepted some of their messages," she responded, defensively.

"I'm your mentor. Remember? After our conversation about Bill Bradley's true intentions, I guessed you, at least, tried to make contact with his Pleiadian mentor. Were you successful?"

Silence, while Pat decided if she was willing to go pass the point of no return. She knew Mitch was only the messenger, but it was the same as talking directly to the President.

"Well, were you?" he repeated, more forcefully.

"I feel certain 'they' received my plea to warn Bill of what he was getting into. I received no confirming reply."

"I figured as much," he said. In spite of his discomfort in soliciting her cooperation, he honestly believed she was probably the only hope for a peaceful resolution.

"No matter what you say or do, *in behalf of the President*," she emphasized. "I will not be forced into getting involved in this situation. Why don't they use a few 'real' scientists, like an astrophysicist, or an astronomer, or even an astronaut?" she said, sarcastically. Then she added for amusement, "If you are desperate, why not Jimmy Neutron, Boy Genius!" Pat was referring to the animated children's TV series of an American boy with an exceptional IQ who fights the forces of evil with stunning science-fiction inventions.

Mitch paused to let Pat come down a bit. Then he said, "We both know the answer to that question." Then a thought popped into his mind. "You know that Garrett Research Fellowship you've always wanted?" The Eileen J. Garrett Scholar award was recognized as the premier acknowledgement in the world of parapsychology.

"Yes. I remember. But that was a long time ago. So much has changed since that time." Pat had always had an interest in the experiential study of consciousness. Her interest had been to expand upon the Global Consciousness Project conducted at the Princeton Engineering Anomalies Research Laboratory. The project had been all but closed down because of a lack of government funding.

"It can be arranged." After all, Dana did ask him "How can we make up for the Star Gate fiasco?" He thought he'd quite surprisingly found the answer.

"Arranged by whom?" Pat asked. "That award is based on academic credentials, as well as research publications."

Mitch continued without responding to her question, "I was thinking two years at the University of Northampton, England, in the Centre for the Study of Anomalous Psychological Processes." He sensed he had her serious attention for the first time in the conversation.

Then she asked, "Why not a faculty position at the University of Arizona. In the Laboratory for Advances in Consciousness and Health?"

"You mean you prefer Arizona over Northampton?" he asked, surprised. Northampton was presently the foremost center of paranormal studies in the world.

"No, I mean both," she replied, calmly. "A year of research at Northampton *and* a permanent position at Arizona afterwards."

Mitch replied, "As you said, we can't appoint you to a faculty. Particularly, without an advanced degree, Pat." He couldn't figure out whether Pat was serious or not.

"I thought the President was the most powerful man on Planet Earth. That is, until the 'Magnificent Seven' showed up," she laughed. She was definitely enjoying her conversation with Mitch. Particularly, after he opened the door to the possibility of a Garrett Scholarship at Northampton.

Actually, Mitch liked the idea that Pat was proposing. Her request would be an acid test of how badly they needed her help. If they refused, both he and Pat would be off the hook. So he said, "Is this a confirmation of your services? I have to be able to present your position without any doubt."

"Yes, Mitch. This is my position," she said smugly, believing her proposal had no chance; even *with* the involvement of the President.

"I'll see what I can do? No harm in telling him what you want." Mitch felt he had done his part, regardless of the stakes she proposed. Now the ball would be firmly in the hands of the President.

"I still can't promise the Pleiadians will reply to me. But I am certain I can make contact with them. That's at least half the deal," she ended. At this point, Pat was actually enjoying their conversation. She was convinced she would finally be rid of them.

"'I'll propose your request to the Man," Mitch laughed. "We'll see how influential he really is." Mitch chose not to reveal that Dana was a go-between. He figured Pat would be more agreeable to any possible participation if she believed her request was communicated directly to the President by him.

✿ ✿ ✿

"She asked for what?" Dana exploded.

"A Research Fellowship at Northampton and a faculty position at Arizona. You did ask 'how could we make up for the Star Gate fiasco.' I think these appointments will do it," Mitch replied, enjoying Dana's reaction.

"I didn't even know credible programs like these actually existed. Especially on American soil," she replied.

"It depends on how you 'spin' it," Mitch said. "The mission statement at the Arizona Laboratory says, 'To investigate the role of human consciousness and its potential applications for personal, societal, and global health.' That sounds like a statement from the United Nations."

"Why don't we use one of them for making contact if they have Ph.Ds. in this stuff?" Dana asked.

"We're talking about the difference between 'applied parapsychology' and 'theoretical, academic study' of the phenomena. Pat's not only the real deal, but she is the best there is *and* the only deal we have. Most of all, she's a proven quantity."

"I guess you're right" Dana said. "But I suspect the President will be surprised, to say the least, by what she is asking for."

"Well isn't He the most powerful man on Earth?" Mitch asked, amusingly. "I would think nothing is beyond his bidding. Do you?"

Dana couldn't help but laugh, in spite of the seriousness of the situation. Then she quickly returned to the role of Secretary of DHS. "Can she immediately begin broadcasting or whatever it is she does?"

"Not until she has a guarantee in writing of the two appointments for her and her lawyer."

"Doesn't she feel any sense of patriotism? After all, she is from Utah," Dana asked, with some degree of seriousness.

"I think her patriotic gene was transformed into self-preservation where the government is concerned with the termination of the Star Gate Project," he replied.

"Okay. I'll let the President know. At least she's willing to work with us," Dana said, believing the President really had no choice.

Mitch said, "She's not working with us. She's working in behalf of the people on this planet."

"Same difference," Dana said, off handedly, and clicked off.

After returning to their table from observing the local police inspecting the Range Rover, John proposed the group divide into three. He suggested that Anwar and Gala remain in the restaurant as a married couple. John and I would meet on the Marina walkway. And Bin would acquire transportation for their travel east to Ras al-Khaimah. It suddenly became clear to the group why John had ordered tea and biscuits for two.

Both John and Bin teleported from the restaurant. I pretended I was going to the restroom and departed through the back door, where I reconnected with John.

The two local police entered the restaurant. They were met warmly by the owner of the establishment. After a minute or so of animated conversation, the police approached the table where Anwar and Gala were quietly drinking their tea.

The police introduced themselves as local law enforcement

who were looking for the owners of the Range Rover in the parking lot. Anwar replied, "I don't know of any Range Rover. My wife and I stopped here for a quiet meal. We plan on catching the bus for Dubai where we will meet relatives."

The police asked, "Aren't you travelling with three other companions?"

"No, we are travelling alone. We have come from Riyadh by bus." Anwar said.

"Let me see your papers," the one in charge asked.

Anwar reached into his backpack and gave their papers to the police, without comment. Anwar avoided eye contact and retained a submissive look, as expected.

"You have different surnames," the one in charge said, in a confronting manner.

Anwar smiled broadly and said, "We are just married. That's why we are travelling to Dubai. To meet relatives of our family. We plan to get the new papers upon our return. Our application has been filed."

Gala looked up shyly, with just a hint of a smile. Then she touched Anwar's hand and quickly looked downward again.

The police gave the papers back to Anwar. They approached the embarrassed owner, said some angry words, and left. When the police walked back to the parking lot, the Range Rover was gone. So they returned to the restaurant to check on the couple. They were also gone.

✪ ✪ ✪

Carlson's contact in the SSA made a call to his counterpart in the UAE. They were distant cousins. After all, 'blood is thicker than oil.' He informed him of the fugitives entering the UAE and the CIA attempts to apprehend them.

"Why do they want them?" his cousin asked.

"I don't know. They claim a situation involving an American

domestic dispute. But, I don't believe them. There is something going on. I'm letting you know so you can be on the lookout for the group."

"What should we be looking for?" asked the UAE counterpart.

"They're driving an old Range Rover. We've had conflicting reports about how many of them there are; anywhere from three to six individuals."

Although Carlson's contact in the SSA didn't say it, the implication of keeping him informed in return was clearly understood.

Shortly afterwards, Carlson's contact received permission to provide military transport for Carlson's team, without explanations or questions. The assumption was that his agency head had spoken directly to Lloyd Pierson, the DCI in Langley.

Carlson's team arrived in the UAE in the late afternoon. They immediately began collecting information regarding the scheduling of air transport out of Abu Dhabi and Dubai. They focused their inquiries on private transport services. The inquiries were quite expensive, aka bribes, given the fact that they did not involve an *official* security operation.

Carlson wished he still had the Israelis as part of the team, but Pierson was adamant about exclusively limiting the security force to the U.S. Carlson noted an anxiety in the DCI's voice that he had never heard before. It was a combination of reluctance and uncertainty.

Pierson had received a call earlier from Kenneth Clarke regarding the CIA operation in Saudi Arabia. The call involved the operation that the President had learned about from the Israeli Prime Minister.

"Hello, Ken," Pierson said, formally. "What can I do for you?"

General Clarke immediately came to the point. "I understand you have active operatives in the Middle East. Does the operation involve the Pleiadian situation?"

"Yes, it does, Ken." Pierson had no intent of playing power games with General Clarke. The CIA depended too much on the military for many of their personnel and operations. But most of all, Clarke was not a person to be toyed with. He had the full support of the President and in turn, fiercely protected the President's back.

"What specifically is your involvement?" Clarke asked, more politely.

If Clarke was asking a question about the *Seven Sisters*, it had probably come from the President; or what he thought the President should know. Pierson could feel the situation getting gradually out of hand.

"I got a call from Dana over at Homeland Security. She suggested we take over the surveillance of Dr. Bradley when the *Israeli Incident* occurred. She said it had gone international at that point. I told her we would do what we could to apprehend the group and bring them back to the U.S."

"Is there anything more," General Clarke asked.

"No. That's it," Clarke replied, beginning to feel uncomfortable.

"When did you plan on informing me?" General Clarke asked.

"When we had success. This isn't a normal operation, Ken," Lloyd said, attempting to move the conversation from a school boy reporting to the principal to one between professional equals. "You are aware we are dealing with people who have unusual abilities."

"Yes, I am aware of that." Moving on Clarke said, "The President learned of your operation from the Israeli Prime Minister. You can imagine his surprise, not to mention his embarrassment, since he had no knowledge of what the Prime Minister was talking about. Most of all, I'm sure the Prime Minister picked up on the President's surprise."

"Sorry about that. We simply couldn't succeed without the Israeli network in the Middle East," Lloyd said, honestly. "Do you want us to continue this operation?" he said, hoping Ken would take the ball and officially pass it to someone else. Then the CIA could continue to "monitor" the situation without having direct responsibility.

"What is your status?" the General asked.

"We know they are in the UAE at this time. However, we don't know their plans or their intended destination," Lloyd stated. "The UAE is probably just a stopover for air transport. Our agents in the field are collecting information as we speak of scheduled flights out of Abu Dhabi and Dubai."

"Yes, continue your operation. But keep me informed. And, no more surprises, Lloyd."

"The truth is, Ken, I'd rather someone else was taking the lead on this one. We have no experience for dealing with extraterrestrials. That's more the job of the military. Although you guys tend to have a one-dimensional approach," Lloyd laughed for the first time in their conversation.

General Clarke said, "Truth is, we may have to become involved at some point. Given what's happened so far, I doubt they're here for a neighborly visit. Talk with you later, Ken" and the General clicked off.

✿ ✿ ✿

Dana immediately put in a call to the President. Knowing his familiarity with technology, she also sent him a text message. All cabinet members had access to the President using this form of communication. It allowed him to be contacted without going through his Chief of Staff. In addition, it provided direct messages from them without anyone's interpretation in the event he decided to respond. The number of characters was limited, like Twitter, so that all messaging would get to the bottom line. Unfortunately, too many of the messages involved passing the buck to him for difficult decisions they should make.

In such cases, he simply didn't respond. As a security measure, his instant messaging address was changed monthly.

His Chief of Staff, Ronald Jameson, received Dana's message to have the President call her when convenient. That was it. She felt certain the President would recognize her call was in reference to only one matter. Ronald Jameson's first impulse was to ignore the message since she didn't state the nature of her call. After all, *he* determined the convenience of the President's protocol. If anyone didn't state the nature of their inquiry, he routinely ignored it.

Ron had been with the President since his Alderman and Senate days in their home state. There were no secrets between them. Yet the Secretary of Homeland Security had apparently established a person-to-person relationship with the President, by-passing him. He knew he had instructions from the President to be contacted whenever she called. Unlike other situations they had been through, he gave Ron no information as to why this particular situation did not require his briefing. He was simply told to inform him immediately if she called.

He also sensed this call should not be withheld from the President. So, he sent an instant message to the President that Dana had called. They were presently in Paris, the first stop of a European tour to devise strategy for Western economic stability.

Minutes later, the President exited the meeting and returned her call on his private secure cell phone. He obviously noticed Ron's irritation about being left out of the loop. But this was one situation the Chief Executive had determined the fewer who knew, the better. As far as the President was concerned, his irritation was understandable, but irrelevant.

When he was connected to Dana, the President walked away to ensure the privacy of their conversation. He came straight to the point without any small talk. "Hello, Dana, what have you got for me?"

"Mr. President, Pat Christensen will work with us."

"That's wonderful news. When can she begin her efforts to contact them?" he asked, anxiously."

"Before she begins, there are requests she wants in writing for herself and her lawyer." Dana knew this was an obstacle the President wasn't interested in hearing, but one that only He could approve.

"Requests?" he asked, taken aback. "What kind of requests?"

"The requests are the conditions for her cooperation. General Clarke informed me to ask her what we could do to make up for the Star Gate shutdown, if that was necessary. As you can imagine, that offer was necessary to secure her cooperation," Dana stated, without emotion.

"Okay," the President said, "What are her requests?"

Dana explained them as quickly as she could, knowing how valuable the President's time was. In addition, she knew his impatience in having people get to the point, a trait of her own.

There was silence for what seemed like a long time for the President. Then he said, "Okay, I'll have General Clarke handle it. Tell Ms. Christensen, we'll have it arranged by tomorrow. We'll expect her to start when we contact her."

"Yes, Mr. President," Dana replied, formally. "I'll wait for instructions from General Clarke."

After disconnecting from Dana, the President put in a call to Kenneth Clarke. He suggested the Head of the NSA contact Dana Hartman for details. He stated that he expected Pat's requests to be handled by the following morning.

❂ ❂ ❂

Bin had no problem securing a tinted window limousine with Saudi diplomatic license plates. He acquired it from a local supplier in Abu Dhabi. Practically anything was available in the UAE for the right price—no questions asked.

Bin first disposed of the Range Rover while the local police were questioning Anwar and Gala. He simply drove it from the lot and deposited it with one of the members of the Middle East Network. It was to be stored in a safe garage, indefinitely.

Anwar and Gala used the rear exit of the restaurant onto the boardwalk as soon as the Abu Dhabi police left through the front door. They did so in an unhurried manner. The owner of the restaurant simply watched them depart without informing the police. He was still trying to figure out how five patrons had magically become two. He did determine that the one who ordered tea and biscuits for only two patrons had something to do with it. On reflection, he concluded, 'He was a strange one—unconcerned and continually smiling.'

When the police returned to the restaurant to question Anwar and Gala about the missing Range Rover, they were no longer there. They summoned the owner and asked about the married couple. He informed them he had been in his back office the entire time. The husband had paid, and they were simply enjoying their tea before departing. He had no interest in repeating the embarrassment of his initial telephone report.

"Where are they going?" the one in charge asked in his official capacity. "We have just learned that they are fugitives who have entered the UAE illegally."

"I don't know," the owner replied. "I asked them that question. They made it quite clear they had no intention of revealing where they were from or their business in our country."

By this time, an all points alert had been issued in the UAE for the whereabouts of the Range Rover and its occupants. The alert was for the apprehension of possibly four men and an Arab woman. Unlike Saudi Arabia, this was a "quiet" alert with no roadblock checkpoints. The UAE officials determined there was no threat to their country's security. They also concluded that there was an abundance of confusion as to what the APA was all about. No one knew for sure or wanted to be held accountable for the actions taken.

The separate teams of John and I, and Anwar and Gala assembled about a mile from the restaurant along the boardwalk shops. After John related telepathic instructions to Bin, he arrived driving their new limousine.

William A. Guillory

Chapter**Sixteen**—The Proposition

G eneral Clarke determined he was out of his element in
personally achieving Pat Christensen's requests. He had
no experience working with academics. In addition, Dana also
had limited experience with university systems, except for legal
briefs with selected faculty of the University of Chicago Law
School, while she was District Attorney. And obviously, she had
none involving academic parapsychology scientists. The only
person he could think of was Mitch. At least Mitch believed in
the whole idea of extrasensory abilities. He also assumed Mitch
had academic contacts from the Star Gate era. So General Clarke
picked up the phone and made the call.

"Hello, Mr. Crenshaw's office. This is Cindy," his
administrative assistant said, cheerfully.

"This is General Clarke. I need to talk with Mitch Crenshaw,"
he said.

"He's presently in an important meeting. He informed me
that he's not to be disturbed. Even if the President called,

General," Cindy replied, with an amusing tone.

"Cindy, I suggest you pass a written note to Mr. Crenshaw informing him that General Clarke would appreciate a moment of his time," the General said, as politely as he could.

"But sir, he gave me specific instructions."

"Cindy, if you don't pass a note to Mr. Crenshaw, you will no longer be taking instructions anywhere in the Federal Government. Do I make myself clear?" His charade at politeness was gone.

"Yes, General. I will pass him the note." She wondered why everyone in Washington attempted to use "power trips" to get what they wanted. No wonder the system was so screwed up. As soon as the economy improved, she would be out of here.

"Thank you," General Clarke said, noting that it was increasingly difficult with each succeeding generation to use his authority in getting what he wanted from civilians. Somehow, respect for authority was no longer part of SOP.

Less than five minutes after disconnecting with Cindy, Mitch Crenshaw had returned the General's call. "General, sorry about the put-off," Mitch apologized. "With downsizing, I have to spend more time coaching and instructing our young, talented workforce. What can I do for you?"

General Clarke came directly to the point. "I've been instructed by the President to fulfill the requests made by Pat Christensen for her cooperation with contacting the Pleiadians. Problem is, I don't have any idea about how to go about making the contacts with the 'appropriate' academic people; either here or in the U.K."

Mitch replied, "I didn't even expect the President to take her requests seriously. I assumed Pat could go back to selling real estate and telling fortunes," Mitch laughed, clearly disappointed they wanted her involvement. Even though he knew at some level, it was inevitable.

"How do we go about achieving her requests? The President

wants to have both accomplished by tomorrow sometime," the General responded, authoritatively.

Mitch smiled to himself and replied, "Let me make a few phone calls and get back to you. I'll see what can be accomplished. These requests are not as simple as the President might assume."

"I understand," the General said. "I do appreciate anything you can do. I'll be waiting for your call."

Mitch decided to proceed from East to West in the terms of time zones; from England to New York to Tempe, Arizona. He phoned the Northampton head of the Parapsychology Department, whom he knew personally—Sir Charles Pennworth. When they were connected, Mitch said, "Charlie, I've got a proposition I'd like you to consider."

Sir Charles responded, "First of all, it's after hours. Second, I've had a few whiskeys, what you chaps call scotch. And third, you want me to engage a proposition under these circumstances?"

Sir Charles Pennworth had a distinguished career in the study of clinical psychology. During the past ten years he had increasingly used trance state modalities for understanding deep emotional traumas experienced by his clients. In the trance state, they quite easily recalled events that had little or nothing to do with their present lifetime. As he followed their lead in these sessions, he eventually came to the conclusion they were recalling past lifetimes. These events led him to his present studies in *experiential parapsychology*; side by side with the more established approaches of *experimental psychology*. The former involved study of the inner workings of the psyche and the latter, external responses and measurements to external stimuli. His overriding passion was to understand the nature of the human mind, wherever it led.

"It involves money. And it has a short window of opportunity," Mitch replied, knowing that subject would get Sir Pennworth's attention, no matter what time it was or his condition.

"Okay, you've got my undivided attention. Let's start with the money first," Sir Charles suggested, in jest, but clearly attentive.

Mitch responded, "You know that renovation project you've been asking of your government for five years. I think I've found a source of funding."

"I'm all ears," Sir Charles said, now fully sober and awake. "Now, what's the other part of the proposition? Before I tell you the cost of the renovation project." Sir Charles noticed that Mitch had not bothered to ask about cost. So, he reasoned that the source must have "deep pockets."

"You remember our discussing Pat Christensen some years ago?"

"Yes. I remember her quite well. She's still the most extraordinary subject I've ever seen in my present work. What's her present status? After the 'Star Gate' came crashing down?" he mused, referring to the English Humpty Dumpty nursery rhyme.

"I've always felt guilty about how our program ended; and our work all but discredited."

"It's only temporary, Mitch. The work we do is inevitable."

"That's what I'm calling about. Pat has been awarded a Garret Research Fellowship and she wants to study with you for a year; a combination of her extrasensory abilities and your theories of deeper states of consciousness."

"Is that the other part of the proposition?" Sir Charles asked, astonished.

"That's the other part," Mitch replied.

"You've got a deal," Sir Charles said; especially if she's coming on a Research Fellowship. There's a project we're conducting now where she would fit in perfectly."

"Great," replied Mitch.

"Now for the renovation costs that comes along with Pat." Sir Charles gave Mitch a number and waited for bargaining. None came.

Then Mitch asked, "Is that in Euros or Dollars?"

"Euros, or course, old boy."

"Then I can offer you 70% of that number in Euros," Mitch replied, which was the going exchange rate. "And I can do so within the next month."

"Done!" exclaimed, Sir Charles. "I think I'll indulge myself tonight, and have another whiskey; neat of course. Keep me posted on what we need to do from this end." After disconnecting, Sir Charles wondered what was really going on. Somehow, the offer he'd agreed to was win/win, but solely from his perspective.

❂ ❂ ❂

Mitch's next call was to the Executive Director of the Garrett Foundation; Dr. Gail Erickson. Mitch liked negotiating financial deals in the latter part of the day because most people's energy level had begun to decline; making them more receptive to deals they were unlikely to make in the morning hours.

When he was connected to Dr. Erickson, he began with an upbeat approach, "Gail, this is a friend from one of your former lifetimes on Planet Earth."

Gail smiled, in spite of the fact that her administrative assistant said the call was untraceable when she picked up. "Who is this? I'm really not in a mood for jokes," she responded, pretending to be official. She knew it was, at least, someone she knew by the use of her first name.

"This is Mitch Crenshaw from the DIA."

"Mitch," Gail replied. "What brings you into the world of fairies and elves?"

Mitch always appreciated Gail's wit. In fact, he was happy this was not a face-to-face conversation, because Gail could figure out things before someone got to the point. "Gail, I'll come straight to the point," Mitch stated.

"Good," she replied, giving Mitch the sense he had five minutes on stage before the trap door opened and the next act appeared.

"I would like to make a proposal to you."

Silence.

"I would like to establish a Garrett Research Fellowship for Pat Christensen; and a second fellowship to someone your board chooses."

The silence continued. So Mitch assumed Gail was telepathing her unspoken questions.

He went on. "The funding would be made by an anonymous donor and available within a month's time frame."

Finally, Gail said, "What's the catch, Mitch? We all know Pat used to run circles around most of the paranormal practitioners. We were just pissed-off she sold herself to the government."

"It wasn't like that at all, Gail. Pat was young, naïve, and patriotic. She believed she was serving her country. Just like anyone in the Armed Forces. She was simply using her extraordinary abilities, just like anyone else who believes in truth, justice, and the American way," he added to give Gail a chuckle. "So, don't blame her. Blame me."

"Oh, don't worry. You are the #1 perp. And those so-called 'establishment scientists' are #2. And just to round things out, the #3 perp is the DIA. They could have continued the program under DARPA—Defense Advanced Research Projects Agency— and no one would have known!" Gail paused, clearly still upset at what had happened to Pat and the Star Gate program. DARPA routinely funded high risk defense research with no scrutiny from the scientific world; or anyone else, inside or outside of government.

Mitch recognized his call had triggered a "hot button" in Gail. Invalidating the Star Gate work was like invalidating the Garrett Foundation and all the work they had done in the field of parapsychology. He also realized that cutting this part of the deal was not going to be solely about money. But also validating the Foundation's work.

"Okay Gail, I'll level with you. Pat continued to improve her extrasensory abilities after leaving the Star Gate program. She contacted me recently to let me know she thought she was picking up telepathic messages *between* Pleiadians here on Earth. She wants to work with Charlie Pennworth at Northampton to bring about a dialogue involving the future of Planet Earth. That's it in a nutshell," Mitch ended. He surprised himself on how smoothly and succinctly he explained the *Seven Sisters* situation; not really knowing how close he was to the truth, excluding, of course, the Charlie Pennworth part.

"What about the DIA? How are you involved?" she asked.

"This is our way of making up to Pat for what happened with Star Gate. This area of interest is closed to the military," Mitch said, reassuringly.

Everything Mitch said to Gail about telepathic messages was obvious to her; except for intercepting messages *between* them. Non-human aliens had been here for centuries aiding the personal awareness of receptive human beings. In fact, the purpose of the Garrett Foundation was ultimately to aid the evolution of consciousness of humankind. She didn't believe for a moment the non-involvement of the military. After all, that was obviously the source of the fellowship funding.

Finally, Gail said, "Okay, we'll do it, but I have to put my own spin on it for the board." The Foundation had been dealing with hard economic times, like everyone else, in addition to apathy with respect to paranormal activities. 'This could just be what they needed to raise interest again,' Pat reasoned.

"That's fine," Mitch said. "You're much better at that stuff than I am."

Then Mitch thought, two down and one to go. He wondered if the President knew what it actually took to achieve his directive to General Clarke, "fix it."

❂ ❂ ❂

The final leg of the triathlon was the Dean of the Arizona Laboratory for Advances in Consciousness and Health. Mitch knew he would have to put on his "game face" to be successful. He had asked Gail to make an introduction to Dean Harvey Blackman about the project the DIA had in mind.

When Mitch phoned Dean Blackman, he was surprised by the positive reception of his call. Dean Blackman began to recount to Mitch all the advances they had made in their study of consciousness. "We are now involved in field studies to show that populations, like American natives, who are receptive to the mind-body connection have significantly healthier bodies. The best way to explain it in layman's terms is 'mind over matter healing'—as distinguished from curing minor ailments."

Mitch said, "Just a minute Dr. Blackman. I'd like to explain why I'm calling."

"Okay," he stated. "But I got the idea from Gail that you were possibly interested in new funding opportunities. I was hoping the government was intending to renew its efforts in our program. Particularly, with the cost implications of the new healthcare bill."

"That's not specifically why I'm calling. But, we don't have to rule out a new funding source."

Dean Blackman had started to become deflated when Mitch intervened, but remained interested in his comment about a new funding source. After all, as Dean, his main job was to "hustle money" for the Laboratory, to put it bluntly. He replied, "Why don't you tell me specifically why you're calling." His tone had transformed from excitement to suspicion.

Mitch began. "Some years ago, the Defense Intelligence Agency conducted experiments to determine the viability of consciousness projection for remote viewing."

"You mean remote spying," interjected Dean Blackman.

'Aw shit. This is going to be a tough one,' Mitch thought. "Well, as you may probably know, the program was discontinued in the mid-1990s. We no longer do research in the area of paranormal studies."

"You think technology is more powerful than human consciousness," Dean Blackman interjected again.

'Patience,' Mitch kept repeating to himself. 'You need to win this one. Let him express his views. Probably, most of it is true anyway. No need to get upset.'

Dean Blackman had just ended his lecture of the power of consciousness in not only healing, but also transforming the nature of human relationships to make us a more humane society. That's why the work of the Laboratory is so vital," he explained.

One thing Mitch had learned over the years in working with academics is that they wanted to tell their story for the justification of any funding they received. It was important for any funding source to understand the impact of their work on scientific exploration as well as societal good. So he listened to Dean Blackman for five minutes more, then he interjected, "Dean Blackman, we are interested in your consideration of a faculty position for a gifted person with extraordinary extrasensory abilities. Is there any possibility of such an appointment?"

"What's his educational background and experience in the field?" Dean Blackman asked, thinking he knew everyone who was extraordinary in the field of parapsychology.

"It's a she, Dean Blackman. And she was one of our most advanced subjects in the government's program that I mentioned earlier. Her name is Patricia Christensen."

"Are you telling me she has no advanced degrees and published research papers?"

"Yes. That is what I'm telling you. Her research has all been in applied studies. She lends credibility to much of the research you conduct."

"I think I heard rumors about her some years ago. She just dropped out of sight?"

"That's correct."

"What do you have in mind in terms of 'funding' this appointment?" Dean Blackman asked.

"I checked with your former agency head here in Washington and suggested we do a five-year renewal of your departmental grant."

"What about ten years? These studies do take time, you know." Dean Blackman had no hesitancy in asking for more. He sensed this was a deal the DIA wanted.

Mitch concluded it was time to play hardball with the Dean. Either the deal was going to happen or not. "Five or not at all," Mitch said.

"There's a hitch," Dean Blackman said. "I have to get my faculty's approval of what she intends to study as well as her position title. This is obviously not a tenure track appointment. *And*, I can't make this decision on my own."

"Okay, let's set up a conference call for tomorrow morning and Pat will explain what she has in mind," Mitch responded. He concluded that this was as far as he could "fix" Pat's requests. She had to earn her way from here.

"Fair enough," the Dean said. "I will convene them tomorrow morning at 8:00 a.m. for a one-hour presentation. We'll have an answer for you by 10:00 a.m. Is that sufficient time?"

"Perfect," Mitch, said. "Be sure to mention to them the financial implications."

Ignoring Mitch's comment as a given, Dean Blackman said, "Oh, one other thing, I will have to get approval for such an appointment from the President of the University. But I think that will only be a formality, since it is not a tenure track." What the Dean didn't say was that the President would be delighted with the extended five-year funding. He'd been desperately looking for support to keep the Laboratory afloat.

Pat began. *"**I*** would like to pursue the study of consciousness as a separate discipline comparable to the study of the material world as we have done since the time of Descartes and Newton."

"What do you mean by separate?" one faculty member asked.

"I mean we no longer subject our metaphysical experiments to the laws of physics. We must and we will achieve real physical world effects and results, but physical world formalisms are not valid. It's like mixing oranges and apples."

"What formalisms do you plan to use, Ms. Christensen?" she was asked.

"I suggest we develop them, the same as our present natural science was evolved over centuries. That's where the experience and ingenuity of this faculty come into play. Again, the same as we did for the present scientific paradigm we *believe* in today."

"What disciplines are you proposing with this Brave New World?" another faculty asked, with an amused smile.

"I propose advanced degrees in *telepathy, clairvoyance,* and *remote viewing* as a start. Those are the ones I personally have the most experience with. I will depend on you, as a faculty, to develop new conceptual and mathematical formalisms to explain the phenomena. The same as we 'invented' calculus and Atomic Theory to explain other phenomena we observed in creating the Newtonian-Cartesian paradigm. And when we produce a genius, we will create a theory in metaphysics comparable to Einstein's Theory of Relativity in physics."

"What plans do you have from an experimental standpoint?" another asked.

Pat could sense a growing interest in what she was proposing, rather than the resistance she originally experienced. Particularly, since her proposal involved the joint efforts of several faculty members who would share in her funding program. "The proper word is *experiential*. The study of consciousness through the development of *innate* extrasensory abilities we all have that have not been sanctioned by Newtonian-Cartesian science. My plan is to develop a body of teachers and students in the mastery of these abilities for practical applications in healthcare; and ultimately in the development of healthy human minds with greater wisdom."

One of the more senior faculty, who had not asked any questions up to this point, stated, "Ms. Christensen, I assume you know what you are really proposing,"

"Yes, I do," she responded.

"I suspect you are proposing a revolution in human consciousness where there will be little separation, if any, between the physical and metaphysical as well as between the mental and spiritual," he stated. "Am I correct?"

"You are correct, sir. Those separations are really artificial anyway. Once those barriers are done away with, we can begin to learn the true capacity of the human mind. This is all within your context of the study of consciousness. That's why this Laboratory is ideal for such an effort."

Finally, he asked, "Where did you come up with these ideas? You have no training or degrees in these studies."

"Much has come through writings I have done. But most is because I have given little thought to anything else since I left the Star Gate Program. I believe the study of 'consciousness' as I'm proposing is the next frontier of scientific exploration."

"One final question, Ms. Christensen. What are your plans if we do not approve your appointment?"

The Dean was visibly upset by this question. He indicated that this question would be discussed following her interview.

Pat chose instead to answer his question. She stated, "In that case, I will take my proposal to Northampton where there is more intense effort than there is here in the U.S."

Even Mitch, who was listening in on the interview, was impressed. Pat had advanced far beyond his realization of her potential. 'No wonder she's able to communicate directly with the Pleiadians,' he thought to himself.

"Thank you for your time, Ms. Christensen. We will have an answer in one hour," the Dean stated. And he ended the video conference.

William A. Guillory

Chapter**Seventeen**—The Sting

It's amazing the freedom and latitude given to an impressive-looking diplomatic vehicle—especially one with tinted windows. Traffic is stopped to allow passage. Salutes are often given as an acknowledgement of official respect. And the speed of the vehicle is only limited by freedom of the road.

We actually began to feel as important as the limousine demanded. We noticed the "silent checkpoints" as we moved along the northern highway of the UAE bordered by the southern end of the Persian Sea. As expected, our transport was not subject to the inquiries of such surveillance.

"I think we should wait for night fall before proceeding to fly out of Ras al-Khaimah," Bin said.

Anwar agreed. He suggested we stop to rest and plan our best exit out of the UAE.

"Since they'll expect us to stay on the move by driving to Dubai, why don't we remain here in Abu Dhabi before proceeding to the airport," Gala suggested.

"Good idea," John said. How do we rest up here in Abu Dhabi? High end or low end?"

Gala responded immediately, "High end, let's keep to our MO, but no registration." Apparently, from Gala's perspective, she was still on vacation, with no spending limit.

"That shouldn't be difficult in this city," Anwar said.

Then Bin added, "Well, if that's settled, I'll take care of our flight out of Ras al-Khaimah. Perhaps, a flight to Qatar for one or two passengers," he said, amusingly.

In spite of the seriousness of the situation, everyone seemed upbeat and positive about our situation. As if some divine source was protecting us from whatever difficulties we might encounter.

"What's a high-end accommodation here in Abu Dhabi?" John asked Bin.

"The Royal Palace Hotel, without comparison. It is actually the most stunning hotel on this planet," Bin replied. "Nothing was spared in its opulence in terms of true decadence."

"We will want the utmost privacy when we arrive," said John.

"No problem. It is designed for such situations," Anwar added.

When we arrived at the Royal Palace Hotel, Bin got out of the car and asked the bell captain, "Can you direct us to the private entrance for our delegation?"

The bell captain immediately responded, "Why, of course. What accommodations would your party require? Or have you made reservations?"

"No, we have not made reservations. We're here on a very delicate mission for a one-night stopover. We prefer no record of our stay for obvious reasons. We would like your most private three adjoining suites." And as an afterthought, he added, "cost is not a factor."

"Why, of course" the bell captain repeated again.

"Could you have someone meet us at the private entrance and escort us to the suites?" Bin asked.

"Yes. I will handle your request myself. Here are the directions to the private entrance."

"Thank you," Bin said, and slipped him two hundred Euro bills.

By the time we reached the private entrance, the manager of the hotel was waiting for us with four attendants. He said to Bin, "I have brought several attendants to tend your luggage."

Bin replied, "That will not be necessary. We are planning an early morning departure, so we'll leave our luggage in the trunk. Can you send us light evening clothing and toiletries for four men and one woman?"

"Why of course," the manager responded. He turned to dismiss the attendants when Bin gave him a slight head signal. He quickly surmised the group wanted absolute secrecy. 'Something big must be going on,' he thought.

The group exited the limousine and followed the manager to the private elevator that took them to the suites. John and I roomed together, so did Bin and Anwar, and Gala was assigned the room between the two suites.

Bin slipped the manager 1,000 Euros. He took the bills, smiled broadly, and just before departing indicated he would personally return with the items requested. After viewing each of the limousine occupants, it was unnecessary to ask about clothing sizes. The manager had years of experience in tending the most unusual needs of wealthy guests. The requests of this group were easy to fulfill.

When the manager returned with our personal items, we each made requests for light food and drink. Again, we were each served personally by the manger after dismissing the attendants who helped bring our dining orders.

When John settled for a nap, I suddenly had the urge to do the same. I wished I could have remembered the echo in my last dream of the grave situation.

Again, I fell into that state intermediate between

the wake state and dreaming. I was surprised how easily my consciousness projected from my physical body. I also sensed the presence of my companion again as I journeyed toward the portal. When I crossed the portal, I immediately sensed the power of unlimited creativity, characteristic of astral space. The telepathic message picked up where I previously exited. 'We are all connected through a complex system of portals throughout the universe. Physical contact is made through 'translation' via these portals. However, physical entrance to a portal is limited by one's level of evolution. What you do on Planet Earth affects us most on Pleiades, as your nearest evolved neighbor.' I responded, 'How have we affected you?' The reply: 'The prevailing consciousness of your planet, driven by a survival mentality, forces us to decide whether to sever the portal to You permanently; which would set You adrift with the attendant consequences.' 'What consequences?' I telepathed. 'You would lose your connectedness to us and our efforts to assist your evolution. But most of all, You would no longer be....' And...again, I was abruptly awakened as if I did not want to learn of the consequences or when they might occur.

After disconnecting the teleconference with Pat, Dean Blackman made a few comments. "We are presented with a highly unusual situation. It is either a gift from the heavens, given our present funding situation, or a questionable decision that could seriously affect our reputation as a Laboratory.

Particularly, at a time when there is tremendous skepticism with respect to paranormal work, even though we've put a 'healthcare' spin to it." With those statements made, he opened the floor for discussion.

One of the recently tenured, well-respected, faculty members asked, "What decisions are we being asked to make, Harvey?"

Dean Blackman replied, "To put it bluntly, Ms. Christensen would like to be considered for a faculty position. This appointment would be in exchange for funding her appointment as well as five years support of the Laboratory from the Feds."

"That's blackmail!" exclaimed one of the faculty members.

"Of course it is," Dean Blackman responded, casually.

"Are we in the business of 'selling' faculty appointments?" another asked, with less emotion.

"When we negotiated to get you in competition with Princeton and Duke, I think the research funding and laboratory space we got for you made the difference. What would you call that?" asked Dean Blackman.

No response.

One of the more senior faculty got everyone's attention. "I think the key factors that distinguish us from other paranormal programs is not only our exceptional academic credentials, but also the quality of the basic research we perform. These are the key factors we consider for faculty hiring as well as tenure."

Harvey responded, "Well, I think we all know what her record is in that regard. If our criteria are solely based upon those two factors, then we've concluded our discussion."

With this statement came a hush over the meeting. Then someone asked, "Just for the sake of discussion, what will be the probable result if we turn down their offer?"

"We'll probably be exactly where we are now," Harvey replied. "Look, the only reason I brought this situation to you is because I was approached by a certain federal official who chooses to remain anonymous. He indicated that Pat actually chose *us* because her abilities matched certain faculty research areas. She also liked our mission statement."

"This whole situation puts us on the spot," another stated. "We have to really consider whether our mission statement is just academic rhetoric or do we really believe it. But most of all, given the kind of work we do, gaining scientific credibility is probably our most important challenge. We are simply not viewed the same as other academic departments on this campus—exceptional credentials or research wise."

Dean Blackman had not expected the discussion to lead to the credibility of the research of the Laboratory or their commitment to the mission statement. But it was obvious that these were concerns of the faculty; making Pat's abilities even more valuable to their research efforts.

Then the senior faculty who had questioned Pat toward the end of her interview raised his hand. He began rather deliberately. "I've not spoken up to this point because I wanted to hear the views of a variety of faculty. Much of what you've all said has influenced the comments I'm about to make."

"I think our greatest challenge is having the public believe in what we do. That our work has practical application not only to healthcare, but to the quality of life they experience. Impressing other traditional academic research faculty is of secondary importance, in my opinion. We can theorize all we want about the studies we perform, but until we can begin to *influence* the outcomes in people's lives, we will be continually challenged and put on the defensive."

Silence. Which he took as a sign to continue.

"I also think Ms. Christensen is correct in proposing that we begin to establish our own formalisms for the study of consciousness. How can the study of the non-material world follow the same rules that we establish for the material world? No wonder we are continually frustrated in our attempts to convince others of the validity of our work."

"One final statement regarding this discussion: she is, beyond a doubt, the most advanced subject we know of *with* these extraordinary abilities. How could we *not* avail her talents in confirming the work we do?" he ended.

Silence, again.

Then Dean Blackman stated, "Before I take a motion for her appointment, I'd like everyone to consider the comment Pat made in response to one of your questions. If we reject her appointment, it will be offered to Northampton Centre, in England. They have already accepted her appointment, but her first choice is us. Apparently, this appointment is critical to someone in Washington. With that said, I'd like to entertain a motion for her appointment to our faculty, and we can proceed to a vote."

❂ ❂ ❂

Dean Blackman went to his office immediately after the faculty vote. He punched in Mitch's private number on his cell phone, as instructed. "Hello, Mitch?"

"Yes, this is Mitch," he said.

"This is Dean Blackman."

"Yes."

"I'm calling to tell you of our decision."

"Okay," Mitch replied, in a detached manner.

"We would like to offer Ms. Christensen the position of Assistant Research Professor of Metaphysics. This position is not initially tenure track. It can, however, become tenure track based upon the results she produces over the five-year period of research funding." Dean Blackman paused to get Mitch's reaction. This was the crucial part of their negotiation.

"So, this is not a regular faculty appointment. Am I correct?" Mitch asked.

"That's correct. There was a strongly expressed feeling that academic appointments have to come with earned degrees and tenure with refereed research publications. In addition, tenure appointments have to be approved by our board. Given your time restraints, we didn't want to open that *can of worms.*"

"I understand," Mitch replied. "Are there any other conditions associated with her appointment?"

"No, there are no other conditions. However, two of our most brilliant faculty members have offered to work with Ms. Christensen. Dr. Stanley Kopeckne is interested in developing theoretical formalisms involving the study of consciousness. Dr. Harvey Anderson is interested in collaborative work involving the systematic development of extrasensory skills as a degreed program."

Mitch responded in a non-committal way, although he was delighted with the Arizona faculty's proposal. He guessed the clincher might have been the lie that a similar offer had been made and accepted by Northampton if they rejected Pat's appointment.

"I'll inform Ms. Christensen of your offer and let you know her response within the hour."

After disconnecting from Dean Blackman, Mitch contacted Pat. "Hello, Pat. This is Mitch."

"I know who you are, even before you call," she laughed.

Mitch took five minutes to relate Arizona's offer. Then he said, "What do you think? Thumbs up or thumbs down?"

After a long silence to create a little anxiety in response to Mitch's detachment, Pat said, "Have them send me a contractual agreement, and we have a deal."

"Wonderful!" Mitch replied, discovering how tiring this entire affair had become.

"I assume the Research Fellowship is also a slam dunk?" Pat asked.

"Done," Mitch replied. "Anything else?" he asked.

"No, that's it," Pat pretended the conversation was complete when Mitch asked, "When do you plan on making contact with the Network Pleiadians?"

"As soon as I receive written confirmation of the two appointments. Is there anything in particular the President would like me to request?"

"I'll get back to you with an answer to that question before you go into *network mode*," he mused.

"Okay," Pat said. "The ball is in your court."

✹ ✹ ✹

"General Clarke, this is Mitch. The deal is done with Northampton, the Garrett Foundation, and the University of Arizona," Mitch stated proudly. "Pat has also agreed to the arrangements offered by each of them."

"Great news, Mitch. Well done." This was the highest compliment General Clarke could give to a reporting subordinate.

"Pat wanted to know if there is a specific communication the President would like her to send?"

"Good question. I hadn't thought that far ahead. I'll inform the President and let you know what he comes up with." General Clarke disconnected and quickly put in a call to the President.

"Mr. President, we have a go with Pat Christensen."

"That's great news, Ken. When can she begin sending them messages?" the president asked.

"Probably within the hour. She wanted to know whether there was a specific message you wanted her to deliver?"

"Well, beyond why they are here and what are their intentions, I hadn't really thought about it. What are your thoughts, Ken?"

"Mr. President, I suggest we set up a 'meet,' possibly at Camp David. That provides us maximum privacy and there's nothing unusual about your going there on the spur of the moment."

"Good idea," the President replied. "Why don't you draft something for me to send to them? I'll look it over and make any changes necessary."

"Will do, Mr. President," Ken replied. He was about to disconnect when a thought popped into head. "Oh, Mr. President."

"Yes, Ken?"

"Should we plan a military briefing with the Joint Chiefs? Or have a greater military presence at Camp David?"

The President thought to himself, 'I would have never considered involving the military at this point. Good thing I have Ken.' "I don't think so, Ken. If we set up a meet, they'll probably teleport in and teleport out. Let's just have the presently existing security at Camp David on increased alert. After all, it is the most secure compound in the world. Okay?" The President was referring to security provided by one of the most elite Marine Corps units.

"Okay, Mr. President."

General Kenneth Clarke put together a communiqué for the President's approval centered on the two critical questions: "Why are they here and what was their intention?" He also added a suggestion to meet, face-to-face, with the President.

☼ ☼ ☼

After the short rest and use of the exquisite health club facilities of the Royal Palace, the team reassembled to plan our exit of the UAE. Bin explained the plan to everyone. Then he called the manager to have the car brought to the private entrance.

"We have decided to have a short meeting in the city. We will return later this evening," he explained to the manager.

"No problem, sir. I will bring the car around myself. You remember how to use the elevator for the private entrance?" the manager asked.

"Yes, we do," Bin replied. "We'll meet you in five minutes."

We headed for the Ras al-Khaimah airport, about 126 miles

away from Abu Dhabi. It was shortly before midnight so traffic was light. We expected the drive would be less than two and one-half hours. Our diplomatic limousine also made it easy to traverse our journey without any apparent incident.

Meanwhile, Carlson's team had been working feverishly to locate the whereabouts of the Network group. After all, the UAE was a relatively small country. The secondary plan of the CIA team was to anticipate the means and place of departure of the team from the UAE—by water or by air. Their major focus was on private air transport out of the country.

So, they split into two teams to handle each of the tasks, with Carlson coordinating their overall progress. They employed a local source for assisting them in both efforts. No local contacts had identified a group approximating the Network team in any private residences.

Then their source got a tip from an attendant who worked at the Royal Palace. He informed the local source that earlier that afternoon there was a private diplomatic group that had checked in, without prior reservations. The attendant doubted this was the group they were seeking because the manager was shown an official document for a meeting the next day with the Foreign Minister of the UAE. The purpose of the meeting was to discuss the initial disengagement of the U.S. from Afghanistan.

The report of such a delegation was very plausible, since the UAE had a long-standing partnership with the Afghani people and government. Dating back to 2002, the UAE had contributed more than ten million dollars alone to water irrigation projects for agricultural development in rural areas.

The local source asked his contact at the Royal Palace to find out as much as he could about the whereabouts of the group and any other information about their country of origin. The contact indicated he would do what he could and report back.

The other team checking for transport out of the UAE was surprised by the number of private flights in and out of the country—especially from Abu Dhabi and Dubai.

Most of these flights were extremely private business deals involving the UAE and other partnerships around the world. The UAE was ideal as a neutral country to conduct such business deals. It was to the business community as Switzerland is to the private banking world. Therefore, getting information about the occupants of private flights, beyond their manifests, turned out to be a difficult proposition.

In spite of these difficulties, the team was attracted to a last-minute arrangement involving a flight to Qatar. The flight plans indicated two individuals flying on a diplomatic mission. The flight was scheduled for a 3:30 am departure. This information was coordinated with the diplomatic group staying at the Royal Palace. They were also planning to leave on an early morning flight. Carlson's team knew that the number of passengers could easily be rearranged at the time of departure.

Plans were quickly put together by the CIA team in coordination with UAE security forces. The arrangement required rather high-level approval for the *Sting* operation. Ultimately, Pierson had to imply that the operation was of utmost importance to the President of the U.S. to get final approval. The head of UAE security was very concerned about an American "cloak-and-dagger" operation exploding in his face, like the *Israeli Incident*.

❍ ❍ ❍

Carlson's team received information from the hotel attendant that the diplomatic group had suddenly left the hotel. He also informed them that the group was travelling in a diplomatic limo. 'No wonder we missed them,' Carlson thought to himself. 'We've been chasing dead ends. It appears we are finally ahead of them at last.'

He dialed Pierson in Langley. "We think we have them pegged for an early morning flight out of the UAE. We now know they switched vehicles. They are travelling in a diplomatic limo. We plan to intercept them at the airport. Do you have any updated instructions?" Carlson asked.

"Just what we discussed previously. No hostile actions should be taken. We don't know what we are dealing with," Pierson replied.

"What specifically, should our actions be?"

"Make sure you apprehend Dr. Bradley and any other 'individuals' who are travelling with his team. You'll have to handle the aliens by ear. Use a diplomatic approach to ensure them that no harm will come to anyone in the group. We simply want to ask them questions about the intentions of our *alien visitors*."

Carlson assumed 'individuals' referred to Earthlings. Key phrases he picked out of Pierson's instructions were "no hostile actions" and "use a diplomatic approach."

Meanwhile, we were en route to the airport for our scheduled departure. Both Bin and Anwar were feeling nostalgic about our departure. We had formed a bond that went beyond friendship or commitment to a common cause.

"What will you do when you reach India?" Bin asked.

"I have given this question much thought," I responded. "John and I have discussed it. I would like the final destination of our journey to be Varanasi, India. It's also been historically known as Benares and Kashi."

"Why there?" Anwar asked.

"It is one of the world's oldest cities; and the holiest place in the world in Hinduism. It's called the center of the Earth. Varanasi is the city where Buddhism was founded and compatibly hosts many other religions of the world. It is for Hindus, what Jerusalem is for Jews and Christians, and Mecca is for Muslims."

"What do you expect to accomplish there?" Bin asked. "Especially as it relates to the Quest."

"I'm not quite sure as yet," I replied. "But I feel it's like going back to the source. A place away from the modern world where I can 'receive' answers to the questions you are asking me. After all, the name Kashi —the luminous one—refers to the city's historical status as the center of learning, literature, and culture."

"Won't the authorities eventually find you there?" Anwar asked.

"Probably," I replied. "But I have a feeling our hiding and eluding authorities is coming to an end. It's time to take a public stand and let our fate take its course."

After these words, we continued in silence to the airport.

The diplomatic-looking group of four men and one woman arrived at the airport. They slowly proceeded toward the tarmac where the Gulfstream G100 private jet awaited their arrival. This was another tip off to Carlson's team. This jet had a passenger capacity of 7, whereas reservations were made for only 2.

The limousine stopped some distance away from the waiting aircraft to ensure they were not walking into a trap. Everything seemed eerily quiet—even for this time of the morning.

After several minutes of observation, they continued their slow approach to the Gulfstream, preparing to bolt and drive away at the first sign of trouble.

When they got within fifty yards of the idling aircraft, the pilot opened the door and began descending the stairway—as had been agreed. This was the signal that all was in readiness, with no complications.

When the limo stopped in the front of the stairway, four armed men quickly descended the stairway. A convoy of four vehicles with flashing lights appeared from the darkness and surrounded the limo. The limo occupants were trapped with no means of escape.

As each of the occupants exited the vehicle, Carlson made it clear that their intentions were to locate an American named Dr. William Bradley. That it was believed his life was in danger. And that their mission was solely one of ensuring his safety.

When all five occupants had exited, none fit the description of Bill Bradley. They were all citizens of the UAE on a private business mission to Qatar—four men and one woman who were members of the Middle East Network Team.

Meanwhile, a nondescript aircraft had left the Ras al-Khaimah airport a half-hour earlier en route for Riyadh. However, the pilot radioed a change in destination, once airborne, for Mumbai, India—far from the commotion occurring at the Dubai airport.

William A. Guillory

Chapter**Eighteen**—The Holy City

We touched down in the Mumbai airport in the early morning hours and taxied to a secluded hanger. The three of us—John, Gala, and I—were well rested after sleeping through the three-hour flight over the Gulf of Oman and then southeast over the Arabian Sea into Mumbai. We were met by the Pleiadian Network member assigned to India, Ravi Patel. He was accompanied by his protégé, Jasmine Singh.

Ravi and Jasmine bowed graciously, with clasped hands, as we exited the plane. They both smiled broadly. Ravi said, "Welcome to India."

John stepped forward and embraced Ravi. Then he looked at Jasmine with a funny look on his face. He knew of her as Ravi's protégé, but they had never met. For some reason, he looked unsettled. That was odd for John who seemed to be unperturbed by anything. Then he turned back to Ravi and said, "It is good to see you again, my friend. I am sure you are aware of our adventures since my arrival here on Earth."

"Yes, we are aware," Ravi replied. I think it will be less adventurous here in India. Our plan is to be 'remote.' You have chosen the ideal city in India for your stay."

"Excellent. I'd like you and Jasmine to meet Bill Bradley and his companion, Gala Korol."

Gala and I stepped forward and were warmly embraced by Ravi and Jasmine. Jasmine placed a wreath of jasmine flowers around Gala's neck and said, "These are for your growth as a vine." They embraced again, as two sisters reunited after a long separation.

Then Ravi said, "The car is waiting, as you requested. You will truly have an experience of northern India on our 1,000 mile drive to Varanasi."

As we travelled across the country, Ravi explained to us that the northern border with Tibet was the snow-covered Himalayan Mountains, dense forests, and fertile plains, "The Dalai Lama took refuge in the northern Himachal Pradesh state after the Chinese occupation of Tibet in 1959." He pointed to the northern mountain range.

Jasmine commented, "We are looking forward to your next blog, Bill. Your writings have caused many conversations throughout Asia; especially here in India among our growing middle class."

"What seems to be the general theme that arouses the greatest interest in most people?" I asked. I was gathering information in preparation for my emotionally provoking blog. I specifically wanted to create a "confrontation" in the thinking of anyone who read it. I felt it was time to stir an awakening or cause many to retreat into their shells of illusionary safety.

Jasmine responded, "I believe the idea that the average person has more power than they imagine. But most of all, together, we have unimaginable power—particularly over our own destiny," she said, smiling and continued. "The idea that we are principally responsible for our fate, and even our station in life has provoked heated discussions, even among our Gurus."

Ravi added, "Here in the eastern part of the world, we have very strong family relationships with extended networks. We naturally support each other. The challenge is connecting these networks across and between caste systems here in India."

As we drove easterly through the towns of Nashik, Dhule, and Nagpur, we detoured through the Pench National Park. We resumed our three-day journey through Rewa and finally into Varanasi.

Ravi mentioned that Varanasi was home to many notable gurus, poets, writers, as well as the well-known musician, Ravi Shankar, because of its spiritual history. Driving across country had begun to transform my sense of reality from West to East.

We finally arrived at an "independent four-bedroom house" near the upscale area of Rathyathra Crossing. This was to be our home for the next few weeks.

❂ ❂ ❂

Carlson's team had finally tracked the air transport of John, Bill, and Gala to the Mumbai airport. By the following morning, they had agents gathering information about the possible location of the trio.

A vehicle travelling along the highway of northern India was most unlikely to be easily located by security sources. The CIA team quickly came to the conclusion they had hit another dead end—at least for the time being.

After conferring with the DCI, Pierson, they again decided to rely on local sources to assist them. These associations were a continual problem because the locals wanted to know the details of the individuals' violations they were seeking; especially those involving international law.

Carlson's team created a story of a group of Americans wanted for questioning regarding possible terrorist associations.

It was emphasized that they were not terrorists themselves, but had possible vital information regarding other individuals. The team also emphasized the necessity for secrecy, location, and apprehension.

There were so many holes in the hastily-created explanation to the Indian Security Force that no one really believed the American story. However, in the sense of cooperation, the ISF vowed to look into the matter and cooperate with the American team.

At this point, Pierson decided it was best to let the President's plan of direct contact through Pat Christensen take over. The CIA would continue its "soft search" for the trio, along with the ISF. The best approach was to use the local "U.S. assets," code for CIA agents, in the Embassy in Delhi—just 425 miles northwest of Varanasi. An intuitive feeling told him, the wider this search became, the more it would turn into an "international incident."

❂ ❂ ❂

Pat Christensen began transmitting the telepathic message to the Pleiadian Network shortly after receiving written confirmation of her requests from the President.

'The President of the United States would like to convene a meeting with you at Camp David at your earliest convenience. He would like to discuss the purpose of your visit to this planet and your intentions regarding that purpose. He would also like to discuss the role of Dr. William Bradley in your plans. He wants to emphasize that this is an invitation, not an order. Please respond at your earliest convenience.' The last sentence of the message amused her most. The part about an invitation and not an order, she interpreted as "Washington-speak;" as if either mattered to the Pleiadians.

Antonio—aka Tony—had received Pat's first telepathic transmission, as had the other six Pleiadians. Finally, after four broadcasts, over several days, he responded by informing her that her message had been received. Nothing more.

Then he proceeded to convene a virtual telepathic conference with the Pleiadian Network. 'Should we respond to this invitation by the President of the United States or simply continue our work quietly with average people until the people of this planet reach the point of no return?'

The responses were varied from hope to possibly returning home to Pleiades. 'Their beliefs are so strongly opposed to each other that the prevailing consciousness is to die for them rather than change,' one telepathed.

Another responded, 'I can see hope with new social networking systems. There is greater peer-to-peer influence than they've ever had before.'

After several more exchanges with no clear sense of a resolution, John telepathed, 'Why don't we let Bill continue his final two blogs, and see what the response is then.' This suggestion seemed to have unanimous approval.

Then Tony telepathed, 'Should we accept the President's invitation?'

Silence, as they each reflected on the question for several minutes. It was a difficult question to answer since it meant singling out an individual leader as a spokesperson for a planetary problem. Most of all, they knew the President's motivation for the invitation was fear and protecting the American people, not the welfare of the planet.

Then Ravi telepathed, 'What else would we expect? After all, he's intellectually and politically astute, but spiritually ignorant, not stupid. Like most humans, his concern is only for those of his own kind. I suggest we meet with him and at the same time continue our efforts on the only true source of planetary transformation, the average person.'

Again, there appeared to be general consensus. Tony then telepathed, 'What about the question involving Bill Bradley?

Should we respond or ignore it?'

Bin responded immediately, 'I think we should respond to that question. It would provide an opportunity to explain why we are really here, in part. I believe we owe them an explanation to help allay their fears. Most of all, to have the President understand that human evolution is the *only* course for their continued existence.'

Bin continued, 'and the obvious Pleiadian to accompany you, Tony, is John, since Bill is his protégé.' Bin's proposal was also accepted unanimously.

At the completion of the meeting, Tony telepathed to Pat their acceptance of the President's invitation. He also indicated they would simply "show up," so no security checks would be necessary. In addition, the President could invite anyone he felt necessary for his personal security; but the fewer involved, the better for secrecy and confidentiality.

Pat was amused by the last statement since she knew the Pleiadians had no hostile intentions. And if they did, it would have happened long ago when humans were protecting themselves with sticks and stones!

❂ ❂ ❂

I readily adapted to the Varanasi climate—80s °F during the day and 60s °F at night, with relatively high humidity. After all, we were situated on the River Ganges. The wet air was no different from the city where I grew up, New Orleans. I knew this city was the perfect setting for my next two blogs. I could *feel* the inspiration, perhaps because of its historically spiritual nature.

So I retired to one of the bedrooms converted to an office and allowed the message to flow through me.

I'm not sure how to begin this message except to

say that we face a grave situation in terms of our existence on this planet. I have a sense that the threat we face goes beyond our disagreements with each other. I'm also not implying historical biblical threats, such as floods and fire, but a threat caused by the intense hatreds we have of each other that reflects our day-to-day living. It also reflects how we use immense resources for intelligence, violence, and warfare in response to that threat. The threat I am speaking of is more in the form of "intuitive questions." "Are we naturally 'connected' to other worlds?" "Do we affect them as they affect us?" "Are we a positive influence on other worlds or a negative one?" "Most of all, do those connections, somehow, sustain our existence?" I realize these are all questions beyond scientific explanations. That's why I called them intuitive. One thing is certain; we are not creating a more compatible planet of people, but just the opposite. The only hope for each of us, as individuals, is to transform ourselves and our world of relationships. If we collectively refuse to change, we deserve our fate. We are all on one small planetary ship.

The Messenger

The response to this blog was swift and polarized. There was such polarization that I wondered if I had made matters worse than I anticipated. However, in the end, I concluded we were running out of time. We needed a "confrontational message," since confrontation was *the* crucial step in the transformation process.

The following responses to my latest blog reflect the polarized points-of-view:

"The Messenger, or whatever he calls himself," is spreading a message of doom and gloom. We don't need any more of these prophets! I suggest we ignore this blog!"

"I am not sure what this blog is all about, but I do know everything is changing. And I don't have to look very far to know, it's not for the better. I'm afraid to predict where we are headed as a planet of people."

"I am a person who trusts my intuition more than my mind. I know my mind can go crazy, but not my intuition. I do believe we're connected to something and that it's a two-way street."

"I'm a scientist. I have always rejected this metaphysical mumbo jumbo. I use my intuition to solve scientific puzzles. I would never use it to make sense of the human condition. I don't think we are capable of the type of change discussed in the so-called Messenger blog, nor is there any need to."

"I am an average religious person. I do not claim any exceptional intellect. I do fear that God is not pleased with the people of this planet. I have faith that He will send us a savior to lead the way out of the present darkness and into the light of salvation. Thank you for allowing me to speak my peace."

"Since I read the first few blogs about my ability to transform my world of relationships, my life has changed dramatically. I don't know if it has changed anything about the world, but if I multiply my experience by a million people on this planet of 6.5 billion, we can change the world."

"I don't *like* messages of fear as a motivator for me to change as a person. That's why I reject most organized religions. But when I get over my reaction to 'fear,' I have to ask myself, 'Do I have a responsibility to create a more compatible world, simply because I chose to become part of this planetary ship?' The answer I got is YES! Perhaps, starting with my own family."

After reading the worldwide responses, I concluded they

were perfect. Emotions were aroused. People were questioning, expressing, and the majority probably just reading the different points of view. This is the public workshop I'd hope to create. The inescapable one of personal introspection. This, I felt, was our *only* hope.

✪ ✪ ✪

Gala and Jasmine established a relationship of sisters. Jasmine was from a middle class, Indian family. She was insistent from very young about her independence. Her father affectionately described her as "a boy in a woman's body." After graduation from college in India, she did graduate studies in the U.S. at MIT in computer science, then post-graduate work at Cal Tech. She was flooded with offers from U.S. high-tech corporations, but decided to return to India to start her own business.

With her father's influence and the support of her brothers running interference, she became quite successful as the brains behind the "family's software business." Her exploring mind propelled her to continually learn; with a focus on inner exploration. Out of curiosity, she attended a lecture by one of the most respected spiritualists in India named Jiddu Krishnamurti.

What attracted her was his insistence that wisdom came from within—when provoked—and not from the spiritual-sounding statements of a Guru. This, she always believed, and his message resonated. The book that transformed her world was his writing, *The Awakening of Intelligence*. It took her several months to read it, such that she thought she understood what it meant.

When she returned to read passages later in her life, the meanings were different. It was then that she realized, the words were the same, that *she* had changed. It was also clear what the word "provoke" meant. Life, itself, provokes confrontation through conflict, and the opportunity for transformation.

Now she had reunited with her sister. She assumed she had an important role to play in Gala's development. Jasmine believed that everything that happened to a person was part of their "fated path" of engagements. And every engagement had the potential for personal transformation. Her engagement with Gala was not an accident, she surmised.

She took personal responsibility to have Gala *experience* the history of Varanasi—the oldest continuously inhabited city in the world. Besides the museums, libraries, and the more than 100 Ghats on the riverfront—considered to absolve people from sin—Gala was moved most by the temples that had etched so much of humankind's efforts to transcend purely earthly desires.

The last temple they visited was Kashi Vishwanath, located near the Ganga Ghats. In this temple resides the guardian of the holy city, Lord Shiva. Lord Shiva is the third member of the Hindu Trinity, the other two being Lord Brahma and Lord Vishnu. Lord Shiva is the Lord of mercy and compassion. He awakens wisdom in His devotees. An experience of this temple is believed to be soul-cleansing and sets one on the path to spiritual transformation.

When they exited the temple, Gala was emotionally moved to tears. Jasmine asked her, "Sister, what is the source of your pain?"

Gala looked surprised by the question since it had such deep implications. "I was simply moved by this particular temple," she replied. "Somehow, it seemed to bring back memories."

"What memories are those, Sister?"

"Memories of lifetimes as a woman?"

Jasmine remained silent, waiting for Gala, her sister, to continue.

"Finally realizing that being a woman in a patriarchal society was really about learning humility," Gala replied, still in deep reflection. "That doesn't come easy to me. In fact, Bill's nickname for me is Fire, which doesn't necessarily imply humility." She smiled.

"Maybe you might learn that humility has the power to extinguish fire," Jasmine replied easily. "It is only through the experience of humility that we understand the insecurity a male has in such societies. They would vehemently deny this, of course." She laughed.

"What do you mean?" Gala asked.

"The realization of the illusion of male superiority is *their* experience of humility. The realization that *every* person is *inherently* equal as a human being. You see, the transformation he experiences plays out in every relationship in his life. Women are the facilitators of a male's transformation."

"I didn't know such a seemly simple relationship had such deep meaning on a spiritual level," Gala replied.

"Yes, you do know. You've simply blocked it so far, in your present lifetime. With Bill, however, the roles of facilitator and student appear to be reversed, at present," Jasmine laughed.

"If you learn silence, particularly with Bill, the roles will be again reversed. And you can be *his* facilitator."

"What does he need to resolve?" Gala asked.

"That's a conversation for another day. Today is about you."

They walked arm in arm, as one, the European way.

As they strolled easily along the streets of Varanasi, they were totally unaware that they were being observed and followed.

William A. Guillory

Chapter**Nineteen**—The Meeting

The hastily arranged retreat to Camp David caught the Press Corps by surprise. In fact, they were not informed of the President's departure until the following morning. The President had made a quick exit in the early morning hours by the presidential helicopter, along with the identical decoy 'copter going in a different direction. They reached the sprawling retreat, perched atop the Catochin Mountains north of Frederick, Maryland, at about 2:00 am.

The forty-five minute trip had him comfortably settled for a quick nap and breakfast by 6:00 am, which was his normal regime. After a rather heated conversation with General Clarke, the previous evening, he had agreed to bring along two additional elite Secret Service Agents who were former Navy SEALs. Although they were both heavily armed, the President wondered if that would make any difference with aliens, especially those with extrasensory abilities.

After reading the complete dossier on the *Seven Sisters*,

the President conferred with General Clarke regarding the objectives of the meeting. They both realized the meeting was probably a one-time opportunity to communicate directly with their visitors; at least they were promised a full day. In fact, there was no assurance that the entire situation wouldn't go public at any time, given the tenacious curiosity of the Press. Fortunately, the two Pleiadians would be simply "showing up," so there was no need for a secret entrance to arouse the Press' attention.

If the Pleiadians could get in and out of the meeting without the Press being alerted, it would be a miracle. At precisely 9:00 am, according to schedule, the President was informed that his "guests" had "arrived."

When the President first saw Tony and John, he was surprised how ordinary-looking they were. He wasn't quite sure what he expected, except the word "alien" did provoke strange looking creatures in his mind. 'Too many science-fiction flicks,' he thought. He extended his hand and introduced himself.

"Thank you for your kind invitation, Mr. President," John stated, extending his hand to the President. "I am John, and this is Tony. He is the leader of our expedition to Earth."

"Both of you are quite welcome. We don't often get visitors to the U.S., or to this planet for that matter, from as far away as you have come," the President said smiling, attempting to create a cooperative environment for the meeting.

The two Pleiadians smiled graciously, both thinking, 'you have been having visitors to this planet for centuries. And more often than you think.'

John replied, "Tony has been here since you detonated the first atomic bomb in the Nevada desert in 1944. He also observed your two detonations over Hiroshima and Nagasaki in 1945."

"That is a part of our history we are not proud of," replied the President, somewhat at a loss for words. The statement by John was not accusatory, just a statement of fact.

The two Pleiadians just sat there looking at the President until he felt a necessity to say something. After all, he had requested the meeting. General Clarke and the Secret Service agents felt a similar discomfort during the silence. The Pleiadians were not accustomed to small talk.

Then the President said, "What brings you to our planet," as though entertaining two unexpected guests who had just dropped in for drinks and light conversation.

Tony stated. "I originally came because we feared the initiation of the 'atomic era' could lead to your self-annihilation as a species on this planet."

"That is quite a conclusion," the President stated, not sure whether to deny or acknowledge the reality of Tony's statement. Then he said in his reflective way, "What can we do to prevent such an occurrence, presuming we still have time?"

"Permanently change your aggression toward each other. In every aspect of your living; families, communities, cities, and countries, right down to person-to-person relationships. This is your only hope," Tony stated, without emotion.

"That's quite an undertaking," the President responded. "We haven't been able to accomplish that way of living in the history of our planet, as I understand it."

"It's your only hope," Tony repeated. "You did ask me what you can do to prevent the occurrence of self-annihilation. You need to learn how to live compatibly with each other. When I say You, you do understand that I am referring to the collective You on this planet. We do not consider you to be the spokesperson for this planet of people."

The President felt like a schoolboy being held responsible for a condition that his buddies had created. The "conversation" had just begun and yet he felt a strong sense of defensiveness. In truth, his "guests" had given him direct, honest, and non-threatening answers to the questions he had asked. He decided to try a different tact to put the conversation back on neutral footing.

☼ ☼ ☼

"I understand that one of you has had the company of Dr. William Bradley over the past several weeks," the President stated. "May I ask the purpose of that relationship?" he asked, like a request, forgetting his guests were not citizens of the U.S. or of Planet Earth for that matter.

John responded, "I have been in a relationship with Dr. Bradley for more than ten years."

"I thought you only recently arrived here. At least that's the information I received," the President responded, with a confused look.

John looked at Tony, not knowing exactly how he should respond to clarify the President's confusion.

Tony said, "Tell him the answer to his question. He needs to know everything, whether he's ready or not."

"Ready for what?" the President asked, not accustomed to others holding private conversations at a meeting where he was supposed to be in charge.

"Mr. President," John began, "I am Bill's, er...Dr. Bradley's Guide for his personal development. We have been in communication for more than ten years."

"How?" the asked President, with a confused look.

"Through a channeled connection. You see, Bill had been preparing himself for our dialogues fifteen years before I made contact. Even though he was not *consciously* aware he was preparing for me, specifically."

"I don't think I quite understand how he could be preparing for you if he didn't know you were going to make contact."

"Most of You have no awareness of your unconscious motivations. *They* control 80% of what you do. Part of your unconscious is controlled by your intuition. Your intuition provokes you to do things in opposition to rational thinking. Bill simply assumed I was there and our dialogue began. It's called channeling."

"That's it?" the President asked.

"When we thought he had developed sufficiently to influence the evolution of your planet, I showed up." John smiled as he completed his explanation to the President.

"And?" the President asked, waiting for John to continue explaining his relationship with Bill.

"I am physically coaching Bill now. That is, as an *apparent* human being. I am also protecting him from the aggression of the people of this planet. Apparently, You do not really believe in freedom of speech," John said, smiling.

Tony looked at John sternly. He telepathed a message.

John said quickly, "I am extremely sorry, Mr. President. I was totally out of line in stating a judgment of the motivations of people on this planet. Please accept my apology."

"I understand, John. The people I work with make judgmental statements about me all the time. I am not offended by your observation."

After an hour or so of continued conversation relating to life on Pleiades, the President paused, and then said, "We've discussed quite a bit of new information for me to process, and I still haven't gotten to the important questions I have for you. Why don't we take a break from this morning's meeting, have lunch, and resume our conversation this afternoon?"

The President pushed back, rose from his chair, and departed with General Clarke and the two agents in his wake. He didn't wait for a response to his parting question. This was a tactical move to clearly communicate to his "guests" that He was in charge.

When the meeting resumed in the afternoon, the President felt prepared and relaxed. He had to admit that his attempt at small talk had not gone as planned. Now he knew how to deal with his guests. The second half of the game was going to be different.

He had also conferred with General Clarke during the luncheon break as they strolled around the grounds of Camp David. Quite to the contrary, General Clarke thought the meeting was going quite well. His tours of duty in countries all over the world had taught him that trying to maintain control of conversations with others having a totally different *worldview* was impossible.

He advised the President to simply go with the flow. Accept the answers given, even if he didn't believe them. And focus on the most important questions: "Why were the Pleiadians here?" and "What were their intentions?" Other than those questions, the more they talked, the more the President's team could learn how to deal with them. After all, the team would analyze the recorded sessions later.

So the President put on his "game face" as he entered the meeting after everyone was seated. He noticed the Pleiadians were amused by the protocol of standing when the President entered the room. And everyone sat after the President was seated.

The President began with a serious look, rather than the inviting smile he had used at the start of the morning session. He came directly to the point, "Gentlemen, is Dr. Bradley being used by you to 'stir up' people on this planet in opposition to legal authority?" General Clarke was somewhat surprised by the President's demeanor. He would very rarely "piss off" an adversary he knew so little about. He was more a proponent of the African proverb, "Speak softly and carry a big stick"—which translated as, negotiate peacefully and subtly threaten with military might.

John looked at Tony, who gave a slight nod. Then John

said in a detached manner, "I certainly hope so. Particularly, if treating each other with dignity and respect, not to mention the preservation of human life, is in opposition to legal authority," John smiled, warmly.

The reply caught the President off guard again. He realized that the tone of his question did not reflect dignity and respect, but that of an adversary. "What I meant is that we've had enough public demonstrations of dissatisfaction with what we are trying to accomplish," he replied in more conciliatory manner.

"Perhaps, you give them the impression you can solve all their problems and cure all their ills. You know, like the song, *Promises, Promises*," John replied with his usual smile.

"That's what they *want* to hear," the President replied, ignoring John's song reference. "Or that's what we have to say to get elected."

Tony responded with compassion, "Don't you think that makes them dependent, like children? They never get a chance to grow up, think for themselves, and take responsibility for helping to create a better world."

This comment did cause the President to reflect rather than respond as he would in a political debate. "What you say makes sense," he said. "I guess we're not quite sure how to handle the ground swell that's occurring from Dr. Bradley's blogs—most of all, the recent one which speaks of 'a grave threat' and our 'connection to other worlds.'"

"What are your concerns?" Tony asked. "After all, both are statements of fact."

"Are you from this other world? And do you pose the 'grave threat' he speaks of?" the President asked in a non-threatening manner. Then he wondered if he really wanted to hear the answers to these questions.

Tony responded, "Yes, we are obviously from the other world. No, we are not the grave threat." He ended with no further explanation.

John filled the silence that followed. "As Bill's Guide, he asks me questions. I simply answer them. On occasions, I ask him questions to provoke his growth and learning."

"Are you saying his blogs are his own ideas?" the President asked.

"Yes, for the most part," John responded. "I am also sure I *influence* his thinking. After all, we *are* a more evolved civilization than you are," John ended, with a stern look from Tony again.

❂ ❂ ❂

After taking a mid-afternoon break, the meeting resumed. The President began again, this time with a more friendly tone. "I would appreciate knowing why you and your Network of Pleiadians have journeyed to our Planet?" the President asked.

Tony responded. "First, you should know this isn't *your* planet. This is the second time you've made that statement. You've simply been allowed the privilege to experience being human; with some elementary degree of intelligence to manipulate technology. If the consciousness of this planet decided to reject you as an inhabitant, it would do so, as it has done in the past through fire, flooding, and a variety of so-called natural disasters. I assume you do realize the planet has a consciousness of its own?"

"If we have evolved and lived here for as long as we can remember, shouldn't we feel it's our planet? I think we have earned the right of ownership."

"Ownership gives you the idea you can treat this planet and its indigenous people as You choose—without repercussions, I might add. The historical natives of this planet have never assumed ownership."

Tony continued, in spite of the President's irritation and confused look at his response. "Second, we chose to meet with you, in the absence of other influential global leaders, because we don't want our visit here to cause widespread panic. We hope that you will confidentially share with other leaders the nature of our presence and explanations we have provided you. You were fortunate in having an individual who could telepath at our level of frequency transmission."

"Thank you. I will," responded the President.

"And third, we are here to help save you from a global crisis and your own self-annihilation as a species on this planet, before time runs out."

"I'm not quite sure I understand what you mean by a global crisis or our own self-annihilation?" the President asked.

"There are several ways You are presently headed for a global crisis, some with greater probability than others. For example, worldwide poverty, resulting from food shortages, even in developed countries; financial instability of money markets will occur again because the root cause is still alive and well: greed; and global economic breakdown, similar to what you recently experienced in 2008; tied, of course, to financial instability. You *are* aware that more regulations will be of little value. The individuals prone to this activity will simply find other ways of circumventing the new regulations. The next time will be even worse. The warning signs are clearly evident, but you choose to ignore the root cause."

Tony paused to see if the President wanted to respond. When he didn't, Tony resumed.

"The crises with greater probability of occurring in shorter time frames are global competition for energy; depletion of the fresh water supply worldwide; and nuclear terrorism. I won't even mention global warming which you choose to debate and also ignore, even when the signs are quite obvious.

"Could you give me more details about the major threats you've predicted. I'm not sure I understand why you classify them as inevitable, in spite of everything we're doing to avoid such catastrophes," the President ended, with a genuine sense of interest.

"For example, all out competition for energy sources is just 'around the corner' so to speak. The middle classes of China and India are growing at a phenomenal rate. They are major consumers of energy-driven services and commodities. At present, the Indian middle class is roughly the same population of the U.S.—about 300 million people. In general, the have-nots of the world will demand a greater share of the world's resources."

"That's an issue we have begun to address. However, I was not aware of a fresh water crisis," the President replied.

"That surprises me," Tony said quite candidly. "You are simply running out of fresh water to supply even those in developed countries. Primarily through pollution of existing sources, such as lakes, rivers, reservoirs, and underground aquifers, but also with the expanding population growth. At present, about 6 billion people use about 30% of the fresh water supply. By 2025, they will use about 70%. You can expect severe water shortages in Asia in the near future. Can you imagine a world without fresh water?"

"No, I cannot," the President replied.

"Our greatest fear, however, is nuclear or radiological terrorism. They have the potential to, not only devastate local areas and create widespread fear, but also set into motion a series of nuclear exchanges. Thereby, making this planet uninhabitable for human existence. We refer to these as 'hot planets.' "

"You've painted a pretty dismal picture of our,...er, this planet's future, Tony," The President said with a deflated look.

"I am not speaking of the planet's future," Tony responded. "I am speaking of humankind's future."

After a reflective pause, the President said, "We honestly continue to look for new ways of creating a world of peaceful coexistence. Admittedly, we have not succeeded. I, for one, will not give up hope," the President said, with a rush of renewed energy.

"The solution is not about creating new ways of functioning. You have been extraordinary in creating ways to maintain the status quo. The solution is about transforming your dominant way of thinking from greed, domination, and power over others to compatibly accepting your inherent differences."

"The President was feeling even more deflated as Tony shared these comments. He seemed to even become physically smaller.

"You do realize this is true of all nations on this planet," Tony stated, "not just yours. We fear nuclear terrorism or a preemptive nuclear attack, justified by defense of one's self, will initiate the annihilation of humankind. We are here to help you avoid these events."

✪ ✪ ✪

Tony resumed, "I believe the other question you asked was, 'what is our intention?' I believe you mean what specifically it is we intend to do to be helpful in avoiding the major threats to your existence."

"Yes, that is what I asked," the President responded, somberly.

"It is our intent to coach the protégés of your planet in influencing the evolution of people everywhere. Our focus for change is on the average person."

"And exactly how do you plan to accomplish the 'influencing of evolution,' particularly, since we, as leaders, haven't been able to accomplish this?" the President asked.

"That's precisely the reason for our focus on the average person. We hope the messages of personal responsibility and the power of mutual support will somehow resonate at a basic human level—beyond survival or self-interest. If not, then we will have failed—both our efforts and your own attempts at peaceful co-existence."

"Why didn't you simply come to us in the first place, as leaders, rather than using clandestine efforts to recruit people from this planet to do your bidding," the President retorted, beginning to feel more like the "leader of the free world."

"We have sent you messengers throughout the history of your present civilization beginning with Shamans during your period of hunting and foraging. A few early messengers include Lao Tzu, Mohammed, Siddhartha Gautama (Buddha), Assisi, and Aquinas. During the 20th century, we sent you Gandhi, Mother Teresa, Mandela, Maya Angelou, and King, among many others. All with the intent of creating a transformation in human consciousness."

"What are you saying?" the President asked with a puzzled look.

"They were all Pleiadians, in human form, of course. You either ignore them, subject them to character assassination because of their lack of mastery of human emotions, or finally you kill them when there is great popular appeal to their message. As in the case of Jesus of Nazareth."

"This is all beyond my comprehension!" the President said. Tony's statements were beyond a simple disagreement. They involved a clash of paradigms. "We have our own explanations of the origins and lives of the individuals you have mentioned. We still honor them to the present day," the President explained. He wondered if he really knew what he was talking about.

"Yes, You honor them, but ignore their message, in practice. You have not changed the predominant human consciousness of this planet from conflict, destruction, and war to human co-existence, which was their true intent. Without such a transformation, You have no hope as a species. That is why we are here."

The President just sat there speechless, as did General Clarke and the two Secret Service Navy Seals. The Seals had long ago wondered why they were there.

"You appear to have no capacity to avoid self-annihilation on your own. We have come to aid You in preventing such an occurrence," Tony ended.

William A. Guillory

ChapterTwenty—The Transformation

"Good morning, Ken," the President said, the morning following their meeting with the Pleiadians.

"Good morning, Mr. President. I trust you had a restful night."

"No, Ken. Just the opposite. I had a very fretful night."

"I'm sorry to hear that, Mr. President."

"On the contrary, I think it was good. If I had slept soundly, it would have meant I learned nothing from our conversations with the Pleiadians. As it stands now, something happened to me during the meeting. I'm not sure what. But I think I'm beginning to see things in a different light."

"What do you mean? A different light," Ken asked, with a look of concern.

"I mean the stock answers I've given to complex problems seem like a very small part of a bigger picture."

"Can you be more specific, Mr. President?" Ken asked.

"I thought you'd ask that question." The President laughed.

"But the truth is I have a bunch of disconnected thoughts at this point. I'd probably only confuse you and myself."

"You don't have to make sense to me, Mr. President. Although I've never said it, I consider you a person of great integrity. I've always felt that you care about the people of this country as your first priority. The same as I have always felt about the soldiers under my command."

"Although you've never said it, I've somehow always known it, Ken" The President paused. "I'm thinking I need to be more than just the President of the United States, or even the so-called leader of the free world."

"What, then? I've always thought that being the President of the United States was a big enough job for any one person."

"I think I need to be *a* leader of the planet Earth," the President said, smiling. Then he quickly added, "Now I'm not sure what that means or how it plays out. But I'm thinking that I need to help bridge differences with our adversaries, rather than just get the best deal for those who think like we do. Does that make any sense, Ken?"

"It does, in an ideal world, Mr. President."

"Dammit, Ken, we have to do *something* radically different. We can't just travel the same road we've been on. I think the Pleiadians are probably right about where we're headed. After all, you know the definition of pure insanity is to keep doing the same thing and expect something different to happen."

They both laughed to break the building tension. Then Ken said, "What exactly do you have in mind? After all, I am military, through and through. We work best with strategy, tactics, *and* action."

"One thing I *have* decided, and that's not to inform any other leaders of the meeting we've had with the Pleiadians. That would simply lead to worldwide chaos."

"I agree totally," Ken replied.

"As a start, I think we need to take a more cooperative

approach in how we conduct foreign policy, while ensuring that others know we're not weak or defeated, but honestly trying to reduce conflict and the threat of war."

"Tony's comments really got to you, didn't they?"

"Yes they did. The more I protested and made excuses, the more naïve I sounded, even to myself." The President laughed. "The conditions he described are all true. It's like our collective planetary report card."

"If it's any consolation, much of what he said made sense to me, too. But being military, I always think of the intent of my adversaries. At this point, they are still our adversaries."

"That's why I need you close to me during this crisis. To give me a different perspective. After all, my number one job is to protect the American people, at all costs."

"Speaking of adversaries, Ken, were you surprised that their voice recording was 'white noise' while my mine was recorded clearly?"

"Not at all. I've prepared myself to deal with an adversary for whom I'm still looking for a weakness or vulnerability. They still have the advantage on us."

✪ ✪ ✪

"How was it, John?" I asked excitedly, when he returned from his meeting with the President.

"Different than I thought it would be," John replied.

"Different in what way?"

"I thought we'd have to force him into believing that a state of urgency exists. That immediate action needed to be taken to put the people of this planet on the right track."

"So, what happened," I asked.

"We talked. He listened. He obviously didn't accept everything we said. But, he listened, seriously."

"How did you expect him to react?"

"I expected him to be defensive and give us endless explanations justifying America's point of view."

"And?" I asked, waiting for John to explain.

"When Tony told him You were headed toward self-annihilation, he asked how You could prevent it. When Tony described the crisis You are facing, he simply listened and asked for more details."

"Isn't that good for what we are trying to do?" I asked.

"Of course!" John almost shouted.

"So why do you have that funny look on your face?" I asked.

"Because something happened to *me* during the meeting." John took on a serious look that reflected something close to humility.

"What?"

"I had memories of my intense personal growth classes as a young boy on Pleiades. These classes are required throughout one's life on our planet. The willingness to change your perception about reality can be humbling. And during our meeting, I thought your President had the same experience."

"How does *his* experience relate to you? I don't quite understand."

"The kind of change I'm speaking of goes both ways. Both parties are changed by unconditional openness."

"Are you saying that his experience of humility triggered the same experience in you?"

"You are learning fast." John smiled.

"Then, how have you changed?" I asked.

"Although I've been quick, and sometimes impatient, to point out your shortcomings, I've also not fully acknowledged your progress as humans."

"Like what?"

"Like your ideas about *equality*, *freedom*, *democracy*, and *human rights*.

"These ideas are a major part of our Constitution and Bill of

Rights."

"I think your founding fathers were trying to provide you with a *framework* for governance. They had no intention of telling you *how* to put them in practice or that what they did in the 18th century works today."

"All this happened as a result of your meeting with the President?"

"Probably," John said, reluctantly. "After all, these ideas are the most important ones for human evolution."

⚘ ⚘ ⚘

"We think we know where they are, General Clarke," Gary Pierson, the DCI, stated by his secure phone.

"Where?" General Clarke asked.

"They are in the Holy City of Varanasi. It's about 494 miles southeast of Delhi."

"How'd you find them?"

"Carlson's team did. He reported that in countries like India, a cousin of a cousin of a cousin is a better source of intelligence gathering than all the high tech stuff we have."

"I don't doubt it. It makes your case for a resurgence of live ground assets in the Agency, doesn't it?"

"They won't listen to us in Congress. They are too mesmerized with youngsters dazzling them with impressive, but useless, high-tech toys."

"I'll let the President know and get right back to you." General Clarke clicked off and shot off a message to the President using his latest high-tech digital toy.

Five minutes later, the President called and asked, "Ken, what do you think we should do?"

"Well, they're making no attempt to hide their whereabouts. Pierson reports that the cousin, named Jasmine, is providing a private tour for Bradley's companion, Gala Korol. That scares me if we attempt a 'snatch operation.' "

"In truth, Bradley's blogs may be doing us a favor. If people get worked up, then whatever actions I take can appear to be the result of public unrest."

'Always thinking like a politician,' General Clarke thought. "So, what should I tell the DCI?"

"Tell Pierson to hold tight and keep them under surveillance."

"Is that it?" General Clarke asked, skeptically.

"Do you have a better idea?" the President asked.

"Not really. Maybe I ought to say something about Bradley being less important to learning about the intentions of the Pleiadians than we thought."

"Yeah" replied the President. "That might work. Look Ken, I've got to go. You handle it with the DCI." And the President disconnected. His way of operating was to depend on capable subordinates to resolve difficult situations. It had worked so far.

"Shit," Ken whispered to no one in particular. He disconnected from the President's line and reconnected with the DCI.

"What the hell does 'hold tight' mean?" the DCI exploded. "Word of mouth occurs in both directions. Carlson's team will be compromised within 24 hours—or even less."

"So, they know that we know that they are there. In any case, Bradley is less important to learning about the intentions of the Pleiadians," General Clarke said, in an off-handed manner.

"Then why have we been trying to apprehend him?" the DCI asked.

"Things have changed. The President is putting a greater priority on making direct contact with the Pleiadians."

"How's he going to do that?" Pierson asked.

"At this point, he's working on it. That's all I can say."

They both disconnected with a distinct feeling of frustration. The DCI reminded himself that this was the reason he didn't want to get involved in this fiasco in the first place.

After relaying the President's instructions to Carlson in

Varanasi, Pierson wondered how much more bizarre this situation could become.

But he wondered more about General Clarke's comment, "Bradley is less important to learning about the intentions of the Pleiadians." Where did that conclusion come from and what were its implications? After all, he was paid to ask questions about off-handed comments people made without thinking.

Spontaneous discussion groups began to form online. The responses to my last blog had created a world-wide *spark*. Everything happened so unexpectedly that no one was ready for the global online exchanges that occurred. On the other hand, anyone could have guessed that the increasing popularity of each succeeding blog was leading to "something" big. Messages flashed with such frequency and volume, the Internet almost crashed.

The comment about "connected to other worlds" triggered communication among the New Age contingencies. The added spice was that the aliens who were already here would soon make their presence known.

The great majority, of a religious persuasion, began to speculate about planetary forms of world destruction, beyond water and fire. The movies *The Day the Earth Stood Still* and *Knowing* naturally entered these discussions. But most were shrouded in "The Day of Reckoning" from the Bible and humankind being called upon to answer and repent; and even a possible second coming.

Ellington sat in his home library following the events on the Internet, with a snifter of brandy next to the liter decanter. The thick orange-brown liquid had provided the calming effect he needed to maintain some degree of composure. He whispered to himself over and over again, "*If* they had only let me handle it, we wouldn't be in this mess." However, the mess he was referring to was the reaction of the financial markets worldwide. Not the Internet exchanges. The market fluctuations provided no sensible means of knowing what he should do to protect his fortune. He had long since forgotten about his investors. He wondered why this situation was happening to him, given the fact that his family's fortune dated back to shortly after the Revolutionary War. He had no intention of being the first of that lineage to lose it.

Discussions also began to dominate most university classrooms as well as spontaneous student campus groups. Town hall meetings were hastily arranged, but no one seemed to know enough to be in charge or what topics should be discussed. There was just a sense that the Earth's human consciousness was beginning to spin off of its well-trodden axis. And change was in the air. A type of change that no one felt could be directed or controlled.

Finally, the President decided he probably knew as much or more than anyone about both Dr. Bradley's role as well as the alleged agenda of the Pleiadians. He decided he needed to find some means to deliver a message to the leaders of the world that also had global implications.

Amidst this background of world-wide upheaval and confusion, I decided to write my final blog.

The first thing I'd like to say is that we're actually

talking with each other. By the fact that it's electronic communication, we're also forced to listen, which might be impossible face-to-face. Every time we read someone else's point of view, we change by some incremental amount. The greater the separation in views combined with a greater emotional reaction results in a greater (eventual) incremental change. This proposition might sound impossible on first thought, but transformation is often aided by an emotional response of opposition. This way of communicating also allows each of us to experience change in our own unique and private way. I am convinced that when we work through the infinite number of missives, we will discover the common themes we probably all desire. They are equality, freedom, democracy, and human rights, in whatever unique way those are appropriate as determined by one's own culture— not some outside source. Our ability to embrace these themes as a basis for all human existence will allow us to endure as a species on Planet Earth. Our unwillingness to do so will result in our self-destruction.

The Messenger

The Internet workshop continued with unabated intensity as more fuel was added to the fire with my new blog. There was something fascinating, and yet unpredictable, about a global Internet exchange relating to fundamental questions about human existence. It was an event that had never happened in human history, particularly, since there was no human facilitator controlling the process.

The interchanges about the four human values—*equality,*

freedom, democracy, and *human rights*—predictably produced accusations of racism, sexism, and homophobia; political, economic, and communication enslavement; exclusive governance by the rich and powerful; and discussions of the opportunity to *pursue* the rights of being human, not a guarantee of such rights.

As I read the responses in "real time," I decided to post an addendum to my last blog. An addendum that would clarify and begin to consolidate the vast sea of information exchanged.

> *I think I need to provide clarifying comments in respect to the four common themes I discussed in the previous blog. First and foremost, they were not intended to illustrate how systematically these are violated throughout our planet—both overtly and subtlety. The intent was to begin using the process of global consensus using this magnificent system for global communications—The Internet. When I think of democracy, it is from the original Greek word "demokratia," 5th Century B.C., meaning "rule of the people." Governing responsibilities are granted by the will of those governed. Two words closely associated with democracy are "equality" and "freedom." Equality, I suggest means all human beings are inherently equal in terms of worth or value— regardless of differences, accomplishments, or birth origin. Freedom is both the quality of one's state of being as well as the exercise of political, economic, and cultural participation and access. The more recent term, proposed in 1979 by Czech jurist Karl Vasak, human rights refer to inherent freedoms all human beings are entitled to by virtue of their existence. These include the vast majority of civil rights that protect one's freedom to actively participate*

in civil and political life, without repression. I am suggesting that probably the overwhelming majority of us share these in common. What are your thoughts?

The Messenger

The furious global exchanges continued. However, it was more like a consensus gathering process. Few, if any, really argued against any of the four themes. Although it was mentioned that there are societies on this planet where people prefer to be told what to do and in exchange, they are taken care of. My thought was, where that truly exists, it is an expression of diversity.

I concluded the global workshop was the best reality show I had ever participated in. It set a precedent for the possibility of global cooperation, compatibility, and ultimately co-existence. I began to get a glimpse of what John had said earlier, "All we need is a spark." I didn't believe such an occurrence was possible in today's world. Now, I was reexamining my belief as yet another example of my own self-limiting way of thinking.

Now, all we had to worry about was "The Matrix!"—if governments around the world began to fear greater exposure of their inner workings, they would take control of the Internet.

William A. Guillory

Chapter**Twenty-One**—The Summit

The president decided to convene a Summit of the original G-8 in addition to selected developing countries because of their rising political and economic power. The Summit included Brazil, Canada, France, Germany, Italy, Russia, Saudi Arabia, South Africa, Japan, China, United Kingdom, India, Australia and the U.S. This group represented approximately 80% of the economic GDP of Planet Earth. They were hastily invited to Deauville, Basse-Normandie, France where plans were already in progress for the next meeting and press coverage could be easily controlled.

The President's invitation stated that he wanted to discuss a grave planetary threat that involved them all. No other details were given. Speculation began to run wild in the absence of accurate information or more explanation. It ran from the large-scale intervention of the U.S into Pakistan to an admission that the U.S. economy was about to collapse, in spite of publicized reports of its recovery. Some speculated it was probably connected to the Internet situation and how order might be restored.

There were even unsubstantiated reports that a deal had been made between the U.S. and China to control the economic climate of the planet. Particularly, in light of the recent visit by the Chinese President to the U.S. over several days. Although the press was fed a heavy dose of their areas of disagreement during that visit, it was speculated that the U.S. and China might be forging an Economic East-West Alliance.

The Summit members were anxious and tense given the apparent urgency of the President's invitation.

The entire event was set into motion when the President called General Clarke about 2:00 am a few days after their debriefing of the meeting with the Pleiadians. "Ken, can you come to the White House immediately?"

After coming awake, Ken replied, "What? You sure it can't wait for a few hours, Mr. President." In spite of the President's continued suggestion, Ken had never chosen to call him by his first name. Probably, because of the military protocol of respect for a superior person in the line of command—regardless of the time, place, or situation.

"No, Ken. I'm afraid I might either forget or decide not to go through with what I'm planning to do."

"Okay, give me forty-five minutes."

"Can you make it thirty, Ken?"

Approximately thirty minutes later, Ken and the President were huddled in the Oval Office. "Let me just put it out there for your thoughts, Ken."

"Shoot."

"I've decided we're no longer going to be the police of the world. We spent $267 billion in 2000 and $800 billion in 2011 just to make sure nothing breaks out anywhere, anytime in the world where we're not the major force involved in controlling its outcome."

Ken just sat there and waited for the President to continue.

"We're no longer the number one economy in the world, China is. Our people are hurting here at home securing jobs and just making ends meet. And *we're* continually making the next generation weapon of mass destruction."

"Okay, you've told me what we aren't going to do. Now tell me what you think we ought to do."

"Just a minute, I'll get around to that. Let me finish giving you my thoughts about reducing defense spending."

"As I said, China is now the number one economy in the world. They're also a military superpower. They have to assume greater responsibility for preventing and resolving major conflicts in that part of the world. Like the never-ending dispute between North and South Korea."

"In order to take better care of our people at home, we also need to make changes in our economic system to one where spending money for stuff we don't need is not considered the solution for a healthy economy." The president paused to catch his breath.

"I'm still listening, Mr. President."

"Ken, what I'm saying is we have no vision for this country that is realistic for the 21st Century. And all I've done is 'mind the store.' We need an American Glasnost or Perestroika—a restructuring of our economic and political system."

"You do realize that the Soviet Perestroika led to the downfall of the Soviet Union and ended the Cold War."

"Yes, I'm aware of those events," the President replied, smiling.

"Do you want to see the downfall of capitalism, as we presently know it?" Ken asked.

"Shit!" I don't know, Ken. But I do know we've got to do something to get out of the rut we're in. I can sense it in the mood of the people everywhere I go. They're looking for something to happen to shake us out of our lethargy. What do you think?" The President was really seeking an out-of-the-box brainstorming session. A course of action that would, at first, shake up Americans, and then have them say, "Yes, that is what we need!"

"I'm just glad I'm not in your shoes," Ken laughed. "I agree we have to do something. Probably dramatic. The people of this country are living in a more self-centered way than I can ever remember. We've always used an external threat to unite us, like starting a war. I think you're right. There's nothing we've offered to inspire the frontier spirit we used to have."

The President noted the "we" in Ken's statements. "I want to make *America* stronger rather than fixing the world. I want us to care about each other more than thinking we each have to go it alone. And I want to win in our foreign policy by what we do to help others—with no agenda—rather than attempting to convert them through money and power."

"I hope you recorded everything you just said. Because those statements are the basis of the vision you're looking for. Now we have to decide how to convince our political leaders to join us, without political motivations."

"Is that possible, Ken? Politicians are, by nature, political!"

✪ ✪ ✪

During their morning meeting, the President and Ken put together a list of five political and business leaders to attend a briefing. The President realized this briefing was the biggest gamble of all. He intended to *inform* them of his plan to move forward with the future of the United States.

The group consisted of the present Ambassador to China, the Speaker of the House of Representatives, the Secretary of Defense, the Senior Senator from Utah, and the President/CEO of a major high-tech American corporation. They were selected because the President and Ken felt that these men and women were visionary thinkers and knew how to deal with the reality of change. Most of all, they were not so "attached" to their present positions as to compromise the best interests of the American people.

When everyone was assembled in the White House conference room, the President began:

"I want to thank you for joining me here on such short notice. I trust you all know each other." He paused for unspoken nods of ascent. Then he continued, "I'll get straight to the point of my invitation. We are at a grave point in, not only the history of the U.S. but, the future of humans on this planet. I suggest we are like the story of crabs in gradually warming water, proceeding toward a rather comfortable ending."

The group sensed a detached seriousness from the President. Almost other worldly. Each wanted to reply, since they were accustomed to *running* meetings, not listening placidly. The ambassador to China was most attentive and nodded his head in approval of where the President was *apparently* headed.

"I believe we require a major change, both in our thinking and ultimately in our vision for not only the U.S. but, for the entire planet. We have been called leaders of the free world. I think we need to amend that description to *a* leader of the world—where we take into account the concerns of everyone. Not only ourselves and those who think like us, but also those we have traditionally considered being our adversaries."

The President paused again to read the individual, nonverbal cues of those assembled. He could see they each wanted to respond or at least ask questions. He put his right hand up and said, "I only have a few more comments, then I would like to have responses from each of you with respect to my observations." He smiled reassuringly.

"I have been thinking about how we use our financial, natural, and human resources. I've even given thought about our major activities as a country and a planet. Just below the surface, my sense is that we live in a constant state of fear. No one wants to say it or confirm it, so we continue to build more sophisticated weapons, increase technology for surveillance at a blinding pace, and fail to adequately provide for the welfare of our people, even though we are purported to be the richest nation, per capita, on the planet."

"Ladies and gentlemen, we have to create a new vision for this country that reaches into the reality of the future rather than desperately trying to hold on to the past. It must represent a 'quantum shift' in our thinking. Now, I would like to hear what you have to say. Why don't each of you take five minutes to respond to my comments. Then let's have an open conversation."

✪ ✪ ✪

The House Speaker began. "We need something more than just the response to a panacea—like 'create more jobs,' " she stated. "We all know that's a temporary fix. We all know that all great civilizations rise and fall. Instead of falling, I think we need to find our place in a 21st century world. And that place begins with the elimination of the adversarial mentality we have, both in society and in our political system. Until we learn to come together as one society of people who takes care of our own, we have little to say to the world that has any influence." She looked to her right to indicate completion of her opening comments.

The Secretary of Defense sat up, straightened himself, and began. "In spite of all the coming together we might desire, at present, we still have enemies that are committed to our destruction. It is my responsibility to ensure that doesn't happen. As long as I am Secretary of Defense, with the resources to carry out that mission, I will use every means possible, by U.S. and international law, to protect the people of this country. I am always interested in 'quantum shift' ways of accomplishing this mission," he ended, with a defiant look—not stubbornness, but resolution.

The Senator from Utah could sense rising tension in the meeting, so he began by saying, "I hope this is a confidential meeting, Mr. President. I wouldn't want most people from my home state hearing my comments." Everyone laughed, somewhat guardedly. He continued. "I will state what I truly believe, not what I usually say to get re-elected. I feel we have gotten away from 'us' and 'we.' Today, it's all about me and my group. If we don't find a way to come together, starting here in the U.S., we have no future." He stopped there.

The President/CEO of the high-tech company began with a pause, as if to collect her thoughts. "I've never really bought into the whole idea of 'beating the competition.' That's why most of our success has been based upon partnerships, joint ventures, and acquisitions of companies that fit our philosophy—not on immediate monetary profit. Our not-so-secret weapon is our human capital. That's where we focus our efforts. I'm sorry to say, because of the economic situation and the polarization of the American society, some of our best and brightest youngsters are immigrating to other countries for work." Then, she turned to the Ambassador to China to indicate she was complete.

He began. "Most of my thinking about the President's statement has already been said. So, I have no additional comments at this time. I am, however, extremely interested in what you have in mind as next steps, Mr. President."

The President said, "Let's have a continued discussion before I share with you next steps. The group shared their ideas about the future of America, largely expanding upon the points they had each made in their five-minute comments.

At the completion, the President stated, "I've made plans to convene to a G-14 Summit in Deauville, France. At that time, I will make known to everyone specifically what I have in mind. I want to absolutely ensure there are no leaks. I will take full responsibility for what I propose, since my comments will involve the world community. Thank you for providing your advice and wisdom."

As they were leaving, General Clarke asked the Ambassador to China to remain so that he could brief the President about the situation in China.

When the President and the Ambassador were alone in the Oval Office, he retrieved two sheets of paper from his desk. He handed them to the Ambassador and said, "Please read these comments and let me know what you think. This is what I plan to say at the Deauville meeting." Then the President walked out of the office.

When he returned ten minutes later, he asked the Ambassador, "Well, what do you think?"

The Ambassador was ashen. He looked up and said, "I'm just glad I'm not in your shoes."

"I've been told that. Tell me something new. Tell me how you think the American people will respond, or even world leaders."

"Mr. President, I don't think that matters. It's really what you truly believe is necessary to head off the cataclysm we're headed for. I can see it more easily since my time in China. I don't know if I would have the guts to do what you're proposing."

"I believe you would, Mr. Ambassador." That's why I asked for your opinion. Besides General Clarke, you're the only one who knows what I am planning to say. I'll expect you to brief the Chinese leaders about the details after my speech."

The Ambassador was about to leave when the President said, "Oh, Mr. Ambassador?"

"The Ambassador stopped and looked questioningly at the President, "Yes, Mr. President?"

"I hope you're the next President." The President paused and added, "after my second term, of course."

"The Ambassador smiled and departed."

Shortly afterwards, there was a knock on the door of the Oval Office. The President replied, "Please enter."

"May I have a few words with you, Mr. President?" Ron Jameson asked.

"Sure, Ron, what's on your mind?"

"Mr. President, I know there's something's going on that you feel I shouldn't know."

"I'm sorry about that, Ron. We go back too far to hold out on you. But this is something that I think you will have a difficult time dealing with."

Before the President could explain further, Ron put his hand up and said, "You know, Mr. President, I think you're probably right. In any case, I have a letter for you to read. If you sign it, I'll know it's time for me to move on. Just let me know by tomorrow."

Without opening the envelope, the President knew it was Ron's resignation.

As Ron opened the door to leave, he said, "You know, I've neglected my family for too long. But it's all been worth it to have served you, sir."

The President moved from behind his desk and embraced Ron for a long final time. "Good bye, Old Pal." Then he returned to his desk.

Ron closed the door of the Oval Office for the final time.

After a half-hour of reflection, The President picked up the phone and called General Clarke. "Ken, would you have Dana Hartman come to the White House ASAP?"

✪ ✪ ✪

The President began his statement to the Summit:

"Ladies and Gentlemen, I humbly thank you for attending this urgent meeting on such short notice. I hope you know I would not take you away from your very busy responsibilities unless there were urgent matters we must handle together. The matters I will discuss with you singly appear solvable. But when considered together, they are a formidable test of our will and skill of working together in a way that has not yet been demanded of us. We will be challenged to set aside our individual interests in preference to the greater goal of human preservation on this planet.

In my invitation to you I indicated there was a grave situation we face that threatens our continued existence on this planet. We are aware of widespread poverty worldwide, in spite of enough food production to feed us all. The financial meltdown we recently experienced is a mild forerunner for what's in store for us—ignited, I am ashamed to say by the greed of financial institutions in my own country—and the aftershock of financial breakdown that leads to widespread economic depression.

More grave than those are three other situations that you are aware of: The diminishing supply of uncontaminated fresh water for domestic, agricultural, and industrial use; the predictable competition for energy, particularly for the growing middle classes in populous countries; and most threatening, nuclear and radiological terrorism. These three, when taken together will inevitably lead to an incident that can result in self-destructive nuclear exchanges that will render Planet Earth uninhabitable. At least nine nations presently have nuclear capability, and the number is growing annually. That, my friends, is where we are today.

It only takes one mistake and we all suffer the consequences. That's the grave situation we face. It would be irresponsible and sinful for us to ignore this situation as leaders in control of those horrible weapons. Our strategy for defense is to continue to build more sophisticated weapons of mass destruction. That's hardly a solution for an intelligent species of people.

As a result, I would like to share with you the future course I intend for the United States to begin to address this situation:

We will begin by shifting 20% of our defense budget to address our economic situation at home.

We will use this government funding to create jobs for reconstructing our deteriorating infrastructure in terms of bridges, railway and municipal transportation, improved fresh water preservation, and the reduction of armaments except for what is absolutely necessary to protect the safety of the American people.

We will begin to redesign the basis of our economic system to focus on conservation rather than consumption. We will work very hard to shift from an engine of greed to one of freedom of creative expression in entrepreneurial efforts.

Most of all, we will attempt to base our foreign policy on supporting the success of others, without expecting them to adopt our political philosophy and cultural values.

Thank you again for your attendance and patience for my comments. I am willing to respond to any questions you might have," he said, smiling. *"I'm sure you probably have many."*

✿ ✿ ✿

At least half of the members at the Summit immediately raised their hands at the invitation of the President for questions. The French President, representing the host country, facilitated the Question and Answer session. He recognized the President of Brazil.

"Mr. President, I commend your courage, if not totally the wisdom of what you have proposed. Who knows, perhaps the world needs something of what you have suggested. I withhold judgment for the present time."

The President replied, "I could not hope for a better response."

Next, the Prime Minister of Japan stated in a low-key fashion. "I hope your decision does not lead to the occupation of the Japanese people," he said, glancing at the Chinese leader.

The President simply nodded and said, "I promise you, it won't."

The Russian, German, and English heads of state sat stoically, trying to assess the implications of the President's comments; and the future of their alliances.

Quicker than expected, there were no more questions. Most appeared to be contemplating and assessing the consequences of the President's statements. They retired for relaxation until their formal dinner that evening.

Swift global reaction was occurring as the President's speech was circulated worldwide at precisely the start of his presentation. By the time he had concluded, Lloyd Pierson, the DCI received a call on his secure line from a European industrialist who headed up a loose confederation of global billionaires. They talked for approximately fifteen minutes. By the completion of their conversation, the industrialist knew exactly where the DCI stood on the President's proposal.

Chapter**Twenty-Two**—The Plot

The Billionaire Club was not a club at all. It was an informal confederation of parties with a common interest. That interest was to maintain control of the overall direction of Planet Earth—from 40,000 feet. The confederation was actually an evolutionary phenomenon that had become more formal as greater numbers of global multimillionaires began emerging in the early 1990s. Especially the *noveau riche* from the younger generation who funded idealistic programs to change the world.

The Club consisted of seven members having residence in the U.S., China, Japan, Switzerland, England, South America, and Russia. Although they had official residencies in these countries, they considered the planet their home. Besides having immense wealth, each of the members had critical influence on commerce, finance, economics, politics, science, and technology. They saw themselves as keeping in place the orderly—and sometimes disorderly—flow of processes and systems for a properly functioning planet; like democracy, socialism, capitalism, communism, global trade, and most of all demand and consumption.

The assumption was that planetary human dynamics had become so complex and chaotic, unpredictable events could easily throw it into a tailspin of conflict over competing national interests. Although the G-6, G-8, and now the G-20 were formed to prevent such events, they consisted of politicians who were far removed from the reality of world order. That was the reason for the formation of the Club in the first place.

They had received continuing reports of the President's situation involving the *Seven Sisters*. Initially, it was observed with amusing interest as the President wrestled with how to resolve the issue of alien visitors. Alien visitors were not a surprising event to members of the Club. They knew that nothing was beyond the realm of possibility. The only question to the Club was the visitors' *intent*. Then appropriate action could be taken. The rest was up to fate, which they realized they did not control.

However, what they had not planned on was the "conversion" of the President to assume he knew what was best for the world order. Drastic changes involving the rules of conflict or the economic system that fueled the world were out of his league. The question the Club faced was whether to let his pronouncements run their course and be rejected by the appropriate political bodies or to stop him in his tracks. The wild card emerging in this dilemma was the reaction of people online to the blogs by *The Messenger*—Dr. William Bradley.

They believed the statement made by Victor Hugo more than a hundred fifty years ago,

*"There is one thing that is more powerful
than all the armies of the world,
and that is an idea whose
time has come."*

Taken together, the world situation could quickly spin out of control. So they agreed upon a two-part plan. Part one: Eliminate the American President. Part Two: Ride the tide of change to its unpredictable conclusion as a result of widespread protests, and maintain control of the ship, if not its direction. If it continued, decide the fate of Dr. William Bradley.

So, the appropriate steps were set into motion for the best time and place for the President's "removal." The Administrator of the Billionaires' Club was charged with this task. All communication with contractors was done electronically through encryption, and subsequently destroyed. He was simply referred to as the Administrator. Obviously, names were never exchanged with contractors. The Administrator's residence, unknown to contractors, was Switzerland.

The President's statements at the Summit caught the American people by complete surprise. Up to the present, he was considered by the country to be a progressive, but certainly a pragmatic President—not subject to unpredictable flights of fantasy.

His pronouncements for the future of the U.S. also caught most of the political power brokers by surprise. Although, some word had started to leak from his meeting with the business and political leaders at the White House prior to departing for France. As a result, some knew something big was about to happen. Most were safe in the knowledge that the U.S. was still a democracy with a balance of power in three governmental branches. Although he was considered the leader of the country, the President couldn't do anything drastic without the advice and consent of Congress.

The President had begun making plans for advising the leaders of Congress of what he presented to the Summit. He had chosen not to inform this group initially for fear of leaks and offensive action against his plan before sharing it with other world leaders. He did, however, want the advice and thoughts of visionary American leaders and those most impacted by his proposal. So the meeting had been held prior to drafting his final notes.

When he met the Congressional delegation, he began by attempting to lighten the mood, "Although it's almost impossible to catch the Washington political scene by surprise, I'm guessing most of you were unaware of my thoughts for the future of the U.S." They all laughed guardedly.

Then the President said, "In truth, I have been thinking for some time that we have been in a kind of sleep state. That we've lost our pioneering spirit that has made us leaders of the world for so long. But most of all, the changes in the world seem to be dictating our future rather than the other way around. So, I began asking myself, 'how do we get out of this rut?' I wanted to initiate this conversation in the most dramatic way, without having my ideas compromised by the usual spectrum of versions from others. I figured that would happen anyway."

"So now that you all know, in broad description, what I'm proposing for our future, what are your thoughts?"

The majority leader from the House of Representatives was quick to respond, assuming his leadership position justified his place in line. "Mr. President, it seems as though you're asking the American people to do a 180° turn in terms of how we have done business for the last 400 years; just here in America." He didn't wait for a response, but continued. "What exactly do you mean by an 'economy of conservation?' "

The President replied, "Well, as a start, we need to produce everything we do in an environmentally-sensitive way, even if the rules have to be legislated. We need to view the environment as an extension of the houses we live in. Secondly, I propose we purchase what we need, within the limitations of our budgets. That we begin the painful process of purchasing what we need rather than spending out of control and creating a personal and national debt as a basis for economic stability."

"Does that apply to the White House?" a Junior Congressman blurted out.

"Yes, it does," the President replied. "We will be taking active steps to reduce the budget deficit and achieve an annual balanced budget; with accountability measures, I want to emphasize." He paused as if to decide on what he was about to say, then continued, "My intention is that everyone, including the rich, will have to make sacrifices to put us back on track."

"What about the cut in defense spending you've proposed? How can Americans feel safe with such a cut?" another asked.

"We will simply have to learn to focus on the most vital surveillance and security measures. As stated in my speech, other major powers of the world will have to take greater responsibility for the safety of the Eastern regions of the planet. We simply don't have the resources anymore to be the police of the world."

"How do you think the American people will react to your proposals, Mr. President?"

"I really don't know. But I do believe that they elected me to lead for the future, not to cautiously lead to be re-elected. I will try to convince them this is a challenge we must face together, as united as possible."

"It appears the Internet exchanges have moved to the streets. Especially in countries that believe they have been denied democracy and freedom," I was explaining to John.

"Yes, I've noticed," John replied.

"I think you were probably right all along. All we needed was a spark to ignite an apparent underlying global desire for the freedom of expression. After all, I believe that desire is fundamental to all human beings." I began to sense a change in my relationship with John. Although, he was still protective of me and Gala, our relationship was evolving into an exchange of ideas between equals—without the necessity of excuses when crucial discussions were appropriate.

"You know movements like these have the potential to take on a life of their own. They don't really need an official leader," John said, openly.

"What are you saying, John? That I ought to remove myself from what is going on?" I asked. "After all the encouragement you've given me to take the lead?"

"That's pretty close. The media has a way of creating leaders and heroes. Then the so-called leaders become the ones with answers. They also become the targets to those in opposition."

"What do you propose I do, John?" I asked.

"I really don't know the answer to that question. It depends on how transformed and empowered people feel they are. I guess your major concern should be to prevent the movement from stagnating and returning to where it was before. It's a delicate balance."

"In all honesty, that would be perfect. I've never fashioned myself a leader. In fact, I feel best when people help themselves. I love to lead from behind."

"Empowered people have a way of organizing themselves. When they stop looking externally for answers and realize the power they possess for self-organization, they achieve the ultimate expression of democracy and freedom," John said.

"In any case, there are spontaneous uprisings pretty much everywhere. Even in established democracies, people appear to want some degree of change in the way they are governed," he ended.

Assuming the conversation completed, I turned back to the flood of Internet exchanges that had not abated over several days. John, however, didn't leave.

So, I turned back to him, and asked, "What's up?"

"I'm not quite sure, Bill. It really began when we were in Paris."

"What began?"

"I guess you call them feelings and emotions. We had no preparation for handling them before coming to Earth."

"Oh, that's no big deal, John. Feelings and emotions are natural for human beings. All you need to learn is how to manage them."

"That's more easily said than done. This body seems to have a mind of its own. I can't seem to control them, let alone manage them."

"Control them when?" I asked.

"Like when I'm around Jasmine, quite frankly. This body begins to do things that I can't seem to manage or control."

"Oh, that," I smiled, appreciating the fact that there was something even the advanced ones from Pleiades couldn't handle. "I think I'm beginning to understand what you might be dealing with."

"With some people, it is stronger than with others. With the President, feelings and emotions were present, but I could handle them. When I'm near Jasmine, it's completely different. Worse of all, I think she knows."

"Yes. I would guess you're right. Women know these things immediately. Remember, we talked about the differences between casual and emotional relationships in Paris? When did this all start? You've only known her for a week."

"It started when we first met at the airport. It was just a flutter then. But as time has passed, I've tried to avoid her."

"I'm afraid that won't work, John. The real question is how does *she* feel about you."

"That's only part of it, Bill. Ravi also knows. There is nothing we are capable of hiding from each other. Even if we wanted to have a few secrets."

"Is that going to be a problem? After all, he's a Pleiadian."

"He's bound to protect Jasmine—body, mind, and spirit— just as I am bound to protect you. I guess that protection now extends to protecting her emotionally—whatever that means."

"Let's not get ahead of ourselves, John. We should first find out how she feels about you. Then, we consider alternatives. Okay?" I asked.

"Okay," John replied, but he already knew the answer to that question."

✪ ✪ ✪

"Initially, I want my message of change to be delivered to the heartland of America, not any of the big cities around the country," the President was explaining to General Clarke.

"What cities do you have in mind?" Mr. President.

"Somewhere central to the country in location. Somewhere that represents good, hardworking people who understand plain, common sense. If I can't convince them, then my proposals have no hope."

"What about Iowa? Dana's home state. It's referred to as the 'American Heartland.' The capitol city, Des Moines, is right in the middle of the state. And also very close to the center of the country, from east to west."

"What about a speaking site?" the President asked.

"That may be a problem. There are no large indoor facilities that hold over 50,000 people."

"What about a football stadium?"

"Well, Iowa State is thirty-five miles north of Des Moines in Ames. But I hope you're not considering an outdoor speech, Mr. President?" Ken looked at him with concern.

"Why not?" the President asked. "What's the size of the stadium?"

"Let me look it up," Ken replied. "But I hope you're not serious."

The President didn't reply. He just waited for Ken to retrieve the seating capacity using a quick Internet search.

"It's about 60,000, more or less, if the football field is used for seating."

"That's perfect," the President exclaimed. "Why don't we see what Dana thinks?"

When Dana arrived, Ken and the President resumed their discussion of speech sites in the Oval Office.

The President began, "Dana, we're thinking of holding my speech to the American people in your home state. Is that a good idea?"

"In what sense, Mr. President?"

"In the sense of the type of reception I'm likely to get."

"Well, to begin with, you won the state in the last election; not by a large majority though. It's slightly favorable to our Party overall, but strongly divided ideologically, east and west. As you know, Des Moines and Ames, where the university is located, are right down the middle of the state."

"We need a tie-breaker," the President said.

"Well," Dana said, "Funny you picked Iowa State University. Its football stadium was recently renamed in honor of an African American football player named Jack Trice. I think it was in 1997."

"Why him?" the President asked.

"He was injured during the game against the University of Minnesota in 1925 where he sustained a broken collar bone. He later returned to the game and while trying to make a tackle was trampled by three Minnesota players. He was sent to the local hospital where he was declared fit to travel by the doctors there. Trice died from hemorrhaged lungs and internal bleeding as a result of the injuries sustained during the game. The stadium was named in his honor in 1997. It's the only football stadium in the country named after an athlete."

"How do you know so much about Trice's story?" the President asked.

Dana smiled and said, "It's my home state. I do keep up with what's going on. Especially a story like this one."

"Yeah, that was a stupid question," the President said, smilingly. He paused, then stated, "Most of the festivities will be in Des Moines, but the question Ken and I are discussing is the speech site; possibly the Jack Trice Stadium. What do you think?"

"What do I think about what?" she asked, truly puzzled. As a lawyer and naturally left-brained, Dana always wanted to know, "What specifically is the question?"

"The question is: Am I in danger of an assassination attempt?"

"She paused, and then responded, "In my opinion, you're always in danger of an assassination attempt. The real question is: Will there be a consciousness in Iowa favoring such an event?"

"Like Dallas with President Kennedy?" He asked.

Dana proceeded cautiously, again as a lawyer would. "I think it is fair to say there was strong feelings against President Kennedy prior his visit to Dallas. Not only there, but throughout the South because of sweeping changes he was proposing with respect to Civil Rights. There were also rumors that he planned to have us pull out of Vietnam. That was not exactly popular with the military-industrial complex at the time."

The President didn't respond, but simply waited for Dana to

continue.

"Will that be the case in Iowa? I doubt it. These are people who work hard, support their families like most in America, and appreciate plain simple talk. They also expect you to keep your word."

"So, should it be the stadium or some indoor facility?" the President persisted.

"I don't think the facility will make any difference about your protection. But I do think the stadium will be a more electric environment."

"Thanks, Dana. I guess you know you are now officially part of the *Heartland America Team*."

❁ ❁ ❁

Monique Rashad and Jacques Lamoreaux were, without question, the best assassination team around. Their success rate was 99.9%. The 0.1% was a mortal wound that achieved *removal* several hours later. That record was over fifteen *engagements*. Most of them involved corporate and government assassinations where corruption or illegal arms or drugs were involved. Their relationship was largely forged out of the incendiary events in the Middle East during the 1990s.

They lived on an undisclosed island in the Adriatic, populated mostly by indigenous people whose family history dated hundreds of years. They were in touch with the world to the extent they chose through high-speed Internet, digital television, and a communication system that would rival the best corporations in the world. Their isolated existence was the result of their chosen profession resulting from a personal tragic event.

Monique was the daughter of an American Marine and a Muslim Lebanese mother. Her father was assigned to the American Beirut base in the early 1980s. Her mother worked at the U.S. military base where they met. Their affair was intense and highly risky, given the strongly divided tensions involving the American presence in Beirut—presumably, in a peace-keeping role. That is until the 1983 suicide bombing of the airport barracks, killing 241 American servicemen and wounding many more. Monique's father was among those wounded. He was flown to the USS *Iwo Jima* off shore and then to a hospital in West Germany for convalescence. Fortunately, his injury was not serious and he was soon able to return to active duty with his outfit in Beirut.

Unknown to Sergeant George Maxwell, Monique's father, was the pregnancy of Sari, Monique's mother. He returned to Lebanon to find her and was told that she had fled to relatives in an outlying area after the attack on the barracks. Sergeant Maxwell had decided to forgo his military career, if necessary, to be with Sari. While conducting his private search to find her, he was suddenly reassigned to Asia. Word of his relationship with Sari and search for her reached his commanding officers. His military career was considered more important to them. He lost all hope of finding her and remained unmarried for the remainder of his military career.

Everyone was told that Monique was an adopted daughter that no one wanted, having obvious American features. Monique had a striking resemblance to her father even with her bronze skin. She excelled in her studies and attended the American University of Beirut. She perfected American English, learned from childhood, without the hint of an accent.

Jacques Lamoreaux was the son of a French General assigned as part of the United Nations peace-keeping force in Beirut. The meaning of his name Lamoreaux, derived from the Old French, was "dark-skinned." It matched the complexion of his handsome, athletic body. He violently opposed the American presence in the Middle East as well as their strong support of the Israelis. He reasoned the French were there because of historical reasons and related best to the people of Lebanon. The French were wanted and respected by the Lebanese as opposed to the Americans who forced themselves into the region for exploitation. While in Beirut, Jacques spent much of his time in the Muslim community, adopting many of their cultural ways.

Jacques' father insisted he attend the AUB where he met Monique. The attraction was instantaneous and intense; as when her mother first met Sergeant Maxwell. Jacques studied electrical engineering and computer science. Monique studied world politics and Western history. Jacques was often perturbed by her intense interest in learning about the Western world. For some reason, the area they disagreed most was in their differing opinion of the Americans. While Monique didn't like their presence there, she felt Jacques had no idea what could erupt without them.

Jacques took pride in teaching Monique military strategy and the use of firearms. It was then that her sharp mind and natural combative skills began to emerge; and even surpass Jacques'. His adjustment to her rapid learning was difficult at first, but he reasoned away his jealousy by thinking of her as his student. One of the most important lessons Monique learned from Jacques was respect for an adversary. That sense of respect was crucial to the meticulous preparation she devoted to every engagement in life—whether it was a competition with Jacques or the removal of someone associated with a contractual agreement. She naturally emerged as the leader of the pair.

One evening when the four of them—Monique, Jacques, Sari, and Jacques' father—were having dinner at an outdoor restaurant, an important government official at an adjacent table was assassinated. The official was a leader in the fight against government corruption, and arms and drug trafficking. Unfortunately, Sari and Jacques' father were both instantly killed by the drive-by shooting. Miraculously, both Monique and

Jacques were unharmed. Their killers were never arrested or prosecuted although it was generally known who they were. Both Jacques and Monique decided that peaceful means of achieving justice was a waste of time; particularly, when it involved the wealthy and powerful. They dropped out of college and vowed to avenge their parents' deaths by taking matters into their own hands. That was the beginning of their deadly partnership.

Their first job was identifying the individual responsible for the deaths of their parents. A powerful Middle Eastern arms dealer. After meticulous research, preparation, and practice, they executed a clean and surgical removal, with no collateral damage. Shortly afterwards, they began receiving requests for high-level contracts. They researched such individuals, confirmed their corrupt activities, and decided on that basis to accept or refuse a proposal. They viewed themselves as "avenging angels" for those without wealth or power. But in truth, their removals served most the endless conflicts between the rich, powerful, and corrupt—both within and outside of the system.

Chapter**Twenty-Three**—The Assassination

Jacques and Monique were meticulous students of *The Art of War*, written by Sun Tzu, more than 2,300 years ago. The writings of Sun Tzu are still unsurpassed in providing a tactical approach to victory over an adversary. An assassination to the J&M Team was not simply a crude act of killing another human being. That could be easily accomplished by simply walking down the street. It was closely associated with wealth, power, and corruption, which were often inseparable.

High profile individuals with highly trained security personnel often lacked the most crucial element in preventing harm to a "principal"—and that was *mental acumen. Preventing an encounter, rather than victoriously engaging one was the objective.* In the case of the President of the United States, however, the American Secret Service was endowed with both exceptional intelligence and highly developed skills of engagement. That is what attracted Monique most to their newly contracted project. After all, the President was no more corrupt than most powerful world leaders. The element that ultimately convinced her agreement was the President's support of Israel, even when innocent people were killed by Israeli military attacks. For Jacques, it was his dislike of American policy and military action in the Middle East, often resulting in considerable collateral damage to innocent people. When such events could not be resolved by denial, families were simply compensated for their loss.

Each of their engagements began with the most important *"Appreciation of the Situation"* from Sun Tzu, *"Every battle is won before it is fought."* It is won through information, planning, and preparation. A thorough knowledge of one's adversary was a necessity—including their tendencies and tactics, and most of all their commitment to die in protection of the principal— the President in this case. Nothing brought out this point more vividly than the famous picture of Lee Harvey Oswald, the presumed assassin of President John Kennedy, being shot by Jack Ruby where Oswald's police guard drew away from the assassin. Secret Service Agents are trained to do just the opposite.

The J&M Team was continually astounded by the wealth of information available about high-profile individuals from the Internet. They wondered how long it would be before stronger security measures would began to seriously prevent the unlimited flow of information. Actually, something more drastic would be required since global hackers seemed to always be ahead of the game. They reasoned it would not be long before the G-8 began to take serious steps to control the flow of information on the Internet—a necessity for a planet dominated by fear, control, and power over each other.

"He's scheduled a two-day trip to the 'Heartland of America,' it says," Monique read to Jacques. "Some place called Des Moines; and followed by a speech in Ames, Iowa, from a football stadium."

"Oh yeah, I think that's Iowa State University. I vaguely

remember the location from a visit to America with my father some years ago," Jacques replied.

"Since you've been to America, why don't you handle the logistics of the physical location? You know, positioning, buildings near the stadium, the President's location, and of course, an exit strategy."

"No problem," Jacques replied. "That makes sense since I have a feel for what the American people are like. Mostly obnoxious and rude! They think the world belongs to them."

"Actually, I don't dislike them. I just think they don't have any idea of our history and don't have an interest in learning it," Monique said. "They're just brainwashed into thinking that anyone who is Muslim is a terrorist. It's mostly ignorance, I think."

"I believe it's more than just ignorance," Jacques replied, thinking 'we've been here before.' "But who knows for sure," he said, pretending to give Monique the benefit of the doubt so they could get on with their planning. "You handle the Secret Service and their plans from the arrival in Des Moines to their 'presumed' exit on the afternoon of the second day."

She responded, "As long as you keep in mind, the number of security people is insignificant. The more they use, the more easily they are subject to confusion. After all, *warfare is based upon deception*."

✪ ✪ ✪

Now that Dana was part of the President's inner circle, she could add another point of view when he and General Clarke disagreed. Not that a majority of two would win. The President usually felt strongly about some things, no matter what a majority might think or what the risks might be. One of his decisions was that the speech would be in the football stadium where he could speak to the entire crowd nearly 360° in the round.

Dana had taken over the duties of Ron Jameson in terms of scheduling and press releases, but she had not moved into the role of holding press conferences. Both her personality and approach with the President had immediate impact, which often happens with a change in personnel. He sought her opinion on most subjects like timing, speech details, his dress, and selected political leaders.

En route to Des Moines, Dana was briefing both the President and General Clarke of the schedule after his mid-morning arrival. "The Governor and top state leaders will be meeting Air Force One and escort you to the capitol building for a short statement to the legislature."

"I'm just pleased to have an opportunity to begin laying the groundwork for 'America in the 21st Century.' I hope it catches on. We couldn't have picked a better place to start," the President said. After selecting Iowa, the President had Dana begin researching the history and concerns of the local political leaders. He planned to make commitments through their Congressional leaders. After all, he did carry the state in winning the Presidency.

"Tomorrow, you're free in the morning except for a short briefing with the two Senators and several Representatives from Congress. Again, to begin laying the groundwork for "America 21st," Dana amended the slogan.

"What's the mood like, Ken? In terms of the people of Iowa."

"I think there is a sense of anticipation, Mr. President. They're beginning to look for details regarding your plans."

"Since Iowa is sometimes called the 'Food Capital of the World,' I have some ambitious plans for the farmers there; they involve not only feeding America, but also the starving and impoverished populations of the world."

"I think the people of Iowa will be a very receptive audience," Dana contributed. "Their response to your speech will be a good indication of the mood of the American people."

"What about security, Ken? Are you satisfied? Once I decided on the outside stadium, you've had complete control of my safety."

"We've doubled the number of security people and feel pretty good about the various perimeters. The Secret Service obviously knows this stuff best. I have complete confidence in the measures they've taken."

Just then, the intercom indicated Air Force One was beginning its landing pattern into Des Moines, Iowa.

✪ ✪ ✪

The day following my conversation with John involving Jasmine, I arranged for her and me to have lunch together. As we walked to one of the nearby restaurants, Jasmine suggested we journey to a place in the older part of the city.

After being seated outdoors at a private table, she asked, "What are your plans now that people are aroused everywhere and the American President is surprising the world? One would think he's had a revelation from one of our Gurus," she said, smiling.

"I'm not quite sure what my plans are. I do know that I'm not running or hiding anymore. With people in the streets and the President trying to shake things up, maybe I can return to a normal life."

"I once read a statement from a Thomas Wolfe novel, '*You can't go home again.*' It means you can never go back to the way you used to be after having experiences that change you as a person. No matter how hard you try."

"That's probably true, Jas," I said, adopting the shortened nickname. "But I don't know what more is necessary for me to do."

"Just stay open. I have a feeling there is a lot about to happen in the next week or so. You may be needed quicker than you think. That's the kind of world we live in today."

"By the way, what's up between you and John?" I surreptitiously slipped in. "Or should I say between John and you. He seems to be a 'little' attracted to you?"

"I would say more than a little," she smiled. That kind of smile.

"What does that mean?" I asked, somewhat, but not totally surprised. After all, John had told me his role was not to interfere in the direction of the planet. I wondered if that included a romantic tryst with Jas.

"It means whatever you think it means. What's your interest in knowing what goes on between John and me?" she asked, a little cheeky.

"Goes on?" I asked. "Is that the place you've moved to?"

"Look, Bill, what I mean is that John and I have a special connection. It happened when we first met at the airport. I've tried to keep separation between us because we're different from each other."

"That's my point, Jas. John is not human. I mean not human like you and I. And he certainly doesn't know how to handle feelings and emotions."

"What makes you think I do?" she asked, with a surprised look. "I've already told you I've tried to keep separation between the two of us. What more do you expect?"

"Something tells me separation hasn't necessarily worked."

She lowered her head, embarrassed by my implication.

"If Ravi finds out, he will be so disappointed in me." And with that admission she began to cry.

"Look, I'm not criticizing you. I don't have the right to judge anyone given the mistakes I've made in my life. But I guess I've grown protective of you, given your relationship with Gala."

Jasmine continued to sob softly. People in the restaurant began to notice. At this point, I decided it was probably time for us to leave. So, I said, "Look, I'll talk with John and Ravi as soon as we get back. Maybe we can straighten this thing out before it gets too serious."

She just cried harder. At that point, I rose, took her gently by the arm, and we left the restaurant.

When we returned, I looked up John. He was in a delightful mood and broke into a smile as I approached. "What's up, Bill?" he asked.

"Something serious," I replied.

"Oh? And what's that?" he asked, innocently.

"You and Jasmine. It won't work."

"Why not?" he asked, naïvely.

"The two of you are different. Not like people here on Earth. I mean you are physically or non-physically different. Not to throw in *very* different in terms of how well you *know* each other."

"She and I are not as 'different' as you think. She's a very old soul with ties to the Pleiades that she is unaware of."

"That's no excuse, John. There is no future for the two of you. You'll be returning to Pleiades. Then what's to become of her life?"

"We're living for the moment, Bill. There is no future."

"That's in your Pleiadian reality! She lives in a human future. In addition, you're like a child where feelings and emotions are concerned, in an adult human body. That's a lethal combination, John."

"Okay, let's talk with Ravi. He's been here longer than me. But let's not bring in Tony as yet."

At that instant, Ravi appeared, smiling. "Was I summoned?" he asked.

"Yes, you were," John replied. "You know the situation. What is your opinion?"

"First of all, John, Bill doesn't know, you've crossed the line in terms of our agreements for coming here. We have to start there."

"Crossed what line?" I asked, beginning to have a sinking feeling in my stomach connected to Jasmine's crying.

John said, with an apologetic look, "I tried to explain to you that we had no training in managing feelings and emotions."

"So what?" I said, "What does that have to do with Jasmine?"

"We had an emotional coupling."

"You what?" I exploded, as it became clear what John was saying.

John paused to collect his thoughts before replying to me. Then he began. "Bill, you don't seem to understand that humans and extraterrestrials have been intermingling for centuries. This is not something new or unusual from our perspective. Perhaps, the greatest period of coupling occurred with your Greek civilization around the 5th century B.C. Because of our extrasensory abilities, some of which you haven't seen as yet, You referred to us as Gods."

That's no excuse, John. You're here to help us discover a better way of living, not to have an intimate relationship with Jasmine; particularly, where there is no future in it for her."

"What do you know, for sure, of Jasmine's future? Let alone your own," John replied calmly.

I sat there speechless with respect to his question. Then a thought jolted me. The thought was about all the emotionally driven events *I* had experienced in my life, where rational, sensible thinking was not even a consideration. And most of all, what basis did *I* have of being judgmental of their relationship. Was being upset really about protecting Jasmine or about the incompletions in my own life?'

✪ ✪ ✪

Out of all the "removals" they had accomplished, the J&M Team believed this one would be their pinnacle. Maybe they would retire afterwards and go into a more legitimate line of work; like starting a global consulting firm. After all, money wasn't a problem. But attempting to live a normal life after what they had been doing was a bit far-fetched.

These thoughts were running through Monique's mind as she lay perched in the crawl space of the Jacobson Athletic Building. It was located at the north end of the football field. Dead center.

She and Jacques had arrived, hours before the final Secret Service sweep of the building, during the middle of the night. They certainly didn't search crawl spaces of the building. The team carefully tended their diets at least days before an "engagement." Their longest waiting period was two overnights.

Jacques had disabled one of the three elevators leading to the west-side skybox suites high above the stadium. As a result, he had free access to the shaft using his mountain climbing gear. He had retired above the elevator during the early morning hours before the President's speech. He would have an excellent view from the top of the shaft where there was a small crawl space and window for viewing the stadium—*information and planning.* Even when the Secret Service inspected the disabled elevator, there was no reason for alarm.

Jacques and Monique had a system for the removal of a "principal." It was called "fire" and "echo." Fire was the lead trigger, while echo shot just afterwards, separated by the speed of sound. They had spent long hours practicing this sequence on their small island with melons of various sizes. Jacques was positioned to the President's right and Monique was directly behind him. In their planning, Jacques was fire and Monique was echo, in the event *adaptation was necessary from unforeseen events*—Sun Tzu.

At precisely 11:45 am, the President and his entourage entered the stadium with the playing of "Hail to the Chief." He was surrounded by Secret Service Agents. The seated throng stood and cheered enthusiastically as the President waved to both sides and center south of the stadium. There was also seating on the field to bring the stadium capacity to 60,000 from the normal seating capacity of 55,000.

The J&M Team were in contact by instant messaging. No verbal communication would be employed until the fixed countdown by Fire—Jacques. When seated on the podium, the President was surrounded by other dignitaries. Jacques and Monique had expected a single row seating. Last minute accommodations were made for other state law makers and local "shakers and movers." This alignment might complicate things for Echo—Monique—since all their removals were surgical, with no collateral damage.

Fire would have to get off a good head shot. No problem for Echo as long as the President was standing. Her job was really clean-up in the event the unforeseen occurred. They both assumed they had one shot each. No use making a mess and jeopardizing their escape. Timing was critical. With the planning and preparation they made, the removal was a foregone conclusion—more like a ritualistic ending. The rush came from the perfection of the plan and its execution. Only divine intervention could prevent the President's destined fate.

After introductions, the President finally stood and began his address. The J&M Team had studied numerous speeches by the President and noted that when a point was made and the crowd cheered wildly, he would stand still basking in their "response" to his "call." It was during one of those intervals that Jacques would initiate the eight-second countdown for his firing. The first time the President had one of these pauses, he took exactly eight seconds. Jacques shot off an instant message to Monique that the countdown would be five seconds, instead of eight. She replied, "Okay, no problem."

The second time this happened, Jacques began the verbal countdown, "Five, four, three, two, and on one, something unexpected happened. The top page of his speech blew off the podium from a spontaneous gentle breeze. At that instant, the President reached down with his left hand to retrieve it, and Josh's shot missed the right side of the President's head.

Monique had an instant to correct her head shot. She hesitated, uncharacteristically, and fired. The projectile entered and exited the President's right shoulder area. Panic erupted as Jacques triggered harmless, explosive devices around the stadium to create mass confusion. He quickly descended the elevator shaft and left his rifle atop the inactive elevator. He entered the elevator through the top emergency door, donned his security uniform, and manually opened the elevator doors and exited. He lost himself in the panicked crowd appearing to give directions to those looking for a safe escape.

Monique, meanwhile, had stripped down to her exercise dress and joined other women who were in the Jacobsen Athletic Building. Most were watching the events on televisions around the gymnasium. She had ample time to make the transition since the panicked crowd prevented immediate search of the Jacobsen building by security personnel.

The pair made no attempt to immediately exit the area, as would be expected by security forces. Their plan was to wait for hours until the commotion subsided and simply drive away with a saddened look.

After being shot through the back shoulder, the Secret Service swarmed the President. They carried him, as in drills, to the nearest exit to a waiting ambulance that is always stationed at one of his speeches. His private physician, who travels with him for such occasions, took over his treatment of blood transfusion.

The bullet had severed the right brachial artery and there was significant loss of blood. Arterial injuries are more severe than venial injuries because the blood pressure is greater in arteries than in veins. In addition, nerve damage can lead to permanent disablement or even amputation of the injured extremity. However, at present, the President's physician didn't have the luxury of a diagnosis. He was dealing with stopping the bleeding and simply saving the President's life.

He was unable to stop the loss of blood completely with heavy gauze. The President was unconscious. General Clarke was the only other person in the rear of the ambulance with the President and his physician. Dana was in the trailing Secret Service limousine. A look of grave concern was on the physician's face. General Clarke had a stoic look of deep regret for not insisting more strongly on an indoor speech. The President appeared to be drifting away and giving up the will to live.

Then Tony appeared from nowhere. The physician was visibly shocked. Tony said, "Allow me to help." General Clarke indicated his okay to the President's doctor. Tony applied the palm of his left hand to the President's shoulder and a bright energy source began flowing through the President's body. The damage process began to slowly reverse; his injury began to repair itself.

Within ten minutes, the president was fully alert as if nothing had happened. He was surprised to see Tony and tried to recall the events of the last half-hour. In surgical terms, Tony had done an end-to-end anastomosis repair of the President's injured brachial artery. No nerve damage was evident, as the President easily moved his right arm.

General Clarke said, "It appears, Mr. President, that you experienced divine intervention—twice in the last half-hour."

Tony said, "I think I'm no longer needed here. I'm sure you and the doctor can create a credible story, Mr. President." Then he was gone.

"The President's physician was in shock. He could only blurt out, "Who was that guy?"

By this time the President had regained his full faculties. He stated to his physician, "I'm sure we have your full confidence in this matter. Let's use the bloodied gauze to confirm the wound I suffered. You will announce that my condition was not as grave as you initially thought. It was a clean shot through and through. You'll be taking me to Camp David for recovery under your personal care. I will fill you in later on Tony. Okay?"

"Yes, Mr. President," the physician mumbled. "I just need a little time to readjust my reality," he smiled. "The most important thing is that you're okay."

"General Clarke, would you detour this ambulance to Air Force One for immediate take off to Washington?" the President requested.

When Jacques and Monique reconnected, they smiled at each other recognizing that this engagement did, in fact, involve divine intervention. Monique was still at a loss as to why she hesitated in executing Echo. What they had not remembered, in all these years, was Sun Tzu's most prophetic statement in *The Art of War, "Above all, the wise leader follows a moral path—The Tao.*

William A. Guillory

Chapter**Twenty-Four**—The Aftermath

When Air Force One arrived near Washington, D.C. at the Andrews Naval Air Facility—formerly known as Andrews Air Force Base—the President was immediately transferred and helicoptered to the Camp David Retreat.

He was accompanied by General Clarke, Dana Hartman, and his personal physician. A press release was distributed to the news media relating his condition as Fair. Furthermore, his physician assured everyone that the President was conscious and alert. He indicated that he would be giving a press update on the President's condition and would answer detailed questions at that time.

Meanwhile, the President had begun discussions with Dana and Ken Clarke regarding the proposed cut in the military budget of approximately $800 billion. A twenty percent cut was roughly $160 billion to invest in the rebuilding of America's infrastructure, creating a wealth of new jobs—similar to the actions taken by Franklin Roosevelt during the New Deal. A significant fraction of this sum could also be devoted to creating new breakthroughs in clean energy sources. These new discoveries would gradually reduce and ultimately eliminate the United States' dependence on oil from most countries around the world.

Since this proposal was the most controversial, he was pleased to have General Clarke as part of the discussion and a major source of the forthcoming resolution. They had begun to put together a coalition of House and Senate members from the Armed Forces Appropriation Committees to begin discussions. General Clarke would deal directly with the Secretary of Defense and the Joint Chiefs.

Closely associated with a defense budget cut was the immense appropriation of $145 billion for the global War on Terror—much of which had been shown to be duplicate efforts. Dana, as former Secretary of Homeland Security, would head up appropriate cuts and submit her recommendations to the President.

The President's strategy was to seize the public tide of empathy and compassion from the assassination attempt. His demeanor would be one of a fallen hero literally rising from the dead. Implying that the attempt on his life was fueled by those who want to retain the status quo, or even go back to the past, during our present unpredictable and rapidly changing times. He couldn't wait to address the American people again and exude the appearance of a recovered warrior.

He put in calls to the Head of the FBI and the DCI, Lloyd Pierson, to learn the progress made in identifying the individuals involved in the assassination attempt. Most of all, he wanted to know whether they were Americans or from some other country. Since he had guarded confidence in the DCI, he also enlisted the services of the President's Special Projects Team. The SPT was a security team reporting only to the President relating to his security and the security of the United States. They had unrestricted freedom in such an investigation, unlike the CIA who, technically, had to report to a Congressional oversight committee.

The SPT was not officially acknowledged as to its existence, its activities, or its budgetary expenditures. It operated solely at the discretion of the President—both in preventative and retributive roles. The President's request to the head of the present team was very simple: "Find out who put out the hit on me." Colonel Darin Thomas had, not only military experience as a Ranger, but also, stints with the CIA and the NSA. He handpicked his team for this particular assignment based on their Special Forces skills in addition to their unquestioned loyalty to the President. He assured the President there would be something to report within a week's time. At that point, his team would be prepared to take whatever action the President requested.

Meanwhile, things continued to unravel—particularly, in the Middle East and Africa. The unrest and uprisings were primarily led by the younger generation—most were under 30 years old—the *Millennial Movement* as it was being called. Their major weapon—connectedness through the Internet primarily on Facebook, Twitter, and YouTube.

As governments countered by closing down these sources as well as cellular phone service, they discovered *they* also became dysfunctional and out of communication. As one protester said on Facebook before it was closed down, "This movement started long ago when the world became connected. We are no longer willing to live under the suppression of free speech about our living conditions."

Our team was following the events by television in Varanasi. I said to the others, "I have a feeling these protesters will not be stopped by tanks or military force."

"I think you're right," replied Jasmine. "Those in power simply refuse to understand what the protests are all about."

"And what's that?" John asked Jasmine, to make sure he was correctly tracking her thinking.

"They are dealing with a no-compromise generation that has been in continual communication with their counterparts from around the world. Just an 'innocent' email from an American or an Australian is *encoded* with the freedom of expression. It's simply taken for granted by those in such countries."

"That's exactly what Bill was saying in his last two blogs," Bin said. "The desire for a more democratic way of living is so great, that it's practically unstoppable, even if it's temporarily sidetracked."

Jasmine continued, "What we are seeing is the beginning of an unofficial global coalition of Millennials—and in some cases they are joined by kids less than 17 years old."

"What are you saying?" I asked Jasmine.

"That their alliance with each other, around the world, probably goes beyond the country they are from—all because of relationships fostered by the Internet and Social Networks," Jasmine replied.

"I wonder if Mark Zuckerberg had any idea what his innocent 'gossip communications invention' would lead to?" asked Ravi.

"That's also why your blogs have been so effective, Bill," Jasmine said.

"What do you mean?" I asked.

"Direct communication that is unfiltered, without propaganda, is one of the most powerful means of connecting people. Whatever measures are used to brainwash us are not as effective as people communicating directly with each other," she replied.

"One thing we haven't mentioned," John stated.

"And what's that?" I asked.

"The impact this movement will have on Americans and others in countries where democracy *is* practiced," John replied. "Remember, transformation is always a two-way street."

"It can only make them stronger as a democracy," I quickly responded. "And bring us together as people."

"That depends on how open and transparent each country chooses to be. You have to keep in mind, your government and news media also brainwash your way of thinking about other cultures and religions of the world," John said.

John's last statement was a conversation stopper. It left everyone speechless. And reflective.

✪ ✪ ✪

The J&M Team returned to their island home, disappointed. The biggest principal ever in their careers eluded removal.

"I was able to make a quick correction on your mark of 'fire,' but I couldn't get a clean head shot when he bent over," Monique said, reflecting on her moment of hesitation.

"Quite frankly, I'm still mystified where that gust of wind came from exactly on my mark to fire," Jacques said, disgustedly.

"Well, that's exactly the reason we're a team, Jacques. *'Always expect the unpredictable.'* When he bent down to retrieve his speech page with his left hand, all I had available was the right side of his back," Monique repeated.

"You still got off a good shot. And we know it hit him."

"I'm mystified why that bullet didn't do more damage than what they reported. That is, unless they're lying. No one has actually seen him except his inner circle," she said. "You know how encouraging they want to be to the American people in situations like these."

"Well, we have other urgent matters to be concerned about. We received half payment in advance for this engagement in our Swiss bank account. What should we do to preserve our reputation?" Jacques asked. "Return it?"

"Hell no!" Monique replied. Our contract specifies that we are guaranteed half if we inflict a grave wound; and full immediate payment for removal. I know that bullet did a lot of damage to his right side. Let's just wait to see if he makes a public appearance before we decide what next steps we need to take."

"Should we contact the Administrator to report our decision or just wait for him to contact us?" Jacques asked.

It had been clear for some time that Monique made the decisions for their operation. Jacques had little ego about her leadership skills and cunning. "We wait for him, or her, to contact us. We leave the half payment where it is for now. But I have a feeling we also need to think about becoming incognito for the time being. We've always wanted to travel to 'out-of-the-way' places where there are no surveillance devices."

"Are there still places like that on planet Earth?" Jacques asked, half joking and half serious.

"We'll certainly find out, won't we," Monique replied, with her devastating smile.

Others were also busy deciding the fate of the J&M Team. The Billionaire Club members were unanimously unhappy about the failure of the engagement. "How much do they know about us?" the Russian member asked during their virtual conference. They were resolute about the secrecy of the Club as well as its membership. They also took extra precaution to avoid being seen together in public; under any circumstances.

The Administrator of the Club replied, "Probably more than they let on. After all, the key to their success is based upon the extensive research they do on any contract they take. It would make perfect sense that they would attempt to know as much as possible about their contractor. The only reference they have is me as a point of contact, by encrypted email, of course."

"We certainly cannot afford the investigation of anyone in direct communication with us." The Russian replied. "Even if they believe it's a single person."

"The member from England said, "Well, I think it's clear what we need to do."

"And what is that?" asked the Administrator.

"We need to immediately close off any link to us." And then, he added for clarity, "As though *they* never existed."

The other members all acknowledged their approval.

"I'll see that it's taken care of," replied the Administrator.

They also decided it was appropriate to become incommunicado until everything was sorted out.

The Swiss Administrator, rarely, if ever, failed at any of the Club's operations. That's the reason they had chosen him for the Club's engagements. Although none of the members even remotely implied it, the failed attempt on the President's life reflected on him as Administrator. And failure was not an option in the Club's activities.

Seeing the situation in that light, the member from England had done him a favor by recommending the removal of the J&M link. In fact, he should have recommended the proposal himself, instead of asking what should be done.

He activated his highly secure computer and sent out two messages. The first message was to inform the J&M Team that there would be a second contract on the President when things settled down. They should retain the half payment. This message also implied they were not being held responsible for the misfire. The second was to a client he had personally employed in the past for the removal of the J&M Team. He instructed that all trace of them and the contents of their residence should be erased—as though they never existed.

When the J&M Team received the encrypted communiqué from the Administrator indicating there would be a second contract on the President after things settled down, Monique knew immediately what was going on.

Jacques replied thanking him for a second opportunity, referencing the hand of fate. And within the hour they had set off to find an "out-of-the-way" place where there were no surveillance devices!

That evening, their secret island retreat was removed from planet Earth—as though it never existed. Shortly before the removal, the villa was fully lit, music was playing, and there appeared to be two individuals relaxing as detected by an external infrared scanning device.

❀ ❀ ❀

The highly select assassination community was relatively small. And, the best of them could be counted on one hand, depending on the target. Based upon his CIA and NSA experience, Colonel Thomas had begun scouring this community for leads relating to the actual hit team. The reports from the FBI had clearly revealed there were two assassins. They were located roughly at a 90° angle from each other—to the right of and directly behind the president.

The bullet that exited the President's body was easily found. Given its shape, the FBI wondered why the President was still alive. The bullet that missed was found after extensive damage had been done to the Iowa State University football field. Ballistic tests confirmed the two bullets were fired from the two rifles left behind.

In the rarified air of highly select assassins, there was only one that operated as a team. In the trade, they were known as "Fire and Echo," because of their operational style. The existence of an assassin team didn't necessarily rule out a possible team engagement. However, the overwhelming probability was that two individuals coming together for a temporary job like this was highly unlikely. It was one thing to identify a possible assassination team, but altogether different from proving it. The President's SPT didn't operate on speculation. Particularly, if subsequent orders from the President required the removal of someone.

Just as the corps of highly select assassins is relatively small, so are the highly skilled artisans who fabricate their weapons. The two rifles left behind were easily traced to a Miguel Borelli, located in Padua, Italy. After a brief conversation with Colonel Thomas indicating the weapons used in the attempted assassination of the President, Signore Borelli confirmed he had designed the two rifles that were shown on a faxed photograph. The search of his records indicated they were a special order from a Post Office Box address in Zadar, Croatia. There was nothing unusual about such a request. Many gun enthusiasts throughout Europe sought his skills. Most were anonymous because of license firearms regulations involving serial numbers.

This information was combined with the mysterious explosion on the small Adriatic island of Susak, along the Croatian coastline. One of the SPT members with family ties to the island, Lola Picini, was dispatched to the quaint island to investigate a possible connection. Susak was located in Kvaerner Bay, southwest of the Istria Peninsula, roughly 75 miles due east of the northeastern Italian coastline. The island is about two miles long and one mile wide. The J&M villa was located at the top of a hill about 322 feet above sea level with an unobstructed view of the Adriatic Ocean. The village population was roughly 200 residents. The island is known for its production of wine and grappa.

Since tourism was the main source of economic activity, Lola Picini moved easily among the flow of pedestrian traffic. Her SPT members called her Pic for short. Her family, formerly the

Piciničs, became Picini after immigrating from Susak to Hoboken, New Jersey, shortly after World War II. Genetic memories made her feel just like a native and back home as she wandered about the island community. She could even understand and speak some words of their unique dialect.

The owners of one of the restaurants were delighted to acquaint her with the island and they fell into easy conversation. She learned that indeed the spacious villa was owned by a European couple; although the woman seemed to have a different accent from the man. They kept to themselves and interacted little with the island people. When the dock needed repairs or the fishing boats required an extra hand for unloading the daily catch, the man named Jon was most happy to help. He was described as athletically built, about six feet, two inches, with dark hair and tan skin.

Monique was about five feet, eight inches, black hair, and a beautiful body, as the male owner smilingly described her. His wife was not amused. "Did they spend a lot of time on the island?" Pic asked.

"Oh, yes. They were here most of the time except for the frequent vacations they took," his wife answered.

"Was there anything unusual about them?" Pic asked.

"Not really," he replied.

Then his wife said, "There was one thing that bothered some of the villagers."

"What's that?" Pic asked.

"They seemed to be shooting enthusiasts. They practiced often on a deserted stretch of the island. Other than that, they were probably just like most of us here—trying to find peace, happiness, and a little privacy away from the crowded cities."

❁ ❁ ❁

The President's physician appeared before a hungry

entourage of reporters. They were hungry for news about the President's condition. He was accompanied by General Clarke and Dana Hartman.

"Good afternoon, ladies and gentlemen," he began. I would like to update you on the President's condition and his probable recovery time." It was clear the physician was not a public speaker and was obviously uncomfortable in the spotlight.

"As you know, the President suffered a severe vascular injury caused by a gunshot to his rear, right shoulder. I reported to you yesterday that the President is in Fair condition. That is, his vital signs are stable and within normal limits; he is, of course, fully conscious, and a little uncomfortable." At this point, the physician was recounting the President's reaction to General Clarke's comment that a 20 percent cut in the defense budget wouldn't fly. He continued, "And all of his vital signs are favorable."

"One reporter asked another, "What the hell did he just say?"

"I don't have a clue?" the other replied.

"Then, Margret Ferguson, a reporter with a reputation of getting to the point asked, "Is the President in critical condition?"

The physician replied, "No."

"When is he expected to resume his normal duties?" she persisted.

"I would expect fairly soon. I think General Clarke can answer that question better than I can," the physician said, attempting to conclude his part of the President's update. "Are there any more medical questions I can answer?"

"Yes, I have one." The room went very quiet and the acknowledged Dean of the Press Corps, Leslie Davidson, asked, "The President looked to me like he was almost mortally wounded. What exactly did you do to help him recover to the state you're describing?"

The physician was silent for five seconds or so, then composed himself and replied, "Sir, I think the President's recovery was nothing short of a miracle. Whatever saved him was out of my hands."

The reporter nodded and said, "Thanks." And to himself he said, 'I thought so.'

Then General Clarke rose and walked to the podium. He was not at all intimidated by the Press. He had years of public speaking. He stated, "It is my understanding that the President plans to address the American people in a few days. Meanwhile, the business of running the day-to-day operation of the country is being taken over by the Vice-President. I assure you, we are in very capable hands. Now, I'll take a few questions."

"What does the President plan on telling the American people?" One of the reporters asked.

"I think he wants to present additional information about how we can cut defense spending and yet have us all feel secure."

"Is the proposal to rebuild America's infrastructure just a 'warmed-over' version of the New Deal?" Another reporter blurted out.

"I certainly hope not," General Clarke responded. "You know as well as I do we're trying to impose new technology on outdated support systems. Our railroads, for example, are not capable of handling high speed trains; which could aid considerably in keeping up with our present transportation demands. Our electrical power grids are an accident waiting to happen, simply because they are outdated for present energy demand. These are just two of the areas the President intends to address."

"What exactly does the President mean by changing from an 'economy of competition' to an 'economy of conservation?' Competition is the fuel that has made this country great."

"Some would argue that point. They might say it's the creativity, ingenuity, and entrepreneurship that have made this country great. Now we must maintain that success while simultaneously focusing on energy and environmental concerns rather than on spending uncontrollably on things we don't need."

When other hands flew up, General Clarke raised his right hand politely and said, "The President can give you better details than I can. Thank you ladies and gentlemen." And the three of them departed.

Leslie Davidson commented to one of his colleagues, "Something is very fishy about this entire situation. And I'm going to find out exactly what it is."

William A. Guillory

Chapter**Twenty-Five**—The Resurrection

A week after the press update on his condition, the President returned to the White House to take over his duties as Chief Executive. He resumed his normal routine. Everyone was astonished by his miraculous recovery; particularly the Secret Service agents who transported him to the waiting ambulance after being shot. However, the word around the Service was, it wasn't theirs to question but to protect. Most of all, he had *not* been lost on their watch.

The President had truly had a "near death experience." The aftermath of an NDE is typically detachment from the consequences of everyday life and freedom to live true to one's self. A result of knowing there is life after death. Most of his aides noted a greater sense of serenity and a genuine concern for others. Previously, he had been continuously preoccupied with his executive responsibilities, sometimes to the exclusion of the presence of those around him.

General Clarke experienced the President as more open and

empathetic to his point of view. As if he saw the issues they were dealing with from a larger perspective. He was more "quietly confident" of the steps that needed to be taken even if those around him were upset by the apparently radical changes he was proposing. The President exuded a sense of determination and purpose that seemed to allay the protests of those closest to him. Most of all, there wasn't the slightest hint of fear. In fact, it embarrassed Ken to acknowledge what he experienced most from the President—love.

"Well, I guess it's about time, Mr. President," Ken said, informing him of his speech to the American people.

"Thanks, Ken. I can't tell you what a supportive force you have been during my Presidency. I honestly don't believe I would have the understanding of our complex system without your insights," the President said, as he proceeded to the Oval Office for his televised address to the American people.

When the cameras came alive, the President exuded an overwhelming picture of health, centeredness, and confidence. He smiled slightly before beginning.

"My fellow Americans, we have been through a traumatic event over the last weeks. An attack on me is the same as an attack on the American people. It is an attack on everything we stand for and our way of life. We have rarely resolved our differences by silencing a voice through assassination.

I will repeat, as I have said previously, we live in a world that is changing faster than we have adapted to it. This is usually a sign that small incremental changes or applying band aids to complex problems are not permanent solutions. We need to rethink the direction we're headed and redefine our place in the world—all with the intent of creating greater cooperation and compatibility with others.

We know it will take time for some to set aside their anger toward us—in some cases justifiably so. During that time, we will remain strong and resolute in defense of our safety and well-being. We will also continue to take preventative measures to protect ourselves and our allies throughout the world—without compromise.

What I want to propose, most of all, is that we redefine America in the 21st Century. History has shown, over and over again, those civilizations that refuse to adapt to change simply fall by the wayside, often into oblivion. I will not stand by and let America be yet another of those experiments in futility.

As such, I will be enlisting the Congress, the federal agencies and departments, and the American people in reapportioning our federal budget, redefining capitalism for everyone's benefit, and rebuilding America to constructively participate in the 21st century. I will be sending Congress the details of my proposed redesign of America for their advice and consent.

That is my message to you. I invite every American to actively participate in this process of Rebuilding America 21st. God bless you and may God bless the American people, and all the people of this planet."

❂ ❂ ❂

The J&M Team got confirmation of Monique's suspicion when they learned their villa on Susak was reduced to rubble. They also assumed that they had only bought time until it was discovered that the two energized robots that Jacques had built, for just such an occasion, were not them.

They had fled to the most populated area of the planet, void of surveillance devices—Asia. They reasoned that the most obvious place to become temporarily lost and still know what was going on in the world was one of the rural provinces of Western China. They had set aside millions in cash reserves which obviated the necessity to make any withdrawals from their Swiss bank account—which would surely be monitored.

They took up residence in a southwestern China city in the Sichuan Province—Yibin, which is located at the junction of the Yangtze and Min Rivers. Its population is roughly 300,000. They were able to obtain an out-of-town residence with most of the conveniences they required.

Their objective was to lie low. Lose themselves in the day-to-day life of the culture. And plan their next move. Monique made it clear they had no intention of living out their existence in that part of the world, constantly looking over their shoulders. Their cover was a European couple—a free-lance photographer and writer—gathering information and photographic shots for a book about the rich Chinese culture outside of the eastern metropolis seaboard. Their simple dress and ease of connection to the local residents led to a rather obscure lifestyle.

When the Administrator learned of the escape of the J&M Team, he instructed his client to simply await further instructions; which was code for making himself scarce. He reminded himself that the failed attempt on the President's life lay at his doorsteps as well as the escape of the J&M team—two strikes. Again, the operational mantra of the Club entered his mind, *failure is not an option.*

Jacques had retained all of the encrypted and supposedly destroyed messages from the Administrator. Although, the Administrator had used a multi-routed system of computer communication, Jacques had little difficulty in finding the source of the computer location. Connecting the computer source with the person was going to be their next engagement. Monique would decide on the method of engagement when he determined the Administrator's identity and location.

✿ ✿ ✿

The Internet exchange of messages among people from around the world began to exceed those within various countries—including the United States. They involved shared descriptions of their life conditions—including income, family, and personal aspirations. Less emphasis was placed on their differing philosophies of culture, religion, and politics. What began to emerge was a confluence of aspirations: to live peaceably, share resources, and create a world where differences were accepted by each other.

This decided shift in thinking was led by the *Millennial Generation*, worldwide. Digital communication was becoming the most lethal weapon of connectedness on the planet—direct communication, uninfluenced and unfiltered by local governments or the Press.

Worldwide support for the American president's speech began to emerge through a coalition of Gen Xers, Millennials, and the emerging 2020 Generation—the latter, less than 17 years old. There were also exchanges that expressed that such attempts to begin resolving differences were naïve. The feelings among some were so adverse that change was impossible. Furthermore, any attempt at changing the presently existing views in some countries would only lead to greater force and oppression than was presently experienced.

I said to the group in our Varanasi retreat, "This is the best thing that could have happened to us. We're finally talking directly with each other trying to decide our future direction—and the possible consequences if we don't change."

Jasmine added, "And it's truly being decided by ordinary people *without* the necessity of a leader."

John simply smiled and said, "It seems like our focus on the average person was the best strategy after all."

"What do we do now?" Ravi asked.

"I guess the most important thing happening for me right now is what's happening in America," I said. "I have been thinking that it's time for me to go home. I've been running long enough. This whole thing has gone way beyond me."

"Just stay open," John said. "I have a feeling we may need more of your involvement before this whole thing is decided."

Jasmine, or the others, didn't miss John's use of the word "we" instead of instead of referring to us as "You." I wondered what that meant.

✪ ✪ ✪

The President's office received an urgent call from Lloyd Pierson, the DCI, requesting an immediate meeting. The DCI indicated to Dana Hartman that it was regarding the assassination attempt. Dana had now officially taken over as the President's Chief of Staff. He was delighted to have her serve in this role. She brought an insight to critical decisions that only a female could contribute. Between Dana and Ken, he had an incredible support staff that also believed the country needed to move forward in some significant way. They both respected his instincts in regard to what "moving forward" meant.

"Lloyd, are you sure I can't tell him what you've learned?" Dana asked.

"Yes, I'm sure," he replied, thinking 'who does she think she is' now that he's made her ceremonial Chief of Staff.

"Okay. I'll cancel his meeting with the Energy Secretary and put you in at 3:00 p.m. He'll determine how long the meeting will be, but I can promise you it won't be more than fifteen minutes." Dana stopped there, reading what Lloyd must be thinking having to go through her to get to the President.

Lloyd simply said, "Okay" and hung up, to send her a message of who he was and the power of his agency.

Dana had begun to get some idea of the sizes of ego the President had to deal with on a daily basis. But this new, transformed President seemed to be amused by the positioning of each of his appointments.

Earlier that day the President had received a call on his private and highly secure cell phone from Colonel Darin Thomas. Colonel Thomas updated the President on their progress thus far. "Mr. President, we are ninety percent certain of the identities of the attempted assassins."

"Who are they, Tom? The President asked.

"They are probably the most skilled assassination team around today. They are referred to as 'Fire and Echo.' Their villa on the island of Susak, Croatia was leveled a few days ago. Probably, by their clients for the failed attempt on your life."

"That was swift," the President replied.

"That's why I'm calling to update you now, before their trail gets too cold. What should we do when we apprehend them?"

"Try to capture them alive, so that we might question them regarding the client who hired them. If capture is not an option then the safety of your people takes precedence."

"Thank you, Mr. President. I'll keep you informed of our progress."

Later that afternoon, Lloyd Pierson entered the President's office with a look of Sylvester the Cat having just swallowed Tweety bird. "Mr. President, I have great news for you. Well great in the sense of the charge you gave us."

"What's the news, Lloyd?" the President pressed, impatiently.

"We are fairly certain we know who your attempted assassins are," he announced with a dramatic air.

"Yes," the President replied, "Who are they?"

"An assassination team of a French national and a Lebanese

woman, known as Fire and Echo. They formerly lived on the island of Susak, Croatia, until it was destroyed a few days ago. The French national is the son of a French General who was killed in Beirut along with the woman's mother. His name is Jacques Lamoreaux."

"What about her background," the President asked.

"We don't know as much about her background, except she apparently has strong American features. Probably the daughter of a G.I serving in Beirut. She met Jacques at the American University of Beirut. After their parents' death, they dropped out of university and disappeared. That's all we know for now."

"How were you able to gather these identifications and backgrounds so quickly?" the President asked.

"Mr. President, when we combine the immense resources of our data base of intelligence with the people we hire, we can identify most anyone from the developed world and their entire background—no matter how well they attempt to camouflage it."

The President just looked at the DCI noticing the look of pride he exuded, and thought to himself, 'Good thing my life is practically an open book, even my pot-smoking days in college.'

"Good work, Lloyd. Now that we know who they are, let's find them and hold them accountable for their cowardly act."

"My field people are working on it as we speak," Lloyd said, again making a pitch for an increase in field agents.

"When do you feel we might apprehend them?" the President asked.

"That may take more time. But, given their identification and backgrounds, we feel confident it won't be but a few more days."

"Thanks, Lloyd," the President rose indicating the meeting was over.

"Oh, one other thing," the DCI said as an afterthought. "Although, the mother claimed the daughter was adopted, there is rumor to believe the woman killed was her biological mother."

The President stopped for a moment of reflection and said,

"Okay, let's find them." And he escorted the DCI out of his office.

The President immediately put in a call to Colonel Thomas in the field. "Darin, this is the President."

"The two assassins are a French national named Jacques Lamoreaux and a mixed Lebanese-American woman named Monique Rashad. The woman's father was probably an American G.I. assigned to Beirut at the time of her birth."

"No wonder she's so good at what she does. Just missing a screw."

"Be careful not to work at odds with Lloyd Pierson's people, Darin? They're officially looking for them also."

"No problem, Mr. President. Their field people are among the best in the world. The only difference is they have constraints and Congressional people to answer to that we don't. So we should be on the same team except for situations where they have to draw the line. Don't worry, we'll make it work."

"Thank you Colonel Thomas."

"Be in touch, Mr. President."

And they both clicked off.

William A. Guillory

Chapter**Twenty-Six**—The Dénouement

After two weeks of seclusion in Yibin, China, Monique decided it was time to go on the offensive. They had split their time between getting lost and following the events relating to the assassination attempt. She reasoned the hunt for them would be relentless and sustained until they were eventually found. The CIA and the team that blew up their home would eventually discover something that would provide clues to their escape. No plan is ever foolproof. It was amazing just how small the planet could become when you didn't want to be found; particularly, by high-tech security forces.

Monique's plan was to use ground transport where there were no surveillance devices and private air transport where there was. They both had several passports from their professional line of work, so movement across borders was not difficult except where there were photographic devices or international tracking systems, like Interpol. Using this system of operation, they easily made their way to Europe using a westerly approach.

Once in Europe, Monique and Jacques changed their natural appearances considerably using hair coloring, non-corrective eyeglasses, facial skin tone, and dress. The identity redesign allowed them to use a single passport throughout European Union countries.

By the time they arrived in Switzerland, Jacques had located the city of Geneva and the street address of the computer used by the Administrator in communication with them. It was a simple, but well-kept, office building with rentals for small business operations. There were no more than twenty offices renting the four-story building. They began their search by systematically visiting each office to obtain official email addresses, business activity, and number of employees. Monique started with the two upper floors and Jacques took the two lower floors. They were careful to get all the information required on one visit to each office. They were aided by small, high resolution cameras to take photographs of the office equipment. Both concluded their assigned floors in two days.

Monique and Jacques began their analysis of the information they gathered. They systematically eliminated fifteen of the offices as legitimate businesses. Of the remaining five, three appeared to be in transition and two having itinerant use. One of the itinerant offices was rented to a Hans Stübler, real estate agent. That explained his regular absence from the building—especially since he was a one-man operation. The other was a Dietrich Steiner. No telephone or address listed. Probably a false name.

They returned the following evening, after hours, entered the building and began a thorough search of Herr Steiner's office. They confirmed his computer was the one used in communication with them. It appeared he had not been there for several days or maybe a week or so. Upon returning to their rental, Jacques hacked into the office rental database and discovered that the only information recorded for Herr Dietrich Steiner was a required cell phone number. He then proceeded to hack into the databases of the most popular business cellular providers and voila! He located the number with a required address for Herr Gunther Friedman at a suburban area of Geneva.

The following evening, the J&M Team paid a visit to the address of Herr Friedman. It was comprised of upscale estates with high-end security systems. No doubt with security personnel considering his recent error in judgment in using the J&M Team for the President's assassination. So they decided to surveil his activities for a few days. The Internet revealed his official line of work as President of a prominent investment firm. He was a well-known financier who contributed generously to the arts in Geneva—a pillar of pride in the local community.

As they predicted, he was chauffeured to work by two security guards that could both easily qualify for the Defender position on a soccer team. As usual, the emphasis was on a successful encounter not a preventative one. Disabling each of these impediments would be easy, although not taken for granted.

When the chauffeured car returned that evening, after daylight, Monique had disengaged the electronic sensing mechanism of the entrance gate. Jacques had followed the trio the entire day. He informed Monique by cell phone that everything was a "go" for the abduction. When the guard riding shotgun got out of the car to check the gate, a predictable but foolish move for a high-end security guard, Monique shot him in the neck with a drugged dart. He grabbed his neck and fell to the ground unconscious.

The other guard got out of the car to check on his fallen comrade. Monique also took care of him. A more mentally astute move would have been to back up the car and take off like a bat out of hell.

Poor Herr Friedman sat in the backseat with a look of inevitability. He wasn't surprised by the appearance of the J&M Team. Particularly, when his client, hired to erase them, confirmed they were not killed in the explosion. Nor were there any clues as to their escape. He certainly didn't expect them to hide indefinitely, and eventually be caught.

"Good evening, Herr Friedman," Monique said politely.

"Good evening, Fräulein Rashad. And Herr Lamoreaux," he replied. "In truth, I've been expecting you." Jacques took over the driver's seat and began a tour of Geneva. Monique sat in the back seat facing Herr Friedman.

"Why is that?" she asked.

"When we were unable to locate you, I knew it was just a matter of time before you would locate me. That's why I contracted you in the first place, your skills and ingenuity."

"Thank you for the compliment."

"What is it you want of me?" Herr Friedman had no intent of suffering through a painful experience where he would eventually give them the information they wanted anyway. He was much too old for such a heroic episode.

"Who put out the hit on us? And our villa?" Monique replied, dryly.

"I did; on behalf of a global club committed to preserving the operation of planet Earth exactly as it is presently. Apparently, the American President had other ideas. You were hired to assassinate him and you failed; and so I failed. The rest is rather obvious. There are no personal issues here," he ended, somewhat arrogantly.

Herr Friedman reasoned that if he appeared to fully cooperate, they might let him live, out of professional courtesy. If they wanted to know the identities of the other club members, and he refused, his fate would be sealed. In truth, his fate was probably already sealed once the other club members learned he had been apprehended by the J&M Team.

"Who are the other members of the Club?" Monique asked.

"That I do not know," he lied with a straight face. "We agreed there would no personal identifications so there would be no link to each other. We use code names and communicate solely by electronic means."

Monique ceased questioning Herr Friedman. She quickly realized he was mixing the truth with lies. She gave Jacques instructions to drive to their rental. When they arrived, they took him to the guest bedroom. He was bound, spread eagle on his back, and stripped down to his undershirt and underwear. For Herr Friedman, this was a humiliating position.

Monique was particularly gifted in the art of painful experiences that she learned during her youth in the Lebanese countryside. Best of all, none were messy, involving blood. It's amazing what one can do to break the will of someone when tampering with the nervous system. Monique applied a few carefully placed acupuncture needles to Herr Friedman's extremities. And indeed, he did prove to have a very low pain threshold. He even offered the identities of the other club members without being asked again.

Next, they wanted to know the identity of the client who was dispatched to destroy their villa. Herr Friedman's emotional state had significantly elevated by this time and he was near tears. But he knew lying under such circumstances would just result in more excruciating pain. So he offered, "The client is out of Marseille. You probably know of him. But I wouldn't worry about him now. You know our rule for employment, 'failure is not an option.' I am sure he plans to disappear for the next few years, if possible. His contract to dispose of you has been revoked."

They both knew that was the extent of Herr Friedman's knowledge since he had already wet the front of his underpants. He was about to faint. So Monique slowly began extracting each of the needles she so expertly inserted. They released him and wished him good luck with his other club members.

❂ ❂ ❂

Colonel Darin Thomas decided to bring his team together for a brainstorming session. After losing track of the J&M Team following their escape from the villa, he decided they should jump ahead and make some assumptions. They had nothing else substantive to go on.

"Let's assume the J&M Team is not going to simply hide out and hope for the best. What would their next move likely be?" he began.

"If they felt they would inevitably be found by the CIA or someone else, I think they would attempt to take action first. These people are not amateurs," one team member said.

"What kind of action?" asked Pic.

"I think they would go after whoever leveled their villa," another offered.

"Yeah, but whoever did that was probably on contract," Pic suggested.

"I think they would probably go after whoever hired them in the first place. That's the most likely source of the bombing. Probably for failing to kill the President," Darin said.

"How do we find out who that might be?" the IT guy asked.

"Probably someone very prominent who opposes the President's recent proposals."

Another said excitedly, "If that's the case, this individual is going to make himself or herself very scarce right now."

"So, one approach is to monitor the disappearance of prominent individuals who might oppose the President's proposals. That's still a pretty small needle in a big haystack."

"There's another approach," Pic said. "If we assume J&M are going to be on the move, why don't we monitor them?"

"How do you suggest we do that?" one asked. "We don't know

where they are in the first place."

"If we lost them in Shanghai, then we monitor private flights from there to their destination during the past week. That should cut down on the number of prominent people we are looking for to certain areas of the world," Pic replied.

The IT whiz on the team quickly inputted the most recent flight requests and eliminated all but those involving couples. There was only one in the last three days that travelled from Shanghai to Poland; a Mr. and Mrs. Jon Lambert. "Well, there's Jon again," Pic said, in reference to the name Jacques used on Susak Island.

"Let's assume they're headed for Western Europe," Colonel Thomas said, "Where to next."

"Why not go to their destination? Why stop in Poland?"

"Regardless of the answer to that question, let's assume Western Europe. If we focus our search on the wealthy, then the number gets smaller. So, we all need to hit the news media as well as the underground gossip mill of the wealthy," concluded Colonel Thomas.

Fortunately, the SPT didn't have long to wait. The scuttle bug, spread primarily by Herr Friedman's bodyguards, was widely dispersed among the wealthy of Western Europe. Primarily, as a precaution for their own safety. Herr Gunther Friedman had been missing since the previous evening when he was abducted at the entry to his estate. At this point, the police were brought in and a massive, but discreet, search had begun for Herr Friedman and his abductors. Even Interpol was notified. There were no news media announcements. However, other members of the Billionaire Club *were* aware of his abduction and its implications.

Colonel Thomas' team immediately placed a blanket perimeter around Western Europe. He asked himself, 'what would the J&M Team do that would be unusual in terms of an escape? Assuming they had to first dispose of Herr Friedman.' At first, he dismissed the thought of their using the "most obvious" mode of transportation. 'Getting lost in plain sight.' Then, on second thought, he asked 'Suppose they changed their appearances and used new passports? Then they could walk right through security and return to China.'

That's exactly what Monique had decided to do with their considerably altered appearances. They decided to take separate travel since the authorities were looking for a couple. She also had a backup plan she discussed with Jacques in the event either of them was caught. They planned to regroup in Shanghai, return to Yibin, and plan their next move from there.

Through the President's intervention, Colonel Thomas was able to temporarily add a new feature to the security gates in the major West European airports. It was infrared imaging of a person's body and skeletal structure. Regardless of appearance or the gain or loss of weight, technicians could use even a partial body photograph to match a person's photographic infrared image. Full length pictures of both Jacques and Monique were obtained from their university records from AUB.

The monitor was near 90% accurate—only an identical twin could beat the system. Jacques and Monique were neither. Monique took the Zurich airport and Jacques took Bern. Unfortunately, Monique was endowed with an extraordinarily unique body that was not easily matched by other women—even in Europe. The red monitor flashed as she walked through the security doorway. She was immediately surrounded by a group of security personnel and whisked off to police headquarters. "Okay," she thought, with a smile, "Plan B."

❁ ❁ ❁

"Ms. Rashad, I am Colonel Darin Thomas. We have been attempting to apprehend you and your partner for the last few weeks."

"Monique just stared at Colonel Thomas, unafraid.

They were alone in a highly secure interrogation room. "I'll come straight to the point, 'Did you and your companion attempt to assassinate the President of the United States?'"

"You cannot prove that, Colonel Thomas," she replied, looking him directly in his eyes.

"I don't need to prove it, Ms. Rashad. If I have enough evidence—circumstantial or otherwise—I will personally see that you are disposed of." 'Damn, she isn't a bit frightened,' he thought. An uncomfortable feeling of respect for her was creeping into the exchange.

"I am fully aware of that Colonel Thomas. I was taught enough about special military units to recognize one when I see it. Why isn't the CIA involved here? I would have expected them to run this show."

"Look," he said, authoritatively, "I'm asking the questions here."

Without replying, she continued to look directly at him.

"Where is your partner?" he asked.

"I don't know. Maybe you caught him." she responded with a questioning look. His non-verbal response said, "No." So she smiled.

He continued to stare at her wondering where to go next. Perhaps, he should simply shoot her and get it over with. There's little question she's one of the assassins. However, this could only be done on orders from the President.

"Before this conversation runs further downhill, I would like to tell you some things regarding the President's assassination attempt. I know who ordered the hit," she offered, to his surprise.

"We already know who ordered the hit," he bluffed. Assuming Herr Friedman was the contractor.

"If you mean Herr Friedman, he is only the tip of the iceberg. He is a member of the Billionaire Club. Eight wealthy and powerful businessmen around the world. The President's recent proposals run counter to their agenda. That's why the hit was ordered."

He noticed she said "He is a member......," when referring to Herr Friedman, not "He was a member." What that meant was that Herr Friedman was probably still alive. "How do you know that?" he asked.

"We questioned him before we allowed him to go free. I have no idea where he is now. But I'm sure his club members are very interested."

"I'll go back to my original question since we both know the answer, "Did you and you partner, Jacques Lamoreaux, attempt to assassinate the President of the United States?"

Monique responded, "The threat to the President is not over. They plan to regroup and try again. We know more information than I have told you about how to find them," she said.

"Are you offering to help us find the other club members?" he asked, astonished by her audacity.

"Yes," she replied.

"Lady, are you out of your fuckin' mind?" the Colonel blurted out.

"Probably. But we're worth more to you alive than dead at this point. They ordered us to be erased; along with our villa on Susak. We have no allegiance to the Club," Monique replied.

"You don't have any allegiance to us either. You nearly killed the President!"

"But we both have a debt to pay to the same adversary. Without us, you will probably never identify them, let alone find them," she bluffed. "They use code names. Most of all, they will not let the President run his agenda—under any circumstances."

"We can always 'waterboard' everything you know that will give us the best chance of identifying them."

"Even then, you won't know everything we know that will give you the best chance of catching them. You probably know that Jacques is a genius at finding people online."

Colonel Thomas was at his wit's end. What she was saying made sense. He was torn between falling out laughing and pulling out his gun and shooting this bitch in the head. Waterboarding someone stubborn often resulted in turning that individual into a vegetable who was useless afterwards. So, he walked out of the interrogation room, pulled out his sat phone, and put in a call to the President."

"Mr. President, we have a situation here."

❂ ❂ ❂

When the President received Colonel Thomas' call, he was heavy into negotiations with House and Senate leaders to pass his legislation relating to defense spending—the fountainhead of his transformation for America.

"What is the situation," he asked, reminding himself again that the only time someone asked for his opinion was regarding very difficult decisions.

"Do you have ten minutes, Mr. President?"

"No, I have five," he replied with shortness.

Colonel Thomas explained the situation in three minutes. Then he asked, "What do you want us to do?"

"You decide, Colonel. If she's telling the truth, recruit her. She's an incredible asset if she's no longer trying to kill me. If she's lying, you must deal with her appropriately."

"What about her partner?"

"We'll deal with him once he's captured," the President replied. "Any other questions, Colonel Thomas?"

"No, Mr. President. I'll handle it."

The President disconnected.

"Shit," Colonel Thomas said. 'This is not what I signed on for.

I take orders in situations like this, not decide them!' he thought. Perceiving the motivations of others using intuition was not his thing. Yet, he knew soldiers, and she behaved like one. There was no emotional plea for her life or side stepping his questions; except for 'Did she attempt to assassinate the President?' Why she didn't answer that one with the directness she did with the others was still hanging on his mind. He simply wanted to get her admission on the record for closure in case he had to dispose of her later.

Meanwhile, the President had done all he could to get his agenda through Congress. He was nowhere near the majorities he needed to push through the 20% reduction in defense spending. The feedback he got was 10% was the limit that was acceptable and even that would be a push; not a guarantee.

'Well, I didn't come this far just to compromise again,' he thought to himself. 'History is full of examples of great civilizations trying desperately to hold onto the past when faced with a crisis of their existence. I have no intention of letting the U.S. become another.'

He retreated to the Oval Office. He sat there looking out the back window facing south, hoping for a revelation. He figured he had one last card to play. It would be a huge gamble. Because if it worked, the direction the country would take would be totally out of his hands.

He picked up his secure line and told Dana Hartman to put him in touch with Dr. Bill Bradley, wherever he might be; ASAP.

Half-hour later, Dana buzzed the President's office. "Mr. President, Dr. Bradley and his team have returned to his Salt Lake City home."

She had put in a call to Lloyd Pierson to find out the whereabouts of Dr. Bradley. Lloyd had commented, "They made no efforts at secrecy during their travels from Varanasi."

Dana said, "Here he is, Mr. President."

"Dr. Bradley, this is the President," he said when they were connected.

"Yes, Mr. President. What can I do for you?"

"Dr. Bradley, as you know, I'm trying to create reform in America."

I thought, 'That's a polite word from what I understand you're trying to do.' So, I continued to listen to what the President had to say.

"Let me get straight to the point because time is running short," he said with a slight pause. "I need something dramatic to happen to have any hope of forwarding my agenda," the President paused.

"How does that involve me? I asked. "You know I don't get involved in politics. Although, I do believe that if we don't dramatically change our way of dealing with each other, we have very little hope for the future."

The President thought he was listening to Tony again. He continued. "What I need is a massive rally on Washington in support of my proposals. Something like we've never seen before."

"Why don't you just call for one?" I asked.

"That won't work. What I do think will work is one of your blogs."

"Wait a minute, Mr. President. I just told you I don't take political sides. That would ruin my credibility."

"What *can* you say and still keep your own integrity?" the President asked.

"Mr. President, I honestly believe you're one of the only hopes we have for changing the direction of this planet. I also believe the only way this can happen is if people want it—without the necessity of a major catastrophe. At that point, it'll be too late."

That's exactly what the President wanted to hear. So, he just said, "Thank you, Dr. Bradley, I look forward to your message."

"Oh, Mr. President can you call off the people who have us

under surveillance? I think it's a little useless at this point. My friends and I are hardly a national threat."

"Yes, I will."

✪ ✪ ✪

I sat down in front of my laptop and just allowed the words to flow through my fingers.

> *Believe it or not, we're at a crisis point. The focus of the crisis has shifted to the United States. Will we prove to be the leader we have always advertised to the world or will we retreat into the shell of desperately holding on to what has worked in the past?*
>
> *The President of the U.S. has prepared the stage for this great challenge to be decided. However, there has always been a basic rule about political systems: "You can't **transform** a system from within the system; You can only change the rules of operation." The job of transformation has always been the responsibility of ordinary people outside of the system. That's the reason for this message.*
>
> *If we want to see a world that is preserved for future generations then those generations will probably have to play a leading role in ensuring that preservation. That can only happen if we go directly to the people who are deciding our future and make our voices heard. We probably need to fill the Washington Mall from the Congressional Building to the Lincoln Memorial, so that our representatives vote in **our** behalf and follow **our***

will.

*It is not for me to say what that will is to be. But once we decide to unite in behalf of a new direction for this country, it will become clear what first steps we need to **demand** of our representatives. I hope to see all of you on the Mall in Washington, D.C.*

The Messenger

The response to my appeal was overwhelming and surprisingly, global. Encouragement from the *Millennial Movement* to take to the streets was the dominant theme, similar to what had happen in other African and Middle Eastern countries. The tables were turned. Since so many Americans had been zealous about what others should do, even with a threat to their lives, the outside world was anxious to see what *Americans* would do.

The response was swift. Funded by a coalition of young American Millionaires and Billionaires, arrangements were made for a day-long rally throughout the Mall in Washington. Support for a 20% to 25% cut in defense spending was the centerpiece of their demands. There was also a demand to preserve Social Security for the coming generations.

The day of the rally had never seen so many Americans in the Washington, D.C. area. Hotels were filled, residents housed relatives, and friends offered their homes to those with no housing arrangements. The crowd was arranged along the Mall according to the alphabetical order of the states. Senate and House members could get direct input from their constituents, bypassing Party bosses and representatives. Most conversations centered on a demand for radical change or they would not leave.

The focus was on the future world the young would inhabit, not on the preservation of present policy.

There was also strong opposition to the prevailing movement that brought most of those to Washington. The President activated as many National Guard troops as necessary to maintain order, short of a show of force. The occasional clashes prompted some foreign reporters to feature their story as "America in Crisis." Most Americans disliked the foreign news coverage, the same as that experienced by foreign reporters in their country.

The measure for a 25% cut in defense spending was defeated in the House of Representatives. The compromise measure for a 20% cut was passed overwhelmingly. This bill was sent to the Senate where the real battle was poised to take place. Instead of focusing on anti-rally demonstrations, the powerful lobbyists and special interest groups had aimed their efforts on the Senate, where strong alliances had existed for decades. This is where the crucial battle would be fought. The outcome would determine America's future.

❂ ❂ ❂

"We're two votes short of a tie in the Senate," the President said dejectedly. "If we pick up two more, the Vice-President can cast the deciding vote."

The President, General Clarke, and Dana were assembled in the Oval Office going over the final tally, before the official vote.

"We've come so far, "General Clarke," said. "I really didn't believe we had a chance to come this close."

"I did," said Dana, emphatically. "I believed we could carry the vote. And I still do."

They both looked at her, wondering where this source of confidence had come from.

"You both have to admit that the events which have occurred over the past few weeks were way beyond our comprehension. I just feel that something is guiding this whole process. And this vote for the President's proposal is the final step. Somehow, I believe we just can't fail."

"Okay," the President said. "Let's go over the list again. Maybe, we've missed reading someone."

As they proceeded to review the Senate commitments, Party loyalty was not first on the list. Ideology and long-standing debts dominated the Senate votes.

Then Dana said, "I believe I can get us one more vote!"

"And who would that be?" asked the President.

"I can't say, just yet," she replied. Dana pulled out her cell phone as she exited the Oval Office. She put in a call to Senator John Carson.

"Senator Carson, this is Dana Hartman."

"Well hello Dana. You operate in high places now that you're no longer at DHS."

"Not high, Senator, more like frustrating. I'm dealing with people I can't tell what to do rather than terrorist plots these days. I'm not sure that I was better off at DHS; with your oversight I might add."

"What can I do for you, Dana?" he asked, wanting her to get to the point of her call. After all, they were not necessarily *aligned* now that she worked for the President.

"Senator, I was wondering if I could convince you to change your vote on the President's defense proposal." Dana said.

"Not a snowball's chance in Hell!" He laughed, thinking, 'This woman really has balls.'

"Senator, I could make your association with Robert Ellington and the Guardian Angels disappear permanently from the DHS' records."

Complete silence, so Dana just waited.

Finally, Senator Carson asked, "You *do* play hardball, don't you?"

"No Senator, it's not personal. I honestly believe this bill is best for the country. We're in bigger trouble than you can imagine."

Senator Carson was a realist. He exercised great power because, he lived by the lyrics from the *Gambler*, "He knew when to hold 'em and knew when to fold 'em." And most of all, "The time for countin' when the deal was done." He asked, "Who else knows?"

"Just me and my analyst. Once your name is erased, who cares, anyway?"

Then he asked, "What about my explanation to the people of the great state of California?" The question implied there was more to the deal than simply erasing his name.

"There's new money in the bill for agriculture and public works," Dana replied. "California should get more than its fair share."

"No, I need a healthy dose for education, health, and services. That's 18% of our GDP. Our education system is hurting real bad."

"Done," she said. "You know my word is gold. We can decide on the details later. Okay?"

"Yeah."

"But first, your vote."

"Okay, you got a deal. I just hope I'm around to collect on it!"

Dana returned to the Oval Office and announced to Ken and the President, "We just got Senator Carson's vote."

They both looked at her with astonishment.

She replied, "Don't ask, don't tell."

Chapter**Twenty-Seven**—Epilogue

After their meeting with the Administrator, Gunther Friedman, the members of the Billionaire Club decided to go into deep cover for three months. This meant absolutely no contact no matter what situations emerged. They felt they could adjust to however the world might change as long as they had money and power. Their influence was from 40,000 feet, not the day-to-day ground-level events.

Gunther Friedman decided he would not return to his home the night he was released by the J&M Team. He went directly to his office, withdrew millions in cashier checks, and headed for his favorite Southeast Asia outpost to begin living in obscurity. He also sent a note to his wife indicating he would be gone indefinitely. She would be contacted from time to time but financially she and the family were secure. They had discussed clear instructions for such an anticipated occurrence.

At this point, Gunther was not the center of attention. What was important now was the legacy of his family name and the assurance that the wealth of his children was secured.

Colonel Thomas resumed his conversation with Monique Rashad. "I have spoken with the President and he has given me clear instructions of how to resolve the situation involving your offer."

Monique just looked at him and replied, unflinchingly, "And?" She had always remembered Jacque's instructions, "Never let an adversary know you are scared, it will unnerve him."

"Before I tell you of my decision, I would like an answer to the question you did not answer. You are correct I cannot *prove* you were part of the assassination team through physical evidence. So, I'm asking you again, "Did you attempt to assassinate the President of the United States?" Colonel Thomas' expression made it clear that this was not a court of law where the Fifth Amendment applied.

She realized his decision would probably hinge on whether she truly *intended* to kill the President. So she decided to tell him the truth. "If I had intended to assassinate the President, he would be dead," she replied.

"What do you mean?" he asked.

"It means I had a clear head shot, but I chose not to use it. Something happened in that moment that I can't explain. Something that's never happened to me before."

"And what was that?" he asked, clearly puzzled.

"I don't honestly know, Colonel. I just couldn't do it!" She never broke eye contact with him.

"So?" Colonel Thomas asked. "What are you saying?" He wanted a clear statement of her intentions to determine if she was lying. He'd had years of experience questioning captives.

"So, I chose not to kill him. I chose to wound him instead."

He looked at her long and hard for a full ten seconds. Then he said, "I'll see what my team thinks." He turned and left the room.

When he returned fifteen minutes later, he said, "You have a reprieve for the time being. We'll deal with your partner when we catch him. Any questions?"

"No," she replied. "But you won't capture Jacques. Our agreement was to think of ourselves in the event one of us was captured. No heroic rescues."

"We'll see," said Colonel Thomas. "We want you to make contact with him. Tell him of your decision to help us find the Billionaire Club members. See if he wants to join you."

"Okay," she said. He started to leave and she said, "Colonel Thomas."

"Yeah?"

"Thank you."

"He turned to leave again and said, "Oh, by the way, it wasn't unanimous. I'd advise you to watch your back."

☼ ☼ ☼

The entire team of Pleiadians and their protégés assembled at my home in Salt Lake City, Utah. Tony began by saying, "I think it's time we shared with all the protégés our ultimate reason for coming to Earth and attempting to influence its evolution."

"When you began your 'atomic era' in the 1940s, you also entered a phase where you began to influence the universe beyond Planet Earth. You never gave any serious thought to the fact that nuclear radiation was projected into outer space every time You exploded a nuclear bomb above Earth. Outer space has weather patterns just as you have here on Earth, dictated by the solar winds.

"Such radiation is funneled into a vortex, and a significant fraction is fed into the portal systems we have described. Filtering systems exist to control low levels of lethal radiation. I use the word lethal, because even low levels that are allowed to enter the portal system can cause incurable diseases to Pleiadians. The obvious solution is to permanently close the portal to Earth."

"What happens if you permanently close the portal? It can no longer be used for space travel?" I asked.

"It is much worse than that, Bill. It means You will no longer be fed by the *life-force*. The *life-force* is the energy current that gives rise to creativity, innovation, inspiration, art, scientific conception, spiritual expression, and the force that drives human beings in service to one another. You call it by various names such as Chi, Tao, Prana, Ki, or even the Soul. In essence, it is the *breath of life*. Without it, homeostasis sets in and You wither and die as a species; including all other animal and plant life."

"If you knew this already, what is your 'real' reason for coming here?" I asked, perhaps, not wanting to know the answer.

"Our journey here was to determine if there was any hope of You evolving beyond resolving your differences through threats, aggression, and ultimately the use of nuclear weapons—whether by accident or through conscious intention. If we conclude you are not capable of human evolution, then the portal will be permanently closed to Earth."

"You must know that the changes which have occurred, since you've been here, give us reason to believe we are capable of changing, " I exclaimed in desperation.

"If we conclude you are capable, but not yet proven, it will remain open and You will be closely monitored."

"So, where are you, as a delegation, on this question?" I figured we might get straight to the point.

"Split," Tony said dejectedly. The Pleiadian Council will not accept a split conclusion.

"Where does that leave us here on Earth?" I looked around to see if I was speaking for the other Earthlings. They nodded their accent.

"John has decided to remain to work to the end, without any direct interference with your chosen destiny. His primary function will be to oversee your continuing development and the safety of you and Gala. He also has a personal motivation. His relationship with Jasmine," Tony said.

"What about you, Tony?" I asked.

"I decided years ago I would not be returning to Pleiades. My primary activity will be my continuing efforts in human evolution on the European continent. In addition, I plan to ensure the safety of the President; without his knowledge, of course. John and I realize that remaining here beyond our original assignment means we can never return to our home. Our fate is tied to yours."

"Are the two of you sure you want to make such a sacrifice? After all, even with your help the odds are they will win anyway—one way or another. It seems money and power determine the fate of this planet, not people."

"We agree that the forces that oppose evolution are immense. Although the challenge is a difficult one, without the continuing efforts of individuals like you and the President, it would be hopeless. The others are returning to Pleiades to present their report to the Council."

Everything was moving so fast, I didn't know what to say. Both Bin and Ravi were about to leave permanently and I was already feeling this overwhelming sense of loss. They, along with the other three Pleiadians nodded and were gone! Just like that. No goodbyes. No hope to see you soon. No hope you make it. Just gone!

Then just as suddenly as they disappeared, Bin and Ravi reappeared. "We've decided to remain," said Bin. "I will continue my work in Africa and the Middle East. If we can transform that area of the world, we can transform the rest of the planet."

"We feel you still need our help," said Ravi. Our work is not yet done. We believe there is still hope. The others do not. I plan to continue our work in India. Jasmine has pledged to continue our mentoring relationship."

Then Jasmine said, "John and I need time to understand what this relationship is all about, beyond the emotional stuff. He catches on fast," she commented with a smile. "Obviously, distance will not be a factor. I am committed to my development and work with Ravi."

Gala said, "Bill and I have decided to live together to understand better a relationship free of dependency, selfishness, and need. We have already experienced these in previous marriages. They have resulted in divorce. But we've agreed to stay together no matter how difficult the learning process." I simply nodded my agreement.

The Earthlings cried unashamedly. The Pleiadians looked embarrassed by the feelings they were experiencing; all except Tony and, of course, John.

❂ ❂ ❂

The President invited Leslie Davidson, the Dean of Reporters, to the White House for an exclusive, live television interview. He decided he would hold a separate Press conference for the entire media, after the Senate vote. But he wanted to provide an opportunity for the American people to have a live explanation for all that had happened to him over the past several weeks.

When they were assembled together prior to the interview, Leslie asked, "Are there any questions that are off limits, Mr. President?"

"None that I can think of, Les. I want to be as transparent as possible with the American people."

"Good. Then I have a few that go beyond the political situation. They may involve you personally," Leslie replied.

"In truth, Les, the two are probably inseparable. I'll try to be as honest as I can without causing any confusion."

"That's all we can ask of you, Mr. President."

"Time, Mr. President and Mr. Davidson," one of the aides informed them.

When they were seated, the countdown began. Shortly afterwards, the flashing red light of the TV monitor came on.

"The Moderator stated, "Good evening ladies and gentlemen. This is a special, live interview between Leslie Davidson of *The Global Times* and the President of the United States. Mr. Davidson."

"Thank you," Leslie said to the camera. Then he turned to the President, "Mr. President, I think I speak for the American people and friends abroad, we are relieved and delighted to see how well you have recovered from the assassination attempt on your life."

"Thank you, Leslie. I am still overwhelmed by the outpouring of thoughtfulness of the American people and people from around the world."

Leslie quickly interjected, "Which brings me to my first question, Mr. President. How were you able to make such a miraculous recovery in such a short period of time?"

"Let me ask you a question, Les. 'Do you believe in miracles?'" Then the President quickly went on. "You don't have to answer that question. I really meant it for all of us. Because, I believe that nothing short of a miracle could have caused the top page of my speech to blow off the podium at the instant the first shot missed. And then to have the second shot only wound me in the shoulder was a blessing."

This is not where Leslie wanted to go with his question, but he had no choice except to follow the President, "Why do you say being wounded was a blessing, Mr. President?"

"Because it allowed me to experience my own mortality. Most of all, it allowed me to become more resolute in attempting to ensure a successful future for America. I assure you, such a commitment could only come from an experience of humility; a traumatic one in my case."

"Let's take a look at your proposal to cut defense spending by 20%. Isn't that a dangerous gamble, given the world we live in today? America still has many enemies who would like to have us let down our guard."

The President momentarily gathered his thoughts, and replied. "If we continue down the road we are headed, the ultimate destination is predictable. I don't think anyone would disagree. We might disagree on when and how, but the destination is clear. In graphic terms, the annihilation of human life on this planet. I'm unwilling to be a continuing participant, as President, in that destination. I also intend to provide a choice for the American people."

"So you're gambling that your departure from our present policies will influence others to change also?"

"Yes, I am. While also holding other powerful nations responsible for their roles in forwarding the course of peace."

"Your proposal also means that American interests in other parts of the world will also be less influential. Are you willing to accept that change?" Leslie asked, becoming clearly agitated with the President.

"We can no longer afford to be peacemakers of the world. As I have said, others have to assume their roles. It's time we focused on the welfare of the American people. In either case, if others don't assume their roles, we have no hope any way. That's where we are," the President ended, smiling confidently.

They continued on lesser issues and then Leslie finally said, "Mr. President, there have been reports of extraterrestrials from fairly credible intelligence sources. Have any of these individuals attempted to contact you?"

"As you might assume, Leslie, we had similar reports from our intelligence agencies a few weeks ago. With the assistance of the Defense Intelligence Agency, we were able to arrange a meeting with two individuals who claimed to be from another star system. They turned out to be ordinary-looking human beings. They stated their concerns about the great challenges we all face on this planet, such as an inadequate supply of fresh water, increasing energy demands, and nuclear terrorism. We determined they were not a threat nor at any time were any threats made. They had not broken any laws; they had no weapons; and they asked that their identities be kept anonymous. We have kept them under surveillance for the present. Finally, we concluded there was no reason to alarm the American people."

"I have another question to ask about the extraterrestrials and extrasensory ...." Leslie's voice tapered off as he looked at the video camera. Then he glanced at his watch.

The flashing red light came on the video camera, indicating the conclusion of the interview. The President said, "Thank you Leslie, and my thanks to the American people." They both dislodged their microphones. The President shook Leslie's hand and retired into the White House to meet with Dana and General Clarke.

Meanwhile, the TV crew was having a discussion with Leslie. None of them could understand why the flashing red light monitor had gone off ten minutes ahead of time.

❂ ❂ ❂

The atmosphere was tense. The gallery was filled to capacity. All the arm-twisting had been done. The pressure of the lobbyists had been immense. Unlike anyone could remember in years. There were considerable threats of recalls if certain Senators didn't vote the right way, from both political persuasions.

Outside of the Congressional building, there were loud chants of "America 21st!" "America 21st!" "America 21st!" that went on relentlessly. Indeed, it did appear that America was, at least, at a crossroads, if not a crisis. An affirmative vote would be the greatest change in direction of American policy since the end of

World War II.

It would be a conscious acknowledgement of really what already existed. We were no longer the largest economy in the world—China was. We could no longer afford to police the world *and* adequately tend the social, educational, and livelihood needs of our people at home. In short, we could begin finding our place in the new world order based upon our strengths as a nation while simultaneously ensuring a positive future for our younger generations.

The President had come to understand that true leadership is based upon *influencing* by example rather than by threats based on domination, control, and presumed power over others. Even military might no longer had the power to control people's minds—and their actions in the face of certain death. The words of the French philosopher, Victor Hugo regarding the power of an idea whose time had come, seemed more pronounced than ever before. People from around the world demanded greater freedom, participation, and accountability from their governments.

And now those inside the Senate chamber were wrestling with three intersecting issues: the pressures of those who supported them over years—special interest groups represented by lobbyists; accountability to those who elected them—presumably, based upon some degree of integrity; and their own personal conscious to do the right thing in preservation of the country's future.

For some, there was no confluence of issues at all. It was who "buttered their bread" over the years, simply a debt owed that needed to be paid. For others, it was the belief that they were there to represent the dominant persuasion of their constituency. For a few visionaries, it was larger than both of those motivations. Those few stood in the shadows of the founding fathers who wrote the American Constitution.

One such visionary who was about to cast the deciding vote was the Senior Senator from Utah. He had skillfully navigated a fifty-year political career by exerting immense behind-the-scenes influence on major legislation. Now he was about to cast the deciding vote against or to affirm the President's reduction of defense spending, and probably end his career. Particularly, in light of his recent promises to the American Tea Party movement.

After his vote, everything went quiet and still within his own reality. There was pandemonium in the Senate and the chanting outside rose to an even increased level as compared to before his vote. Something deep within him that had always guided him on critical issues arose to overtake the consequences of rational thinking. He voted from his heart this time. He voted affirmatively for the President's cut in defense spending.

"Well, it's done," the President said to Dana and General Clarke, as they observed a televised showing of the Senate vote. "The question now is will people everywhere do their part in bringing about the transformation we need?"

He smiled, although his thoughts had already shifted to the Billionaire Club and others like them. He surmised that they would resort to whatever means necessary to stop the *America 21st* movement from achieving critical momentum. He had decided, since his miraculous recovery, there were some things he could influence and others only fate could control.

He said to Dana, "Please get Dr. Bradley on the line for me. I want to thank him for his blog. I would also like to share a few ideas I have in mind for moving us forward."

Now that the President had won his battle for *change*, the quest for a *transformation* in human consciousness now clearly rested with ordinary people. The question was, were they ready and willing to take on the task of creating a planet of peaceful co-existence or consciously continuing on the road to self-annihilation.

Colonel Darin Thomas, in concert with Agent Carlson of the CIA, had formed a special coordinated team. Their objective was to identify, locate, and eliminate the Billionaire Club members. There was no intent to capture them for trial. The intent was to locate and quietly eliminate each of them. Thus began the greatest manhunt in the history of an invisible adversary with unlimited resources—*The Hunt for the Billionaire Club.*

Acknowledgements

First and foremost I acknowledge the encouragement and support I received from Galina throughout this project. She has instincts far beyond those of an earthly nature. I appreciate the work done by LaRay, who typed the entire manuscript and continued to give me ideas—as well as suggested actors for a movie version of the book. My sister, Barbara, read the manuscript several times and made valuable suggestions. She was also a major source of encouragement as well as my two daughters, Lea and Kayla. I appreciate the feedback Phil provided throughout the project. He provides a perspective I'm often blind to. Linda McPharlin, my editor, was invaluable in making sense out of what I was trying to express; although I do not hold her responsible for the final manuscript. Beckie as well as others made valuable suggestions. Finally, I would like to say that writing this book was a personal joy for me. I hope it provokes our attention to the preservation of the people on this wondrous planet.

Other Titles by the Author

Realizations

The Guides

It's All an Illusion

The Living Organization—Spirituality in the Workplace

Animal Kingdom

Living Without Fear

Diversity—The Unifying Force of the 21st Century

How to Become a Total Failure—
The Ten Rules of Highly Unsuccessful People

Center for Creativity and Inquiry

The Center for Creativity and Inquiry is a non-profit corporation organized to access and draw upon interdisciplinary resources to inquire into humankind's social and spiritual needs and to then produce creative and innovative responses as may be appropriate. The Center is currently run by the Executive Director, Dr. William A. Guillory. Programs of the Center include:

- Individual Study Sponsorships (Personal Inquiry)

- Small or Group Inquiries on Subjects of Present or Future Interest (Collective Inquiry)

- Creativity, Innovation, and Quantum-Thinking Seminars

- Publication of the Newsletter, *Out of Context*

- Leadership Programs for the Socially and Economically Excluded, and Modest-Income Groups

- Invited and Sponsored Speaker Series

- Advanced Leadership Seminars

- Service – An Advanced Retreat

The programs of the Center seek to understand the relationship between human transformation and service to humankind, to understand how to create human compatibility, and to promote the unlimited development of humankind's intuitive and creative abilities in order to discover solutions to problems which minimize global conflict.

For more information regarding the Center, please contact us at:

The Center for Creativity and Inquiry
5442 South 900 East, Suite 551
Salt Lake City, UT 84117
Phone: 1-801-274-2885
Fax: 1-801-274-2916

Please visit our website, pleiadiansbook.com.